JOHN DU

DREAMGUARD
the trilogy 1

St.Giles's FAIR

SAMARA PRESS 2000

© Samara Press

Mayfield Road Tarago NSW 2580 Australia

First published by Samara Press

Tarago NSW /London UK / Portola Valley CA USA

phone +61 2 4849 4562

fax +61 2 4849 4636

email <john.dutton@bigpond.com>

homepage www.dreamguard.org

National Library of Australia

Cataloguing-in-Publication data

Dutton, John.

St Giles's Fair

ISBN 0 9577556 0 0.

ISBN 0 9577556 3 5 (set)

I. Title. (Series : Dreamguard, the trilogy ; 1).

A823.3

Cover design by msquared with Simon Flynn

using photography by Montgomerie, back cover

illustration by 'John', photographed by Wildwater

Printed and bound in Australia by Australian Print Group

coille uaine tir nan sgeul ... .

the green wood of the land of story ... .

Somhairle MacGill-Eain

acknowledgement

With gratitude to Autumn Stanley for her belief in this book and her constant encouragement.

dedication

this trilogy is dedicated to its characters

humans   to John, whose love gave Bear his life,
to Charles, who found a pathway through time,
to Susan, diviner of languages, who solved the riddle
of the word-spider

animals   to Bear, dreamguard, embodiment of the Lord Buddha,
to Seal, who hears the Voice in the World,
to Hippo, who meets the darkness unafraid with laughter,
to Tiger, his one love lost, who gives us music ever new
and an island free from killing

forces   to Murgatroyd, cat, and once prince over darkness,
in love both with good and with evil,
to Megan, the witch, who fed on the feelings of children,
and for them made the unreal real,
to Grayach, the spider, imprisoner of souls with words

and last, but foremost, to Sacramento, the poet sea-lion,
whose songs make what he sings live

J. D.

• contents

• the museum

CHARLES KNEW his mother and father were not getting on together. Things had happened, and he had watched them. Things that one does not mention, even in the pages of the story. His efforts to help had not helped.

Most of the time he could forget it. Sunshine came into the living-room on the first floor. His electric train ran in and out of the green-purple mountains on the train-board, papier-mâché mountains he had built up on scrumpled chicken wire. The river flowed by outside the window. There was Hippo to talk to.

Everybody put a good front on things. Sometimes his elder brother John took him out in *Cressida* up the Thames that winter. It was an empty time, winter. They would watch the Canada geese with their blue-black necks, and stare at the green-grey water swirling where, in the summer, water-lilies would be growing again.

Their father worked in his study, played chess with him, or drove him on Saturdays to the stables in the hills for riding. He dreamed of the thunder of hooves on the long meadow, and of the branches going by overhead as they walked the horses through the forest. Of his horse's ears flicking in front of him. Of wondering what was in the horse's mind.

Other days they went out shopping with their mother. It was a great game, trying to get her to buy them things. She was usually sensible, but sometimes she was impulsive. Like the time she had bought John a second stuffed seal as a wife for his first one. They always ended by having tea on the top floor of Allison and Lovells, a place full of old ladies playing at being upper middle class. And talking loudly, just to make sure you could hear what they were saying.

Their mother gave parties where she sparkled. He and John were allowed to offer chocolates around, and to fill up the guests' drinks. Sometimes they got a little drunk themselves, and wandered about in dressing-gowns and bare feet till long after bed-time.

They went with her, too, when she gave readings from her poems. Charles was proud he could sell more of her books than any adult could, standing behind the trestle table piled with volumes. The urchin's appeal in his eyes was hard to resist, and he knew it. But the eyes were sharp as well. He did not make mistakes with the change — ever.

But things were wrong at home, and getting worse. Something was going to collapse. Suddenly. All he could do was watch it, feel it, coming.

That afternoon, heaviness seemed to be in the air, like the silence above the snow on a slope before an avalanche. He felt restless, and stupid. Eventually, for no reason he could explain, he wandered off down Meadows Road to the University Museum. As if he were sleep-walking.

There was almost no one about inside. For a time a young man fidgeted with thumb-tacks, putting up a poster for the World Wild Life Fund. Then he left. The felt-covered door thudded shut behind him. The glass cases ached with boredom in the sunshine and silence.

Charles wandered around. His senses were dazed. The atmosphere was too fusty to breathe in easily. He looked at the stuffed egrets. They looked back at him. The knobkerries had worn handles. Stained, too. So once they must have done mischief on human heads. Real, bloody, painful heads.

Next to them were spear-throwers that made your arm longer, and the spear go farther. And shields painted with flattened-out totem animals. As if they'd been skinned. Shuttered masks opened to show a second mask beneath, a mask with a different face. Why had he come to look at these things? His eyes felt stiff. Sometimes he couldn't see the world around him.

Only the dinosaurs seemed to speak to him. The skeleton of a pterodactyl hung from the ceiling on threads. Tens of millions of years ago it had skimmed the waters, looking for fish. Painted blue oceans and pink-brown land on maps showed how different the continents had been in the earlier ages of the earth. No bulging Africa, no Asia pegged out like a hide, but strange smooth coastlines and imagined names — Pangaea, Laurasia, Gondwanaland.... A small box, nested with cotton-wool, held fragments of dinosaur eggs found in the dry sands of the Gobi. Laid by a mother dinosaur....

In front of him stood Triceratops, armed with his multiple horns and his curved collar-plate of bone. He was looking up, surprised, from a dinner of museum ferns. A skeleton of Tyrannosaurus towered in the next case. He had shrunken forearms and a huge, dragging, tail. His jaws grinned, still hungry after seventy million years. A model of Diplodocus waded through the blue perspex of a swamp, under frond-like trees. Plastic trees. His tiny head seemed to sway at the end of his long neck. No wonder he'd had to have a second brain, at the lower end of his spine.

Most of them were bones, fixed on plexiglass struts. More accurately, casts of bones left in the hardened mud by accident. They had no descendants alive.

Charles looked at them with his mammal's eyes. Why had they perished? Had the weather grown too cold? Their hairless skin was a poor protection against a winter night. Had it been deadly radiation, trickling in when the earth's magnetic field had faltered? Was it because they had no taste-buds, and had poisoned themselves on the beautiful, new, uneatable flowers? Grandmother said that another planet had hit the earth, and darkened the sky for years with dust. Green plants that needed sunlight had withered; the dinosaurs had frozen and starved. It was odd that not one of them was left. — How much longer did human beings have before they too vanished? His mind considered a future when human beings were absent, and what meaning it might have.

Stegosaurus seemed more approachable than the others. But why did a double row of what looked like dinner-plates run along his back? Charles had no idea if they were there for defence, or for warming up in the sun, like a sort of solar panel, or for cooling off in the breeze, like a radiator grille. The friendly look on the stegosaur's face appealed to him. The face was only a skull, but no matter. He felt, if he'd been back in the Mesozoic, or whenever those times had been, he could have talked with him. It would have been company. Like Hippo.

As his eyes searched about, he noticed something missing. Glass panels are full of reflections. Full of ghosts from the real world —bright windows and polished floors, and fluorescent lights — that haunt the cases but slide away as you approach them. Today, he could see straight into the Stegosaurus. Someone had taken a panel out. Probably the caretaker. Perhaps he'd had to clean the case, or re-stack the heaps of rock inside. Then he'd forgotten to put the glass back, or gone away leaving the job unfinished. These things happen.

Charles put his hand in, and twisted the last vertebra off the stegosaurus's tail. He held it in his fist, clenched, down in his trouser pocket. The bone felt warm and comforting. He separated his fingers, and let it drop to the bottom. He had committed a small, apparently pointless, crime. If he hadn't been feeling miserable, he wouldn't have done it. Charles, being Charles, stayed outwardly serene. He walked around in the museum afterwards as if nothing had occurred.

He looked at a fossil archaeopteryx with its fern-like tail. Then at some blood-stained shrunken heads, like Punch-and-Judy puppets. He admired a tray of gold coins stamped with the profiles of self-satisfied rulers, tyrants no doubt. It was difficult to concentrate on them. A feeling was tingling inside him, which took hours to go away completely. Though he did not know it — yet — he had just caused a change in the path of his future.

He was to have forgotten the bone, and you will have forgotten it too, when — later — it made a difference. Between living death and escape.

———————

• other minds

THE SUMMER HAD PASSED with the thunderstorms of late August. Fitful storms that had made the air uneasy, heavy, and oppressive. Then darkness had begun to come earlier, and the sunlit evenings seemed — already — long ago. It was cold enough for sweaters again. The autumn had turned restless, golden and brown. The winds spoke of time passing, of things not done, and that never would be done.

Saint Giles's Fair had come in early September. The Ferris wheels rotating with their glittering lights. The con-men barking encouragement at the reluctant public — buy! shoot! have a wonderful time! Their hooded lids had almost hidden the contempt in the eyes beneath. And the greed. While the Fair-women — wearily, desperately, cheerful — had twirled the wispy pink sugar-floss for the children, who watched them with hungry faces. Then the Fair had gone.

It was October now.

Night.

Charles and his brother John sat at the top of the stairs, bare toes dug into the carpet. They were in their pajamas and meant to be asleep. They had served drinks to the guests downstairs, been kissed by their mother, and said goodnight to. But the night was warm, and something in it not still. The moon in the moving clouds seemed to float like a buoy above the river Thames. Wind noises, traffic noises, slipped in through the garden trees.

From below their feet a fan of light shot up. It splayed through the banisters, and cast a shadow woodland on the walls. The trees overlapped each other, in blackish greys and half-greys, in half-half-greys and misty whites. The boys could imagine themselves walking there, along those soundless avenues. Other selves, other times. The water tapped in the pipes of the heating system, like messages between prisoners in a jail. Chatter and laughter drifted up from the grown-ups' party below, and the smell of fresh cigarettes.

They felt like young animals, full of unused energy looking for a purpose. When Charles spoke, it was as much to himself as to his brother.

"What'you think it's like, being one of them?"

"Like who?"

"Like *them*," said Charles. "Grown-ups. What's it feel like inside?"

"Don't know," said John. "They never seem to be doing the things they really want to be doing."

5

"What sort of things?"

"Don't know if they know," said John. "I sometimes think they've forgotten, themselves, What you see's different. Just their outsides."

"So?"

"Always wanting to be well thought of," said John. "In the end, they live and die by that. We will, too, one day."

Charles scratched his head.

"I could be a grown-up," he said. "I think. But I have a feeling there's something more. Some secret I don't know yet."

"What sort of secret?"

"Not sure. Their laughter, maybe. Specially when it's on the other side of a door. Urges working in *them* that I don't feel in *me*."

"You're keen on money," said John. "And that's a grown-up thing. True, you're too young for a love-affair."

"Who'd want one of those! The're too many round this house as it is. No. Nothing like that."

"You tell me, then."

John was losing interest, but Charles shrugged slightly.

"I have the suspicion," he said, "that they want the world to make sense."

"Doesn't it?"

"Give me one good reason why it should."

After a long pause, John answered:

"Maths."

"*Maths?*" said Charles contemptuously. "You can prove whatever you want with that. Remember Daddy's introduction to algebra?"

"Of course I do," said John. "A half-full glass is the same as one half-empty. So — half-full equals half-empty. Multiply both sides by two. Then full equals empty. He's slightly mad, for a grown-up."

"Mad or not," said Charles, "that's maths for you."

After another silence he resumed:

"D'you think even Mummy wants to be well thought of?"

"Not *even*," said John. "More than most. Poets like to be remembered. Think what happens when she gets a rejection slip."

"Stage one, ashy-faced silence," said Charles. "Stage two, walking very quietly to the bookcase, getting down the latest copy of *Stanzas*, opening it at pretend random, and reading out someone else's poem that's been accepted. Stage three, asking Daddy, and anyone who happens to be around, if it's better or worse that the one of hers that's just been sent back. Hmm? Stage four, we all agree that, of course, the poem in the mag's far worse. Stage five...."

"That's enough," said John. "Stage seven or eight is having a drink, or two drinks, and getting it over. Or kicking us first. See what I mean?"

"Actually," said Charles, "she's right to be upset. Her poems *are* better than Andy's or Craig's. If you read hers out aloud, they sound right. I'm not just being loyal."

"How can you tell?" said John. "We're her sons. We're programmed to be loyal."

"You're programmed to think we're all programmed," said Charles.

John humphed, but didn't answer.

They sat without speaking, listening through the open window to the wind, to the people passing, and to the boats, creaking at their moorings.

FOOTSTEPS shuffled on the sidewalk outside. They heard an old woman's voice crooning a song — a mournful, bitter song it was, with a sharp edge to it.

"Drunk," muttered John. "Like those meths-swigging tramps that sleep under the canal bridge and frighten you when they smile at you."

"Sshh!" said Charles. "She's not drunk. Crazed, maybe. Not drunk. Listen! You can hear what she's singing."

But a fragment was all they could catch. The lines rose and fell, tuneless as a keening at a funeral. What they meant was hard to say:

Made sightless from heart's greed, a seer second-sighted,
Master yet prisoner of glittering words,
Many-souled, centreless, magus and rabbi,
Dreaming the dream of the real.

Desirer and hater of others,
But also grimed glass of the lantern of Law,
Its flame hidden by filth, yet unblown by time's wind,
Destroyed by creating, made whole by its loss.

Only light from the time before Time ever was
Is now, long ago, dissolving your powers,
Has given back sight, reawoken the day....

The rest was lost as she moved on.

"Weird," was John's comment.

"Do you realize how weird?" replied his brother. "She wasn't singing in English. Yet we understood her."

"Sounded like English to me," said John. "What else could it have been?"

"*Eer dah-hyowlugh goon-hyowlugh, a vriarun launrach....,*" murmured Charles. "How should I know? It seemed to me I saw her, in a cottage full of peat-smoke, where the chickens roosted on the rafters, and iron hooks and plaited creels hung on the walls. She was speaking those words over a cradle. *In Gaelic.* Outside there were mists, and paths that disappeared into the mountains. And my name then was no longer Charles, but Siari."

John laughed.

"I wish you didn't have such an imagination," he said. "For a moment you almost convinced me."

"She was giving a prophecy," Charles continued. "Prophets speak of the future as though it were the past. For them, what's to come has happened already. The baby's name is Grayach. Some time in the future we have had something to do with him."

"No wonder some people think you're odd," said John. "So would I, if I didn't know you."

"No odder than you," said Charles. "What do you think people think when they see you, with straightened-out wire coat-hangers in your hands, looking for water or metals, or lines of force in the earth?"

"Dowsing's perfectly respectable," said John. "And sometimes it works."

"You probably won't dare to do it when you grow up," said Charles. "It makes other people too uncomfortable."

"Maybe you're right," said his brother. "I think, sometimes, that grown-ups are caricatures. Caricatures of themselves. They've thrown away all the things they could have done, except for one or two. And now — that's all they are."

Charles sighed.

"Do you think they like each other?" he asked.

"Not much," said John. "Except for sharing dislikes, maybe. Nothing superglues a friendship like that. Remember the College Secretary in Saint Raymond's. She hates snow. If the snow's just fallen, she says to you, 'Isn't it awful weather!' And you have to reply, 'Yes, Pam, isn't it!' Then she beams. If you said, 'Actually, I think it's magical and beautiful,' she'd hate you. So you don't."

"If that's how it is," said Charles, "there's not much of a future for us. I like lots of people for themselves. Why can't it go on being like that?"

8

After a few moments, he added:

"Do you think Daddy and Mummy like each other?"

"They tolerate each other," said John. "When things are going well. And when they're not, you know what happens."

Charles shuddered. Then he added:

"Yet Daddy still loves Mummy. I'm sure of that."

"I think so," said John. "I think so. But in some place deep inside him, and hidden away. The other way round's not true. Must have been once. But not any longer."

The younger boy dropped his head onto his knees. The pajama fabric felt warm against his cheek. He lapped his hands around his ankles. His ankles were cold. He sighed again.

"I wonder what those words referred to," he said. "And why did we hear her just then?"

"Accident," said John. "A chance glimpse into somebody else's life. Two worlds — hers and ours — passing each other by. A different past, a different future, for each of us. Even a different present."

Charles raised his head and shook it.

"No. No," he said. "Those words were meant for *us* this time. What I want to know is, whom did she speak them to for the first time? And who is Grayach? Events cast their shadows in front of them."

"Oh," said John, "so you do think that life makes sense? A different sense from the one we see?"

Charles did not answer, but changed the subject.

"Listen to that hubbub," he said. "All having a marvellous time. Or pretending to. Why don't they let *us* stay up for the whole of a dinner party? We're not kids any more."

"We're a nuisance," said John. "We distract them from important things."

"What do they have to say that we can't understand?"

"If you knew, you wouldn't be kept away."

Charles gave his brother's solid shoulder a karate-chop.

"Rat!" he said.

John was unmoved.

"I don't get the hang of it any more than you do," he said. "I'll tell you what: why don't we slip down and eavesdrop? It'll probably all be boring nonsense, but — who knows?"

"We could try," said Charles, "but there's no way of getting close enough to hear them without them spotting us."

"There is. Have you thought of the serving-hatch? There's that cupboard underneath it that opens on both sides, one side into the kitchen and one side into the dining-room."

"And if they do see us, what then?"

"Let's take Bear and Tiger with us. For protection. Some of the guests haven't met them yet. We can say we came to introduce them. They'll be amused. Even Daddy will think it's funny. He's a soft spot for the animals, though he doesn't like to admit it. We might even con a glass of wine off him. So — want to try it?"

Charles nodded.

"Why not?" he said. "Why not? I like doing things that are disapproved of. Makes me feel more alive. Anyway, it's too early to go to sleep."

BEAR AND TIGER were two animal sleeping-bags. They had stuffed heads for pillows, with wide cheerful smiles. That, at least, is how they had begun their lives six years earlier when they'd arrived for Christmas. Now they had characters of their own, stronger than most of the flesh-and-blood people you meet every day. Even when you hadn't touched them, their expressions seemed to change according to what they were thinking. Or you were thinking.

The boys lifted them gently off the beds in their rooms, folded them over their arms, and padded down the stairs. The parquet in the hall was cold under their feet, and its wax squeaked. The linoleum on the kitchen floor was warmer. They crouched down and sidled into the cupboard under the hatch. It was a cramped and forgotten place, where old newspapers filled the dark with a sour smell.

John tugged the doors shut on the kitchen side; and Charles, cautiously, eased the doors open on the dining-room side. They swung out, three or four inches, into the grown-ups' world.

A world full of magical odours. Of heavy tweed suits and bitter-sweet French tobacco. Of newly cut, fat-crisped beef, of mustards and sharp horse-radish sauce. The silicon tang of furniture polish. The aroma of oil paint from the pink-fleshed nymphs and the muscled satyrs beside their dark river-pool, warmed by the lamp that curved down from the frame to light them. They saw human legs touching each other among the fluted mahogany table-legs, set on their brass casters. They saw the movement of hands among the scrumpled white napkins, and — once — the sparkle of a suddenly shifted decanter.

Bear smiled up at John in the darkness of the cupboard. He was enjoying the outing. Tiger's blue eyes shone like pools of water or sky. Charles glanced down into them. As always, he saw sequoia trees, and sunlit glades. Tiger's mind lived in another world, untroubled by the unreal life of reality.

"Life," a man's voice broke in, a voice deep and pleased with itself, "is a war between dreams."

"Who's that?" Charles whispered.

"Dr Homely-Sage," John husked back.

"What a ridiculous name."

"He's Mummy's word-therapist. He has an institute somewhere."

"Doing what?"

"He once stopped me in the hall," said John, "gripped my arm just below the shoulder, and said 'Be careful about your words. Words speak louder than deeds. That's what words were made to do. *We are what we say.*' Then he stared at me, let me go, and walked away."

"His voice makes me uneasy," said Charles.

"He tries to be friendly," John added. "He's said he'll teach me boxing."

"'Tries' is the right word," said Charles. "And I still don't believe that 'Homely-Sage' is his real name."

While this conversation was going on in the cupboard, the Doctor was being answered by a man with a Scottish accent. The Scotsman's words were blurred but sharp, like rocks coming through a mist.

"Life," said the Scottish voice, "is determined by necessities. By food, tae begin with.[1] Talk tae a starving man about poetry and he'll no' listen tae you.[2] When the human animal's been fed, it has tae defend itself. And once it's safe, it usually happens that it feels the urge tae reproduce itself. Dreams, your dreams, are no more than the smoke off a fire. Dreams, my dear Doctor, have tae burn on solid fuel."

"Don't you play chess, McQuark?"

(Homely-Sage was speaking again.)

"Indeed I do. What of it?"

"Let me put a question to you, then. If the Black side and the White side have the same number of pieces and pawns, is the game always equal?"

"Certainly not. It depends on the position."

"A position," the Doctor resumed, "is not a solid thing. You can't touch it. You can't pick it up. You can't weigh it on a pair of scales. It's abstract.

---

[1] 'Tae' = 'to'.

[2] 'No'' = 'not'.

No more than a pattern. Yet it's decisive, just as you've said. How can you believe, then, that only matter matters?"

"A game," said McQuark sharply, "is no' tae be confused with real life. What happens in a game is no' real. Imagine, by way of contrast, burning the wooden chess pieces tae keep youself warm on a cold night. In a game, you can lose, then set the pieces up on the board again, and start another. But you cannae burn them twice."[3]

The boys heard the Doctor chuckle.

"Games are kinder than life," he said. "I agree with you there. The dreams of real life can be cruel. Why do the Arabs fight the Jews? Why do Catholics and Protestants kill each other, and each others' children, in Northern Ireland? Because they dream different dreams. The other differences between them are of little account."

"Dreams," said a woman's voice, "can even change the power of your body to do things."

Her voice was husky and seemed to have the colour of honey.

"Who's she?" Charles asked John, under his breath.

"Maria di Pasiphaë," came the whispered reply. "She's one of Daddy's friends. Travels everywhere and does the things the natives do. Or tries to."

"In Japan," they heard Maria saying, "I used to watch people walking on fire, with their bare feet. The most ordinary people. Grandmothers with faces like little crab-apples, businessmen with their trousers rolled up and their briefcases still in their hands. I was going to try it myself last year, but lost my nerve. I don't believe in the spirits enough yet. They scolded me for dodging it. Scolded me. Said I'd catch colds in the winter if I didn't."

"Did you?" said a young man's voice, teasing and friendly.

"Colds?" said Maria. "Yes, of course. I always do."

"Who's that chap?" murmured Charles.

"Frankie Edgbaston," John murmured back. "You've seen him at parties. Black eyes, curly black hair, rabbity front teeth. Refused to take over his father's steel window business because he prefers to write."

"What's he write?"

"Short, funny, cruel poems," said John, "which Mummy thinks are quite good, and drooly slushy novels to make money, which she hates."

"If the little grandmothers don't get burnt," said Frankie, "why can't you believe in the spirits?"

---

[3] 'Cannae' = 'cannot'.

"It's not so simple," replied Maria. "They told me about a young Christian missionary. Maybe as a warning, maybe to test me. He used to sit watching them dancing across the coals, with all the chanting going on, and the banging of gongs, and them hugging each other, and laughing. It seems that it got on his nerves. One night he jumped up and pulled off his sandals, and shouted 'My faith is a great as yours!' Then he stamped his way across the coals. He was three weeks in hospital being treated for his burns, poor fellow."

"Is that true?" said McQuark.

"My dear Norman," said Maria, "they all believed it was true. Why don't you just enjoy it?"

"Tell us something you do believe in," said Frankie, "before we have a boring argument about truth."

"I'll tell you about something I've actually seen, then," said Maria. "Close up. One day our landlady in Yumebashi came in, terribly excited — which was unlike her, she was usually unimpressed with everything. She insisted we go with her to see some True Light priests taking baths in boiling water."

"How long for?" said McQuark.

"About a minute."

"Biologically impossible, if they were unclothed and survived afterwards."

"Exactly," said Maria. "There was an Italian journalist one day who refused to look at it, because he knew it was impossible. Knew. Stood there with his back turned. If he didn't believe in it, he wasn't going to risk seeing it. But it happened. Each one of the priests got psyched up in turn, into a sort of trance, as the chanting got louder and louder. Then he'd fling off his cotton robe and lower himself into the cauldron."

"How do you know the water was boiling?" said McQuark.

"Because I was scalded when one of the priests splashed some at me playfully. It's not like boiling oil, which is easy to fake. With oil, you just let steam bubble up through the cool liquid, and it looks like a scene from Hell. But it isn't. Oil's quite comfortable actually. But not boiling water."

"What's the point of soft-boiled priest?" said Frankie.

"Blessings," said Maria. "After about a minute in the cauldron a couple of assistants pull him out, red and puffy, with his eyes rolled back under his eyelids. The crowd rub their hands over his steamy, exhausted body — to take the magic off it. They think it brings good luck for a year. The competition's brutal to get at him."

"Mass hypnotic suggestion," said McQuark, unimpressed.

"That's why I could never believe in gravitation," said Frankie.

"Why not?" said McQuark, unaware he was being teased.

"Gravitation is a mass hypnotic effect induced in school-children by science teachers," said Frankie. "It doesn't actually happen."

Several chuckles erupted around the table.

"There's a simpler answer," said Homely-Sage. "Their dreams keep the priests alive. As Maria said, their dreams give their bodies the power to survive conditions that would kill any of us. Tell us, Maria, haven't you also seen dreams that kill?"

"You should be stopping on egging her on," said an Irish voice the worse for drink. Charles recognized it. It was Katie Boru's. Katie spread chaos around her like a tidal wave. You bobbed up and down for some days after she'd passed by. She knew just what she was doing, though. And enjoyed it. She had a knack of persuading their mother to lend her money.

"Some of us like unpleasant stories, dear," said another woman's voice, rich and ratty with middle-aged cynicism.

"That's Netty Pinckney," whispered John. "Daddy says she did *disgusting* things for the Secret Service during the war, and has been bored ever since. I bet she did them well. Hates children. Loves gardens."

"I *enjoy* being egged on," said Maria's voice. "Don't you realize? I'll tell you about something else I saw in Japan. One of my meditation teachers took me to a cave. Inside there was a sort of hollow smell, from all the old incense that had been burned for hundreds of years. When we went deeper in, it was mixed with the sweet-bitter stink of fresh incense still burning. Dozens of candles were stuck in the sand, yellow flames sputtering. And lots of old women, and a few old men, who paid us no attention but just kept muttering, 'Namu Amida Butsu! Namu Amida Butsu!'"

"What's that mean?" said Frankie.

"Prayers to be reborn in the Western Heaven. Anyway, just in front of us, there was something quite still in the flickering, jerking gloom. With tawny highlights. At first I thought it was a huge glacé peach, shrivelled with time, but still shiny. It wasn't, though. It was a little dead man. He was sitting there, nude, with his long white hair over his shoulders. And his body was perfectly preserved. My teacher began to worship it, and I had to pretend to do so too."

"Bodies rot when they die," said McQuark. "Unless you embalm the cadaver, or freeze it, or salt it. What had they done to this fellow? Gutted him? Stuffed him with herbs and spices? Lacquered him?"

"Nothing so crude," said Maria. "These people had discovered that if you live only on fruits and nuts — no bread, no rice, and of course no meat — you starve slowly to death. It takes about five years, and is said to be exquisitely

14

painful. But there is a chance, when you die, that your body won't rot. The corpse has to be kept in a dry place, of course, like that cave, and it's still a gamble. If you win, you become a god. People worship you."

"And if, after all that, you do rot," said Frankie, "what then?"

"It's a sign you're not a god," said Maria. "That you've been pigging rice in secret, or had some hidden wickedness. They chuck your body out."

"Where's the fun in being worshipped after you're dead?" said Frankie. "I want to be worshipped while I'm still alive."

"The dream," said Homely-Sage. "It is the dream of god-hood that keeps them going."

"The Japanese are not human in the way that we are," a weary club-land voice broke in. It belonged to an elderly man the boys called 'Goat', though his real name was Priestley.

"Perhaps they are *more* human than we are," said another new voice, Penny Bran's. Penny demonstrated against nuclear bombs, and tried to grow vegetables on an allotment, more because she thought she ought to than because she liked doing it.

"They have a unique intensity," she added.

"It's not just the Japanese," observed Netty Pinckney in her leathery way. "We're none of us really human. Closed worlds to each other. I couldn't even understand my husband, in spite of years of trying. Don't know why I married him now. Wasted effort, all of it."

There was a munching sound as she pushed some roast beef into her mouth.

Then Emer, the boys' mother, spoke for the first time. Her speech was clear and light. It seemed to them like a mountain brook running over the grumbling pebbles of the others' conversation.

"Being a poet," she said, "I like to get inside the life of everything. Not just people. I was out near Penny's allotment the other day, listening to the crackle of the old men's bonfires. I saw a little black dog, with half-cocked ears. He was nosing about in a mound of rubbish. For a moment I forgot who I was, or that I had ever existed. I encountered the world through his eyes, and his nose, and his paws, as if I were him. With him, I licked the powdered coffee encrusted at the bottom of a jar, tasted the sour corroded terminals on an old car battery, and crunched the rotting stalks of Brussels' sprouts plants. We sniffed together at slime moulds, snail-shells, and damp paper bags. We watched earwigs scuttle away, and tracked the hot leathery whiff of rat odour.... I, or he, whoever it was, was having such a marvelous time that I was surprised, when his owner whistled, to find myself a woman, and clutching

15

a shoulder-bag by the roadside."

She laughed, and added:

"I like to get into people, too. It's a sort of professional hunger. I always want to go deeper in, to *be* them, to make their movements with them as they make them, even to get torn by their feelings...."

"Forgive me, dear lady, for saying so," put in Goat Priestley, "but what you are describing is self-deception. If I am foolish enough, even at my age, to prick myself with a pin, how can *you* possibly feel anything of the pain that *I* am feeling? It's mine. Private."

Emer was at a loss for an answer, but Doctor Homely-Sage defended her.

"How do you know," he said, "that she *doesn't* feel it?"

A second young man's voice entered the conversation. It was Andy Quells, another poet. John and Charles called him 'Glamour Boy' behind his back because of his golden hair and Greek-god profile. And the fact that he knew how handsome he was. And used it.

"Small boys and grown-up torturers," said Andy, "get pleasure from inflicting pain. What is it that they get a kick from?"

"I do *not* get a kick from hurting people," Charles whispered fiercely to John. "Though I enjoy outwitting people who want to hurt me."

"If what you say is true," said Emer to Goat Priestley, "I couldn't go on writing poetry. A poet is a magician. She makes spells with words. Not just descriptions. Not just arguments. *Spells.* She uses her words to call up spirits. She conjures up moods in her listeners. By some means or another, her feelings are transferred. You believe that we are completely cut off from each other. Can't you even feel my feelings now, in this conversation?"

"Outside, dear Emer, only outside," said Goat. "Inside remains a mystery. Look at me now. Over seventy years old, and fit for nothing any longer except eating and drinking. I am going to swallow a mouthful of your excellent claret. Tell me what *you* feel when *I* sniff it, and then let its juices trickle past my tongue and down my throat."

The boys heard him pick up his glass, snort over it, and down a mouthful of wine, rather noisily. They could imagine his eyes, half-closed in concentration on his pleasure. Their mother had once described him as a smiling vulture.

"Well," said Goat, "feel anything?"

"Of course not," said Emer.

But Doctor Homely-Sage would not let the argument go.

"As a matter of fact," he said, "it *would* be possible for me to experience your pleasure, given that the appropriate arrangements had been made first.

Whether I should want to is another question."

"You would need to be a man of some discrimination," said Goat, "to match my gourmet sensibilities. Just tasting my wine is not the same as tasting wine the way I do"

"Doctor," said the boys' father, "you are making an extraordinary assertion. Is it based on theory, on experience, or just hearsay?"

"None of those," said Homely-Sage. "I say it on the basis of repeatable experiment."

John and Charles heard a soft rustling noise, then two clacking sounds. The Doctor had folded back the table-cloth and placed two empty wine-glasses side by side on the polished mahogany. A pure ringing note sang out as he rubbed the rim of one of them with a fat moistened finger. Then, suddenly, he damped it.

"Listen to the other glass," he said.

The second glass, untouched, was singing with the same note.

"Resonance," said Homely-Sage. "One instrument can impart a sound to another like it, if they are set to the same tuning. And if one sound, a sequence of sounds. We human beings are similar instruments, more or less. We only need a little tuning to respond to one another. To pick up the experiences of a bat, though, or a dolphin, or a snake, is virtually impossible. Too few signals come through to make sense."

"I have known shamans," said Maria di Pasiphaë, "soul-travellers, who claim to have been all those, and more."

"I did not say that it was totally impossible," said the Doctor, "but they live in a world of senses so different from ours that their inwardness is all but unimaginable. Bats and dolphins know their surroundings as patterns of reflected sound-waves. Pit-vipers know them as variable fields of heat. Bees can see in the ultra-violet, where plain yellow daffodils have stripes. Pigeons feel the magnetism of the earth. So I am sceptical, simply sceptical. There is not enough in common."

"You are going too fast for me," said the boys' father. "To say the least, men and women are more complicated than your wine-glasses. How is such tuning to be done?"

"The premises are preposterous," added McQuark, "but even were I tae accept them — which I do not — there is no way in which as simple a problem as colour-blindness could be overcome. If one person's mind cannae tell red and green apart, how can you convey tae him the feelings of one who can?"

"I am faced with such doubts," said the Doctor, "that I should like to

17

show you how it happens. We have finished our main course, and very good it was, too. If dessert can wait a little, would you care to see a demonstration?"

A hush fell. John and Charles sat still, fearing that the creaking of the cupboard boards might give their presence away.

"I think it would be interesting to see," said their father.

There was a nervous murmur of approval from the others.

"Bear in mind, then," said Homely-Sage, "that it is you who are agreeing to it. My professional code of conduct forbids me to impose it on anyone, or to practise it without giving the following warning. You think that cigarettes are addictive: a familiar, calming jolt that clears the mind, quickens the thoughts, and then, little by little, a pleasure that becomes unbearably necessary. Something you have to have. You think alcohol is hard to give up, that the world is too bleak without the glow of its companionship, without the softening warmth that makes other people endurable. So they are, but soul-travelling is much more compulsive. Much. Once you have experienced it, it is almost impossible to break free from the sweetness of becoming other people, of feeling the tunes playing in oneself that are, in a sense, another 'him' or another 'her'. Let that be understood. It is a hunger that never lets one alone ever afterwards. Is there still anyone brave enough to want to try it?"

"I am addicted already," said Emer. "It will not make much difference to me."

"*No!*" hissed Charles under his breath. "Mummy, don't do it!"

"Not so loud!" whispered John. "You'll give us away. It'll only be some sort of parlour trick. Hypnosis maybe. He can't possibly really do what he says he's going to."

"I don't even want him to hypnotize her," said Charles. "She'll become his slave."

"Calm," replied his elder brother. "We're best off listening here in secret. He can't hypnotize *us*. That's a safeguard against mischief, don't you see?"

Charles pursed his lips and tensed his shoulder-muscles, but did not answer.

"Well, then," continued Homely-Sage, "anyone else who wants to experience it can take their turn later. Who do you want to be, Emer?"

"Why don't you become me?" said their father to their mother. "Why don't you find out how I really feel?"

"You?" said Emer, laughing. "I know you too well already. No. No."

There was a silence as she surveyed her guests.

"I should like to become Andy," she said at last. "Andy, and know what sort of poetry he feels. If he doesn't mind, that is."

"You're welcome," said the young poet, "but don't be shocked at what you find. It's pretty awful, being inside me. Lots of things I don't let people see. Don't even let myself see, if I can help it. Do I feel anything, Doctor?"

"Nothing at all, Mr Quells," replied Homely-Sage. "Just sit back and watch her, like the rest. All I am going to do is to sense your emotional meridians, and then bring Emer's into balance with them. Are you ready?"

Andy must have nodded, because they heard the Doctor push back his chair and walk round behind him.

"Lean your head back into my hands," he said. "Relax. Think of nothing in particular. Good! That's fine! A little more relaxation. Good. There we are. There we are. I am just going to touch the emotional centres below the sylvian fissures in your skull. Very lightly. There. Beautiful. Then the front and back fontanelles. And the cervical vertebrae. Excellent! The body can do things the mind would never imagine possible. It's your turn now, Emer."

The boys heard their mother sigh as she tossed her head back and let it rest between the Doctor's palms. They imagined him pressing and rubbing her skull, and waited for what would happen next.

"I can't feel myself becoming Andy," said Emer. "I am just the same as before."

"Patience," said Homely-Sage in his professional soothing manner. "It is easy, but not that easy. The two of you are in tune now, but there is another stage. I have to turn down your own personality. It is quite strong, and Andy might find himself becoming you, rather than the other way around. For this stage we shall need the lights off, and complete silence, please."

Someone got up and turned off the overhead lights and the picture-lamp.

"I am laying my fingers on two special points on her temples," said the voice of Doctor Homely-Sage. "Her working-life energies are draining away. It is like earthing an electric charge. She is sinking into a passive tranquillity. Little by little. Her mind and her body are now ready to resonate with Andrew's."

While this was going on, something else had happened. With slow, deliberate motions, more noiselessly than a cat, Charles had opened wide the cupboard door. He had slid himself onto the carpet, Tiger cradled in one arm. He had drawn his feet in under him, stealthily. Then he had risen, so cautiously that nothing had creaked, until he could sit on a spare chair. John, with Bear, had followed, equally slowly. They sat there in the darkness, side by side, unseen by the guests, and gazing at their mother, whom they loved so much and who seemed so far away from them.

Doctor Homely-Sage was shining a pocket-torch on Emer's neck and face from below. She seemed to be in a trance. Her breasts rose and fell, with a deep but unsteady breathing. Once or twice she shuddered, and clenched her hands. Behind her loomed Homely-Sage, a shadow in the shadows, a puppet-master standing over his marionette.

Emer grunted. The guests looked at her sharply, and chills ran down their backs. Her fine oval chin was thickening and developing a cleft. Her slender curved nose was becoming straight and sturdy. The tops of her shoulders were already swollen with unfamiliar muscles. The mist of fine black hair had hardened into a tangle of golden boyish curls. The cool smooth skin was coarsening, growing sweaty and salty. She was turning into a copy of Andrew, crude but recognizable, a man in a woman's evening dress.

The dress tore across the shoulder. What had seemed no more than a theatrical dream in the light of the Doctor's torch became real with the noise of the fabric ripping. Maria buried her head in her hands. "Sainted Michael and Mother of God!" muttered Katie, "it's horrible!" Netty narrowed her eyes and watched with a clinical pleasure.

Doctor Homely-Sage took off his jacket and laid it around Emer's shoulders. The brown-purple tweed made her-him look grotesque....

"MUMMY," said a frightened husky voice, "come back. It's Charles here. Charles *and Tiger*."

Emer's faced jerked at the last two words. Her eyelids lifted a moment. Half her mouth opened, as if a dentist's anaesthetic had left the other half numb.

"Come back!"

Charles's voice was stronger now. It rang with a note of command.

"It's Charles and Tiger here!"

Emer sat up, groggily. Invisible water seemed to be streaming over her, washing the Andy out of her face and body as though carrying away a layer of clay. The blue-grey eyes opened fully; and stayed open.

"Charles," she said, and her voice was strange and flat, "why, why did you call me? It was so beautiful, so exciting."

She glanced at the jacket that swathed her shoulders. Then she tossed it onto the floor. The ripped dress slipped sideways, but she ignored it.

"Excuse me, everyone," she said. "I must go upstairs to change into something more suitable. Dessert will be served shortly."

She stood up, elegant, and seemingly sure of herself. Then she went out, casually flipping the lights on as she did so. The door shut, and the eyes that had followed her turned back to look at John and Charles.

"Well, lads," said McQuark drily, "so you broke the hypnotic spell. Good for you."

"It was not hypnosis," said Maria. "It was soul-travelling. I've seen it before."

The boys' father was tapping his finger on the table. Up and down, up and down. He glanced at the cupboard doors swinging open, and pursed his lips. Several times he seemed about to say something, but checked himself.

Doctor Homely-Sage's hair-covered hands were gripping the back of the empty chair in front of him. He was trying to look affable, but Charles could see he was only controlling his anger.

"Good evening, adults!" said John cheerfully. "Sorry if we interrupted something. We've come down to introduce Bear and Tiger. To those of you who haven't met them before."

The boys stood up and bowed, holding the two animals.

"I used to have a bear," said Frankie. "I told him stories. He was a good listener."

"Helpful animals," observed Maria di Pasiphaë. "Every shaman has to have his helpful animals to guide him when he travels in the other world."

"It is impossible not to be in a good mood when Bear and Tiger are around," said John. "They also — ahem — enjoy a little wine."

"They look the worse for drink already," said Netty Pinckney. "The stitching in their necks is coming undone."

"Take them around quickly and say hello," said their father, his voice unsteady. "Then stop fooling and get back to bed. You've already helped to serve drinks this evening, and that's enough."

Bear and Tiger made a circuit, saying how-do-you-do, and being admired. When Charles reached Doctor Homely-Sage, the Doctor took Tiger in his arms for a moment.

"A remarkable beast," he observed. "What does he eat?"

"He's a vegetarian," answered Charles. "All blue-eyed tigers are."

"I see, I see," responded the Doctor, handing him back. "Much safer in the nursery. But you will have to look after him if he is to stay healthy."

Charles flushed at the word 'nursery', but kept his cool. He hugged Tiger and moved on.

Their father came with them upstairs, and saw them to their rooms. As he was about to turn Charles's light off, he remarked:

"You were in that cupboard long enough to know what was going on, weren't you?"

"Enough to know I didn't like it," said Charles.

He looked at his father with a mulish jut to his jaw.

His father only smiled.

"I know just how you feel," he said. "And I'm not angry. But what you did might have been dangerous. People who are dreaming, or sleep-walking, should not be woken suddenly. They may not be able to regain contact with themselves."

"Why didn't *you* forbid her to do it, Daddy?" said Charles.

His father thought for a moment.

"You may be right," he said. "You often are. But these days I cannot forbid her to do anything. You know that."

He shut the door, and his footsteps went down the stairs.

Charles waited till the sound had stopped. Then he picked up Tiger and went through into John's room. John was sitting on his bed, looking out at the moonlight through the half-open curtains.

"Poor old Daddy," said Charles, "living with all sorts of problems that he won't talk about and thinks we don't know."

"I still don't believe it really happened," said John. "McQuark was right. It was some sort of illusion. Or else Homely-Sage *was* hypnotizing us."

"Maria thought it was real," said Charles. "Remember what she said about those priests bathing in boiling water? It can't happen, according to science. So, when it's in front of you, you won't even look at it."

"It was too theatrical," said John. "Why did he have to have the lights off? It was some kind of fraud, though I've no idea how he did it."

"Oh, no!" said Charles suddenly, and stood up, his face pale.

"What's wrong?" said John. "You hurt?"

"Sort of," said Charles. "Don't, whatever you do, touch Tiger. I'll be back in a moment."

He went out to the bathroom and returned carrying a pair of rubber gloves, tweezers, and an old china saucer. He switched on the bedside lamp and pulled the gloves on. He laid Tiger flat on John's bedspread and began to examine him with the minutest care. He brushed through his fur inch by inch with the tweezers. Tiger looked at the ceiling, taking it calmly. John wondered if his brother had gone more than usually mad.

"Got it!" said Charles with a grim satisfaction.

He held down Tiger's chest with one hand, lowered the tweezers, pinched the blades together, and tugged — delicately — at something. Millimeter by millimeter a bodkin appeared, until it was as long as one of his fingers.

"Good God!" said John. "It was right in his heart."

Charles nodded matter-of-factly, and laid the bodkin in the saucer. It twisted up suddenly like a match burning in an invisible flame, then shattered into fragments.

Charles patted Tiger on the ear.

"You should be all right now," he said. "It was a good thing you told me."

"Whoever put that ugly thing in him?" said John. "Whoever did it must be out of his mind."

"Apart from me, only one person handled Tiger," said Charles, "and that was Doctor Homely-Sage. He also made a remark about Tiger's health. Said I should look after him. But why should he stick a needle in Tiger's heart?"

"Look in Tiger's eyes!" said John.

Charles glanced down. Where there were usually only sequoia trees and sunshine he saw a volcano with rivers of fire still running on its slopes. And a cloud of smoke clearing slowly above it into the blue sky.

He drew his breath in.

"There has been the most terrific fight," he said. "And Tiger has only just won."

"I think we can guess," said John. "When you first tried to call Mummy back, your voice was weak and husky. Then you mentioned Tiger's name, and at once your voice became stronger. Like a man's. You're going to have a voice that can give orders when you grow up. That second time you spoke, you *were* giving an order. And it was obeyed. I've never heard you speak like that before."

Charles brooded.

"There's something in what you say," he said. "I don't know why, but I felt I had to use Tiger's name as well as mine. And when I did so, I felt the power surging through me."

He patted Tiger again.

"You're a helpful animal," he added. "Just as Maria said. Thanks."

"Something serious must have gone wrong to make Doctor Homely-Sage hate a stuffed-animal sleeping-bag," said John. "He's our enemy now, and that's not a pleasant thought."

Stirred by an impulse, he walked to the window and looked out. What he saw made him draw back.

"Come and look, Charles," he said. "But not too close to the glass. We don't want to be seen."

His brother joined him.

On the stone-paved terrace below, half in the moonlight and half in the odd-shaped shadows cast by the ornamental trees, were a man and a woman, walking together. It was Emer and Doctor Homely-Sage. They were holding hands.

"I thought as much," said Charles. "Evil is afoot."

"We'd better follow them," said John. "My tracksuit's black, and yours is navy-blue. If we pull them over our pajamas we'll be invisible."

"We'll need black sneakers, too," said Charles, "which you've got, but I haven't. My football boots will do, I suppose. And we'd better take our Swiss Army knives."

John nodded. They smeared bootpolish on their faces, like commandos in the films, then let themselves down through the snake-thick ivy-branches that covered the wall of the house.

But finding their mother and the Doctor was not as easy as they had thought it would be. The terrace was empty again. Nothing but moonlight on the stones and the leafless rose-shrubs with one or two last roses.

Had they gone back indoors, to join the other guests in the drawing-room? The boys looked in through the French windows, at a careful sideways angle. No. They were not there. Katie Boru had gone to sleep on the sofa. Drunk. Nettie was fingering the small Hamada bowl, and looking around from time to time, in a way that suggested she had half a mind to steal it. Everbody else was laughing and talking. But there was no sign of their mother or Homely-Sage. — Only their father wandering around with the coffee-pot, pouring people more coffee, and smiling all the time, with a strange empty look in his eyes.

Emer and the Doctor were clearly still outside.

The boys knew every detail of their garden. They had squirmed, hundreds of times, down the two-foot-wide alley at the back of the sheds, where the boards smelled of creosote. They had sidled, and crawled, on dozens of occasions in the summer, along the trackways inside the rhododendron shrubs, from where you could watch visitors without them watching you. No cat knew its territory better. They moved, silent and unseen, through the outer trees, keeping the house under constant watch. There was no sign of a human figure.

Halfway round they came to the rhododendrons. If their mother and the Doctor were anywhere outside, they had to be here. John lay on his stomach and wriggled forwards, imitating the war films. Charles followed, in the same way. Before long they reached to the clearing where the elms grew, and paused at the edge. The clearing was lit by slowly moving shafts of moonlight, as the elm-branches swayed in the wind.

Hanging from a branch was what looked like a silk-cocoon, a huge silk-cocoon, bigger than they were. It was suspended from a white thread, and it shimmered like luminous milk.

There was no doubt that wound inside the silk was a human body, its knees hunched up. It was stirring slightly, and the cocoon was turning. As it turned, they saw the face. It was their mother's, and she was smiling at them.

A cold sickness clutched at John's stomach.

He forced himself to be calm.

He stood up, and walked over to the cocoon.

"Are you all right?" he asked.

"All right," she said drowsily. "All right."

It did not sound as if she knew what she was saying.

John frowned. He pulled out his knife and flicked the biggest blade open. Then he hacked at the thread above her head. The cocoon jerked about sluggishly, but the thread was too tough to be cut. He tried to hold it steady with his other hand, but it stung him with a cold pain that made him wince; and he let it go at once.

"Damn," he said. "Damn."

"Mummy," said Charles, standing up, anguish on his face filthy with boot-polish, "what's happened to you? How did you get into this thing? — These horrible sticky-slimy threads?"

"Dreams," said Emer. "Beautiful dreams. Dreams of being someone else."

"She doesn't know what's going on," said John. "We've got to get her down from the tree, but I can't do anything with this silk. It's too tough."

Charles peered at the shimmering strands. Then he used the magnifying-glass attached to his Swiss Army knife.

"This stuff is weird," he said. "Look at it under your glass."

John did so, and gave a start.

"It's... it's crawling with words," he said. "Words all moving about. It's not made of silk at all, but of letters, letters interwoven with each other, writhing in and out of each other. What on earth is it?"

"*Vriarun launrach*," said Charles. "Remember the old woman and her Gaelic song? These are the *glittering words* she spoke of. What else is there to come?"

"Departure," said the voice of Doctor Homely-Sage from somewhere near them. "I am taking her away, of her own free will. Away from this dreary place, full of dreary anxious people. I am taking her to my Institute, where her special needs will be understood, and where she will receive the treatment and professional care that she deserves."

He stepped from the shadows where he had been observing them, and plucked the cocoon off its branch with no apparent effort.

"You're not taking our mother away from us," said Charles. "You can't."

"You are quite right," said the Doctor, his eyes glittering like a spider's from behind his pebble-thick glasses. "I can't, but she can. *She* is leaving *you*. Don't try to interfere with us."

He held the cocoon, swinging from one enormous hand, and marched off through the rhododendron bushes. The boys stumbled after him, their knees feeling so weak they almost buckled under them.

The end came too fast to be unbelievable. Homely-Sage strode across the lawn to a Mercedes parked at the edge of the driveway, a Mercedes black like a hole in the night. He opened the rear door, slung their mother in like a bag of weekend shopping, and slammed the door on her. Then he opened his own door, climbed into the driver's seat, turned the engine on, but not the lights, and drove off in a spatter of gravel.

John had raised his hand to throw his knife at the wheels. It was a futile gesture. He let his arm down again, the knife unthrown. It was too late. She'd gone, like that, and they had done nothing.

The two of them stood side by side on the grass, feeling foolish and helpless, tears dribbling down the boot-polish on their cheeks.

John wiped his face slowly. He felt numb inside. Blank. He looked up at the islands of stars betwen the drifting clouds.

"We don't live from even a tick to a tock for one of those stars," he said. "There are more colours in the world than our eyes are made to see. More sounds, and our poor ears hear only a handful of octaves. Yet we think we know what reality is."

He looked around him, and wondered in what sense any of what he saw existed.

"SNAP OUT OF IT," said Charles. "We need to do something fast, not dream. What's that?"

A piece of paper lay on the driveway, tread-marked by a muddy tyre.

He pounced on it.

"Need to get nearer the house to see what it is," said John. "There's not enough light here."

They walked underneath a window, and Charles peeled the folded sheet apart. Slowly, because it was damp and sticking to itself. The ink had run along the edges of the letters on one side, but it was easy to read.

"It's a poem," he said. "The first draft of a poem. It must have fallen from her bag when he pushed her into the car."

"Or been dropped on purpose, perhaps," said John. "What does it say?"

He looked over his younger brother's shoulder. The sloping handwriting was their mother's, that was clear enough. It read as follows:

A hoard of worlds lies silent in my heart.
At times I speak a world. Then what I speak of is.
A world unspoken of stays dark.

A gift once given's no more mine to give,
But treasures too treasured waste impoverished.
And so I speak. These hearts where I invest,
Yield, taken over, priceless interest.

Mirrored in others' glass, my self is whom they see.
Let me be them, if they'll believe in me.

"Do you understand it?" asked John, after looking at it for a few minutes. "It's more like a riddle than a poem."

Charles thought a little. Then he laughed.

"It's about what the trouble with poets is."

"Which is?" said John.

"That they think they make the world we live in, and are worried that no one is paying any attention."

"It's actually a sort of humourous poem," he added. "I think she's making fun of herself, and of other poets. Read it again later."

He folded the paper up, and slid it into his tracksuit trouser pocket.

"I'm keeping it with my stegosaurus bone," he said. "Maybe one day, one day when I understand the grown-up world, I'll know what it really means."

"Look after it for her, then,"said John. "For when she comes back."

Charles shook his head.

"Comes back," he said. "Comes back? I don't think anyone knows yet whether she will, or will not, come back. It is still to be decided. Meanwhile...."

His jaw set suddenly, and the dreaming look vanished.

"Remember what Hippo says. The only way forward is forward. *Multa milia passuum!*[4] — The journey. The journey, *no matter how long it takes.*

---

[4] Latin for 'many thousands of paces' or 'miles'. See the *Waysong of the Hippos* in "The Sea of Bones" in volume 2.

The first step is we have to tell Daddy what's happened, and he will tell the police. After that...."

"He won't believe us," said John. "Nor will they. We'd better leave out the cocoon and that cold, stinging, silk made of words."

"No," said Charles. "No leaving out. If they don't believe us at first, that's their fault. Not ours. If we give them false information, they can't help making mistakes."

"We're in for a rough ride, then," said John. "The police won't like it. They'll say we're fibbing."

"Don't think I don't know it," said his brother. "We have to set ourselves standards that they will never understand."

Charles led the way back to the terrace. Two oblongs of light from the French windows fell slanting on the flagstones. The glass door was opening. They could see their father there, looking out anxiously, and hear the self-satisfied voices of the guests — suddenly louder.

• murgatroyd

LATE NOVEMBER. Another evening. Yesterday's rain was still drizzling down, and the curtains had been pulled early in a lamplit room on the other side of the city. Under a circle of yellow light, two elegant, oval-nailed, hands were going through a batch of photographs.

For a moment each glossy square would tremble between them. Then it would be laid, face down, on the growing pile that lay on a polished table.

The fingers paused. They were empty. Their tips pressed together.

"Any more? There's nothing very satisfying in these."

It was the voice of a lady — old, well-educated in the style of past times, but not yet weary of life. The answer came in a whisper out of the dark behind her.

"I have a few more, Madam. Taken fresh today."

"Put them on the salver, then. I can wait a few minutes before my evening programme."

Five or six new pictures dropped onto the silver tray. She reached for them and considered them briefly. On the last, she stopped. It stayed irresolutely in her hand.

"Any luck, Madam?"

Had she smiled?

Somehow he had sensed the inner surge of pleasure that she always tried to keep hidden.

"Luck?" she said disapprovingly. "Come, come. You have been with me long enough to know that we don't believe in luck. One long chain of compulsions, some sweet, some bitter, — that is the world we live in."

"I mean, Madam, have I been able to give satisfaction?"

"Of course. Look over my shoulder."

A shadow draped itself on the back of her armchair.

"Excellent photographs, are they not?" she continued. "What do you think of the elder one? An athletic build, with brown hair and long eyelashes. He'll be a dear boy — while he lasts. A pity that youth must be so brief! I'm not so sure now that I care for the stubborn look on the face of the younger one."

"He has a wide forehead, Madam."

"So I can see for myself. It is not necessarily a sign of intelligence. You might have added that his fringe needs cutting."

She sighed.

"Are they vulnerable?"

"Delightfully so, Madam. Their mother disappeared last month. It would appear that she ran away with a doctor, or some sort of professional gentleman, masquerading under a false name. They have disappeared without trace. The police are doing nothing. They maintain that, since it seems that she left of her own free will, it is no business of theirs."

"Did she?"

"There is some disagreement. The boys say she was wrapped up in sticky shining threads, made of words, and dragged away like a fly by a spider. Needless to add, they were punished for telling lies about such a serious matter. And punished again for sticking to their story. Not only are they lost inside themselves, not knowing where they are going, they are resentful. It is a resentment that is — of course — usable."

"Most interesting. Most. If that's who it is has taken her, they will be fortunate to see her again. Or, if they do see her again, perhaps not so fortunate."

"Quite so, Madam."

"What of the mindfield?"

"The father," continued this same deep whisper, "is coping. A little grimly perhaps, but coping. The boys have withdrawn into themselves. They have stopped seeing their friends, and talk mostly to each other and to various stuffed animals. They are, in my opinion, ripe for our allurements. And for what comes afterwards."

A faint smile, like wintry sunshine, passed across the old lady's face.

"Beautiful," she said. "Beautiful. I look forward to having them here. Both of them."

She put the photograph down on the table, picture side upward, and rubbed it with her finger, as if she was touching them.

"Meanwhile, I need my fix. We can discuss the details of the operation later this evening."

She leant forward and switched on a television set that stood in the middle of the floor on a Persian rug . When the screen had begun to glow, she dimmed the table-lamp. The picture came slowly into focus, a window into another world.

Murgatroyd the cat looked into it with a distaste born of familiarity.

A MOON hung low over silver birch trees and dark rocks. The twigs were trembling and shaking. Flickers of brown and purple shadow ran across the ground. A girl in a torn tunic was walking there, her bare feet stepping on the dead leaves.

Around her were deer and fawns, their dappled coats flowing in the broken light.

The herd and the girl came together down to the stream. Its waters glittered and rippled as it poured itself over the shallow pebbles. The deer put their heads down to drink from the deep pools, while she sat on a flat rock, and trailed her fingers in some rapids only a foot or so high. The drops sparkled as they sprang up and fell back onto her forearms.

"Lovely," murmured the cat. "Quite lovely."

"No more than pretty-pretty," said the old lady sharply. "That girl's giving me no real feeling any longer."

She coughed abruptly, and raindrops began to spatter in the forest. This was the first sound to come into the room from that other world. It was so clear that Murgatroyd glanced down to see if they were wetting the carpet.

On the surface of the stream, silver pits winked here and there, and here again, disappearing as fast as they came into existence. A wind shook flurries of raindrops from the branches. Several of them hit the girl's face, and she tossed her hair back from her forehead in a gesture of displeasure.

The old lady nodded her head in mild approval.

"Better," she said. "At least, somewhat better."

The rain fell more heavily. Its staccato rattle fractured the slower gushing sound of the waters of the stream. It was coming down hard enough now to sting the girl's shoulders and soak her tunic, which clung to her sides, sodden and miserable.

The deer forded the shallows and scrambled up the opposite bank, where they stood shivering under some thick branches. She followed them, but stumbled and cut her foot on a rock-edge.

"Isn't it a pretty thing, that wound?" said the witch. "Look how the water washes it to a clean line every time she dips her foot. And when it comes out, it bleeds again."

The rain stopped as swiftly as it had begun. Low mists began to cover the ground like a moving blanket. The dripping birch trunks rose out of them like ships' masts. The mists reached the shoulders of the smaller deer, whose heads looked out of them as if they were swimming. Above the deer the moonlight was still soft and good-natured.

One of the fawns took fright at something, and nuzzled against the girl for comfort. She stroked its ears and its neck, and it gazed back up at her out of its huge brown eyes.

"Now!" said the witch, in a voice of cold relish.

The fawn's eyes clouded over. They became a white milky colour. Drops of pus trickled out from under the lids. Its teeth drew back in a silent snarl, and it wrenched free of her embrace. The girl raised her hands to shield her face, and gave a cry:

"No!"

"Oh, *yes!*" said the witch. "And look at the others, too. Mmm."

The eyes of the other deer were clouding over, and a fungus the colour of wet charcoal was rising up their hindquarters, like mould eating away at a tree. The girl was looking from one to another in disbelief and terror.

The old lady's eyes had almost closed, but her mouth was half open in a smile.

"At last," she said. "The flow of real feeling."

After a few minutes she opened her eyes wide again and sat up straighter.

"Not really too nice to look at," she observed. "Let's turn her off. I need warm, friendly, emotions if I'm to keep myself in shape. Some love, some excitement, even some pleasant surprises. Poor Sylvia only gives voltage when she's scared."

She flipped off the switch and turned up the light.

"You see why I need some new children."

"It is very evident, Madam."

The old lady permitted herself the ghost of another smile.

"It's a cruel game, hunting, isn't it," she said, "my hypocritical cat? Yet — exciting like nothing else. *You* hunt birds and mice. That's what they are there for. *I* hunt children. That is what *they* are there for. What would happen to us without mice, and birds, and youngsters?"

"We should wither away, Madam."

"Yes. We should wither — a painful process to contemplate. So, we owe it to ourselves to keep alive, and well, do we not? It is is, as you might say, all a part of the scheme of the Creation."

"So I have always been disposed to believe."

"There has, of course, been progress," the witch went on. "Not so long ago, witches actually *ate* children. Like grilled lamb chops, or chicken legs. You can read about it in *Hansel and Gretel*, and other stories that innocent parents think so suitable for the little ones in the nursery.

"These days we are more refined. What we feed on are the energies of the young. Fresh energies, like new saplings or buds. You know how some youngsters have a sort of light coming off their bodies and faces? That is the magic energy we need to absorb into ourselves, if we are not to dry up.

"Witches in the bad old days used to confect folksy cottages — with chocolate beams, and barley-sugar panes, and marzipan flagstones underfoot — to ensnare their sweet young victims. Today we are subtler. We use television sets as our milking parlours, where we keep our boys and girls. Ready for us at the flick of a switch. And — once we have milked them of their emotions — we let them out again, all their feelings gone, to become what are called 'adults'."

The black cat sprawled on the back of her chair stretched out his claws luxuriously.

"Maybe, one night, Madam Megan, we shall learn to be as generous to mice."

"That, my dear familiar, would be — as we say — the night."

Megan's fingers stroked her black silk neck-scarf, held together by a turqoise-and-silver brooch of Quetzalcoatl, the plumed serpent that devours the sun.

"And now," she added, "if you have your wits about you, we have to devise some suitable means for their capture."

"I STILL DON'T BELIEVE," said John, "that cats put ads in papers. And I still don't believe that they answer letters. Someone else does it for them. It's just a joke. Charles."

They were sitting near the back door at a low circular table made of varnished plywood. It was their table for doing things on. Seal and Hippo looked down at them amiably from the top of a chest of drawers.

Charles shook his head, tossing his fringe slightly.

"I don't feel it that way," he said. "It's real."

He spread out the clipping from the *Oxford World* and re-read it:

> CAT SEEKS FRIENDLY HOME WITH CHILDREN. UNHAPPY WITH PRESENT OWNER. OFFERS AFFECTION, SIMPLE MAGIC. REPLIES, WITH PHOTOGRAPH, PLEASE, TO MURGATROYD, BOX 9.

Then he laid the reply next to it:

> *Dear Charles,*
>   *Thank you for your invitation to come and stay with you and your brother John. I have received many offers, but I like the look of your photographs best. I will come to the back door after supper on Friday, when the stars are up, and meow three times.*
>   *I look forward to making you my friends.*
>   *Yours sincerely,*
>   *Murgatroyd.*

The signature was followed by a pawprint, and a postscript:

> *I am sorry I have no photograph to send you in return. I am black all over, with green eyes, and am quite a bit heavier than a normal cat. I talk to children, but not to adults.* M

"It's after supper now," said Charles. "If it's a joke, we'll soon find out."

"If it's not a joke," said John uneasily, "then something creepy is going on. Cats don't, in fact, talk. Cats don't, as it happens, do magic."

"You do dowsing with bent wire coat-hangers," said Charles. "Didn't you and Daddy dowse the Rollright Stones and find a spiral pattern? Isn't that magic?"

"Someone from the *New Scientist* did it after we did," said John. "They found it was a magnetic spiral. Using magnetometers. No magic about it."

"I don't mean the dowsing," said Charles. "I mean the pattern being there in the ground in the first place. Who put it there? Druids?"

"I don't know how it got there," said John. "But my not knowing doesn't make it supernatural."

There was a meow outside the door.

— They waited.

"I wonder," said John, "if that was the *only* copy of the *World* in which the ad appeared. We should have bought another."

There was another meow.

A long silence this time.

— Then a third.

Silence again.

John looked at his brother.

"I don't think you should open that door," he said. "It's too dangerous."

"That's because you think you know what's what," said Charles, "and you don't like anything that makes you uncomfortable with your own ideas."

"Don't go," said John. "Don't."

Charles hesitated.

As he hesitated, the latch turned of its own accord. The door swung open. In the entrance-way, lit by the lamp in the brick arch, stood a black cat, tail erect.

"Good evening," he said. "I hope you were expecting me. My name is Murgatroyd. May I have your permission to come in?"

His voice was deep and beautiful, almost royal. A voice that made you happy to agree with it.

"Please do," said Charles.

The word 'no' died on John's lips.

The cat was inside the threshold so fast he didn't even seem to have moved.

He sat down, and looked at them.

"So you're real," said John.

"As much as you are. Perhaps more than you will be."

Before John could ask what this last observation meant, Charles broke in:

"I have some cream in the fridge," he said. "And some delicatessen trout. Would you care for a snack?"

The green eyes glowed for a moment.

"How singularly thoughtful of you," said Murgatroyd. "May I sit near the fire as I eat? It's pleasanter there."

"Oh, please," said Charles. "I'll be back in a minute."

As the cat walked across the mustard-yellow carpet to the fireplace, the door closed behind him and snibbed itself shut without a sound.

John looked at Murgatroyd intently.

"Did you make the door open just now?" he asked.

"Yes."

"With magic?"

"Yes."

"How does magic work?"

A shadow of surprised passsed over the cat's face at this question. His eyes rested on John's for a moment. He could see the boy was serious. That, already, was unusual. Stranger still, he could see no bottom to the depths in the gaze that faced him. They seemed to go down, without any cloudiness, forever. The thought crossed his mind that such a child was unlikely ever to be one of his mistress's young customers. He could hardly be expected to give satisfaction. At least of the normal kind.

"The opposite way from science, or more or less," the cat answered softly. "In science, you have to be able to repeat what you do. It gets easier as you learn how. With magic, the more often you do a trick, the harder it gets."

"You mean, the world somehow remembers what's happened before?"

"The effects remain, which is much the same thing."

"What do you mean by 'gets harder'?"

"That every time you repeat a trick, you have to put more magical energy in," said the cat. "There's a simple formula, which is almost but not quite true. After a certain number of repeats, depending on how hard it was to begin with, you reach the point where you don't have enough energy to do it again.[1] The improbable becomes the impossible. That's why the easiest magic is the new magic you invent for yourself."

"I see," said John. "That's why miracles are difficult to repeat."

"Correct."

"There's a problem with before and after," said John. "For people in space-ships moving very fast in opposite directions, the before-and-after of two magical events could be reversed. At least if you use flashes of light to send the news. That would make the formula impossible to determine."

"Deep," said the cat, "but not deep enough. Magical events don't happen in one place but in a sense everywhere."

"You've lost me," said John. "Is there an exact formula for that?"

"Of course." [2]

At this moment Charles returned with the cream and the trout. He put them down carefully in front of Murgatroyd.

"Could you make these with magic?" asked John.

The black cat looked up, surprised. There was already an uneven line of cream on the underside of his mouth.

"Yes," he said. "But it would be a misuse of energy. Besides, I like the taste of reality. Real stuff. Real friendship."

He put his head down again and finished off the snack with relish. The boys watched him without saying a word.

Murgatroyd then stretched himself out on a couple of cushions the boys' father had brought back from somewhere — Thailand probably — the year before. Silk cushions, with circles enclosed in squares on them. Lustrous dark blue and white. He gazed up at the boys curiously, puzzling them out. They didn't seem as defenceless as the network had told him they were. But he could see why Megan fancied them for her TV set. In fact, he rather liked them himself. *A disturbing but exciting thought.* Why should Megan have them?

---

[1] Murgatroyd later wrote down the so-called classical formula for the magical energy m required for the $n + 1$ th performance for John on a paper napkin. It is

$$m_n = m_0^{(n+1)!}$$

where m_0 stands for the magical energy needed to do a trick for the first time, and n is the number of times that it has been done before. Thus the original performance is counted as number 0. The exclamation mark indicates the factorial:

$$n! = 1 \times 2 \times 3 \times \dots \times n.$$

[2] For security reasons, the exact formula, which predicts magical quantum-mechanical non-locality *and* apparent relativistic effects, is not given here.

Charles and John sat on two low-level chairs that grandmother had given them for sitting at their work-table, and gazed back at Murgatroyd. Charles was bubbling, but controlling himself. John was wondering what they had let themselves in for. If it was a joke, it was not at all an ordinary one. An ad in just *one* copy of a newspaper? Perhaps.... Perhaps.... Was somebody targeting them? Why go to such expense? But the cat fascinated him. Quantum magic — that would be something worth learning.

"Murgatroyd," he said, "who was your previous owner? Is she going to make trouble for us if you come here?"

"An amateur witch called Megan," said the cat. "She's not very bad. Not as bad as she'd like to be. But she's not pleasant. And she's incompetent."

"What do you mean by that?" said Charles.

"The only spells she does that work properly are the ones I do for her. She'll be annoyed that I've run away, but there's nothing she can do about it. I've put a spell of untraceability on myself, and I'm cleverer than she is. There's nothing to worry you. Nothing at all."

Why didn't he leave her earlier, then? thought John.

"Why do you want to come and live with us?" said Charles. "We'll be kind to you, but won't you get bored?"

The green eyes seemed to smile at him.

"In a way," said the cat, "that would the rarest of all treats. Just to be bored. Ordinary cats love to be bored, for hours on end. Look how they lie in the sun with their eyes half-closed, while all sorts of interesting things are going on around them. Though I'm sure I won't really be bored. Not with you two. I'm not an ordinary cat."

For some reason or other, he glanced up at Hippo. And had a shock. A powerful personality was coming out of those eyes. It was angry. It did not approve of him.

Hmm.

He washed his left paw with his tongue. Rubbed his left cheek with it. Reflected.

"Put it this way," he went on.. "If you'd lived lives like mine, you'd feel there was nothing stranger and more beautiful than being ordinary. That's why I want to come here. Are you surprised?"

"What does Megan make you do for her?" said Charles.

"Much of it's too nasty to talk about," said the cat. "But all of it's petty and spiteful. One of her favourite tricks is to mix people's clothes up. If she takes a dislike to a girl, for example, she'll have me visit the girl's bedroom at night and take away all her own clothes out of the closets, and off the backs of chairs. Then I swap them around with the clothes of some other girl with whom she doesn't get on too well. When the first girl wakes up, full of plans for the day, and finds nothing to wear but the clothes of someone whom she dislikes, that girl feels weird. You've no idea how upsetting a thing like that can be to a kid. She starts wondering who she is. And who's doing such things to her without her being able to see them. She can even have a breakdown. It's harder than you might think, making yourself put on someone else's clothes in the morning because it's all you've got."

"I can imagine," said Charles. "How does she watch what happens?"

"Through the TV set. Or the mirror."

"Why does she do it? I mean Megan. Why?"

"She's made that way," said the cat. "She's a witch."

"Why did you do it for her?" asked John. "Aren't you cleverer than she is? Did you enjoy it, too?"

Murgatroyd hung his head.

"Part of me did," he said. "And part of me hated it."

John went on looking at him, and the cat understood the unspoken question.

"No, I haven't run away before," he said, "because I haven't known which side of me is stronger. The last few months, I *have* known. My bad side doesn't do me any good. I want to get rid of it. To forget it. I want something I've never had before — a friendly, warm, and cheerful family."

Charles bent down and stroked him.

"If that's what you want," he said, "we'll really look after you well."

"What you've just said means more to me than I can say," said Murgatroyd, smiling at the double meaning in his words. "Thank you. Thank you from the bottom of my heart."

He arched his back under the stroking and purred. He was playing them just right — on a long, long line. In a few days he'd be ready to reel them in.

Like that.

"Why did you go to work for her in the first place?" John asked.

"I was banished," said the cat.

John looked puzzled.

"D'you say 'banished'?"

"Yes."

"Where from?"

The cat looked from one boy to the other. He could see he had them interested; but he had to be careful not to shock them. A small part of the truth would do.

"I don't know why I'm telling you this," he said. "I'm not proud of it. But you seem to understand me, and trust me."

"We do," said Charles, stroking him again.

"The answer is —."

Murgatroyd paused.

Then he finished his sentence with three words, spoken softly but clearly. *"From the Fire."*

"You mean Hell," said John. "Come on! Do you expect *us* to believe *that*? Our father says that there's no such place."

"It is nonetheless the truth," said the cat. "Where else do you think my magic comes from? Why do you think I can talk? For my eighth life I was a Prince over the Darkness. What I did, what I was, was something that I sometimes cannot believe myself now — though I know it was so, once."

"Is this your ninth life, then?" said John.

Murgatroyd half-closed his eyes. He seemed to be looking inwards, into himself.

"I watched people being tortured for so long, for so long," he said. "Every cruelty you can think of. Many you cannot even think of. And it seemed to me wrong that people should be punished for ever. Even if they'd done some foul things, and, believe me, most of them had. It wasn't fair: for limited crimes, a limitless punishment."

"So it isn't," said Charles. "You were right."

"I was right," said the cat. "That was the first of my crimes. To be someone that HSM[3] himself could could not find an argument against. My second crime was proposing a small improvement. My idea was that we should stop the tortures every seventh day. It would have been good for them, of course, but also good for us. Torture does almost as much damage to the torturer as it does to the victim. But some people like it. My third crime, the worst of all, was persuading some other ... um ... some other entities to think about it the same way I did. That was politics. Practically rebellion. So, I was punished."

"How?" said John.

"By the humiliation of being made to live in the human world as a cat. For my final life I was sentenced to serve a witch as her familiar, and an incompetent witch at that. Don't forget: I was once a prince."

"Is living in our world worse than serving the Fire?" said Charles.

"It can be," said the cat.

He smiled a strange cat-smile.

"But I won't accept that it has to be," he said. "Not with your help. That's why I'm here now. It's wonderful to be free."

---

[3] His Satanic Majesty.

John's eyes narrowed as he thought of something.

"But you can still do magic," he said. "Don't you have to give up magic to be free?"

The cat shook his head.

"The line is drawn in a different place," he said smoothly. "So long as I don't make spells that affect living things — affect them directly that is — doing magic doesn't make me rot inside. For example, there's no problem with *this*."

His empty cream-bowl, a shimmering salt-glaze dish, and his china plate with the blue-black head and the backbone and tail of the trout, rose into the air. At the height of about two feet they began to drift across the room, around the edge of the door that opened politely for them, and vanished from sight.

"I've sent them to the kitchen," he added.

"Will they be washed up?" said Charles.

"Can be, if you like."

He raised a paw and made a circular motion.

"There you are!" he said. "Dried as well, and put away in the cupboard."

"But you mustn't touch people," said John. "Is that it?"

"It is possible to lay spells on living beings," said the cat, "including animals, and not just people, but only if they give me their complete and informed agreement. In practice, that means I can't, and don't."

"So you can't do magic on us if we don't want you to?"

"If I did it would stop me being what I've told you I want to be," said Murgatroyd.

"That," said John, "is important to know. I hope you don't change your mind."

"Even if I did," the cat went on, "you're such tough characters it would be difficult. Not just for me. Even for a witch. Magic needs more than knowledge. It needs will-power. And you both have remarkable will-power. Even if you were grown up, your will-power would be out of the ordinary. Among youngsters — I've never seen anything like it."

"How can you tell?" asked Charles. "You've only just met us."

"Your auras. They come off you for several feet around, like a sort of electric field. With most kids it's barely an inch or two, if that."

"Can you see auras?" said Charles.

"There are ways of making them visible, if you want to," said the cat, "but I don't bother. I feel them. They're like a magnetic field round a magnet. You can make a magnet's field visible by scattering iron filings on a piece of card, holding it just above the magnet, and tapping on it till all the filings have re-arranged themselves. You'll see they form nested loops around each end — with shapes like those of a weather-ballon filling out as it rises into the thinner air."

The boys nodded.

"The odd thing is," the cat went on, "that your hippopotamus — the green one, with the patch on his wounded paw — has an aura too. I've never seen a stuffed animal with a will-power aura before. How did you give it to him? My professional curiosity is aroused."

Charles took Hippo down from the chest of drawers and cradled him in his arms.

"He gives *me* will-power sometimes," he said. "Not the other way round."

"Does my Seal have an aura?" John asked.

The cat looked up at the Seal, at the deep brown eyes, the gentle face, and the slightly crumpled whiskers.

He shook his head.

"Nothing that comes out at you, and makes you feel smaller and under a sort of pressure," the cat replied. "Not the way Hippo's does. But there's something unbreakably strong inside him. Love, I think, John. Love for you, and bravery to the point of madness."

"You're talking about our animals the way no one else does," said John. "No one else, not even our father, who makes a good-natured pretence, actually knows they're alive. His grown-up friends make fun of us."

The cat's eyes brightened with an inner light.

"They most certainly are alive," he said. "By any magical standards. I would't touch them without their permission, and I'm not even sure I could, even if I went back to being what I was in the Black Years again. I have met a lot of children's animals in my time — weary Teddy Bears with hanging heads, stupid-faced fluffy rabbits, dogs with hair over their faces and looking like toothbrushes without a handle — all of them loved, of course — all doing a job to the best of their ability, but never, never, with the...the presence of yours. One turns and talks to them as a matter of course."

Charles patted Hippo's nose.

"Hippo spends his life fighting the darkness," he said. "Darkness in people's and animals' hearts. And darkness out in the world. His weapon is laughter. No one tells funny stories the way he does. The stories he tells us in our dreams."

He smiled at Hippo, and Hippo seemed to be smiling back now.

"Tales," said Charles, "tales about Sir Bustopher Barnacle, the Mad Baronet. Or Hai Ai-Queue, the Chinese Detective Super-Intelligent. Not to mention the Great Guru, Maharupee Bankcheckerji, who can make dollar bills fly in and out of bank accounts like birds. Stories so funny they make the world bearable — a world without our mother in it. Bearable, at least, while the stories last. We lead two lives: one life awake, and one asleep, with our animals to keep us company."

"When most people sleep," said John, "it seems as if they've died for a little while. Their minds are blown out. If they dream, it's only for a few minutes. When they wake up, they don't remember much. Our minds never go out. Our bodies may be resting, but our minds are always wandering somewhere else."

"And we don't forget what happens," said Charles.

Murgatroyd nodded.

"That fits," he said. "There are holy men who keep warm naked among the snows in Tibet, and who have passed whole lifetimes sitting cross-legged in meditation, trying to reach such a state of perpetual wakefulness, and failed. And here you are, doing it naturally, as if it were second nature to you."

"Why should one's mind go to sleep?" said Charles. "It's more interesting to keep it awake."

AT BED-TIME Murgatroyd curled up at the foot of Charles's bed, on the old Icelandic rug woven with diamond patterns in dim orange-browns and greens. He looked so much at home you could have imagined that he'd been there for years. This was where their father saw him for the first time.

He had come in, bleary eyed from desk work, to tell them a good-night story in Charles's room. Instead he stood in the doorway, looking at the cat.

"Where did he come from, Charles?" he said. "Did you let him in?"

"He's called Murgatroyd, Dad," said Charles. "Please, please can he stay?"

"He's your cat as much as ours," said John. "Stroking cats is good for high blood pressure. The *New Scientist* says so. It would help you if you stroked him sometimes."

"Since you wouldn't get another dog after Whisky was run over," said Charles, "can't we at least have a cat instead? He won't be as much trouble as a dog."

Their father shook his head. He had heavily set legs, but delicately shaped hands and a thin, humorous face. His glasses glinted as his head moved.

"Two problems," he said. "First, he almost certainly belongs to someone else, and they'll be angry if they find we've kept him. He's not a stray. You can see that just by looking at him. Beautifully kept. Fed, combed, at ease with people. Second, animals are a responsibility. When we go to grandmother's, who's going to take care of him?"

"Mrs Grey would feed him, if you asked her," said John, who was sitting on a chair in his dressing-gown.

Charles had the feeling their father was not quite as much against

Murgatroyd staying as he was trying to sound.

He started a new line of argument.

"Cats own themselves," he said. "As long as he's free to come and go, no one could say we were keeping him."

"It's not so simple," said their father. "If you feed a cat, it gets attached to you."

"Cats do rounds from house to house," said John. "They take food from whoever gives it them. It doesn't mean they get *owned*."

"True," said their father, but he sounded doubtful.

Charles caught a flash from Murgatroyd's eyes, and this gave him another idea.

"He's a useful cat," he said. "He can find things you've lost."

"How do you know?" said his father.

"He just told me," said Charles.

His father let out a breath, pursed his lips, and attempted not to look annoyed.

"I know it's tough," he said, "but try to keep a sense of reality."

"Just try it," said Charles. "Try it. Know your black-and-gold cufflink that went missing? Why don't you show him the other one and see if he can find the one that's disappeared?"

"Oh, don't be ridiculous, Charlie," said his father, though in a kindly voice.

"At least we can try it," Charles repeated. "If nothing happens, well — nothing happens. It's not the end of the world. I'll get the link that's still left, if you'll tell me where it is."

"On my dressing-table. Left-hand side," said his father.

Charles slid his bare feet out from under the covers, and edged himself out of bed so as not to disturb Murgatroyd. Then he padded off down the corridor.

He was back almost at once with the cufflink.

"They were a present from Father Severo, weren't they?" said John.

"Yes," said their father, "though I think someone else gave them to him. Priests have no use for cufflinks. One of his flock probably gave them to him. So he passed them on to me."

"They were rather beautiful," said John. "Especially against the white shirt with wine and grey lines on it. It's always the beautiful things that disappear."

His father smiled, without answering.

Charles held the remaining cufflink under Murgatroyd's nose. The cat was sitting up now and pretending to look at it intently.

"Murg," he said, "find pair. This cufflink. Find pair. Please."

The cat stretched his shoulders slightly. Then he jumped off the bed.

"Does he understand?" said their father to John, giving his elder son a sideways glance. "It almost looks like it."

"Can't tell, can one?" said John. "But he's a smart cat."

Murgatroyd ambled over to where the skirting-board turned a corner near the book case. He paused, lifted his head in the air a moment, then clawed back a flap of the carpet. A flash of black and gold shone up from something lying on the underfelt.

Their father walked across, bent down, picked it up, and examined it. Then he compared it to the other one, which Charles had left lying on the Icelandic rug, holding the two of them side by side.

"He can stay, can't he?" said Charles.

"It's uncanny," said their father. "Too uncanny to be comfortable."

He looked at Murgatroyd, who was sitting by the bookcase, not moving. Then he put the cufflinks into his pocket.

"I suppose so," he said. "I suppose so."

The thought crossed John's mind that there might now be *three* such cufflinks in existence. But he kept his mouth shut.

THE STORY that night was about the cedar forests of the Lebanon, the great forests of which nothing remains today. Their father sat on the edge of Charles's bed, some way down, outside the pool of light from the lamp on the bedside table. His voice rose and fell like a spoken song.

He told them how, four thousand years ago, Gilgamesh, King of Uruk, had wished to do something too hard for anyone else to do. How he was resolved, whether he succeeded or died in trying, to leave such a name behind him that no one would forget him.

Yet Gilgamesh had been forgotten. For two-and-a-half thousand years his story had slept in the fire-scorched tablets of the ruined library of Nineveh. His story, written in languages no one remembered, and cut in a script of wedge-marks impressed in clay. The city of Nineveh, once on the upper waters of the Tigris and capital of Assyria. Sacked six hundred and twelve years before the present era.

Only in recent times had scholars put the fragments together again. Only slowly had they relearnt the lost tongues, and brought the king back to life. And these labours, too, written on dry paper, might themselves vanish before too long, as people lost interest in them. Here was what had happened.

Gilgamesh had crossed the desert with his friend Enkidu to confront Huwawa, the monster who guarded the cedar-trees. The boys in their mind's eye saw Huwawa, lurking in the green depths of the forested hills, knee-deep among the dark channels of running water. They glimpsed his eyes, whose gaze dissolved the strength of men. They saw him overwhelmed by the winds given to Gilgamesh by Shamash, god of the sun. They heard him pleading for his trees, then taken captive and killed, his body offered in sacrifice to the gods. Gods without a conscience. The boys' minds echoed to the crash of the cedars as they were hewn down with axes. They saw the hacked trunks dragged across the desert to the city, to serve there as beams for its palaces, and shining planks for their floors. They saw the hill-slopes of the Lebanon, now bare, and the rains washing their soils away year after year, leaving a land half lifeless.

Murgatroyd lay in the darkness at the end of Charles's bed, thinking his own thoughts, but saying nothing. He remembered Gilgamesh and Enkidu as if it were yesterday. They had been great men, kindly towards cats, warriors, builders, and skilled at having themselves remembered, in songs, and in stone sculptures along the temple walls. But it was the poets who had made the story. The poets who had put imagined feelings in their hearts, and speech into their mouths. It was the poets who had filled the skies with powers like Shamash, the sun. Shamash had never existed. Sculptors who had determined what faces they should have in others' minds. Faces unlike the real ones. And there had — in fact — been no Huwawa, only the mysterious life of the trees themselves.

But Murgatroyd had learned something new. How this overstressed middle-aged man, with his high blood-pressure and uncertain temper, lived serene in his inner mind. How even his bed-time tales opened a vision of the world that gave his boys an understanding so far beyond their years. Megan, he thought, Megan — I wonder if you should not be careful with these two....

He pretended to sleep. Then at three o'clock in the morning he crept down the stairs and turned on the television set in the sitting room.

A face appeared. It was weary and hungry for something, but sharp-witted, very much in command. Megan's face.

"When will they be ready?" she demanded.

Murgatroyd sat to attention. *Am I really going to be a traitor?* he thought. *Or shall I doublecross them, as planned? I don't know my own mind.*

"In a few days, my lady," he said. "In a few days at most. Maybe sooner. Good game needs hanging before it is fit to eat. I have been invited into the house. I have won their trust. Their father has been persuaded to let me stay. All that I have to do now is to work on their greed a little more, to get them used to having what they want, and to having it immediately. Then they will be ready for our Garden of Delights."

"Don't take too much time about it," said the witch. "My heart is starving inside."

"What sort of nonsense are you telling them?" she added.

"You will be aware, my lady," said Murgatroyd, "that is has always been my policy to tell the truth as far as possible. It is more artistically satisfying to mislead by telling the truth — not, of course, ever the complete truth — than by the manufacture of even the most delightful falsehood."

"I am not sure I entirely believe you," said the witch. "But that is of no great importance. You will be judged by results."

The look she gave him made his stomach go cold inside. Then she vanished.

He turned off the set, slipped back to the bedroom, and once again curled himself up on Charles's bed with every appearance of affection.

Which way am I going to to jump? he wondered. *Has it been predestined for me? It will be interesting to see.*

THE MORNING was filled with golden sunshine. The branches of the trees were sharp-outlined and sparkling. At Charles's suggestion they went shopping for Christmas presents. It was typical of him to think of these things in advance, in November.

Travelling in the car with Murgatroyd was not ordinary driving. The cat perched on the back of the driver's seat, wedged against the head-rest. He made sure there were never red lights, and from time to time — when safe and convenient — arranged that the one-way street signs reversed themselves.

Their father seemed not to notice, so far as Charles could see. Probably dreaming about computing again, he thought. They parked in the Institute parking-lot, from which it was an easy walk to the shops.

Since the Science Patio was the nearest, they went there first. All sorts of instruments and curios and novelties were arranged round the walls of a glassed-in courtyard. There were dipping ducks that drank and swallowed non-stop from a bowl of water. There were models of molecules made of dozens and dozens of red, green, yellow, and black balls joined by rods. There were plywood dinosaur kits; and steel balls suspended by threads in a frame that clonked back and forth against each other, showing the conservation of momentum. The pocket calculators on display did more things than you could think of a use for. There were Tarot cards for telling your fortune; Xener cards for practising telepathy; and slinky springs that walked down steps once you started them off. Star-charts showing the constellations on a night-blue background — Orion's belt, Pegasus's stable-box, Cassiopeia's folding chair — and a moon-chart that told you the days when other people went a bit mad, and the days to avoid when making decisions. There was an endless treasure-trove of sensible, foolish, and fascinating things. It was also the best place to start when you couldn't think what to buy for someone.

After changing his mind a few times, Charles bought a sunlight spinner for grandmother. This was a clear glass bulb with most of the air removed from it. Inside the bulb, and poised on a needle-point, was a tiny four-armed weathervane with a square leaf of metal foil at the end of each of its arms. One side of each leaf was silver, and the other black. When you put it in strong sunshine it started to spin by itself, often so fast it seemed like the whirring of insect wings. No one quite agreed why it worked. Maybe the black side got hotter, the last little bit of air there expanded, and pushed the leaf away? In any case, he imagined grandmother's bedroom in the early morning as the sun came in, with the spinner starting to spin on the table under the window, so she would think of him often.

John bought a nugget of iron pyrites — 'Fool's Gold' — fat and gleaming, to remind grandmother of her days in the Sierra Nevada.

Charles noticed that both presents were remarkably cheap. It crossed his mind that Murgatroyd was altering the price-tags. This worried him. He knew Mr Fox who ran the Science Patio. He was a kindly man, and he didn't like the idea of his losing out. He resolved to keep a watch on this at the next shop.

The next shop was the Arran Wool Centre across the street. Charles bought a stone-coloured jumper that was too small for him. Murgatroyd was puzzled by this. He was sitting on the counter between piles of tartan tammies, and when Charles bent down to stroke him whispered something in his ear.

Charles smiled and shook his head.

"It's not for me, cat," he said. "It's for Josh. His last sweater's falling to bits, and Stella can't buy him a new one since she's lost her job on the fire brigade switchboard."

When he paid at the cashpoint he noticed the price had gone down. He noticed something else as well. To judge by the notes still stuffed in his wallet — most of a year's savings — he hadn't spent anything yet. But of course he had. The cat — *presumably it was the cat* — was filling it up as it emptied.

This gave Charles three different feelings, all at the same time. One was that he could now get everyone what they needed, and this was wonderful. The second was that the new banknotes might be magic forgeries, and he hoped the cat had made them properly, so they wouldn't get caught. And the third was, rather miserably, that the cat shouldn't be doing this and nor should they.

John didn't buy anything at the wool shop but at Clipsilver's, the hardware store, he got grandfather a Burnish-Master Colour-Spray Electric Shoe-Care Gun. This was a sort of plastic pistol with a circular electro-magnetic head. By putting the current on with a button you could pick up circular brushes, applicators, and buffering-cloths without getting your fingers dirty. The head rotated with a burring like a small airplane. If you took enough time and care the Gun made shoes startlingly shiny.

"Grandfather's always cleaning shoes," John explained. "I think he'll like this."

Charles shook his head.

"He'll say thank you very much," he said, "and never touch it again."

"Why?" said John. "It's dead simple to use, and it does a much better job than polishing shoes by hand."

"Grandfather's not like us," Charles explained. "He didn't grow up with gadgets. He can't even change a plug. It's just not in the way he thinks."

John looked dismayed.

"I've bought it now," he said, "so I'll have to give it to him. I hope you're wrong. At any rate, I suppose I can always use it for him when I'm staying there. I wish presents were not so difficult."

He examined his wallet, and Charles saw him give a slight start. He guessed that Murgatroyd had been refilling his brother's wallet as well.

"Plenty of money?" he said cheerfully.

"Too much," said John. "I must have counted it wrong, or something."

They ended the morning with an armful of presents each, and wallets as full as when they'd set out. While they were watching football on the television after lunch, Murgatroyd asked them a question:

"Why," he said, "didn't you buy yourselves anything?"

"It was a Christmas-presents expedition," said Charles. "We didn't have time to think of ourselves. Other people will give us something."

John nodded absent-mindedly as the ball hit a goal-post and rebounded.

"Don't you want to get something for yourselves?" said the cat. "We could go out again this afternoon. There's time."

"Of course we want some things for ourselves," said Charles. "I want a Japanese sword when I can afford it. But — ."

He stopped, and John filled in the rest of the sentence.

"With our own money, Murg. Not forged notes."

The cat's jaw dropped.

"They're perfect imitations," he said. "It's one of the tricks I'm best at. No one, certainly no ordinary human being, can tell the difference. How did you know?"

"How we knew's not the point," said Charles. "We're grateful to you, but it's embarrassing. It's not our money. If we buy things for other people that's — well, perhaps — sort of all right. But not for ourselves."

The cat flicked his green eyes from one to the other. He was intrigued and — though he didn't like to admit it to himself — impressed.

"You don't really need my magic," he said. "That's sad."

Charles put his arm around the black cat.

"Murg," he said, "that is just not true. We've got ever so many things to ask you to do with your magic, if you're willing."

The cat's eyes brightened.

"Like what?" he said.

"Like old Mr Hill-Brown who lives three houses down the street," said Charles. "He can hardly get in to work on his dictionaries any more."

"You want to do it now?" said the cat.

"Why not?" said John. "It's not much of a game."

He stood up and switched off the set.

"OK. What do you want me to do?"

"If we keep a look-out at the end of the driveway," said Charles, "there's a good chance we'll see him going by. He takes a short walk every afternoon on Saturday. He tells me he's done so for more than fifty years. These days the best he can manage is to get to the bank of the river. He has a rest there and watches the water pour over the weir, or chats to the moorers in their boats. Then he goes back the same way, very very slowly."

"Why so slowly?" said the cat.

"He has to use a walking-frame. You'll see as soon as we see him. Every step he takes, he has to lift the frame, move it forward a few inches, lean on it to take his weight, and shuffle himself a bit closer to it. Then he has to do it again, hundreds of times, just to make it down the street. If he fell over, he couldn't get up again, unless somebody helped him."

"Odd how he's always cheerful," said John. "Or almost always. In a way, that makes the whole thing sadder."

"What is it you want me to do?" said Murgatroyd. "I can't cure his disease, whatever it is. Remember, my magic only works on things that are not alive."

"We want you to put a spell on his walking-frame," said Charles. "It must not fall over, unless for some reason he wants it to. It must be able to stop any car or truck in its tracks, so he can't get knocked down. Some of the drivers round here never think, or care, where they're going. Our dog, Whisky, was killed by one last year. Most important of all, you must make the frame take the work out of walking. If you can make him feel almost weightless while he's walking along — but safely, mind you — that's what we want."

"That's quite some request," said Murgatroyd. "It makes counterfeiting seem easy."

He put his head on one side, reflecting, and rubbed at his whiskers with a paw.

"Yes!" he said at last. "It's the first time it's been done, so it ought to be possible. Please don't ask me to try it a second time, though. Certainly not a third!"

"That's wonderful, Murg," said Charles.

He picked him up and hugged him Then he put him down again, and the three of them went down the driveway in the sunshine and sat on the low wall at the end of the street.

It was quite a while before Mr Hill-Brown appeared, so they talked of this and that. At other times they were silent, simply enjoying each others' company. Murgatroyd was aware of a strange feeling inside him, a sort of nameless excitement. He wondered what was happening to him. It was not unpleasant, but it was odd. Maybe the good inclination inside him was winning.

When the old man appeared, he was moving along even more slowly than the cat had imagined. But his eyes were bright and quick. He seemed to be noticing everything. The last mauve chrysanthemums in Mrs Moss's garden, stirring in the wind. The silhouette of a hawk on a post in the field across the river. A crumpled paper bag, glittering white, being blown in starts and stops along the gutter, lifting suddenly above its shadow, then dropping down onto it, to rest again.

He probably sees more in a hundred yards, thought the cat, than most human beings do in a ten-mile trudge.

When Mr Hill-Brown was level with the boys he stopped, and readjusted his hat.

"Good afternoon, Mr Hill-Brown," said John. "Beautiful day, isn't it?"
Charles smiled and nodded too.

"Afternoon, Mr Hill-Brown," he said.

"Good afternoon, boys," the old man answered. "Is that a new cat you've got?"

"He's called Murgatroyd," said Charles. "He didn't get on too well with his last owner, so he's living with us."

"Very particular animals, cats," said Mr Hill-Brown. "He looks happy and in good condition now."

He examined the cat.

"'Murgatroyd' you said his name was?" he asked.

Charles and John nodded.

"I wonder if perhaps his real name is 'Margalit', meaning 'pearl'," said Mr Hill-Brown. "He is a magnificent animal. Wonderful eyes. Or maybe 'Margelot', 'the end of a bed'? Cats like to rest, you know. Or perhaps — ."

His face darkened.

"Perhaps 'Meragel', 'a spy'," he added. "It is strange what names can tell you. People will inform you that I am an old man gone crazy from making too many dictionaries, and that the sound of a name is accidental. That the meaning is just what you choose it to be. But I have never found it to be so. Names always tell you something about a person, don't you think?"

The boys nodded a second time.

"Well," said Mr Hill-Brown. "I must be moving again, as best I can. Bodies are such an embarrassment at my age. But I have to make it to the weir and back before it becomes dark."

"Mind if we walk along with you?" said Charles.

"Not at all. A great pleasure," said Mr Hill-Brown. "But as soon as you find my pace too slow, please feel free to be on your own way."

As they moved towards the river, Murgatroyd followed behind making little magical adjustments to the walking-frame. He did it carefully, to avoid mistakes.

Mr Hill-Brown walked perceptibly faster. Then faster still, until he was almost up to the boys' ordinary walking speed.

"You're going well today, Mr Hill-Brown," said Charles.

"You're quite right. I am," said the old man. "I feel more energy than I when I set out. It must be the effect of meeting you."

He seemed delighted, and the boys felt their own delight at his happiness.

"Look at the water," said the old man as they came up to the weir. "Nobody really understands how it flows."

They watched the sleek green torrent pouring down, the tumbleback, and the downstream undulations.

"Don't scientists?" said John.

"They have some rough-and-ready rules," said Mr Hill-Brown, "but the real nature of water escapes them. It is slightly sticky, you see. It sticks to itself just a little. That's why there are all these drops flying about, and the threads and strings you can see in the flow. But its movement also pulls it apart. Have you ever looked at a large waterfall, moving your head down fast, so the pattern seems to be motionless? No? What you see is an open network of water, partly pulled apart, partly sticking together. It is an art to see things, you know."

The boys nodded, and Mr Hill-Brown's eyes sparkled.

John glanced up and down the riverside path. Up-river from the lockgates two runners in dayglo shorts, and with mud spattered down their calves and thighs, were being overtaken by a twelve-year-old girl on a bicycle. Steam was floating from the black chimneys of the narrowboats moored by ropes and iron pegs to the bank. Panels of roses and castles and meadows were painted on their sides. Crude but pretty. Two bicycles were lashed upside down, next to each other, on one of the narrowboats' roof. Wetness was shining from the lower trunks of the riverside trees. The effects of the wash of a passing boat? Four or five ducks were rocking up and down in the water under the mouth of a rusty downpipe. Is this what Mr Hill-Brown sees, I wonder, he thought to himself. Or something different?

The old man was breathing in the air deeply.

After a few minutes, he turned his walking-frame around and began to go back, quite briskly.

They followed.

Murgatroyd caught Charles's eye, and Charles gave him a nod. The cat jumped up on his shoulder.

"Will that do?" he whispered. "I don't want to make it too obvious."

"It looks great," said Charles. "Is it steady?"

"Like a rock," whispered the cat. "I promise."

"Thanks!" said the boy softly. "Thanks very much indeed!"

Ten minutes later Mr Hill-Brown stopped at the door to his house.

"Would you like a cup of tea?" he said. "Rivka's still got some hot water in one of the thermoses. It shouldn't taste too thin."

"Very much," said John. "If it's no trouble."

"No trouble at all," said the old man. "We always have plenty of hot water on hand on Saturdays in case somebody calls."

He let them in. It was dark inside, but he did not turn the light on, and after a while their eyes became used to the gloom.

The old man put tea-bags in four china cups, while his grand-daughter unscrewed a thermos and poured warm water into them.

The gift of making the ordinary something exceptional, thought the cat to himself. I remember when they were making it all up, but I never understood it till now. It makes you think of something else, beyond you, in every act of your life.

Framed drawings crowded together on the walls. Drawings of old-fashioned typewriters, and flying-shuttle looms, and farm machinery, and also hook-tined teazel-plants and turned-over dandelion leaves. Complicated details precisely observed and rendered in sharp pencil lines.

"By my wife, Nushen," said Mr Hill-Brown, when he noticed their interest.

"She died ten years ago, so you probably don't remember her. I still forget myself sometimes, and talk to her. Milk in your tea? Sugar? Can't really believe she's not here."

Milk, they said, but no sugar, thank you.

The old man also poured some milk into a saucer for Murgatroyd. As the cat saw the old man anchor one hand on a chair-seat for support, and bend down painfully to put it on the floor for him, he felt another wave of the nameless sensation he had experienced before.

John took a sip. The tea was lukewarm and hadn't infused properly. No matter.

"Why dictionaries?" he asked, gazing at the stacks of filing-cards and books on the desk.

Mr Hill-Brown looked at the boy intently. What sort of an answer did he want?

"Why do you fall in love with a particular girl?" he said. "A particular woman? I don't know why I fell in love with Nushen, except that I found I got on with her. That life was better when she was around. In the same way, I suppose you could say that I get on with dictionaries. That life seems to get on better when they are around. Does that explain it?"

"Not really," said John with a smile. "But please don't think me rude if I say so."

"I will try again," said Mr Hill-Brown. "Words are like electric wires. They carry a current from the past. My task, as a dictionary-maker, is to see that the meaning flows as strongly as possible. That the resistance to the flow created by people's ignorance of words, or by their half-understanding, is kept to as little as possible. Does that make more sense?"

"I think so," said John. "But why is the past important? Can't we just let it be? There's no way of changing it now."

"Now that is a serious question," said Mr Hill-Brown. "We forget too much these days." He leant back in his stiff old armchair, lifted his hat up an inch or two and rubbed his forehead . "It deserves a serious answer."

"We were spoken to clearly once," he went on. "A long time ago. It has never happened again. Words are all we have to remind us that it did happen — once. And of what was said."

Murgatroyd looked up at the old man sadly. He thought to himself: Here am I, a cat on the floor now, sitting silently, drinking his milk, and I can remember — from my own memories — what he is talking about from his religious books. The volcano erupting on the edge of the fault between two continental plates that runs up the Sea of Reeds. The sky covered with smoke, like smoke from a potter's kiln. If only he knew! But God was not talking, not God at least in any ordinary human sense. Red-hot rock was shifting in the depths of the earth and driving up outbursts of lava. If I were to tell him, he would not believe me. If he did believe me, it would destroy him. And he is a wonderful old man. All I can do is to keep my silence. My silence. And to wish him luck and happiness for all the days he has left. He has a beautiful grand-daughter.

John, too, said no more. The conversation was going too deep for him. After a while he heard Mr Hill-Brown singing under his breath. It sounded like the prayer when the day of rest is over.

Then the old man stood up.

"It is dark now, boys. You had better go home," he said, "or your father will start to wonder where you are."

He patted a small metal lion screwed to the doorframe, holding something written in its paws.

"Have a good week!" he said as they left.

Something weird flipped in Murgatroyd's heart. He wondered if the good inclination had won. As he looked back he saw Rivka, her dark eyes shining, putting the lights on and the whole of the little house ablaze with light. That was another kind of magic.

THAT NIGHT, when the bed-time story was over, and their father had wandered back to his computer, the cat asked the boys to stay awake.

"I've something important to tell you," he said.

"I'm sleepy," said Charles. "Can't you tell us it in our dreams?"

"No. Wake up," said Murgatroyd. "It's a life-and-life matter."

"'Life-and-life'?" said Charles. "What do you mean?"

"Life of the body and life of the heart. You can die while you're still alive."

Charles pulled himself up in bed. He doubled his pillow in two and leant back against it, with Tiger on one side for company. John sat on the edge of Charles's bed, with his hand on one of Bear's paws.

"Tell us," he said.

"Listen," said Murgatroyd. "You are about to fall into a trap. Like your mother. The witch whom I work for feeds off children. Not their bodies. She doesn't touch their bodies. Their *feelings*. She captures children she likes the look of, and puts them in a television set. A set with an enchantment on it. There she plays with them. Like little sugared mice. She changes the world around them, so they react. Sometimes with ecstasy, sometimes with terror, or with laughter, or else sadness. She squeezes the feelings out of them, like you squeeze lemon into China tea. She needs them, as a kind of soulfood. Then, when she's had enough, she switches them off. They exist after that like ghosts, or less than ghosts, mere flitting potentials in the circuit-cards, until she turns them on again.

"When she's taken from them all that they have to give, she lets them go. By this time they are adults, or almost adults, but empty inside. Empty as a split nutshell without the nut. You've probably met some of them, and wondered what was wrong. That's what's wrong. *You two* are next on the list."

The boys felt their hearts freeze.

Murgatroyd went on:

"It's my job to catch new kids for her. Kids still alive inside. I win their confidence. Charm them with purring and affection. Then I fascinate them with a little friendly magic. Like finding a lost cufflink. And then — then I betray them. Megan has a program, the Garden of Magical Pleasures. No kid can resist walking into it, of his, or her, free will. Once inside, they are in her prison. You know how Africans catch monkeys?"

"What's that got to do with it?" said John.

"They put some fruit in a gourd with a small hole in it, a hole just big enough to let the monkey put his hand in empty. Not big enough to let him pull it out if it's holding something. They fix the gourd to a nearby tree. The monkey comes, smells the fruit, puts his hand in and grabs it. All he has to do to escape is let go the fruit, but he never does. Kids are the same. My final task is to get them to watch this program. Once they look, that's it: it's all over."

"Grief," said Charles. "I am completely cold inside. Why are you telling us this? I thought you were our friend. I have never — *ever* — made a mistake about something like this before."

"Nor have you made a mistake this time," said the cat. "Your sixth sense, your sense of truth, is still running true. Something has happened inside me. Something to do with my being with you. I cannot go on being what I have been. I have decided to betray betrayal."

"But you've said that before," objected John. "Said that you wanted an ordinary life."

"I was lying to you then," said Murgatroyd. "This time it's true."

"How much of what you told us before about yourself was false?"

"Very little," said the cat. "It is more artistic to mislead with truth than with lies. I did leave things out. Megan is not an incompetent witch. She is old, resourceful, humorous as only the totally wicked can be, and dangerous. Under her elegant manners, she is without pity. Nothing else needs changing — much."

"Our problem," said John, "is to be sure you're not deceiving us again. How can we be confident of that?"

"Fair question," said the cat. "All I can offer you as a proof is this. Tonight, at three o'clock, I will turn on your television set. By this time even your father will have gone to bed. Before I do so I'll set up a mirror so you can see the screen indirectly. On no account — *on no account* — look at it directly. Otherwise *she* will be able to see *you*. And, if she runs the Garden of Magical Pleasures, you will not be able to resist, at least not unless I help you. Or someone has lashed you to the mast, like Odysseus listening to the song of the Sirens as his ship sped by their rocks, the rowers' ears plugged tight with wax. Hear how we talk. Then judge for yourelves."

"What's going to happen?" said Charles.

"I will cringe and cower in front of her," said Murgatroyd, "pretending still to be her faithful servant. She will want me to fetch you at once. She is impatient. But I will say that you are away in the world of dreams, with Tiger and with Bear, and that I cannot get you back. Tomorrow you must tell your father to get rid of the television set immediately. It is dangerous to have it in the house."

"As bad as that?" said John. "What reason do we give him?"

"Tell him you can't concentrate on your homework for school," said Murgatroyd. "He'll be pleased at that. Impressed, too."

"After that, what happens?"

"I will put spells of protection around the house," said the cat. "She'll still try to get in, and on no account must you invite her in the way you invited me in. If she forces her way in, which she can, she cannot bring her power with her, only her art of persuasion. I will try to stop even that happening. And neither of you must go out alone at any time, or — under any circumstances — on foot at night."

"Sounds frightening," said Charles. "What would happen if we just left? Went to grandmother's, for example. And you told her we'd disappeared?"

"Fatal," said Murgatroyd. "She'd find out the truth in a few hours, then get you. You're safest in your own home, where your powers of resistance are strongest."

"You make it sound serious," said John.

"Haven't you been listening to what I've been saying?" said the cat. "It's more than serious. It's deadly. Don't you understand? *You are being hunted. For food.*"

THE RIVER had flooded. The water stretched across the fields, sometimes on one side, sometimes on the other, sometimes on both. Only the higher parts of the towing-path, which ran along a dyke, and above the drowned grasses and the reflected sky, showed where the channel was. As did the faster flow of the current.

Cressida edged against it upstream. She moved past the stands of reeds, and past the cracked willow-trees where, in the summer evenings, swallows swoop-circled for insects. Now Charles could see only a single, shrug-shouldered, heron. Alone, on a shore of sloping mud. Waiting, unmoving. Also for food.

It was cold. Early morning. Fuzzed reflections here and there showed where ice had formed in the shallow fields. The outboard motor putt-putted at their backs. Noisy, but also reassuring. It gave him the feeling that they were in control — as long as they were careful. One flurry of unexpected wind could blow the light hull scudding sideways, maybe against the bank.

Charles watched his father watching the water. His father's fingers kept easing the wheel — this way, then that way, that way, then this way — holding *Cressida* on her course. A strange man. Charles wondered what was going on in his mind.

John and Murg were down in the cabin. They were listening to the water rushing past the fibreglass sides, watching the floodscape travelling by outside the portholes, and enjoying the warmth from the safety-gas heater high on the bulkhead wall. It was hissing to itself, and the sound combined with the sounds of the outboard motor and the passing water into a kind of music.

From time to time they talked. Mostly they said nothing.

It was the school half-term, and they had taken the boat in order to enjoy a few days of safety. So long as they stayed on board, Megan could not cross the water to get at them, even when they moored at night. Or so Murg said.

Charles liked to stay on deck, to feel the wind lift in his hair, to let his eyes drink in the space. The sky was grey, with cumulus clouds on the horizon, piling up beyond the spire of a church in some distant village.

Canada geese were riding at anchor in this reach of the river, like ships — or so it seemed to him. Two or three hundred of them, with their brown-blue brindled backs and black neck-stockings, were drifting among each other, moving about but going nowhere.

How different this was, he thought, from what they had seen in the mirror three nights before. The witch's face, twisted with wanting, spitting out her orders at Murgatroyd. John and himself to be brought, at once, to the television set. Glimpses of her Garden of Magical Pleasures — pleasures which, when remembered, seemed terrible — not beautiful at all.

The power for a boy to command, to torture, and to kill. What every boy wants, if he's not a cissy. He had seen himself for a moment as the World-Emperor, making all humankind perfect under his control. Then a vision of his own tomb after his death. A black granite pyramid, a mile in height, at the South Pole, a place where only one tomb could ever be, looming above the crevasses through the blizzarding snow, or else visible fifty miles away at midnight in the days of the summer sunshine. A unique tomb, with no other like it. And in gigantic capital letters, cut like those on Emperor Trajan's column, was his name. Only his name. **CHARLES.**

Then the Garden had faded, and he'd seen Megan's face again. Next, a black paw, switching her off.

He blinked. The world around him reappeared. The winter elms raising their arms against the sky. The gap-toothed walls of what was still called a nunnery, torn down four hundred years ago when King Henry the Eighth had made the nuns marry. The swirl of the waters around the sturdy mooring-posts where *Cressida* was easing in sideways to rest her fenders against them.

He stayed on board, keeping hold of both mooring-ropes, while his father leapt ashore to work the lock-gates. He heard the crank-handle rattling in the gearbox, and saw the water, as the sluices lifted, arching out in gushers from the vents in the stone lock-sides.

Later he went below, his face tired by the wind, to talk with John and Murg. Their father remained at the wheel. *Cressida* chugged past the swimming-place, under the trees above the lock, where old tyres hung down on ropes from the branches, their rims now caught at and tugged by the water. Their father remembered the flash of bodies in summer, of kids hugging their knees as they leapt out as far as they could, the sound of their splashes, the yelling and laughter.

Now — a grey silence.

Here and there, moorhens.

Not even a mackintoshed fisherman, hunched on a canvas stool, surrounded by nets and rods, and boxes of bait, his soul fixed on a red-and-white float in the water.

Nothing.

"We've survived," said Murgatroyd. "Survived. So far. But what comes next? I've encircled the boat with a spell. In any case, the witch can't cross running water. When you go back to school, it will not be so easy. She'll be tracking you in her car. She'll find some means to tempt you to enter it, with its smell of warm and sleepy leather. Don't get in, whatever you do."

"What sort of a car does she drive?" asked Charles.

"Black Mercedes," said the cat. "And she chauffeurs it herself. But tomorrow it may be something else. Don't trust to it being black. Or a Mercedes."

"Of course, if the car fails," he added, " — and the smiling offers of lifts, the accidents that need *you* to help her, all the familiar bag of tricks — she'll twirl the Bolas of Shadows against you."

"The Bolas of Shadows? What's that?" said John.

"A bolas," the cat replied, "is made of three iron balls on leather thongs, joined to a central point. The Argentines of the pampas-lands, where you need to ride on a horse to see over the top of the grass, use it to bring down animals. To bring down humans, too, if they want to. They whirl it a few times around their heads, then throw it, spinning. If it even brushes your arm or leg, the balls whip round you, round and around, and bring you down. It's harder to dodge than you might imagine. The Bolas of Shadows is a magic form of the same device, enchanted to be invisible."

John shuddered.

"Why does so much thinking go into cruel things?"

"Life feeds on life," said Murgatroyd. "Even on a day like this, when everything seems in its winter sleep — except for us — there was a heron out. And what was she there for?"

"A meal," said Charles.

"Precisely," said the cat. "A meal. Like Megan. Don't think it will ever be otherwise."

"Don't you wish it could?" said John.

"I wish I could imagine what it would be like," said the cat.

They listened to the putt-putt of the outboard, and said nothing.

A shadow swept over the portholes as *Cressida* went under a bridge. They could see the light-ripples from the water dancing on the underside of the arch. Then they were out again.

"Murgatroyd," said Charles, "do you know what's happened to our mother?"

"I can guess," said the cat, "from what the network has told me."

"What's the 'network'?" said John.

"Megan uses birds as her spies. They also report to me if I have a need to know. An owl told me what happened. The sticky webs of words, the body trussed up like a spider's prey, the screech of tyres on the driveway gravel. I know about that."

"What I mean is, what happened after that?" said Charles. "Where is she now? And who is Dr Homely-Sage?"

Murgatroyd was lying sprawled across the top of a life-jacket. His fur seemed like a black nothingness, an empty hole in the orange colour of the padded vest. As he replied, the silhouette of his head turned slightly.

"We only know of one person — except that 'person' is not the right word to describe him — who can do what's been done. Dr Homely-Sage is one of the outer forms of a Word-Spider who lives in the City of Fogs and Machinery. His central human self, if he has one, goes by the name of

'Grayach'."

The cat stopped speaking.

Charles clenched his fist at the sound of that name.

"You haven't answered my question," he said quietly. "What has this thing done to our mother?"

"If I told you," said Murgatroyd, "you would need more strength than you have to bear it. If you could bear it, it would burn in your mind all the days of your life. You'll be happier not knowing. Believe me."

"There is no choice for us," said Charles. "Not knowing is burning us away as it is. If we can know, we must."

The cat looked at John, who nodded, his face white.

"Such knowledge," said the black cat, "comes with a price you pay forever. It is not like a tag in a shop I can mark down for you."

"Go on, please," said Charles. "We paid that price long ago, and are on the journey. *Multa milia passuum.*"

The green fires kindled in Murgatroyd's eyes.

"Oh," he said, "so you know the waysong of the hippos. Well, then. Well, then, your mother is in a soul-cage."

"Explain," said Charles.

"In such a cage the links between your soul and the world outside are cut. You can only see, or feel, or hear, the things that you can imagine — out of your own resources: what you can remember or dream up out of nothing."

"You mean a perpetual dream?" said John.

"Almost, but not quite. It is solitary confinement in one's own mind. Without new colours or new sounds, or fresh smells or sensations of touch, to feed it, without unexpected insights from one's friends, the brain grows dulled and simple. Blurred. There is nothing left to be discovered. Your seeing loses the power to tell things apart. The soul falls into a special form of torment, where only the obvious can be seen at all. Primary colours: red, blue, and yellow; squares and circles, triangles with equal sides, rhythms of four-time repeating and beating without any variation, no change of loudness. A boredom with itself, beyond any imagining."

"It doesn't sound nice," said John, "but is it really so bad? Compared to real torture, that is?"

"I haven't expressed it well," said the cat. "What it means is that everything becomes without interest. But the memory of what interest once was remains. And the memory of what it once was to be in touch with the world. The suffocation of the heart is indescribable."

"Why does Grayach put souls in such cages, then?" said Charles. "And how does he do it?"

His voice was unmoving and hard, like iron at absolute zero.

"Grayach loves beauty," said Murgatroyd. "At the same time, he hates it. This is because he cannot create it himself. He seizes the souls of those who can, like your mother. Not only poets, but also those who make colours speak, and whose fingers give life to forms of ceramic and stone. He likes to empty their hearts out, for a kind of revenge against the world. To enjoy the pleasure of showing himself that, clever though they may be, he is cleverer than they are. He laughs with himself when he sees their sufferings. To laugh only with oneself is to be demonic."

Murgatroyd paused, then went on.

"As to how," he said, " — first of all he catches them with his skill in words. He can use a word the way a fisherman uses a bright-feathered fly. The victim's mouth closes around it, and, so doing, is gripped by the back-barbed hook. He can turn words into wires, wires that are shiny and sticky and cold. You've seen them. He binds them round a victim's flesh so it burns, but is never consumed. How the cages work, however, I can not exactly tell you."

"How do we find Grayach?" said John. "And how do we kill him?"

"I do not know if either is possible," said the black cat. "On your own, you can do neither. But I am on your side now, and that changes everything. I give you my word, my word as one who was once a Prince, even if over the Darkness, that I will do all within my magic to find him for you, and — if any means can be contrived to set you mother free — then, by my honour, so to contrive them."

His low cat's voice had taken on an unaccustomed strength. For a moment — and this was the only moment this ever happened — they had a sense of him as he had been before his banishment, before he had been doomed to shrink into the shape of a cat. Blackness on fire, neither kindly nor terrifying. Simply — unimaginably other. He had, indeed, been great, greater than they could conceive of.

The moment passed. There he was again, Murgatroyd, their black cat, talking to them from the top of a padded orange life-jacket.

Charles wiped his forehead with the sleeve of his old Arran sweater.

"Murg," he said. "I love you. How do we start?"

"By surviving Megan, first of all," said the cat. "That's going to be difficult enough."

"Look," he added, "I'll tell you something else, even though it may not be of much use. If you ever do get captured — HSM forbid — you can still fight back. Not with your bodies, but with your imaginations. Given the will, you can make the world inside her television set do what you want, not what she wants. And, if that happens, she will either have to come inside the set herself to meet you, mind to mind, or it will explode and you go free. If she confronts you — well, she has never met her match yet, and I wouldn't bet on your chances. The loser is turned into nothing. In the future, though, who can tell? With Hippo at your side.... But you have decided to know, rather than not to know, to walk a path of loneliness among your own kind, knowing what they do not. So I am giving you what information I have. Be warned, though, it may destroy you, rather than help."

"Meanwhile, I take it," said John, "that it's one thing at a time."

Murgatroyd nodded.

"Like a break for sardines and cream," he said. "You couldn't ask your father to tie up somewhere, could you? I don't want to use up energy making sure the saucer doesn't spill."

EARLY AFTERNOON. They were higher up the river. The flooding was gone, and the banks had drawn closer together. The wind had passed, and their father had let Charles take over the wheel, though he stood nearby in case of problems.

There were none. Charles was a canny and cautious helmsman. *Cressida* made her way steadily between banks of reeds, past meadows where horses cropped the cold grass, and from time to time through the narrow stone bridges with only a foot, or so, of space on either side.

Round a bend the river widened. Their way was blocked by a drifting flotilla of Canada geese. Charles shifted the engine to neutral, his finger poised to send it into reverse.

The boat's appearance startled the birds. Wings beating and clamouring, they took off from the river, one after the other, and rose into the air.

Two gunshots broke the silence.

Ke-chaff! Ke-chaff!

One of the geese wobbled, six feet above the water, then fell with a splash.

Charles slammed into full astern.

Back leapt *Cressida* like a rearing horse.

The rest of the geese rose in a mob and streamed away over the hedges.

The dead goose lay in the water, rocking.

Two men in khaki jackets broke from the cover of some bushes, carrying guns, and dashed towards a road.

Weird bluish light, like static lightning, enveloped the boat.

Charles eased down the revs, backing away round the bend.

Murgatroyd sat on the cabin roof — no one ever saw how he got there — paw raised in the line of the running men.

"Good thinking, Charles," said his father. "Those bullets would tear through our fibreglass hull like paper."

The boy saw the cat shake his head and give him the flicker of a wink. But his father saw nothing.

"Take the wheel, please, Dad," he said, still holding it steady.

But the moment his father's hands were on the wheel, he collapsed into silent tears. His shoulders shook, and he gripped and ungripped his fists as he tried to control himself.

His father swung *Cressida* around, and began to move downstream.

"Control yourself, Charles, if you can," he said. "People do these things."

"No, Dad, no," said Charles. "It was me. If we hadn't...."

He choked, fought for control, then started again.

"If we hadn't come round the bend, those geese would have stayed on the water. Those men wouldn't have shot."

He leant on the top of the cabin doorway, still shaking, and made himself take several deep breaths.

"He was so beautiful, that goose," he said. "So beautiful. I don't think I'll forget him so long as I live."

His father patted him gently on the back, keeping the other hand on the wheel.

"Charles," he said, "don't ever, ever blame yourself for what those two men did. They were waiting there, behind those bushes, deliberately, until a boat came or the geese took off of their own accord. They would have shot sooner or later."

"I suppose they would have," said Charles. "But why did it have to be me at the wheel? — Excuse me. I'm.... I'm going below."

In the cabin Murgatroyd looked up at him from his life-jacket.

"You did well," he remarked. "Nerves A1. Caught *me* by surprise, though. I thought it was Megan attacking. You see my protection spell?"

Charles nodded.

"It's immensely strong," said the cat. "But, if it had been Megan, rather than those oafs, it would have been too late."

He mused.

"We'd better keep our wits about us."

The rest of the afternoon passed uneventfully, however. When they moored for the night, nothing else had happened.

THE TILLEY LAMP sent its yellow glow into the corners of the cabin. Whenever the boat resettled its balance, as someone moved, or the current shifted, the shadows would alter their shapes along the curved cabin walls.

One of the doors was half open, to let the air in.

Night-time was stirring outside, full of small noises, of sticks that cracked for no reason, or the munching sound of a cow suddenly clear as the wind changed direction.

They lay on the cabin cushions, drinking hot chocolate, and talking of this and that. They said nothing about the goose. His death was too close for them to want to mention it. The conversation turned to other matters.

"You know," said their father, "we look at this countryside, and we think we're seeing it, but its memories are hidden from us. The boats that go tomorrow round the bend where the goose died will know nothing of him. The river will seem as beautiful as it always does. And yet behind every house, every broken wall, every field, there's a story. But you have to know it to know it. Just looking tells you nothing."

Murgatroyd, curled up against Tiger on Charles's bunk, nodded in agreement. Of course he said nothing.

"What do you mean?" said John.

"Not long after we set out we passed a couple of old boathouses," said their father. "With baskets of flowers hanging from their eaves. Remember?"

"Long Eyot, you mean?" said John. "Baulks of wood on the bank and some empty boat-cradles?"

"It's got a 'For Sale' sign up," said Charles.

"Closed down," said their father. "Brown and May have split up."

"Split up?" said John. "Brown and May? Why?"

"Brown's gone off with another woman. So it's on the market."

"I thought they got on so well," said John. "Why did they quarrel? Was it the campaign against them? All that hate in the papers and at meetings?"

"Could be," said their father. "They'd fought it so long together, the whole thing had been so bitter, that perhaps when he looked at her, all he could think of, in the end, was those years of battling. And, in the end, couldn't stand it any longer. But it's guesswork. There's no way we can really tell."

"I never understood that campaign," said Charles. "To say that two little boathouses were destroying the meadow.... The meadow's enormous. Getting hundreds of people angry about it for years, when it's not even true.... How could they believe a thing like that?"

"Meadow's in bad shape," said their father. "Too many animals been grazing on it. It was smart of the people who own the animals to turn the resentment against the boathouses. Other interests at work, too. A farmer who owns land nearby fancied the idea of running the boathouses himself. He thought if things were made nasty for Brown and May they'd sell up, and he could get them cheap. The people who run the city government have hated Brown for years. Too sharp and independent for them. They like businessmen here to do what they're told to do, and — so it's said — make it worthwhile for them to treat the businessmen nicely. They helped the hate-campaign from behind the scenes. Some of the local politicians, too. Claimed to be keen on the meadow, in the hope it might get them some votes."

"But important people have joined in," said Charles. "Famous people. Why don't they know better? Sir Jeremy Troutman, for instance. The head of St Jacob's College. And that Green Heritage woman. Angel Greypool. Have you seen how she glares at you, Dad, when she thinks you're not looking? But she's done some good things, too. She's not just batty. And there's that botanist against them. She's been saying there's some sort of bladderwort, that's at risk from Brown and May's boathouse. How can a plant be at risk from a boathouse? Why do people talk rubbish?"

"People love ideals. Often good ideals. The meadow's a good ideal. So's the environment. Even bladderworts. What people can't be bothered to do is to look at the facts. Facts take time, work. When you find them they can turn your ideas upside down."

Their father drank the last of his hot chocolate, reached over and put the mug in the galley sink. Then he leant back and resumed.

"They made a myth of the meadow. Said it was ancient common pasturage. In fact, not so long ago, the end where the boathouse is was a garbage-dump. You can see it was, even now, by looking at the bumps and hillocks under the pasture. They said Brown had stolen his land, sneaking a foot or two each year. In fact he made the land by putting fill into the river, with permission. The city even stopped him planting trees, at his own expense."

"Stopped him planting trees?" said John.

"Scared if he made the place look pleasant, it might be harder to get people to hate him."

"Didn't the campaign people try to burn the boathouses down?" Charles asked.

"Twice," said his father. "It happens that leaders redirect the good feelings of good people for their own purposes, and ugly things result."

"But didn't Brown and May win?" said John.

"The campaign failed," said their father. "Not one argument stuck in the courts, or the public enquiries. The campaigners won all the same. The pressure they put on broke Brown and May. Made them destroy themselves."

He sighed.

The water was lapping on the bank by the boat. Every now and then, as the boat rocked, the mugs clinked against each other in the sink. The gas fire hissed softly. Murgatroyd was purring as Charles stroked his shoulders. Somewhere in the distance was an owl.

"May was a hero, too," their father added. "Something the people who leaned on the boathouse gate and spat at her never knew; and she'd never have told them."

"What did she do?" said John.

"Carried information through a war-zone in the Middle East," said their father. " She pretended to be a housewife out shopping, and if anyone asked her questions, to be scatty. What she had in her shopping-bag would have cost her her life, if it had it been discovered. She has cold courage — the hardest kind — the sort the bomb-disposal experts need. And that's the heart that's been broken by the people of this city thinking they're doing good."

"Yet a few years from now," he added, "when people look at those boathouses, that's all they'll see — boathouses. Maybe with flowers still hanging in baskets under the eaves."

He put out his hand and rubbed Murgatroyd between the ears.

"I like your new cat," he said. "He gives me the feeling he's thinking. Not like any cat I've known before."

Charles nodded.

"Maybe, if he could speak," said their father, "he could tell us tales about other places along this river. Stories buried in the land, or in old houses, or the woods. Stories, perhaps, from the cat-world, different from ours."

"Perhaps, some day," said John, "he'll talk. But that will be his decision, not ours."

Ten minutes later the boys were asleep, in their sleeping-bags on their bunks, with Bear and Tiger pulled across their shoulders. Their father turned the Tilley lamp down slowly, and out. Then he rolled himself in some blankets, without taking his shoes off, and went to sleep. The owl was still hooting in the distance.

Two green eyes glowed in the darkness, awake.

"How does he see so deep?" thought the cat to himself. "Grown-ups shouldn't care about such things."

Then he remembered something. And smiled.

"Of course," he said to himself. "Of course. It was that old stuffed rabbit of his, Egger, who became the Administrator of Dreams. So, for thirty years or more now, he must have talked with the power that is. On first-name terms. He may even have half an idea who I am. How the criss-crossing chains of cause-and-effect run hidden through time."

NEXT MORNING, it was raining.

The drops pattered on the cabin roof. If you opened the door, you could hear them hitting the surface of the river.

In such weather, there was no point in moving on. At least, not until they had to. They stayed in their bunks, drinking cups of tea, and enjoying the warmth from the gas-fire. The sound of the rain outside filled them with a sense of contentment, a feeling that it was pleasant just to be where they were. Doing nothing. Or nothing much.

Charles sniffed the draught of cool air from under the door running across his face, and pulled up his sleeping-bag under his chin. He dreamt he was in a space-ship, hurtling towards the stars. For half an hour, he slept again.

Murgatroyd browsed through a book of chess games the boys' father had put down the night before on the side-shelf of varnished wood. He let the moves trickle through his mind, and the possible variations. He had no need for pieces or a chess-board.

The boys' father sat at the cabin table and looked at the pages in a ring-binder he had put together when he himself was a boy. Pressed flowers, from along this same river bank. He remembered the bicycle rides he had made with his mother, up and down the towpath, more than thirty years ago, to find new plants. The common names were entered in his own scrawl. Sometimes crossed out, when wrong. His mother had written the families below, in her own neater hand: *Ranunculaceae* — buttercups, *Rosaceae* — roses, *Cruciferae* — cross-bearers, like cress and wild mustard. And so on. It had all seemed richer, more magical, then.

Some flowers had crumbled to dust, and parts of flowerheads scattered as he turned the pages. Others were almost as tough as they had been the day they were broken off, folded in tissue paper, and flattened under stacked encyclopaedias and dictionaries. That dock, for example, with its fibrous stem and its leaves, dark-purple now, like dried blood. Family *Polygonaceae*. The blue climbing vetch. Family *Leguminosae*. Arc-leaping stalks, and serried lines of parallel leaflets.

He glanced up and noticed the cat reading the chess book.

"Best game of all is number 124," he said. "Réti versus Alyokhin."

"*Alékhine*," the cat corrected him. "Sasha always pronounced it French-style himself. *Not* like Russian. I remember the game well."

"People have trouble with that name," said the boys' father. "It's useful to have the question settled. Thanks."

He went back to gazing at his old flowers, and wishing that, thirty years ago, impatient child he'd been, he had not stuck them on the pages with scraps of gummed coloured paper.

The cat turned on to Game 124 and lost himself in the opening moves. He'd known their father had known he could talk. From the little politenesses in the way he had acted. It was easier, he reflected, now they were talking to each other. Easier than pretending to be an ordinary cat. Strange man — he hadn't even seemed surprised.

John lay on his back, watching a part of the bow-rail against the grey sky. Suddenly there was a kingfisher sitting there. Sharp and clear as if he'd been in a nature film. A glimmer of sunshine lit up the blue-green feathers. Rain must be clearing, he thought.

Flick! The bird was gone. The rail was empty again. He remembered how he'd painted it last summer. Metal undercoat and three layers of white on the tubing. Streaks of rust already coming through again.

Sad about the kingfisher.

Flick! He was back. This time with a fish held crosswise in his beak. He gave an upward jerk with his head, turned the fish through ninety degrees, and swallowed it — longways on — in one gulp.

Then he sat there for a while, looking pleased.

John lifted himself on his elbows to get a closer look. There shouldn't be kingfishers at this time of year. The movement disturbed the bird. Flick! He had gone. This time for good.

John remained still, to fix the memory in his mind. His body was full of a feeling he knew well but which had no name. It was the feeling of having been allowed, for a moment, to see something secret perfectly clearly. To really see it. It was like an omen or a religious moment, except that it wasn't.

The ordinary world returned. He lay on his back on the bunk, his eyes shut, dreaming of the kingfisher for as long as he could.

About half-past eleven, their father went to the cabin door and looked out.

"Almost stopped," he said. "I'll put on my oilskins and take us back. You chaps have to get ready for school again tomorrow."

School, thought John sleepily. A world without kingfishers.

Whirrum-putt-tutt.

The outboard motor was refusing to start. It sometimes did that when the weather was damp.

He imagined his father winding the starting-lanyard round the engine-capstan again.

Whirrum-putt-tutt! Whirr-urra-urra-ummm!

It was going now, second time, but it didn't sound too healthy. Enough to get them back — unfortunately. There were times when he thought he'd like to live on the boat forever, watching the water go by, not trying to do anything, disconnected from the rest of the world.

He wriggled his sleeping-bag down his legs, swung his feet out, and pulled on some trousers. Then he folded Bear so Bear was comfortable, and made his way up outside.

Cressida was churning along through the downstream current. The problem now was to avoid being swept in the wrong direction, against a mud-bank or into the pier of a bridge.

The shallow-flooded lands passed by, sometimes on one side, sometimes on the other, sometimes on both. He watched the Long-Eyot boathouses go by them, then drop behind. In another hour or so, he thought, we shall be at our moorings. Our half-term trip will be over.

CLEARING THE BOAT UP was when the fun finished. A weary business. Only a certain pride made them stick at it.

When it was done they slumped into the estate-car and their father drove them back home. He helped them unload. A hillock of clobber — sleeping-bags, dirty clothes, rubber boots, garbage in plastic bags, spare food, books, radio, empty bottles, full bottles, towels, zippered-up holders with toothbrushes and toothpaste — all the things you need on boats. Then he left to do some shopping.

The time was about four o'clock in the afternoon.

John set a hot bath running for himself in the upstairs bathroom. Charles got a towel from the cupboard, and some clean clothes. He was about to turn the taps on in the guest bathroom downstairs, when the doorbell rang. He put on his dressing-gown and went to see who it was.

There is no way to describe what happened next.

When he opened the door he saw his mother. Except that it wasn't his mother. The person standing there was a bad imitation of her.

Emer smiled and held out her hands.

"Charlie," she said. "My darling! It's been so long. I've been so worried about you. Can I come in?"

He was just about — in spite of himself — to throw himself into her arms, to feel that she was there again, that all that had happened was just a nightmare, when the last four words rang a bell in his mind. A sudden but deep, slow-echoing bell whose reverberations go on and on for ever.

He stepped back. Looked at her again.

It was *not* Emer. It was *not* his mother.

"I'm giving a party this evening," said the thing with Emer's face. "A wonderful party for you and John at my new house. Get a clean shirt on and a jumper — you can't come like that — and I'll drive you both there."

She held out her hands towards him again.

They seemed like his mother's hands.

He hesitated.

"Why don't I come in and fix your clothes for you while you're having your bath?" she said.

Again, the need to be invited in.

Charles's body felt like sand. He seemed to be falling apart, as if nothing could hold it together.

Then his mind cleared suddenly.

"Charlie," said the thing, "don't you love me any more?"

Her hazel-green eyes looked at him as they'd looked so many times before. The eyes that had always been there to notice him, to take care of him. They were her eyes. They were.... And yet.... *They were not.*

"You," he said, in a ghostly, rasping voice, "*You* are not my mother. You have no right to be here. You may not come in, now or ever. Go away, and do not — ever — come back."

It seemed impossible to lift his arm, but somehow he did it.

He shut the door.

The face vanished behind it.

The thought lay cold in his mind: Have I shut my mother out of her own house?

No.

He gritted his teeth and turned the deadlock with the key.

And took the key out.

Then he lurched, exhausted, onto a hallway chair. The chair-feet made a grunting sound on the floor as it shifted back under his weight.

"Thank HSM you made it," said a cat's voice from the darkness. "I thought you were a goner. Me, too. If you'd asked her in, there was almost nothing I could have done."

"It wasn't a good enough disguise," said Charles. "The face was right, but the smile was wrong. Something — I don't know — like trying too hard. The voice was right, but it didn't speak the sweet and laughing way our mother speaks. The clothes, yes, they were her clothes, but she moves more gently when she's wearing them."

The cat looked at him in something approaching awe.

"You are barely eleven," he said, "but you have X-ray eyes. Eyes few adults have, and no child I have ever known. Where did you learn to see like that?"

Charles did not answer. He was still recovering from shock.

"Let's get upstairs," said the cat. "She still needs watching."

Charles followed him up to his father's study. They stood well back from the central window and looked down.

She was standing half way along the drive, facing the house, and drawing lines in the air with her hands. White gloves had appeared on these hands, but otherwise she was still dressed in Emer's clothes. They could see her black car parked in the street beyond.

"What's she doing?" whispered Charles.

He noticed John had joined them, and was looking from behind over his shoulder.

"Megan is putting a Spell of Siege on this house," explained Murgatroyd. "Think of it like the noose round the neck of a man on the gallows, except that it tightens slowly. Not in one deadly jerk, but many. She hopes she can pull it in hour by hour. First, you will be confined indoors, unable to leave. Then, in a room. Finally, to one spot in that room, in an invisible prison. Then, as your will weakens, she will try to come in and get you. Don't worry. It won't happen. Counter-magic is already in place."

"Does a spell like hers need a lot of magic energy?" said John. "Like that formula you told us?"

"It's been used so often, so long," said the cat, "that the $(n + 1)!$ is astronomically high. She will have to stay here in person to keep it in force, and with the counter-magic, my own invention and so low-energy, we can outlast her. I think."

"She's going," said John.

The witch was walking away down the drive. She climbed into the driver's seat of the black car, but then stayed there without moving.

"What's she doing now?" said Charles.

"She's probably felt the counter-magic," said Murgatroyd, "and wondering who might have put it there — like her favourite pussycat, for example. And she'll be thinking of some other way of attack, unless my sixth sense is mistaken."

"Ah, yes," he added after a long silence. "Something horrible, something unspeakably horrible. You are going to have to fight for your lives now."

• bear

THEY WAITED A LONG TIME, well back from the window, while the evening faded into darkness. Then the car drove off.

John moved towards the window to see better.

"Don't open it!" ordered Murgatroyd. "She's gone, but *they* are out there."

"They? Who're they?"

John had turned back.

"The windhands," said the cat. "Her strangest servants. Invisible. And with no fixed shape. They can stretch themselves thin, like mist from an aerosol spray. Or thicken into liquid glass, like see-through plasticine, and enclose you as if you were an insect in amber. They've no eyes, no ears. They only smell and feel other things. Hear the wind?"

"Eerie. I thought it was warm this evening, but the gusting makes me shiver."

John was standing back from the window again, surveying the tops of the trees.

"Not moving," he remarked.

"There is no wind," said Murgatroyd. "*They* are making that noise."

Somewhere a door slammed shut. The house was filled, like a sick person's body, with an uneasy creaking that seemed to fade when they listened to it intently.

"What are they doing?" said Charles.

"Trying to get in."

"Will they?"

"No."

"Why not?"

"My spell's too strong for them. Actually, it's hardly magic — not much more than an electric barrier. Like the wires that farmers use to keep cows in a field."

"What would happen to us if we went outside?" said Charles.

"In a car you might escape them," answered Murgatroyd. "They don't move fast. If you were on foot, the air would soon thicken around you. You'd be unable to breathe. Soft fingers would wrap themselves about your legs and arms, and throat. They'd tighten, and you'd faint. When you woke up again, you'd be the witch's prisoners. Probably inside her television set, among her imaginary gardens and glades. Allowed to live when she felt like switching you on."

"Does anyone ever escape?" asked John.

"When she'd finished with you she'd set you free, but you'd be a lifeless husk, fit only for some office job."

John shuddered.

"What can we do about the hands?" he said. "Are we trapped here?"

"Don't worry," said Murgatroyd. "My spell cannot easily be broken, and the hands have no power once the sun is up. Light seems to dissolve them, or thin them to a mist. If we do need to stir out after dark, there are ways to fool them."

"How?" asked Charles.

"I could make a couple of pillows into imitations of you two. Dress them up in your clothes. So long as they smelt of you. Old clothes are best. And pillows can seem alive when you make their wrinkles move. The hands have no minds. Can't think. What fills them is the desire to grasp whatever she's told them to. To sniff it, then crush it and hold it tight. Nothing else. They'd carry off the clothed pillows to Megan without realizing there was nothing more inside them than feathers. The house would be unguarded for a while, and we could make our getaway."

"Sounds risky," said John. "We might never get back in again."

"It *is* risky. But indoors there's little danger."

"What if she comes back?"

"She's in no hurry. As far as she's concerned you're guarded till morning. She can take her time working out the next way to get you. So — have a good night's sleep. We can lay more plans tomorrow. She won't make another appearance tonight."

BUT THE WITCH'S CAT was mistaken.

The moment John had closed his eyes in bed, Megan's face appeared. Her eyes looked at him. Hungrily. Then her face began to grow larger. Larger. He could smell a stench coming off it, like old, bitter, wet leaves. Next he heard her voice, which rose and fell from a low pitch to a high one and back again, expressing an upper-class arrogance and assurance:

"I imagine you understand what's happened. It is unfortunate for both of us. One would not have thought it, not after what, at least on the surface, seemed to be so many years of faithful service. But ambition eats at the hearts of servants. They want to be better than those who are their masters. Poor Murgatroyd! I was so kind to his failings, his bad head for heights, his drinking, his fits of sentimentality. He doesn't know what he's let himself in for, deserting me for Grayach's service. You'd be doing him a kindness, persuading him to come back to me. He can't really imagine that evil man is going to teach him the higher levels of magic. A mere cat? The idea's unthinkable.

"But you and your brother, now — I am *most* concerned about you and your brother. Look at the terror you're in after three or four days of his lies! Do you really believe that my Garden of Magical Pleasures is a prison? Hundreds of children have been happy there. Ask any one of them. And to assert that I've been chasing you! With loathesome creatures like windhands. What an imagination that wicked animal has! One could almost admire him for it if the effects were not so harmful. Surely, though, concoctions like this are too much to swallow in this modern age, particularly for such intelligent children as you are.

" I *have* been chasing Murgatroyd. Any employer has the right to pursue an employee who runs off to a rival with trade secrets. Even so, were he to come back to me, of his own free will, he would find me all forgiveness. Do see if you can't persuade him.

"As for my invitation, which he was instructed to convey to you, for a very special party, it would give me the greatest pleasure if you could see your way to accepting it. It would make up, in no small measure, for the disappointments of the last few days. My dear John...."

John jerked himself awake with an effort. The witch's face had vanished, and with it her lies, her horribly believable lies.

The darkness around him seemed safe and comforting. He did not dare to close his eyes again, but lay there listening to Charles's breathing through the open door from the next room. He wondered what to do next.

A thought ate at his mind. Murgatroyd in *Grayach's* service? Could it be true? He reflected. The witch — assuming she was a witch — had said the windhands were something the cat had made up to terrify them. That, at least, could be tested.

"Murgatroyd?" he called softly.

"Yes?"

The cat's voice came through the doorway, from the shadows beside Charlie's head, where he'd curled up for the night.

"Could you do that pillow trick you mentioned?"

"Why?"

"I want to see if the windhands are really there. I don't believe in them."

"They're there all right."

"I can't sleep. I want to go for a walk in the garden."

"Don't."

"Show me why not."

He heard the cat drop onto the carpet.

"All right," he said. "Put an old sweater and a pair of jeans on your pillow. Ones you can spare losing."

The cat paced slowly about John's room until the dummy was ready. It didn't look convincing.

"Tie a pair of gym shoes to the ends of the legs," he said. "That's better. All it needs is a head. How about a cushion from the sitting-room, and a woolly hat from the hall cupboard?"

The result was more lifelike. In the darkness of the bedroom, it could easily have been mistaken for a body.

"We need the vacuum-cleaner," added Murgatroyd. "Bring the attachment that's used to clean fluff off the furniture."

"Won't the noise wake up Charlie?" said John.

"It won't be plugged in."

John trundled the vacuum cleaner along as quietly as he could. The cat spoke a few words and the bag blew up tight with air. A sound like a rush of wind came from the attachment tube.

"Right. Put the end where his mouth should be. Now!"

Whooff! The dummy sat up. Its sweater arms puffed, flapping like windsocks on an airfield. They bent softly when they hit him.

"Keep the end of the tube on the mouth," said Murgatroyd. "No. Keep it there."

The dummy rose to its feet. The legs of the jeans seemed too frail to support the swollen pillow-stomach. The knotted ankles twisted limply to one side. But it was, or so it seemed, *alive.*

"OK. Put the vacuum down. Open the window."

John pulled back a curtain. Outside the night was clear, with a brilliant moon. He nudged the window-catch free. No sooner was it loose than the lower section shot up and banged against its frame. He stepped back, hands trembling.

"Exactly," said Murgatroyd. "It's best to keep away from the opening. Let's go now!"

He jumped onto the chest of drawers, and murmured in the dummy's ear. The thing began to walk, if 'walk' is the word to describe how it limped and dragged itself across the carpet. It reached the window and lifted itself over the sill. For a second it sat, with its back to them, legs outside and feet resting twisted on the rose-trellis.

"Looks as if he's admiring the view," said John.

There was a squishy hiss. Invisible fingers bent the dummy's neck down till its forehead pressed on its chest. The arms were folded behind its back, like those of a shirt pressed and pinned at the laundry. Then the legs were forced up till the knees touched the shoulders and the feet drooped level with the hips.

"They're packing him up," said Murgatroyd. "You see? They'll be off in a moment. Yes. There they go!"

The bundle was lifted from the sill. The next instant it vanished. Nothing was to be seen but the moonlight, shining undisturbed on the lawn and among the motionless leaves of the elms.

John sat down on his bed and patted Bear's ears.

"No pillow now," he said. "Sorry!"

Then he shook his head.

"So, Murg," he said, "you were telling us the truth,"

"Did you think I was making *them* up?"

"It did occur to me you might be."

"Why should I do such a thing?"

John told the cat how Megan had appeared to him in his sleep, and what she had said. Murgatroyd's tail swished angrily.

"You were lucky to escape," he observed. "She's a persuasive liar. A deadly one. Next time you may not wake up soon enough."

"I don't think I dare go to sleep again. At least not just now."

"You must have sleep," said the cat. "If one is tired one loses one's powers of judgement, and one's will to fight back."

"But, if I do sleep, there she is — waiting for me."

"So," muttered Murgatroyd, "we are still under attack. But on a different and even more dangerous front. How easily our defences were penetrated! Well, there's only one answer. You can't go without sleep. You must have a dreamguard."

"What's that?"

"Different in every case. It depends on the person. On what you believe in. As for you — let me think a moment."

There was a long silence. John could hear slow, regular, sleeper's breathing coming from Charlie. He hoped that *he* was not having bad dreams, but Charles had peculiar powers, and could probably look after himself.

At last Murgatroyd spoke:

"Do you love Bearie very much?"

John looked down at Bear. His eyes were two overcoat buttons, one hanging a little loosely. His cheerful smile was mostly darning thread, the original cloth patch having cracked and broken away in pieces. His body was a flat, fur-covered sleeping-bag, with paws at each of the four corners. His neck had been strengthened with a length of sacking, and his zip was broken. John kissed him and laid his head against his face.

"We're both very fond of each other," he said.

"He's getting old, isn't he?"

"Over six."

"Would you like him never to grow old? Would you like him to be always at his best, or even better? To be with you wherever you are?"

John looked sadly at Bear.

"I'd like nothing better," he said. "But it's not possible. As my father says, everything gets broken in the end."

"It *is* possible," answered Murgatroyd, "if you will let me make him your dreamguard. You'll only have to shut your eyes to see him, and nothing inside you will ever be able to frighten you again."

"But what would become of the real Bearie?" said John, giving him an anxious hug.

"Real?" said Murgatroyd. "He is real because you believe in him. You are his life, in every sense. But if you mean, what will become of his body?, he'll be all right if you look after him. And *he* will look after *you* in your dreams."

FEELINGS OF EXHILARATION and fear came and went hot and cold in John's body. He hoped that he was not doing something dangerous. He watched Murgatroyd making the preparations.

"It will be all right, Bearie. It really will," he whispered.

The cat had drawn a circle on the carpet with a stub of white crayon. In the middle he had placed five treasures from the top of the boys' bookshelf. There was a conch-shell with a gleaming, pearly interior, two sea-horses preserved in separate plastic pyramids, and two model Venetian gondolas. Their lights had been turned on — blue, white, red, green, and yellow — and were reflected in the pyramids.

"He must take objects he knows with him on his journey. Then he can find his way back," said the cat. "Place him in the circle with them."

"Promise me he'll be all right?"

"I promise."

Very gently, Bearie was laid alongside the treasures, his body rolled up under his head.

"Don't touch anything, and don't try to call him," ordered Murgatroyd. "It might go wrong if you do, and we'd be heartbroken. Beyond any calling back."

He began to run round outside the circle. For two or three minutes nothing happened, and John began to wonder if perhaps the cat had the magic wrong. Then Murgatroyd stopped running and sprang onto the bed, panting.

"It's started now — don't touch, please — please. All — all right," he said between gasps. "It wouldn't move at first."

John stared. There was no doubt about it. Bearie, the shell, the sea-horses, and the gondolas were rotating slowly as if they were on the turntable of a record-player. He followed them round and round with his eyes. Little by little the speed increased. The ring and everything in it were spinning, a glittering merry-go-round. As they span, they grew smaller and smaller. At last they contracted to a single point, which became intensely bright, and then went out.

John was blinded by the return of the darkness, and groped along the bedcovers. Bear wasn't there. A cold panic gripped him.

"Bearie!" he called. "Bearie!"

"Don't call him!" hissed Murgatroyd's voice beside him. "Be patient. He won't be long in coming back."

"What can I do?"

"Lie down. Close your eyes. Think of him."

It took John some time to settle. His pulse was still racing with the excitements of the last half-hour: Megan in his dream, the seizure of the dummy dresssed up to look like him, the magical disappearance of Bear. He envied the cat's ability to drift off to sleep anywhere, any time. In the end, though, drowsiness overtook him. He began to breathe softly and steadily.

He found he was walking in a pine-forest. There was a warm wind and a sweet, resiny smell. The trunks were dappled with sunshine.

In and out among them flew large blue butterflies. Far off he could hear the sea, and gulls crying. A joyous yet troubled expectation of something stirred inside him. He quickened his pace.

The path wound over brown needles and sand. It ran across clearings covered with grassy knolls. Then it wandered out onto a low headland where it disappeared. He found his way down a steep shoulder, pushing between thick-leaved plants that smelt of mint and fennel. Bright red flowers grew upright on their stems like paint-brushes. Small stones clattered under his bare feet. The beach, when he reached it, was full of irregular boulders and hidden pools of tidal water. Along the channels that ran into the sea were bunches of different kinds of seaweed, some with surfaces like wet leatherette, others like shiny brown plastic.

At a comfortable height above the water he sat down with his back against a rock, and watched the waves coming in. The warmth of the stone seeped into his legs. Overhead, the sky was immense and blue.

"It's beautiful, isn't it?" said a voice at his side.

He had never heard that voice before, but he knew at once who it was.

"It's a dream, Bear, isn't it?" he said, not daring to look round yet.

"Shut your eyes for a moment," said the deep, gentle voice.

John shut them. The sunlit seashore vanished. He was somewhere in darkness, lying on his back. He realized it must be his bed. The ruckussed blankets looked like mountain-ranges. Their long grey ridges fell away into pitch-black cliffs and valleys. A thought hit him like a cold thunderbolt. He glanced downwards.

Thank Heavens! He was there, the same as ever, his head resting on the overturned sheet, button eyes staring at the ceiling. He let out his breath out abruptly, and sank back onto the sheets. Then he firmly shut his eyes again,

The rock was as warm as ever, and the sky still blue. A flock of gray-brown birds was streaming away along the edge of the sands, a few inches above the waves.

"It's here whenever you want it," said Bear's voice. "And I shall always be ready. For now I shall live as long as you do, my dear master."

At last John turned. Can you imagine what it would be like if the oldest of friends were to meet for the first time ? There is no way to describe that moment.

There stood Bear. He was on his hind paws, as comically good-natured as in real life. Both brown ears had flopped forwards over his yellow face. His furry stomach bulged gently. But on his chest there gleamed something that had *not* been there before — a dazzling medal of gold, hanging by a ribbon of red silk.

"Bear," said John uncertainly, "what's that?"

"Read it."

John held the medallion between forefinger and thumb, tilting it till the light fell right. Around the edge, in raised square letters, it said:

"OFFICIAL DREAMGUARD BEAR."

"Oh, Bear," he said, "Oh, Bear, you've made it."

They hugged each other, wiped away the tears, and sat without saying a word. It was Bear who broke the silence.

"For a long time," he said, "one lies in the factory. It's dark. One's box smells of mothproofing and cellophane. One wonders what one's owner will be like. It's the all-important question. Will he be spoilt? Friendly?

Quarrelsome. Kind? Stupid? Clever? Will his mother know how to mend one properly? Will he be fond of one? Above all, will he believe in one? In the end, of course, one is bound to wear out and be thrown away with the rubbish, or made into rags. But if something warm stays behind in the heart, that's all that matters. No one asks for more than that. But dreamguard — not one in ten thousand gets made an official dreamguard. Not one in ten thousand."

"It was Murgatroyd," said John. "You should thank him."

"Murgatroyd is a good friend," answered Bear. "But it was your faith in me that made it possible. *He* told me so."

"Who told you?"

"The Administrator of Dreams. When you and Murgatroyd had vanished into the spinning darkness, I rose through a green sea into a world full of bright music. Tubas growled, and bass strings throbbed beneath my feet, like swell pouring through broken rocks. Around me I could both hear and see tunes from innumerable horns. They were tormenting and intense, zigzagging into the distance like tinsel streamers. Bright particles glittered above me, scattered notes from singing harps. Perfect silver bubbles floated past. Melodies from flutes, each bubble reflected in another's sides. Soft xylophone mists folded me about, or lit up suddenly in bursts of blue flame that flashed from the cymbals. As I listened, I heard him speak to me.

"'Your master is a master of music,' he said, 'one who makes dreams walk on the earth. Into the perilous places he goes, into the dark, he must not go alone. You are now his dreamguard, comforter, and friend.'

"'But,' I answered, 'I'm only an old stuffed animal. My zipper's broken. I'm good for little but laughing at everything, and with everyone. What use would I be?'

"'That you will learn,' said the Administrator. 'Thanks to you his heart will not grow cold. He will not forget who he is as he wanders in the Emptiness. Be with him, time out of mind!'

"Then I found myself sinking. The music faded. The air grew lighter and warmer. I landed here, and you were sitting on this rock."

"What does he look like, the Administrator of Dreams?"

"You wouldn't believe me if I told you," said Bear.

"I would."

Bear just shook his head.

"It sounds too odd," he said.

"Bear, *please*!"

"If I tell you, you mustn't be surprised."

"I won't."

"He is an old rabbit, with a blue waistcoat, silver buttons, and a walking-stick. When you see him you know that, in some strange way, *he has seen everything*. He is very kind, and very frightening."

"Why frightening?"

"Because, although he speaks softly, what he says *happens*."

John thought for a while. The he asked:

"Did he have one blue ear and one yellow one?"

"Yes," said Bear, a little surprised. "He did."

"Then I know who he is. He used to be our father's dreamguard when he was young. I'm glad he is watching over us."

Bear nodded.

"I'm only just learning the job," he said. "But I doubt if any evil power, no matter what, would be a match for that old fellow."

"Hasn't he made us a beautiful world!" said John, gazing out over the sea.

"Beautiful," said Bear, "but I'm sure he didn't make it."

"Didn't he?"

"There'd be no need for dreamguards if he had," said Bear with a smile. "Why don't we explore?"

"Yes!" exclaimed John. "Let's explore it together. There may be parts that no one's ever seen before, and we can give names to the places. Which way shall we go first?"

He was standing up, eager to leave.

"Just a moment, master," said Bear. "If I'm an Official Dreamguard, I have to see proper preparations are made. I'm hungry for the first time in my life. It's an interesting feeling. I think we should both have a snack before we set out."

"A snack?" said John. "All right. But where are we going to find it?"

He could see no sign of any food.

For an answer, Bear undid his zipper. (It was working perfectly.) He reached inside himself with a paw. Out came two slices of melon, two sizzling hamburgers, and a baked alaska made of hot meringue with cold icecream inside it.

"I say, Bear, that's a useful trick," observed John, looking at the meal spread out on the rock in front of him. "I never had any idea that you could do that."

"Nor had I," said Bear, with a look of pleased surprise on his face. "It's the first time I've done it."

AN HOUR LATER the forest and the seashore lay below, shimmering in haze. Bear floated at two thousand feet, letting the wind blow him along. His back was warm and furry. He had turned the sides up, like those of an inflatable boat, so there was no danger of John falling out. Sometimes John simply lay there, staring up at the sky. More often he rested his elbows on one of Bear's shoulders and watched the countryside passing below them,

Not far away they could see a broad river winding through a maze of mudflats and waterways into the sea. The sun glinted off its surface like the flash from a tilted knife-blade. Tall reeds bordered its motionless lakes, scattered with islands of moss and creepers, and flocks of pink flamingoes. Higher up, the river's course ran through low hills covered with bluish-grey shrubs. Their smell came drifting up through the air, like warm cinnamon. On a bank was a ruin of some sort.

"Fly lower, Bear," said John. "I want to see what that is."

Bear swung his nose down into a gentle dive, and the ruin came swimming up.

It was a Roman amphitheatre, made of white stones. One side was still complete. Level after level of curving step-like seats rose up to a crown of columns, two of which were still joined by a stone lintel. As they came nearer they could see tufts of grass growing between the cracks. Here and there daisies had rooted, and small purple flowers. Once it must have seated thousands of people, who clapped or cheered or gasped as young girls sewn inside deerskins were ripped and bitten to death by lions, or maybe who yawned and chattered, already bored by it all — in what was now a sunny silence.

John and Bear alighted near the top, and watched a lizard hurry away into a crevice. They were standing on a walkway, worn down with the passing of countless sandals. Gutter-holes had been cut in its sides to let rainwater flow away. On a parapet nearby someone had carved some letters, but they made no sense to John. Somebody's name? he wondered idly. Somebody's girlfriend? I wonder why he scratched it, and what happened to him? Then a thought struck him.

"Bearie," he said, "do you think this place ever had a real past?"

"What do you mean?"

"Could it have been made, from the beginning, exactly the way it is now? A ruin from the start, with stairs worn smooth *by no one*, words cut in its stones by *people who never existed*?"

"I think they existed," said Bear. "Look!"

Down on the sands of the arena, something was moving. It stopped. Then it moved again.

"It's a man," said John. "And there's something else, too."

"Looks like some sort of animal to me," said Bear. "Let's go nearer.

Quietly now, so as not to attract their attention."

They edged down the steps in the shadow of a line of statues. Halfway to the bottom they hid behind a broken wall. Some of what had once been its stones had tumbled into a stairwell, which was choked solid.

No doubt about it now. A man was kneeling on one knee on the sand. Against his breast he was clutching something. Five meters away, on its haunches, sat a tired-looking lion, gazing at him.

"Why doesn't the man run?" whispered John. "He'll get eaten if he doesn't."

"Perhaps he wants to get eaten," Bear whispered back. "I don't think the lion is hungry enough to want *him*."

Just then the lion rose to its feet. It was old. Mangy. It took a few stiff steps towards the man, then sat down again, its shoulders sagging.

The man had bowed his head. In prayer, or in resignation. He was wearing nothing but a torn sheet that covered one shoulder, and was tied round his waist with a rope. He stayed like that for a long while, head bowed. From outside the amphitheatre they could hear the chirr-chirr of the cicadas on the bushes. John noticed the arena gate was open. It had been torn off its hinges and leant against the wall. Through the gap he could see the hills outside, grey-green then grey-blue in the distance and the afternoon sun.

The man raised his head and looked at the lion. Something seemed to pass between them. Like the flicker of an electric impulse. The hand at the man's chest unclenched and dropped to his side. John and Bear held their breaths.

Slowly, so as not to frighten the lion, the man got up. He walked across to the animal, step by step, put out his hand, then stroked him between the ears. The lion lowered his head, and rubbed his shoulder against the man's legs. Both seemed filled with a subdued excitement.

Without a word — or even a gesture — and completely together, they walked over the sand, out through the gate, and towards the hills. For a while they could be seen, going up along the path that climbed the valley. Then they were lost to sight, too small to be picked out against the bluish-grey.

"Whatever was that about?" said Bear after a long silence.

"I don't know," said John, "but I read a story in an old book once. It had a pale blue binding, and letters impressed on it in gold, and both black-and-white and coloured illustrations. It was grandmother's, I think. Long ago, when people enjoyed being cruel, the emperors used to have Christians fed to the lions in open-air theatres like this. It was like a live video."

"Why Christians in particular?" said Bear.

"The emperors made people call them gods. Only the Christians refused to worship them. They said there was only one God. So the government had to have them killed. Ordinary Romans came and watched, clapped their hands and ate toffee-apples. If they had toffee-apples then."

"Why did it matter so much?"

John smiled.

"Something tells me, Bear, he said, "that we can only ask that question now that the circus is empty. But we could only know the answer if we were here when the seats around us were full. They seem absurd and horrible to us — *today*, but we would have seemed absurd and horrible to them — *then*, for not believing. Maybe they would have even thrown us in along with the Christians."

Bear frowned, his honest face puzzled.

"What has your story got to do with these two? The ones who've just disappeared."

"I think they've forgotten the answer. That's why they've become friends."

"Forgotten the answer? Was the gate always open, then?"

"Who knows?" said John. "Maybe no one looked. Until the Last Lion and the Last Christian."

There seemed nothing more to say, so they took off again.

THE LEMONADE trickled down John's throat. He had been thirsty and it tasted delicious. They were coasting back down the river, towards its mouth, barely a hundred feet off the water.

"What shall I do with the bottle, Bearie?" he asked, wiping his mouth.

"Give it to me."

Bear reached round for it. He unzipped himself and popped it in under his arm, where it disappeared.

"I wish we could fly higher, into a cloud. It might cool us down."

"There are no cloud-meadows today," said Bear. "It's too hot. The streaky white ones above us won't be very cooling. Why don't we drift out over the sea?"

"O.K."

An hour later the last land had disappeared from sight. They floated along in the afternoon sun, half asleep, and surrounded by a blue silence.

AS EVENING approached the wind began to rise. The slow swell below them grew into heavy hillsides of dark water. Bear advanced hardly at all, merely keeping his nose pointed into the wind, as if he were an airborne sea-anchor.

It was no longer hot. John's hair was being ruffled. He could feel Bear rocking and swaying as up-draughts of air tugged at him. The horizon was loaded with clouds. Underneath them came the red-golden gleam of the sinking sun, catching the crests of the waves as they lifted above the gloom of the water-valleys. It was beautiful and excitingly frightening.

Before their eyes, a marvel appeared. Above the oncoming swell sparkled battlements of ice. Higher and higher these battlements rose until, almost on a level with them, John and Bear saw a translucent castle riding on the surface of the ocean. Its towers and spires seemed to have been carved from the heart of a glacier. Melting ice glistened as it ran down their walls. Water in the courtyards was sloshing back and forth, swifter than the slow tremblings of the huge bulk in which it was confined.

Sometimes the castle lurched. Cataracts of spray spilt into another enclosure, or leapt the outer walls to fall into the sea. Fissures had opened in the ice-buttresses. Each time the castle leaned a little on its side a hundred waterfalls would pour through them. Then, as they emptied, the castle would right itself and ride a little higher, the sunlight behind its pinnacles splintering into millions of watery diamonds.

The ice-castle sank down on the near slope of the swell. It was now directly beneath them. The sky shone up reflected from its pools as if these had been windows.

"Follow it, Bearie!" cried John, shouting to make himself heard above the wind. "Land on it if you can!"

Again the castle came up into the light, half-melted towers leaning out at a fearful angle. John saw one, top-heavy with an observation turret, snap and fall, smashing the arch of a bridge below it. The fragments swilled in a courtyard lake like loose pack-ice.

"Try the square tower in the centre, Bear," he directed. "It looks the strongest."

Bear hovered above it. The roof was as large and flat as a football field. But even when it was level, as now at the top of a wave, it was dangerous to land on. Parts of a parapet were breaking off in the wind, sending a stinging hail across its slippery surface. One upper corner was pierced by a diagonal crack. There was a sense of irreversible destruction proceeding at a break-neck pace.

"Try lower down," shouted John.

A line of windows opened in the side of the tower. They were circular arches divided by twisted columns. A few were still covered with panes of ice-glass. Most were broken. Fragments like teeth stuck out across the openings.

"Be careful, Bearie!" said John.

86

Bear found a window that looked safe, allowed off for the force of the wind, and flew in at an expert curve. Inside it was startlingly light, and incredibly cold. They flew slowly along through a great hall. Puddles of water lay on the floor. Strange-shaped humps looked as if they had once been tables, or altars. The roof was spiralled vaulting. Ice chandeliers still hung unbroken here and there, their turning pendants flashing at moments in a gleam of filtered sunlight.

But it was the shining outer walls that held John's attention. Every inch of them had been carved from within, like glass, into a design of seabirds, transparent, and detailed to the last feather. As the light swayed through them, they seemed to be flying. Fulmars and petrels, puffins and gulls, fairy terns and plunging gannets. Some were soaring, wings outstretched; others were resting on the surface of the ocean. Lit for a moment by the dying sun, their multitudes sped past like a vision of unearthly beauty.

For an instant only. John and Bear had hardly realized what they were seeing, or believed it, when the floor tipped, shadows swept across the vast room, and the birds were extinguished. The ice-castle was driving down into another trough between the waves.

To their amazement they heard a voice. Looking through the gloom they saw people. Or a sort of people. Dozens of them, without clothes, but on whose skins grew a thick white fur. One of them sat on a throne of ice. The others clustered on the wide steps below him. It was he who was talking, composed amid the commotion.

"True, there are few of us now left. Year after year the currents have carried us into the warmth. Our city has melted. Almost all that was the glory of our people lies dissolved in the waters. Now you tell me that our citadel is breaking too."

A bent white figure rose.

"King of the City of Ice," he said, "crevasses are opening in the deeps. The passages and watchways are twisted, broken, and impassable. Is it not time at last to ask ourselves how we may, perhaps, survive?"

"*Survive?*" answered the King. "That is as it ever was — a self-deception. Man's life is a comet that blazes in the skies — extraordinary, explosive, brief. When death approaches, extravagance is wisdom, thrift folly."

"I only meant, Sire, we have no wish to drown."

"Comfort yourself, Alethaias. We may reach safety. Further south, the seas grow cold again. Beneath our feet lie many million tons of ice on which the sun will beat in vain for years. Perhaps we may yet replenish our bulk through the long winters. Our sons will carve new miracles that make our fathers' handiwork look rough. Or, then — perhaps not. What difference can it make? Does danger alter truth? One can live only for beauty. How can one live for survival? Where is the meaning in such timidity? I am not changing."

The councillor bowed. As he did so there was a sound like an explosion. A mountain of water rushed past the tower windows, Bear, with John on his back, spun round and shot out the window through which they had come in. For a thousand feet he rose vertically. Then he paused, and they both looked down.

The ice-castle was listing on its side, riven by a crack from end to end. It shuddered and split into two pieces, each one of which rolled over in the water. The black waves washed across them, and they were carried away into the night.

THE LAST LIGHT had faded, and it was impossible to see. There was no moon, and not one star. Blackness had closed in and seemed to be touching them. Only the golden beam that shone from Bear's medallion like a headlight illumined the cloudbanks, and the highways of mist that opened before them as they flew.

They had no idea where they were going.

"Can't we land?" whispered John. "I'm frightened by this nothingness."

"The earth is smelling beneath us now," said Bear. "Tree-smells. Sweet pine and bitter fir, *Pinus* and *Abies*, beloved of bears. But I warn you, it will be as dark down there as it is up here."

He descended so slowly and carefully that when they had landed it took John a moment to realize that they were no longer moving.

"Is it all right to get out?" he asked.

"Quite safe, if you move cautiously."

John put his foot out. There was a crackle, and he withdrew it in alarm.

"That's only bracken," said Bear. "And ferns. I'll extract some rugs and sleeping-bags. They'll be very comfortable and springy on top of the plants. What kind of soup do you want? I'd recommend the onion, with the thick cheese topping."

"Sounds delicious," said John, laughing. "Can you manage me an extra sweater first?"

Bear could, and soon they were installed, sipping soup by medal-light, and listening to the dry creakings that came from the surrounding trees.

"What's in this forest?" said John, feeling better fed and more confident again.

Bear held his medal in his paw, and let the beam probe between the trunks. The trees were overgrown with creepers, snake-like branches, some of them as thick as an arm. As the light pulled away from them, the shadows would lengthen suddenly. For a moment the branches would writhe in confusion, then there would be blackness again. It felt as if there were no birds or animals in there. There were no night-movements, no rustlings or stirrings.

They had landed in a clearing, but getting out, at least on foot, was going to be tricky. Their look-around had shown no tracks, no paths through the trees.

"Do you have any power over forests, Bear?" said John.

"I can only try and see," smiled Bear. "But forests are the home of bears. I expect they will obey me."

The sleeping-bags and rugs were returned to his inside, along with the soupbowls and spoons. Then Bear stood up. He raised his paws, pressed them together, and pulled them suddenly apart. A shudder ran through the wood. The trunks and branches drew themselves in tightly, and a path opened in front of them. Bear bowed.

"Thank you," he said. "Come on, John."

They set off together, holding hands. As they walked, they heard the forest closing behind their backs.

Faint lights glittered far ahead of them, and Bear dimmed his medal so they could see them better.

"Like a handful of red fireflies," said John, "only I'm sure they're not. Too low for stars."

"They're not moving," said Bear. "Or, rather, they are. A little."

Coming nearer, they saw the red lights were windows. Five, or maybe six, small diamond windows. The number changed from time to time. It was not clear what sort of a building they were in.

As they approached, Bear brightened his beam again. They gasped. Not fifty meters away rose a square black tower moving restlessly about. That was why the number of windows had seemed to change, as one or two of them had been hidden from view, or reappeared. The reason the tower was moving was that it had four black human feet. Each toe was the size of a car, and the skin was wrinkled.

"A walking castle," said John. "Who do you think lives there?"

"Feel like ringing the bell and finding out?" said Bear with a chuckle.

"Not much. I might get trodden on."

John did not have to ring, however. The feet spread out and twisted, turning the tower. An iron drawbridge thudded out to the ground. Behind it was a dim red glow and a portcullis, like a black papercut. The portcullis rose up out of sight with a clang. The lights in the castle faded. A harsh laugh sounded from inside, and somewhere a whip cracked.

Down from the gateway slid a sleigh made, not of twisted blacksmith's iron, but of snakes, all undulating. They were coiled around a stone mortar in which a tall, top-heavy, woman stood, a skull on a short iron chain hanging from a rod in her hand. Out of the skull's eyes blazed a red light.

She drew the snakes up beside them, and looked down, smiling, but the snakes were still hissing like dry leaves.

"Tourists, I suppose?" she said.

"Travellers," said Bear.

"We have a festival going on at present. Very interesting. Would you like to watch it?"

"What is it?" said John.

"Come on board and I'll take you there."

John shivered slightly. Bear gave him a wink and pressed his hand with his paw.

"That's very kind of you," said Bear.

They climbed up over the quivering backs of the snakes. Once they were standing in the mortar next to her she gave a strange, fierce cry and the sleigh set off at a terrifying pace straight into the blackness ahead. A warm wind gusted around their faces, and the forest seemd to be crashing in front of them and behind.

"How do you avoid the trees?" John asked.

"They are swept away in front and swept together again at the back."

They came out into an avenue lined with torches on wooden stakes. The ground was guttered with deep ruts of dried mud. The sleigh jolted and juddered. The shadows of the trees ran wrinkled across the ruts, tugging at their moorings in the shaking torch-flames. Smoke stung their nostrils, like the smell after a fire.

"Where are you taking us?" said John.

"To the Wooden Fortress of Brozha," answered their guide. "Look ahead!"

The smoke lifted a little, and underneath it appeared a line of palisades, and a wooden gateway, lit by more torches and guarded by some soldiers. Torch-light flashed from the tips of their spears.

"This is the outer wall," she said. "It is made of pine-trunks in a double row with earth rammed down between them. The work was done by prisoners of war captured by Khorgiz the Great. Few wooden fortifications of the later period are as skilfully made. The sacrifice of the slaves after it was completed was also beautifully done — they were impaled — and enjoyed by many visitors. Ah! Here we are at the gate."

As the sleigh came to a stop it was surrounded by guards. They were filthy, with sharp eyes, and dressed in furs, with bandages wound round their legs. Their jabbering, thought John, sounded like nothing so much as the garbage-grinder in the sink at work on nutshells. The woman barked out an order for silence. Then she turned to John and Bear.

"You'd better buy a few postcards at least," she said.

"Postcards," said John, amazed. "Where do they get those from?"

"I supply them as required. They're quite good. Buy a few and you'll see."

Bear rummaged under his arm and produced a pawful of bronze coins. A crowned bear's head was stamped on one side, with the letters ODB intertwined on the other. The woman pounced on them.

"These are nice," she said. "I've never seen coins like that before. Raised milled edges, too. They'll give you a good rate for these. Get down, now, and do your shopping."

The soldiers held out single cards on the flats of their hands for the tourists to inspect, grinning at them. The photographs were in colour. Most of them showed people being killed in battle, necks skewered by flint-tipped arrows, or heads smashed open with axes like soft-boiled eggs under an impatient breakfaster's spoon. One or two showed girls in skirts embroidered with flowers, scowling at the photographer, and one or two were of boys, smiling.

John was both disgusted and interested.

"However did you get such photographs?" he said.

"They were posed for."

"You mean, they're not real?"

"Oh, no, you can be assured they're real all right."

After hesitation, John and Bear bought a picture of a girl, another of some flowers, and a third of a warrior in battle finery but not actually fighting. The soldiers were disappointed with this choice, and made expressions of contempt to each other, shaking their heads.

"Why are they doing that?" John asked Bear. But it was their guide who answered.

"They want to know why you don't buy a battle-scene. They're very proud of those. They cost many lives to make. They think maybe you are not a man."

"Is it manly to kill people to make postcards?" asked Bear.

"You have it the wrong way round. Because they can make some money by selling postcards, it is possible to keep the old virtues of manliness alive. Otherwise there's too little left to fight about for battles to be worthwhile."

"All right," said John. "I'll buy a battle-scene."

Bear laid his paw on John's arm.

"No, master," he said. "You won't."

John looked at him in surprise. Bear's medal, which had been almost too faint to see, was glowing a gentle gold again. And Bear had never spoken to him like that before.

"Why shouldn't I?" he said, his voice faltering a little.

"Because, if you buy, it only encourages them to go on doing it. Let's go somewhere else."

Their guide interrupted swiftly.

"Come, Master Bear, there's no need to buy the battle-scenes if you don't like them. We still have the fortress and our festival to see. Let's not spoil the outing with a quarrel."

Reluctantly, Bear and John helped each other back into the mortar. The tall woman gave a cry, and the sleigh slid between the gates. They were now on a road lined with marquees and tents, and with booths and stalls, most of them boarded up. Everything was in darkness. Only some widely separated torches burning in iron brackets on poles cast a light on their path.

"Where are the people?" asked John.

"Inside the main walls. The festival is a serious matter for them, and a good deal depends on the outcome."

As she was speaking they passed by a circular mound with a flat top, and ringed by a deep ditch.

"What's that?" enquired Bear.

"Something that might interest you," she replied. "Every New Year they have bear-fighting there."

"*Bear-fighting?*" said Bear. His voice had dropped to a bass growl and held a hint of menace. "Between bears and bears, or between bears and men?"

"Between a bear and a man," she answered, "but it's fairly balanced. The man gets killed almost as often as the bear. Any poor fellow who wants to make his fortune is allowed to have a try. There's always a huge crowd, and the King gives gold to the winners. It's a test of skill — and courage."

"Does the bear volunteer, too?" said Bear.

"Gracious, no. You would hardly expect an ordinary bear, straight out of the woods, to understand such things, would you? — What happens," she went on, "is this. The King's hunters put a bear on the island. There's no water in the moat around it but the sides are too steep for the animal to climb. The man who is to fight him walks across a gangway which is then removed. He is only allowed to have a spear. When the bear makes a rush at him, he plants the base of the spear against the inside of his foot and lowers the point at just the right time for the onrushing bear to skewer himself on it."

"What happens if he doesn't get the timing right?" said John?

"He doesn't usually get the chance of a second attempt."

The walls of the fortress were now looming up in front of them. Tree-trunks, with bark still on them, had been pounded into the ground, and braced with supports. Some of them had collapsed, half-pulling the others down with them. Piles of rubbish were everywhere. John could see old car-springs and pools of oil, gutted mattresses, rusty prams, and broken bottles. The stench was stomach-turning. Charcoal braziers burned at each side of the gates. Their stinging fumes, which made his eyes water, were almost a relief.

The guards at the gates waved the snake-sleigh through, and they found themselves in a square criss-crossed by walkways of wooden planks. It was crowded with men and women dressed alike in dirty brocaded skirts, with tattered furs tossed over their shoulders. Most of them were eating out of paper bags. One or two were chewing corncobs. There seemed to be almost no children.

Their guide put a referee's whistle to her lips and blew a sharp blast. When the crowd heard it, they crouched and put their foreheads on the ground. The snakes, curveting and plunging, writhed their way over the tumble of human backs, while their passengers in the mortar swayed and shook.

"It prevents the snakes from cutting themselves on the broken glass," observed the tall woman. "The people here drink more imported beer than is good for them, and are filthy in their habits."

The sleigh glided through streets of low houses built of overlapping boards, then through a square full of foodstalls. Skewers of roasted meat and red peppers were laid out on grills; tubs steamed with hot water; and bundles of dried herbs were hung overhead. Here, too, everyone, dropped to their knees, and meat and vegetables went rolling in the dirt.

A hubbub arose in front of them. They passed under a wooden archway, carved like a birthday cake and with hundreds of candles blazing on it. Shouts and applause greeted them as they advanced onto an open parade-ground paved with slabs of black and white stone in the pattern of a chessboard. The torches here sent out their light through bowls of water mounted on brackets in front of them, so the square board and the ocean of faces around it were interwoven with stabbing beams of focussed light.

They climbed out of the mortar, and their guide went with them to the far side of the square. Two armchairs draped with white sheeets had been placed on a platform, and she motioned to them to sit down. As they did so, a young girl appeared and said something to them in a language they could not understand.

"What's she saying?" murmured John to Bear.

"She is asking if you would like a manicure or hot towels before they begin," said their guide.

John shook his head, and the girl dropped her eyes and sidled away.

A hush fell on the assembly. Trumpets rang out, harsh and exultantly cruel. Two servant boys, their heads on their shoulders twisted back to front, paced across the chessboard carrying an incense burner. They placed it in front of the tall woman, bowed, and departed. She lifted its lid, made of enamel and rust-coloured gold. A smell spread out in waves, like honey mixed with vinegar. John's head began to ache, and the blood pounded in his temples.

The trumpets sounded again. A corpulent man, naked as a parsnip except for black elbow-length gloves, took his place beside the tall woman. He was fondling the handle of an axe that rose above his chest as he rested the blade on the ground.

Once more the trumpets re-echoed. Two files of human chessmen walked with a measured tread to their places on the squares. They, too, were unclothed, except for eyeless helmets of lumpish and misshapen metal that covered their faces. Half of the the helmets were silver, half black. The crowd watched them in a hungry-eyed silence.

The trumpets spoke a last time, one rising, one falling, until they met in a major second that hurt the ears. Two men dressed in robes of bloodstained fur proceeded with impassive expressions to the centre of the board, where they bowed to each other and turned away, one going to the left and the other to the right. One of them was bare-headed; the other was wearing a crown. They mounted ladders to seats on raised stands, like umpire's chairs at a tennis match. They were the combatants. Combatants of the mind.

The tall woman rang a bell. It had a melodious sound, deceptively innocent. The game began. The crowned player with the white pieces barked out an order. One of his men moved forward. There was a pause, then the reply came, equally sharp. A black piece moved in response.

"They're fighting for control of the centre," whispered John to Bear. "It's an interesting way to play chess, isn't it — with living pieces?"

But Bear's merry eyes had gone hard. He didn't answer. The player with the white pieces was thinking and Bear was watching him. After ten or twelve minutes, the crowned man spoke abruptly, and a black piece left the board. It was the first capture. A sigh, like wind dying in a forest, went through the crowd.

Bear stood up. His right paw went to his chest. The golden medallion blazed out, brighter and brighter and brighter still, like the sun rising at midmight. With a gulp of horror John saw the captured piece kneeling front of the naked man with the axe, holding in its hands a freshly plaited straw basket to catch its own head when it was lopped of.

"Stop!" said Bear, and his growl was like thunder in the hills. "Executioner, put down your axe. Pieces, leave the board and dress. Players, take off those robes and get down from your chairs. Witch-grandmother, lay aside your skull with its burning eyes, and close the lid on your incense-burner. Now, and forever."

He spoke with such authority that John looked Bear at him, amazed. Was this *his* Bearie? His dear old Bearie? — Yes, *and also no*. Bear and something else besides. They were obeying him. The axe lay flat on the pavement. The pieces were walking from the board. Some had tugged off their helmets and were even laughing. The players were wrestling free of their heavy robes.

A chill and venemous voice cut in:

"*Continue!*"

It was the witch-grandmother.

"You will do as I have said. All of you," repeated Bear in a voice that did not argue. He spoke as if it was no more than a fact.

Then he turned the full light of his medal straight on his adversary,

"I am an Official Dreamguard, ma'am," he said. "None but the Administrator of Dreams himself has authority over me. I am a simple old bear, and I shall remain a simple old bear, but evil from good I can tell easily enough. This dream is discontinued. It must be remade."

The tall witch-grandmother looked at Bear intently for the first time. When she spoke to him it was in an altogether different voice.

"My congratulations on your appointment," she said. "I am sure you will make a success of it, before, at the end of your time, you come to the Valley. No, don't ask me what that means. You will find out — too late. A dreamguard, well, well! No one should be blamed for being a little clumsy at first. It's a skilled business. Dreams are not easy to understand aright. There is more to this game than meets the eye, much more. Do you know why some have uncovered heads, and some uncovered bodies?"

Bear said nothing, so she went on:

"Only those who make the moves are permitted to have faces and personalities. Those who are moved are merely fodder for the axeman. Do you know why they play at chess with living men whose lives are forfeit when they are taken?"

Once more Bear was silent.

"No?" she said, smiling. "Then let me tell you. They are playing for the kingship of this kingdom. Whoever wins becomes king, or remains so if he is king already. The loser becomes one of the pieces in the next game, his face covered, taking his chances till his time for execution comes."

"Why do you have to kill the pieces when they're captured?" asked John. "Couldn't the king and his challenger just play an ordinary game to decide the matter?"

"If they did," answered the witch-grandmother, "then mere cleverness would win. What is needed in a king is not just cleverness, though of course he must be clever. What is required is sharp wits, and a cool head in a difficult situation. He must be willing to sacrifice lives for victory. He must be able to think without being befuddled by pity, or by fear for himself. Killing the captured pieces, and making the loser serve as a piece himself, is not caprice. Nor is it barbarity. *It is necessary.* We have the ritual to make it understandable, even beautiful. Those who die are content to die. They know their sacrifice is for the good of all. May we continue with our game? You would be interested to see how it finishes."

"I know the end well enough, without seeing it," said Bear. "You want my master to sit in one of the contestant's chairs and play for the kingdom himself."

He reached under his right arm and pulled the zip down the full length of his side. A cold breeze blew past John's shoulders. It was blowing into the nothingness that Bear had opened.

The chessboard began to shake. The bowls of water on the torch-poles shook. So did the players, the pieces, and the people watching. The scene flapped this way and that as if it were no more than a painted backdrop caught in a gust of wind.

The witch had opened her mouth to speak, but she could not utter a word. Her face was anguished with terror as she gazed into the void. Unlike the others, she knew what was about to happen.

Steadily, like a cloth being pulled off a table, everything slid into Bear and disappeared. When the last wooden palisades and the last trees had vanished, the two of them were left alone in darkness lit only by Bear's medal.

"We can breathe again," he said. "We can breathe again. Such things are made in our minds, and our minds must destroy them. Now, we need a new dream. One that is beautiful and simple to understand. I am going to make that dream tonight, the first of all *my* dreams."

Out of his inside he drew three beehives of silver, and set them down on the grass.

"Starlight!" he called softly, and out of the hives flew silver bees. Three spiralling streams of bees joined into one unending line, rising and rising above them till Bear and John were bathed in their light.

"In our other world," said Bear, "night after night the stars make the same patterns. Here, in my world, they will trace new constellations by the hour. Anyone who wants can lie and watch them, from sundown to the sun's rising, dancing their steps across the dark heavens, and never repeating themselves."

The sky was aready full of stars. As Bear had said, they were moving. The patterns seemed simple, but when John tried to follow them he was lost in their complexities.

"What do they show, Bear?" he asked.

"Anything you like to see in them."

"No. Really."

Bear smiled.

"They show the numbers at the heart of things," he said. "The numbers in the growing spiral shell, the numbers in the moving dunes of sand, forever re-creating themselves as the wind blows grain over grain, the numbers in the thickening branches that support the ever more distant twigs. The numbers that rule the waves of light from invisible red to invisible violet. They're all there. When I say you can see anything in them, I mean it. I set them in motion, but even I have no idea how they will end."

John put his arm around Bear's shoulders.

"It is a beautiful first dream," he said. "Is there more to come?"

"Only one thing more," said Bear. "Sit down a moment and I'll tell you a story."

They sat for a while, watching the stars.

"Once, long ago," Bear went on, "there was a king's son. He had all he wanted but he was always sad. A wizard that came by, on a lame horse, told his father that his son would never be happy until he had found the Bear on the Golden Swing. But where the Bear was, he refused to say.

"So the prince set off to find him. He wore out three pairs of iron shoes, and slipped and scrabbled up and down several glass mountains, and all the things you have to do in fairytales. There were days when he thought he saw the Bear — on a distant hill or on an island. But when the prince went closer, there was nothing to be seen. After seven years had gone by, he was riding alone through a forest on a milk-white mare, ready to give up, when he found the Bear. By accident almost. Or so it seemed at the time. The Bear was in a clearing, sitting on a golden swing.

"When the swing went up, the Bear told the prince stories, with the blue sky falling beneath their feet. And when it came down, and the spruce and the birchtrees rose like a green tide to meet them, the Bear sang him poems. He made the prince laugh so much that he forgot he was unhappy. It was only after more days than can be imagined, that the prince in the end remembered who he was, and asked the Bear how to find his way home.

"'Just round the trees ahead,' the Bear told him. And so it proved. There was his father's palace garden as it always was, with its statues and fountains and flowers out on parade, all the same heights and colours. The Bear had been close by all the time. Or maybe the prince had just imagined all his travels....

"In later years, when he was king himself, he still sometimes felt sad. His courtiers told him lies, the piles of government papers gave him headaches, and sometimes he made mistakes which hurt someone. On these occasions, he would take a piece of honeycomb, or a small barrel of Russian beer, and visit the Bear and listen to his tales and poems on the Golden Swing. When he came back he was always cheerful, and no one ever understood how he did it. In spite of a few mistakes, he was a good king, and didn't die till he was over a hundred years old."

"It's a nice story," said John.

"Maybe it's time it came true," said Bear. "Some of it at least."

He held out both paws in front of him, and there, besides the Beehives of the Stars, was a Golden Swing on golden ropes that hung unattached from the sky.

"Whenever you feel sad, my master," he said. "Remember this place. I will be here, and I will tell you stories like the one you've just heard. Maybe poems, too, if I can think of any."

They swang up and down for a while, then sat beneath the stars, laughing and chatting together until, at last, the bees circled down from the dawn skies, and the sun rose above the horizon.

IT WAS MORNING again. The light filled John's bedroom. Bear drowsed on a pillow, smiling to himself at the memory of their adventures, but Murgatroyd was sitting on the chest of drawers. He had a cup of tea beside him, covered with a saucer to keep it hot.

"Terrific stuff, the pair of you," he said. "Particularly on Bear's first night out. Megan launched an attack with three of her deadliest dreams, but Bear was too strong for her. Beyond question, a natural professional. *The Last Lion and the Last Christian*, *The King of the City of Ice*, and *The Game of Chess*. There is enough dark wisdom in those tales to last an adult's lifetime."

He blinked his eyes in the sunshine.

"I shouldn't be surprised — really I shouldn't — if you haven't destroyed some, at least, of her power for ever."

• st. giles's fair

IT WAS LATE in the summer holidays, almost a year later. A year that had slipped away uneventfully, almost unnoticed, though the boys were bigger and stronger. Megan seemed to have vanished into the darkness doomed for her by Bear.

The sun was shining in the garden, and Charles lay rolled on his back in a deck-chair. His knees were up, and his heels jammed against the wooden crossbar holding the canvas seat.

There were blackbirds somewhere.

He stared at the sky through his spread-apart knees. It was blue.

Blue.

"Are you good, Murgatroyd?" he asked suddenly.

The cat was slumped half-asleep on a garden table. Half his mind was on the blackbirds and their nest, now empty, four feet up in a nearby bush. It would have been an easy jumping height. Half his mind was elsewhere.

"What did you say?" he asked, waking up slightly.

"I said," Charles repeated, "are you good?"

"No," said Murgatroyd. "Not as much as I should like to be. Are you?"

"I don't know," said Charles. "What does 'good' mean? And, if you want to be good, why can't you?"

"Two questions," said the black cat. "Actually, they have the same answer."

Murgatroyd smiled to himself. He could feel the warmth in the table-slats flowing into him from underneath. He wondered if Charles would ask to have the puzzle explained.

Charles said nothing, however, but stared at the blue sky. Why was it blue?

The cat began to go to sleep again. He remembered the three little nestlings. The mother had urged them out of the nest too early. One had flown down from the branch where it was meant to shelter and landed in the long grass. He still could see, in his own mind's eye, that little eye there, staring out at the world, so frightened, so hopeful, wondering what life was going to bring it. He'd left it alone, but the crow had taken it.

He sighed.

"I was thinking of grandfather, before he died last year," said Charles. "He used to take me for rides on the tractor. When we were staying at the hill place. He even let me drive it."

Murgatroyd opened an eye, to show he was listening.

"I found a book by him in the house," said Charles. "Yesterday. An oldish book, with a dark blue binding. It's about being good. I tried to read it, because I wanted to hear his voice again, coming out of the pages. We used to have all sorts of talks. About building barns, and clearing the pasture. Whether to hang the swing from a different tree-branch. What the rocks at the top of the hill really looked like. Where to find chanterelle mushrooms. All sorts of things. I miss him, you know. But the book's too difficult. That's the reason I asked."

"What does your grandfather say?" said Murgatroyd, interested.

"Oh, something like this," said Charles. "If I say to you, it's 'good' to give money to poor people, or not to cut down trees, what that means is, I *like* giving them money, or not cutting the trees down, *and* — I think *you* should feel the same way about it, too."

"What's wrong with that?" said the cat. "He was a philosopher, wasn't he?"

"I didn't say anything was wrong with it," said Charles. "It's just that.... Well, suppose I wake up tomorow and feel that giving money to poor people is bad for them, and that cutting down trees is fun, and you should do it too. Then the meaning of 'good' will have changed."

"Isn't it always changing?" said Murgatroyd. "From time to time, and from person to person? Don't cats and blackbirds have their own different goods?"

"If that's true," said Charles, "then nothing's really good. Not like the sky is really blue. For everyone. And I'm not sure I quite believe that."

The cat said nothing, but continued to look at the boy. Had Megan thought she could take this mind into hers? Draw a sweet sap from it to nourish her own cold, pitiless life? It would have killed her.

He was weird — Charles — thought the cat to himself.

He loved him. It had been a wonderful year.

Charles was not a child. He was a fellow-adventurer through the darkness. He was an ally. So there *were* new things, the cat reflected, sometimes, under the sun, no matter what the preacher in past times had said.

"Do you think my grandfather was wrong?" said Charles.

"Not wrong. That's how the word 'good' is used by people, in fact. Pretty much so. These days at least. But —."

He paused.

"If you want to go deeper, I'll tell you how we saw it when I was a Prince over the Darkness in my earlier lives."

"Before you were banished?"

"Before I was banished to ordinary life," said Murgatroyd. "To live my last days as a witch's cat."

"So?"

Murgatroyd drew in a breath.

"To be good," he said, "is to have a feeling for what is outside your own self. To live, at least a little, for other people and other animals. For plants. Even, you know, for stones and stars. You can test whether something is good or not by whether it draws you out of yourself — just a fraction, perhaps — into the rest of all that is, or whether it shuts you up more tightly inside your own mind. Whether it makes something inside you a little more sensitive, or a little more numb."

"Is that all?" said Charles. "It doesn't sound very difficult."

"It is difficult to go more than a little way," said Murgatroyd. "Though the little that most people have is quite resistant. We had to work hard, in my dark years, to kill it off in their hearts. To make sure that they were forever shut. Those we closed down most easily, more often than not, were the proud and stiff ones full of their own virtue, who loved to cut a public figure of being good. You can never tell from the outside, though. Some of them were still alive inside, even after our best efforts."

He sighed.

"One drab, exhausted, housewife who comforts an unhappy child, who feeds her cat, or even pours water onto a dried-up plant, is richer in goodness than all of those."

"But isn't she really looking after herself?" said Charles. "*Her* child, *her* cat, *her* plant?"

"It doesn't matter," said Murgatroyd. "So long as the barrier between them and her is removed. However short the moment before it reappears again."

He stretched himself, cat-fashion, backing his hindquarters away from his forepaws. Then he settled down once more. The noise of the lunch-time traffic, he noticed, was growing louder in the river-side street outside.

"Why is it so hard to go further?" said Charles.

"Wickedness is needed for the world to go on," said the cat. "You wouldn't even be here, but for a little agreeable wickedness once upon a time. Anyhow —. Imagine that a person, or any being, is drawn into an awareness of all that is, of living for It more and more, and for themselves less and less. That state is not like the wind blowing on your skin or on my fur, though that's how it begins. It's like the wind blowing *through* you, or me, and, one day, finding nothing there. After a certain point one dissolves. Like sugar in hot tea."

"You mean, if you are completely good, you die?" said Charles.

"Long before that point. That's why a mix of good and evil in the world is necessary. We have to be imperfect if we are to exist at all. I'm not going to give all my cream and fish away. Some, maybe. If I give it all to others, my 'I' vanishes. I perish of hunger. It's as straightforward as that."

"And those who're completely closed off," said Charles, "what happens to them? Those who are, if I understand what you're saying, in a sort of prison inside themselves?"

"Another kind of death," said the cat. "The death of the soul, if you want to use an old-fashioned word. Actually, it's more like being unable to drink that flow of invisible, magical water that keeps you alive inside."

The tone in Murgatroyd's voice made Charles glance into the cat's eyes.

"You seem to know what you're speaking about," he said.

"With half a life left," said Murgatroyd. "I am still trying to open that well inside me. But every time I begin to succeed, there's a flurry of wind from somewhere and it gets choked up again, with sand, and with dried-up leaves."

Charles stroked Murgatroyd, and rubbed him under the cheeks. For a moment there was no barrier between him and the cat. Then he looked at his watch, an underwater chronometer from his aunt Diana.

He lifted his heels off the edge of the deck-chair, stretched his legs out straight, and jumped up.

"Lunchtime!" he said. "Let's see if there's some tennis on the TV."

They left the blackbirds chirruping in the empty garden.

SOME WEEKS LATER, long after midnight, Murgatroyd had a sudden splitting headache.

It was a witch's headache.

He'd almost forgotten the agony they caused. He knew what it meant, though.

He was being summoned to the television set.

"Like a kid's remote-controlled car," he muttered to himself as he slid off Charles's bed and pattered downstairs, his head like a balloon full of petrol about to burst into flames. "So it's not all over. She still does what she likes with me. I wish they'd got rid of it as they were going to."

The screen was swirling with a turbulent sea of dots when he reached the sitting-room.

He composed himself and sat down in front of it, front paws neatly together. His heart was jumping about like numbers from the random-number key on a pocket-calculator. He tried to breathe more slowly. Get some control of himself. Keep his head clear.

Agony.

Megan's face appeared suddenly.

She looked at him with empty eyes that seemed to be reading his mind. Her lips tightened. So did the muscles in the cheeks under her eye-sockets.

The year vanished as if it had never existed.

"You know the penalty that is imposed on servants who disobey?" she said.

Her voice seem to cut the words out of the air. Separately. As if she was using a knife.

Murgatroyd nodded. But only with great difficulty. His neck was stiff with fear of what was coming next.

"Don't nod. Answer me," she said. "What is the penalty?"

"Imprisonment in a time-loop, my lady."

"Exactly. Like a loop in a badly written computer program," said the witch. "With no condition determined for ending it. With a FROM command, but no TO. And why is it so special, pussy-cat? Now you've had your holiday, tell me that."

Murgatroyd's eyes blinked. Irregularly. He couldn't control them. His voice had dried out.

"Come on!" she snapped.

"Because —," he gasped. Then continued, "Because it solves the freshness problem."

"Of course," said the witch. "Freshness. I'm glad you still understand. Before we perfected the time-loop, pain used to act as its own pain-killer. The sufferer's mind and body wore out under torture. Became, shall we say, like a rag-doll, incapable of receiving any further input of pain. They escaped us. Not now. At each restart of the loop, both mind and body begin fresh, all over again. Capable of infinite agony. Literally infinite. Is that your understanding, too?"

"Yes, my lady."

"How many times have you assisted me with inserting someone into a time-loop since you were assigned to my service?"

"Uh. Some hundreds, my lady. It's hard to remember."

"Seven hundred and ten," said the witch. "It is easy to remember. You have never had trouble remembering in the past. Do you think there is a case for a seven hundred and eleventh?"

"My lady, I do not know what you mean," said Murgatroyd. "By His Satanic Majesty, I have done nothing but serve your interests since I have been here. You have been inaccessible."

103

"Almost a year," said the witch. "While I was ill. Why didn't you come back to look after me? No results here either, it would seem. If I hadn't got myself my Chinese girl — actually only half Chinese, my favourite mixture, with Chinese beauty and European character — I don't know what I would have done. She plays the violin so beautifully. Sings my old soul to sleep. And makes my meals. One day she'll run out of tunes, though. But you, you wretched disloyal and incompetent quadruped, what do I find has happened once I've sufficiently recovered to relish a little variety in my pleasures? I discover a spell round the boys' house. A professional job. The wind hands can't get in. *I* can't get in.

"Oh, how I want to choke and throttle their sturdy young necks! Then release them just before they expire from a lack of oxygen. I want to watch the pretty blush of life reviving in their cheeks! Aiya! A large number of times.

"But there's worse torment still. That Bear. That fat, ludicrous dreamguard with his golden medal and self-important airs. I can't even get at them in their dreams now. Who put him there ? Why didn't you stop it? Why not?"

Murgatroyd smiled smoothly. "It was the Administrator of Dreams, my lady. He was their father's dreamguard once, as I am sure you are aware."

"Old Egger," said the witch. "I see. Well, possibly. I was not aware of that, as it happens. No doubt connections with the right people help in dreams as much as they do in what these human baboons think of as their real life. Possibly. But the timing is suspicious, Judas puss. Am I meant to think it's a coincidence?"

"My lady, please, my lady," said the black cat, "What can I do to persuade you that I am, as ever, devoted to your service? It is a source of almost infinite solace to me to see you well again and as evilly disposed as ever. These two lads are tough, though, incredibly tough. You should think of feeding on some sweeter-tasting kids."

"The flavour of the chase, you fawning, hypocritical cat," said Megan, with a downward-twisting smile. "*You* should understand that, of all animals. The harder the struggle, the sweeter the taste. Just get them to me. *Just get them to me*, do you understand, and all is forgiven. How are you going to do it?"

Murgatroyd dropped his eyes, and thought. His hopes for his last half-life seemed to be going. He could sense her magical power surging like current in a fully recharged battery. His dreams of opening the well even to a thin trickle of water — no, not in the face of this fury. If he tried to kill himself, it would be admitting guilt. She would simply revive him again, with patiently amused cruelty, and loop him, to make sure he suffered to the universe's end. There would be no one to protect the boys. They would be sacrificed one way or the other. No point in being sentimental about that.

Survive! He had to survive. But now he was locked inside himself again. About to betray those whom he loved. And to help the witch whom he hated. The terror of the time-loop left him no argument. He knew too well what it was like.

Too much bad karma from his past lives for him ever to escape. Deserved, he reflected, if anyone ever deserved anything. It is my destiny, he thought, to be evil. Better at least, by one degree, than suffering uselessly.

For no particular reason, his mind turned to Bear. The Bear of the Golden Swing. Warm-hearted towards all beings. And, he muttered to himself, at least I've done something good. One small act of good karma before I go under. Helping him make dreamguard. Before I say goodbye to everything I want — that I wanted — to be.

"Well?" said Megan's voice. It could have frozen a tray of ice-cubes. "You are taking your time."

But he barely heard her. *Bear's face had appeared inside his mind.* Just for a moment. It was unsmiling, but not unkindly, and full of understanding. A message passed from those brown eyes, an unspoken message. Clear, exact, and useful. Murgatroyd nodded. No wonder Bear had already surpassed the destiny once given to him. No wonder. Sixth sense had told him of the danger, as he roamed with his mind on other things, far away in the immensities of dreamland. And some power had given him speed to come here on the instant.

What was Bear now? He seemed an incarnation of something both old and new? Something forever recurring, so strong and serene it left no room for despair. Maybe — even — that prince who, centuries ago, had sat beneath a tree in India. Sat, and resolved not to move again until he gained enlightenment? Felt compassion for all who suffered. Was it possible? — Bear? Hardly. And yet, what else?

Murgatroyd shook his head. But Bear's idea.... It was, at least, a hope. And subtle, too.

"Speak up! Are you incapable of saying anything?"

Megan's voice brought him to his senses, and Bear's face vanished.

"I was thinking, my lady," he said, with all his charm. "And I do indeed have a plan. May I be permitted to submit it for your approval?"

"It had better work," said the witch. "Or you know what will happen."

"It will function perfectly," said the cat. "By HSM, it will, and all the little demons in Tartarus. What's more, we shall have a lot of fun doing it."

"Well?"

"It goes like this," said Murgatroyd. "As follows."

His eyes were shining again, with the joy of craftsmanship.

The witch watched him warily. A resourceful pussycat, no doubt, but what was giving him so cool a charm? She felt safer when he was frightened. She had noticed the speed of the change.

"The boys are extremely careful," said Murgatroyd. "They stay together. They will not go out at night, nor alone. They are well aware, from that stuffed-up panjandrum of a sleeping-bag bear, of whom nothing too vile can be said, that they are in danger. So, point number one: no more attacks. Let them think it's all over. Give them a sense of security. A false sense.

"Second point: as it happens, in three weeks' time it will be Saint Giles's Fair. People lose their souls at fairs more easily than in most other places. I have yet to understand just why, but it is a well-observed fact."

Megan nodded, but continued to look at him sharply.

"The boys love that fair," continued Murgatroyd. "And they love it especially at night, when the lights are on and the crowd is at its thickest. I will persuade them, with all my feline charm, to accompany me to the Fair, or rather, to take me to it, because, I will give them to understand, I have never seen it before. I will promise them my protection from unfriendly things, like wind-hands and witches. I shall also promise them some tricks that will make it like no fair they have ever seen before. Or, indeed, will ever see again."

"I like the irony," said the witch. "You seem to have recovered some of your old spirits and your wits, my dear familiar. Permit me to hope that it is a good sign. They will, indeed, never see it again."

"The next part depends on you, my lady," said Murgatroyd. "You must be gracious enough to condescend to call into existence two wooden automata, statues of those fat boys who fought a battle in Lewis Carroll's *Alice Through the Looking-Glass*. You remember them? A nice Oxford touch."

"You mean Tweedledum and Tweedledee?" said the witch. "Of course."

"Yes, indeed, my lady," said the cat. "Those two. They will need to be about nine feet high, on wheels, or able to walk, with chubby red cheeks, stupid expressions like schoolboys, straw hats, and painted in bright and friendly colours. They will also have doors in their stomachs, and behind each door — lockable from the outside — will be just enough space to keep one boy prisoner. No. Better make room for two boys. The hands, which will be movable, require care. They should be capable of grabbing but not of hurting."

"What do we do with these complicated little monsters?" said Megan.

"They become just another of the shows at the Fair," said the cat. "Once

106

every fifteen minutes or so they have a battle, boffing each other with huge pillows and shouting."

"Do people have to pay to see this?" said the witch.

"No, of course not," said Murgatroyd. "It's for charity. Starving cats in Africa, or any other worthy cause that tickles your covenish fancy. Get a couple of nice kids to take collection-boxes around. Pickings on the side, eh? Keep the car handy for them, too? And, of course, if you still find it all a little tedious you could take bets from the public as to which twin was going to win each time."

"Rigging the results wouldn't spoil the plan, would it?"

"Not in the least," said the cat. "It would help it. Add to the confusion and excitement. Get nicely pulsing waves of greed going through the crowd. No reason why it shouldn't be profitable. You can chalk the results of the last few fights on the board, and give odds according to whether Tweedledum or Tweedledee seems to be on a winning streak. Tell the marks[1] the results are determined by random numbers in the University computer. They'll believe any nonsense like that."

"I do not anticipate encountering any serious problem in summoning the automata you require into existence," said Megan. "But how do you propose we make the kill?"

"There are a few extra details that need attending to before we come to that," said the cat. "You'll need a standard FO spell to keep the Fair authorities off your back for taking up Fairground space without a permit."[2]

"I had already thought of that."

"Less magic is also required if you take electricity from the generator of one of the nearby shows," the cat continued, "rather than producing it yourself."

"Of course."

"That completes the preliminaries. I will lure John and Charles near to Tweedledum and Tweedledee, and then distract John's attention. It is important to secure Charles first."

"But he's the younger."

"I know. That's why I mentioned it. He has a very strong will, and needs to be subdued before his brother, in conditions of complete surprise, or he could spoil everything."

---

[1] Fairman's slang for members of the public attending a fair.

[2] 'FO' may be taken to stand for 'Free Operation' if so desired, though this is not its original meaning.

"If you so advise, I shall act accordingly. I trust you know what you are doing."

"Tweedledum," said Murgatroyd, "grabs Charles and stuffs him into his stomach. The door shuts. I say to John, 'Where's Charles?' He looks around. 'Over there, I think,' I say, and lead him near to Tweedledee, who beams benevolently down. We go a little nearer, and bingo! Tweedledee grabs John, stuffs him into his stomach, and off we go home, and into the TV. Easy."

"I wonder if the onlookers will not attempt to rescue them," said the witch.

"I have already made provisions for that," said Murgatroyd. "We put up a sign that says

RIDES IN 'DUM 'N' 'DEE. 5 MINUTES, 50 PENCE. ALL PROCEEDS TO CHARITY.

Make eyeholes in their buttons — but glassed over, so the screaming can't be heard. Fit a control panel inside. Then anyone going for a ride can make the statue sing and wave its arms about. When you grab Charles, you announce on the loudspeaker, 'And now, ladies and gentlemen, the lucky winner of our mystery draw! Five minutes free ride in the mighty Tweedledum. Five minutes to work the computerized control panel. Special effects by Oxford University Computing Lab. There he goes inside, ladies and gentlemen! Let's see what he does now! Yes! There we are! Off he goes! Isn't he doing well! Let's all give him a big hand! A big, big hand! Thank you! Thank you! And we'll see him when he gets back.'"

"You'd do well at a fair," said Megan, smiling in spite of herself. "Yes. I think there is a chance that it might work. Might. Of course, if you bungle it, you do understand that there are certain consequences? For you."

Murgatroyd nodded.

"It will work," he said. "My life depends on it."

"Not your life, my dear familiar," said the witch, "but the pleasure — or otherwise — with which you continue to lead it."

The face on the screen vanished and was replaced by the swirling waters. These gathered themselves into a smaller and smaller circle, and rotated down an imaginary plughole. The screen went blank.

Murgatroyd stayed crouched on the carpet. Then he pulled himself together and muttered:

"The valley of the shadow of darkness."

He padded wearily up the stairs again, just managed the jump onto Charles's bed, curled his tail around his nose, and slept till the morning. He felt he had become two cats inside, neither of which had anything in common with the other. A good inclination and an evil one.

THREE WEEKS LATER some delicate mind-bending was going on:

"Look, I've never let you down, have I?" said Murgatroyd.

"No, you haven't," said Charles. "Of course not — but it is getting dark."

He was looking down from a window at the river. At the place where Alex had saved John from the thugs when he was still too young to handle them. At the water lapping on the feet of the mooring-posts. It was below the usual level, and the decayed part was showing. The water, too, was more mud than water. It had been another dry summer, with the locks shut for days on end.

A yellow leaf zigzagged down from a willow-tree and hit the water lightly. It spun round once or twice, then lodged on a shoal and stuck.

The sun was sinking. Long shadows from the bridge reached out across the water.

"It's not sense going out at night," said Charles. "You've been telling us that for months."

"You can't be a prisoner to fear forever," said the cat. "She's lost interest. I hear she's got some new kids, including a Chinese girl she dotes on. Gives her a kick just to look into her eyes, or slide her hand — slowly — down between her shoulderblades."

"How do you know?" said Charles. "You been talking to her?"

"I have to talk to her from time to time," said Murgatroyd. "Keep her happy about me. I tell you, she's no longer interested in a couple of tough nuts like you any more. Not with a Dreamguard Bear."

"You could put protective spells around us if we did decide to go, couldn't you?" said John.

"Nothing easier."

The cat was smiling.

Charles turned away from the window and looked back into Murgatroyd's eyes. The red light of the evening seemed to flash there, then fade. Deep in his own mind Charles knew there were fires there, burning. He wondered why.

"I wish you weren't so keen to go to the Fair, John," he grumbled. "We've seen it all before. Last year. Year before, and the year before that. It's just a waste of money."

"But you haven't been with *me* to a Fair before," said Murgatroyd. "I want to see what it's like. I promise you, I'll do things that will make it different from last year, or next year, or any year."

"Oh, come on, Charles!" said John. "It'll be fun. Murgatroyd may not even be here next year. We've been so bored staying in. Like being under house arrest."

"For our own safety," said Charles. "Who's to tell that Megan isn't just waiting? Just pretending she's bored. Until we get careless, and she can pounce. Mmm?"

"I can tell you, for one," said Murgatroyd. "I worked for her, years out of mind. She's not that patient. Not a whole year. Not where kids are concerned. She's got to have fresh ones quick, or else."

"Or else what?" said Charles.

"She gets out of control. I've known times when we've walked past a children's sports shop with a rack of track-suits hanging up, and she's said to me, 'See it?' And I've said to her, 'See what?' And she's said,'That one, there!' And I've said, 'But that's just an empty track-suit, my lady.' And she's said, 'Oh, no, it isn't. I can feel the body that's going to fill it. So warm, and strong, and cheerful. Oh! — Oh!' She's not patient, Charles, Megan isn't. Believe me."

"I'm going to go, Charles, even if you don't," said John. "If you come, I'll treat you to two rides. Anything you like."

Charles shook his head.

"It doesn't feel right," he said. "I think Megan's still out there, waiting."

He looked through the window again. It was darker than before. Far away he could see the top of a circle of lights turning. It was a Ferris Wheel. Uneasy excitement stirred inside him. He seemed to hear the fairground music in his mind's ear.

He put his hand in his trouser pocket and felt the stegosaurus bone. The turning lights and the night faded. He saw tree ferns, and cycads, and sequoia trees. Recklessness flickered in his mind, like flaming brandy circling a Christmas pudding.

"Well," he said with a smile, "maybe one shouldn't always run from adventures. Maybe one should leap headlong into the abyss. And — with luck — come out the far side."

Murgatroyd shot him a strange look, half worry, half affection. Charles always saw deeper than anyone. Without even trying. He wondered what the boy had seen, and what it meant for him.

Aloud, he said: "There's no adventure about it. Not in that sense. Just fun and a little mischief. Magical mischief. As you'll see!"

THAT, AT LEAST, was true enough.

An hour or so later, they began to make their way through a crowd that thickened like a sauce the closer they came to the Fair itself. Murgatroyd rode on Charles's shoulder, as usual, so he could see over people's heads, and whisper in Charles's ear without anyone knowing he was talking.

The noise grew louder. The hubbub of voices. The bass growl of the generators. The screaming of the girls on the roller-coaster as it plunged downhill. The non-stop fizzy harmonium jollity of the merry-go-rounds as their horses lifted and descended. The bang and clatter of the whiplash carts like hammers careering into a million anvils. The explosions of crackers.... These dizzied their minds into a trance and a tingling, wild elation.

"We're like the cells of a slime-mould swarming together," smiled John to himself, "possessed by urges we don't understand."

His eyes blurred. There was already too much to see at the same time. Different stalls begging for attention. Pink twists of candy-floss, as big as a baby's head. Roll-a-ball competitions for prizes of tea-services decorated with roses. A man in old-fashioned breeches, with a cape round his shoulders, standing by a weighing machine. "I GUESS YOUR WEIGHT WITHIN 2 POUNDS CORRECTLY, OR I GIVE YOU GENUINE GOLD PERUVIAN RING: 50 P." The Ferris Wheel turning slowly with its rims and spokes outlined by lights — red, green, orange, and white. Some going down and some coming up. Shiny metal slide-towers like blunt corkscrews with kids twiddling round and round down them, and pspitt! out the bottom, pspitt! one after the other. Dark green wooden ducks jerking along at the back of a duck-shooting stand. *THE HAUNTED HOUSE. OVER-16 ONLY. WE TAKE NO RESPONSIBILITY.* The Ghost Train. The Wall of Death. A stall selling hundreds of cuckoo-clocks with metal pine-cones as weights. Pendulums waggling at different speeds. All showing different times. A hot-dog van, with huge pots of mustard the colour of dayglo khaki. FRED AND MILDRED, HEAVIEST MARRIED COUPLE IN THE WORLD. COMBINED WEIGHT OVER 56 STONE. 75P....

Just let it happen, thought John. Let it happen. I can't take it in all at once.

"Let's start with this one, shall we?" said Murgatroyd's voice in his ear.

"LADY IN A BOTTLE?" said Charles, overhearing. "It was here last year. It's just a swiz. There's this fat lady in a bikini in a big glass bottle, but the bottle's on a base, and there's obviously a trap-door in it. So what's so wonderful about that?"

"Carrie'd say it ought to be HUSBAND IN A BOTTLE," said John.

"That's probably what she'll do to her husband, if anyone ever marries her," said Charles.

"Would you tell her that to her face?" said John.

Murgatroyd coughed.

"Your half-sister is extremely understanding of cats," he said. "She helped me when I fell off Megan's vacuum-cleaner two years ago."

"You fell off Megan's vacuum-cleaner?" said Charles disbelievingly. "You *fell off?* You never told us that. How did it happen?"

"I was drunk," said Murgatroyd. "Pilfered her whisky."

"You were *what?*" said Charles.

"Drunk," said the cat. "I loathed working for her, and thought whisky might help. It didn't. It destroyed my sense of balance. Luckily for me, I landed in the Thames."

"And Carrie helped you?" said John.

"Yes. Fished me out. Dried me off. Brought me back under her jumper and gave me a can of Borden's. I didn't talk, so she didn't know who I was. But I meowed and prouked and said 'Thank you!' in the usual cat way."

"She never told us about that before she left," said Charles.

"Stranger and stranger," said John. "Our fates seem to be intertwined in so many ways. No wonder you found our house so easily."

"We can talk about Carrie later," said Murgatroyd. "I wish I'd kept in touch with her. Didn't realize she was going to go away. But let's push in now, and see if we can't make this bottle-lady's life a little more fun. OK? I can't think of anything less amusing than lying in a hot bottle all day and being peered at by blotchy pink faces, can you?"

John paid the entrance fees, without much pleasure, still thinking about Carrie.

Inside it was as Charles had said.

The dark canvas roof of the tent sagged like a belly above them. Pink and blue spotlights shone down from one of the poles onto a clear glass bottle about eight feet long. It lay with its shoulders raised on a rack a foot or so off the ground, and sloped slightly downwards towards its base.

Inside lay a plump white woman in a two-piece purple swimsuit. It was almost lost in the rolls of her flesh. If you didn't look closely she seemed to be naked. Her face was bored and contemptuous, but could have been pretty. Under her was a strip of cardboard painted yellow and tan to look like sand, with a blue and turquoise strip at the bottom to represent the sea. Six small cut-out palm-trees, notchy-trunked and their fronds curved upwards like little V-signs, were anchored in wooden blocks wherever there was an empty space. Sometimes she twitched her toes. Otherwise she didn't move.

Most of the onlookers seemed a little embarrassed; and after pausing to make sure they hadn't missed anything, pushed out the flap on the far side without waiting for very long. A pudgy, pop-eyed man rested on his elbows on the far side of the bottle, watching the marks go by, and saying nothing.

"You see," said Charles, rather too loudly, "fifty pence to see that!"

The pop-eyed man heard him, and suddenly began to speak.

"As the young gentleman says, as the young gentleman says," he announced, wagging a finger into the darkness around him. "Only fifty pence to see a sight unique in the universe. In this glass bottle, this bottle, ladies and gentlemen, is the only woman ever to make her way in — and out — of a bottle whose neck is only two centimeters wider than her head. Two centimeters, ladies and gentlemen! Without breaking it. You doubt that? Here is a tape-measure, ladies and gentlemen. A tape-measure. Measure the neck of the bottle for yourselves. You, Sir! Would you be so kind as to measure the neck of the bottle? No? Then, Madam, would you? No, again? I take it we're all agreed that the neck is so narrrow that no ordinary human being, no ordinary human being, ladies and gentlemen, could go in and out of it. But Esmeralda, ladies and gentlemen, Esmerelda is no ordinary human being. She is a snake-lady, a human rubber-band, and passing in and out of that aperture is no more for her than going in and out of a door is for you or me."

He paused for effect.

A young man with fat, disdainful lips, observed: "Doesn't it just come apart?"

"My friend here," said the pop-eyed man, "My friend here asks, Does it come apart? A very fair question, a very fair question, ladies and gentlemen. And I will surprise you by my answer, my absolutely truthful answer. *Yes.* This bottle *has* come apart. *Once!* In 1965. Since then it has been sealed. Please examine the seal on the seam of the glass. It is signed by the Chairman of Pilkington's himself. Pilkington's Glass, I should explain in case some of you have not heard of this famous company. Since that date, September the First, 1965, ladies and gentlemen, that bottle has been in one piece. Examine the seal. Examine the date. Don't take my word for it. Check for yourselves!"

A few people bent over the bottle to look at the seal.

"If she's a human rubber-band," said the young man, twisting his lips as he spoke, "why doesn't she come out now? To show us how it's done."

The pop-eyed man assumed a grave expression.

"This, Sir," he said, "is decent, all-family entertainment. You are asking me to ask Esmerelda to show you how she takes herself apart. That is not only improper, Sir, and I am sorry — for you — to have heard you ask for such a thing, it is also quite terrifying. There's not a child in this tent would sleep for a week were he or she to witness how she stretches, how she slides one arm up under her neck till it rests where her throat is now, how she slides, and stretches, the other arm down, down, till her shoulder nestles in her stomach. How she rotates one side of her pelvis up, and one side down, making one leg long, and the other short, like this! And then, with a wriggle, and a dexterous shift — from this side to that side, and to this side again — extricates herself slowly, delicately, painfully, as if the bottle itself were giving birth to her, out, out of the neck. And, then, gradually, reassembles herself again into the normal, the lovely, the entrancingly lovely lady that she is. No, Sir, no! I am sorry, but basic human decency forbids, and I must ask you, Sir, to be so kind as to leave now out of respect for her feelings."

The young man gave an expression of disgust, tossed his head slightly, and, as he walked out, spat sideways into the sawdust.

"Walk around! Please!" cried the pop-eyed man. "Take your time to look! Every angle! Something you'll never see again. Twice around if you want to. Three times. Any number of times. So you make sure you remember every detail. Every detail. But keep moving, please. Let the folks behind have a look. Don't forget there's a queue waiting. In this glass bottle, ladies and gentlemen...."

A scream came from the bottle.

The barker stopped.

He peered down.

There was another scream.

"Harry! Help! Let me out!"

The woman inside the bottle was drawing her knees up, and twisting back and forth. She was trying to avoid something.

She had already squashed the six little palm-trees flat.

Charles looked at the bottom end of the bottle and began to laugh.

"You rogue, Murg!" he said to the cat on his shoulder. "You absolute rogue!"

He began to shake with laughter, trying not to make too much noise. The cat had to dig his claws in to stay on, like a sailor caught on the mast in a squall.

The blue and turquoise on the cardboard strip had turned into real water. Miniature waves were rolling in and breaking on the beach. Flying-fish the size of houseflies were leaping out of the sea and landing on the woman's legs. No wonder she was screaming to be let out.

The pop-eyed man put his mouth over the top of the bottle and said something. Neither boy could hear his words, but they sounded unpleasant. Whatever it was he had said, it stunned the woman. She forced a smile onto her face, lay on her side and began to flick her toes in the waves.

"Look at her enjoying herself!" cried the barker. "Look at her playing with her pet fish! Never, ever, ladies and gentlemen, did you see a flea-circus with an act to match this one. Look how the surf comes surging in, just like the real sea you go to on your holidays! Move along please now! Let the folks behind you see the show! Thank you! Thank you! And be sure, when you get out, to tell your friends, the one, the one and only, Lady in the Bottle with Magic Sea and Magic Flying Fish!"

"He recovered himself quickly," said John to Charles.

"Yes," said Charles. "He's smarter than he looks, old pop-eyes. A lot smarter. Listen to him having them on."

Another scream came from the bottle.

"Harry! Harry! That's enough! I can't take any more!"

Hibiscus shrubs, their red and yellow buds half-opened, were pushing up through the sand around her. A pair of parrots, the size of ten-pence pieces, were skimming up and down the bottle, shrieking and swinging upside down on the shrubs. The woman was trying to fend them off, and shouting at them.

Harry lifted up a huge cork from somewhere in the darkness and pushed it, gentle shove by gentle shove, into the neck of the bottle. The screams faded into silence.

He dropped his voice and smiled at the onlookers.

"See how she enjoys her tropical paradise," he purred. "See how she disports herself with her birds. There is absolutely no deception, ladies and gentlemen, no deception. What you see is what you get. Keep moving, please. If you don't mind!"

"He's going to suffocate her," said John, "if he doesn't take that cork out."

"Calm down," said Murgatroyd. "There's an air-supply in the base. She's not in any danger."

"Thank goodness. What are you going to do next?"

"Get ready to go, I think," said the cat. "Sad. I'd no idea it would upset her so much."

"You can't just leave her there," said Charles. "Break the bottle open, why don't you?"

Murgatroyd reflected.

"You're right, I think," he said. "Harry's not going to let her out. Not while he's raking in the money."

He glanced around.

"Let's get up on those boxes there. The mineral-water crates. OK? — Now, watch!"

The boys looked down over the heads of the other spectators.

"There's nothing to it," said a man in front of them to his wife. "They use those miniature Japanese trees. *Bushi,* I think they're called. Something like that. Grow nineteen to the dozen, they do."

"I thought they took years to grow," said his wife. "And had to have their roots clipped to keep them small."

"That's the trees you're thinking of," said the man. "Tree *bushi.* Trees — yes. But the flowers — no. They're quicker."

Gulping noises broke out among the spectators, and cries of "Look out! He's going to come ashore!"

An extremely small Loch Ness monster was rippling up and down the strip of sea just below the woman's toes.

The next moment she had fainted.

"Why such a panic?" said Murgatroyd. "It's only a baby plesiosaur. Oh, well, then."

He raised his right paw.

There was a cracking sound, and the bottle split apart like an oyster shell.

The parrots flew off into the darkness.

The Loch Ness monster vanished, and the hibiscus flowers turned into plastic imitations.

What was left of the sea dribbled out into the sawdust and wet the shoes of three or four spectators.

Charles and Murgatroyd slid out the exit, followed by John, who was panting.

Outside, the noise and lights of the Fairground seemed a relief, after what they'd been through.

Charles mopped his brow with the sleeve of his sweater.

"Can't you be gentler next time, Murg?" he said. "That was brutal."

"Why should I?" said the cat. "Listen to them in there. They're still clapping. Clapping to the echo."

He steadied himself on Charles's shoulder, claws gripping into the windcheater for balance, and surveyed the fairground, the world of illusion, the world of lights and music, and underneath it the crowd, less happy than it wanted to be, swirling slowly along like a black underground river, breaking

116

into pools and eddies and backwaters.

"How about the Ferris Wheel next ?" he said. "Oh-oh!"

A heavy man man in a raincoat half-tried to bump into John. John shifted his weight at the last moment, and the man stumbled into the back of a woman, who gave him a look.

Murgatroyd frowned, raised a paw, and pointed it at the man. He traced a half-circle in the air. There was just enough light for them to see the man's ears rotate on the sides of his head until they were back-to-front. In their new position they made his face look streamlined, like that of a bad-tempered rabbit.

The rotation must have tickled, because the man stopped and began to scratch at one of his them. But either his finger felt nothing unusual, or he didn't believe what it felt. He would though, later, thought the cat to himself, smiling. Wait till he looks in the mirror tomorrow when shaving.

Both the bad and the good side of Murgatroyd felt pleasure in what he had just done, for different reasons This gave him an agreeably double sense of satisfaction.

John meanwhile was gazing at the faces of the people in the swinging benches around the rim of the Wheel. Some of them looked elated. Perhaps it was the way, he imagined, the towers and rooves of the colleges fell away below their feet, then rose up again, then sank once more. But others looked scared, and others just bored, waiting for the ride to be over. Some of the faces were lonely, others very much together with each other, seeing things through each others' eyes. Lives, he thought, coming and going, one after the other. Lives.

Aloud, he said: "So, what are you going to do to the Ferris Wheel?"

"Something gentle," said Murgatroyd. "Something poetic. Look!"

The circling lights above them began to twist like streamers. The dance of splitting chromosomes in our biology book, thought John. Splitting and doubling. What on earth is Murg doing with them?

The strings of light on the rims came apart, crossed over each other, and joined up again. The spokes began to twinkle like seesaws. Or scissors. It was very odd.

Some of the people in the chairs were now upside down, moving around like reflections underneath the others who were still the right way up. Gravity appeared to be pulling them in the opposite direction.

He watched them carefully. Odder still. There was only *one* line of them. If you waited long enough, and kept your eyes on a single point, everyone came past that point the right way up. So, somewhere, they turned over.

117

And they weren't exactly reflections either. The faces above and below were different. And yet it was close to reflection. The right hands of those above were mirrored by the left hands of those below.

John followed the lines of light with his eyes, struggling to stop them escaping from his mind. Then he laughed.

"Advanced math, Murgatroyd. A single-sided surface. Right ?"

The black presence on Charles's shoulder chuckled.

"Neat, isn't it? The Ferris Wheel has become a Moebius Wheel. Like a strip of paper in a paper-chain looped back onto itself and joined, but this time with only a *half*-twist. So each time the chairs come back to the place they started, the people are facing the opposite way. Inwards rather than outwards. And the next time round they are facing out again."

"It's the spokes of the Wheel that confuse me," said Charles. "They seem to be shifting from one side to that on the other without ever becoming detached, either from the rims or the axle in the middle."

"There is only *one* rim now," said the cat. "And it runs along *both* sides, if you can imagine it. So the spokes at each end of the axle have to rotate *through* the wheel as they turn. But they stay fixed at both ends, the hub and the perimeter. The shimmering effect from the strings of light-bulbs, all those blues and whites and oranges, is beautiful, don't you think? Like reeds in the wind."

"Weird," said Charles. "It shouldn't be able to happen."

"But beautiful," said the cat.

"Maybe for us," said Charles. "But now see what you've done."

The wheel had stopped.

A young woman in a leather mini-skirt and dark green woolly tights was screaming and sobbing as the operator helped her and her husband get off. She had too much make-up on. Her tears had made a mess of it, like raindrops on a windscreen caked with dust.

She was clutching a toddler in a dark blue romper suit.

"You never told us your wheel made us go through other people."

She was crying and screaming at the same time.

"Don't you realize what was happening? Going round mixed up with people facing the other way? He could have been knocked out of my arms!"

The operator was putting a brave face on it, and patting the toddler's head.

"He was 'aving a lovely time, lady," he said in a cheery voice. "Little hero, he is. Proper little hero. Don't you worry, me love. He enjoyed every minute of it."

He patted the boy's blond curls.

"Keep your hands off him! Keep them off!" she screeched at him. But her voice was as dry as sandpaper, and could hardly be heard above the growl of the fairground machinery.

The young man took a clumsy swing with his fist at the operator, who rocked his head out of reach and then kicked the young man hard, but not too hard, on the side of his knee, so he collapsed on the ground with a yelp of pain.

The operator put his hands under his armpits and dragged him up again.

"You keep your hands to yourself," he said. "And look after your missus instead of trying silly stuff with me. Ach, you. Get off now!"

He pushed the young fellow away. He was limping badly, Charles noticed.

The operator wiped his hands up and down on the legs of his trousers to calm himself. Then he eased a lever over, and started the wheel turning again.

"Murgatroyd," said Charles softly, "you are not being kind to people this evening. Let's go home."

The cat turned his eyes on Charles, trying to imagine what was going on in the boy's mind. Then he thought of something, and shuddered. Time-loops.

"We've hardly begun, Charlie," he said in a sugary voice.

The music of the merry-go-round blared in the distance through its loud speaker. The cars of the Whiplash banged and bumped. The deep frequencies of the diesels running the power generators made the surface of the street throb. A confused swell of chattering and shouting and calling swilled around them. Then, suddenly, there was a sound of screaming. Happy screaming. And a tinny roaring of wheels.

"Roller-coaster's started again," said Murgatroyd. "Listen to them! That's the girls squealing on the downhill bits. There it goes once more."

A second crescendo of screams tore through the air like a streamer of sound.

"Why do girls like screaming?" said John. "Or do they just do it without knowing why?"

There was a third round of screaming, fainter this time.

"I don't know," said Charles. "I think it's time to go home. Now."

"One more chance?" said the cat softly in his ear. "One more. Please. I've been doing my best. It's not my fault that people sometimes get scared."

Charles glanced up at the Ferris Wheel. It had returned to its normal state, lights turning slowly against the stars, far above the rest of the fairground glitter.

"A lot of people are going to think they went mad this evening," said Charles.

"It's only poetry," said the cat. "My kind of poetry. Real-life poetry, not just words on a page."

119

Charles smiled.

"Some of your ideas *are* beautiful, Murg," said. "And strange. But people can't take much poetry."

"Wait till you see what I've got for the roller-coaster," said the cat. "Everyone will love it. No one will get angry or hurt. Promise."

"All right," said Charles reluctantly. "One more."

He didn't see the cat raise his eyes slightly, or hear him blow his breath out very softly — with relief.

Standing in the queue was boring. And quite a number of people were trying to queue-jump. Eventually the boys gave up being good-mannered, and pushed and twisted their way up the wooden steps, and got to the front.

"Sit at the back, if you can," whispered Murgatroyd into Charles's ear. "You'll see more of the fun."

He slipped off his shoulder and out of sight between people's feet while John bought tickets for two.

They were the first in for the next journey, and had — for a moment — that luxurious feeling they could choose whatever seat they wanted. Then they heard feet behind them.

Three cars were standing at the platform. The boys quickly clambered into the back seat of the back one and sat down next to each other.

The car was uncovered and open at the sides. You could look over the edge of the wooden running-board and down through the openwork track at the grille of braces and struts that held it up.

"Seems about a hundred years old, doesn't it?" said Charles.

John did not answer but looked up at the iron trelliswork above his head. When he moved his head back and forth, the different levels of trelliswork seemed to move back and forth against themselves in the opposite direction and at different speeds. It was satisfying that things followed laws, even trivial laws. But repeatable.

Some way in he could see another part of the track shining, and the place where it looped the loop, and the centrifugal force pressed you into your seat even though you were upside down. Shaped like a kind of snail-shell. A snail-shell? Another real-life joke.

There was nothing to hold onto except a sort of iron rung set in the back of the seat in front of them. It was cold to the touch, and greasy. The heat flowed suddenly out of his hands when he gripped it experimentally.

An enamelled plate was screwed into the seatback below it, except that two of the four screw-holes were empty. VIROL, it said, ANAEMIC GIRLS NEED IT. A smell of dampness rose from the floor, and old cigarettes. And other things.

The cars in front had filled up, mostly with teenagers who were bigger than they were. No middle-aged people, thought John. Old people don't like roller-coasters. Why not? He couldn't think of an answer.

The train gave a jerk, then stopped. The couplings clanked as they were thrown back, then forwards, against each other. The cable-grip caught the next time, the couplings stretched out taut like vertebrae on a spine, and the three cars began to climb the incline ahead.

The whole of Saint Giles lay spread out below them. The two dark churches at each end seemed like ships in a dry-dock, waiting for the flood of lights and people to rise up and float them off.

There were no guard-rails at the edge of the track. If anyone had fallen out they would have dropped straight through the air onto the street below.

"One of these things came off its rails a few years ago," said Charles. "Going round a corner too fast. At Battersea Fun Fair, I think."

A girl with dark hair and rabbit teeth turned round and looked at him with dislike.

"Everyone was killed," said Charles, smiling at her.

She pursed her lips and turned her head back. Her companion, an older girl, glanced at Charles, but said nothing.

The cars had levelled out at the top by now, almost at a standstill. The rails dipped into a valley of darkness below them, like a pair of silver chopsticks. They could feel the wind ruffling their hair.

"Too late to change your mind now," purred a familiar voice.

Murgatroyd was sitting on the back of the seat between them. He half slid, half dropped down.

"Worse than being on a broomstick," he remarked. "You can feel the whole contraption swaying in the wind up here. Especially when you're sitting on the back coupling."

The other girl in front looked round reproachfully.

"Do you have to?" she said. "You're making her ill."

Charles pretended to be studying the fairground, and not to have heard what she said. Anyway, it was the cat's remark not his, though she couldn't be expected to know that.

The train began to gather speed.

They felt it tilt downwards, pointing them at the abyss.

The abyss grew slightly larger.

Then their stomachs left them. The slipstream hissed past their faces.

Their minds went blank. They felt weightless, helpless, exhilarated and terrified at the same time.

John's knuckles whitened as they found themselves gripping the iron rung.

Instant by instant they went faster and faster. The black trelliswork exploded up past them on either side.

The girls began screaming.

But — as they did so — their voices vanished. Streams of fireflies poured from their mouths instead. Cool shimmering green and icy mauve. They burst into the air like millions of droplets from a smokestack, hanging above the empty tracks behind like clouds of vapour.

The train hit the bend at the bottom, levelled out, then flipped round the loop-the-loop so fast they didn't know what was happening until it was over. It jerked round a bend. The girls screamed again as they were thrown outwards. Another cloud of fireflies lifted into the air, red-gold this time, like millions of tiny eyes.

The train plunged down. It wriggled like a dragon over a series of bumps that left them feeling weightless each time they came off the top. At each bump the girls screamed, and left puffs and streamers of fireflies behind them. Pale yellow this time, and drifting away till they were lost in the confusion of the other lights.

The train was trundling now, losing speed as it climbed the gentle gradient into the station.

Murgatroyd looked sideways at Charles.

"Didn't I keep my promise?" he said. "Wasn't that beautiful?"

"I wish all screaming was as nice," said Charles, laughing.

The train had come to a stop. The rabbit-toothed girl in front looked round at him again. Then she spat over the side of the train.

"Oh, come," said Charles, "I'm not as bad as that."

The girl looked at him.

"Dead fireflies," she said. "You don't expect me to swallow them do you?"

She walked off with her companion before Charles could think of an answer.

He climbed out, slowly and awkwardly. John followed. The muscles in both their legs were stiff with nervous tension.

"Well," said Charles. "Home."

"Of course," said Murgatroyd. 'But there's something we ought to do on the way back."

"What?"

"I noticed a shooting-gallery on the way in," said the cat. 'It's got exceptionally fine Chinese porcelain vases for prizes. You and John are dab shots. You know how much your father likes porcelain. Why don't you win him a piece or two as a present? It's cheaper than buying it in a shop."

"Nice idea," said Charles, "Our poor old father needs something to cheer him up. OK. Let's do that."

"It's fake, isn't it?" said John.

"Oh, yes, I suppose so," said the cat, "but it's so good a fake it doesn't matter. Almost everything that's genuine is in the museums by now. And they're full of fakes, too."

"The museums full of fakes? You mean they can be fooled?"

"No, no, no," said Murgatroyd. "They know they're fakes, or most of them. They can't refuse gifts from rich people. That's the reason. The rich people's collections are a mixture, half fakes, half real stuff. So, if the museums won't take the fakes and pretend they're genuine, the rich people get offended and won't give them the real stuff either. That's how life works."

"Well," said John, "in that case let's win our father a fake. Do you think the shooting-gallery's got honest sights on its rifles?"

"How could they afford to?" said Charles. "Odds are they've knocked them out of alignment on purpose. Couple of taps with a hammer's all that's needed. But you can compensate. Just needs a few careful ranging shots."

Murgatroyd glanced at Charles and smiled. With surprised admiration — like old times.

POT-A-POT CHINESE SHOOTING ARCADE it said. Two painted dragons writhed their way up flats on each side of a counter where half-a-dozen old .22 rifles lay, each attached to a heavy staple by a short chain. The dragons had pearls between their fangs, and whiskers trailed from their mouths.

A wizened little man was resting his head on his hand, elbow on the counter, looking out at the world. He had no customers, but this didn't seem to cause him concern. His eyes flicked from person to person in the passing crowd, like a snake's tongue, fastening on a face for a moment, then letting go and flicking to another one.

Behind him five life-size painted figures rocked back and forth in unison. Each one was different. The first was a white-bearded immortal with a domed forehead and a crane perched on his shoulder. The second was a lady in a robe, haughty-faced, like a demon or a princess, with two long trembling feathers arching above her head. The third was a moon-faced young man with a box of books tucked under one arm. The fourth was a general in armour that bulged at his shoulders and breast and stomach, and whose belt had a demon's face scowling from its clasp. The last was a plump child, his head shaved bald except for a central quiff of black hair. He was gripping a stick of pink coral; and a string of copper coins with square holes in them was slung around his shoulder. All of them had one thing in common. Their right hands held a small jar, about the size of an apple, with a Chinese character painted on it.

A display-case of porcelain vases stood at one side, with a label on each of its shelves — Sung, Ming, Ch'ing — three Chinese dynasties, the earliest about a thousand years ago.

John watched the figures rocking.

Chinese music came from a small tape-recorder on the counter. It sounded to him like the squeaky two-stringed fiddle whose bow goes above one string and under the other — cheerful, cocky, wry, and lugubrious in turns.

A small folded card, stuck to the counter with transparent tape, read 50₱ PER SHOT.

"What d'you have to do?" he asked the wizened man.

The man looked at him, sizing him up.

"Pot a pot," he said.

"What d'you mean by that?" said John.

The man lifted a rifle.

"Use this to shoot a pot out of the hand of any one of the figures," he said. "You've got to break it. So it smashes. One hit gets you a Ch'ing vase from the cabinet, two a Ming, three a Sung. Your selection."

John examined the sights on each of the six rifles, squinting along the barrel of one after the next. Every one was kooked. He flicked his eyebrows up a fraction. Hmm. It might take a few shots to get the hang of one.

"OK," he said. "I'll try half-a dozen bullets please."

He laid three one-pound notes on the counter.

The old man flipped up the notes with the speed of a card-sharp removing cards from a green baize table. Then he counted out six bullets into a dark green plastic ashtray and put them in front of John. He watched to see how well the boy handled the gun.

John's fingers slid the bolt open and the bullet in and the bolt closed with a single sliding movement. Charles, looking on, noticed the old man's eyes narrow. Not much. Just enough to be noticed.

Murgatroyd was still sitting on Charles's shoulder. His tail flicked and his left eye gave forth a faint spurt of green light. The sight on the rifle in John's hands straightened itself until it was perfectly true.

John rested his left elbow on the counter, left hand steadying the barrel, eye sighting the immortal, and right forefinger caressing the trigger. He swayed a little from side to side, to pick up the rhythm of the swaying figures. Concentrating.

He noticed the rhythm had changed. That it kept changing slightly. Not much but just enough to throw him out as he swung the sight to follow the jar. He suspected the old man had a control of some sort hidden under the table, a pedal perhaps. So! There was more to this than met the eye.

He judged the end of an oscillation. For an instant all five figures were still. His finger had squeezed even before his mind was aware of it. Bang!

The immortal's jar lay shattered on the ground. He noticed that it was almost solid stoneware.

The old man's expression did not change.

"One Ch'ing," he said. "Are you going for the Ming?"

"I'll take a Ch'ing to start with, please," said John. "I think that shot was a fluke."

"Well, in that case," said the old man, "take your pick. Which one do you want?"

John pointed to a tall jar with a deep white glaze and overglazed in dark blue and orange.

"That one, please."

"Ah," said the old man, almost looking pleased, "a very discerning choice. The girl on a tightrope. One of my own favourites."

He took it off the shelf, holding the rim in the V between his thumb and his forefinger, with his other hand under the base, turning it one way, and then the other, to show John the scene.

A girl in trousers, balancing herself with a pole held horizontally in her hands, was picking her way, feet turned outwards, along a rope that sagged in a deep curve between the branches of two trees.

John put it to one side, thinking how much pleasure it would give their father. Then he slid the second bullet in and prepared to shoot again, this time at the jar in the hand of the lady whose head was crowned with the dancing peacock plumes.

He never had time to do so.

"John! *Help me!*"

It was Charles's voice. Controlled, as it always was. But with a note of desperate urgency.

John twisted on the spot, on the balls of his feet.

His brother was dangling three feet off the ground. He was gripped by his waist in some huge pink fingers.

Wooden fingers.

Behind the fingers was a figure, about nine feet high. Of a fat boy. With a smirking, ugly, self-satisfied face. More painted wood. It was sticking its tongue out and wagging it mechanically from side to side across its lips. Its stomach was bloated and it wore breeches.

John's first thought was that it was a fairground exhibit gone mad. Tweedledum, out of Lewis Carroll's *Alice*. Or Tweedledee, perhaps. What was it? What was it trying to do? Why Tweedledum? Or his twin?

Charles was fighting to free himself, but the wooden hand was too strong.

It took John no more than half a second to size the situation up.

He rolled forward across the counter on his stomach, dropped to his feet on the far side, still holding the .22 on its chain, and turned.

Now he could point it outwards.

It was already loaded.

He jammed the butt into his shoulder and lined up the huge wrist in the sights. It meant aiming very close to Charles, but the weakest link was there. Probably.

His nerve held.

For a fleeting second he relaxed, and breathed out.

Then shot.

The wooden wrist sagged. Something inside had been broken. A servo-mechanism, a heavy-duty rubber belt, a spring — at any rate something that gave it its strength.

Now gone.

Charles wrenched himself free from the fingers, and went sprawling to the ground. He rolled to his side and was up again in a single motion, hands raised to defend himself.

Then he darted behind the cover of an ice-cream stand.

The huge wooden boy, still smiling unpleasantly above its swollen stomach, began to move towards him. Its damaged hand dangled at its side, but the other one was stretched out like a claw. It shifted the ice-cream stand aside as if were doll's-house furniture.

Charles backed away behind a heavy iron lamp-post, watching the shuffling legs. He decided that his only hope was to change direction constantly, like a banderillo evading a bull in a bull-ring.

John had already slipped another bullet in. Now he fired again. This time at the other wrist.

There was a gaping gash of splinters, and the hand went limp.

John began to load again.

126

Suddenly he felt a grip on his own shoulder, screwing in like a carpenter's vise.

"Put that bloody thing down! There are people out there. You could kill someone!"

It was the old man. He was hissing with a mixture of rage and fear.

But Charles's danger gave John a strength beyond his years.

He twisted and drove the heel of his palm at an angle under the old man's nose. *Hard up*. And backwards.

The old man lost his grip and reeled into the cabinet of vases. Three or four of them were shaken out and broke into big pieces, their bases rolling off like mouths with jagged teeth till they hit something and stopped.

John finished reloading and shot again.

This time he aimed at the knee-joint. Just above where the breeches were buttoned down above the swelling of the calf-muscle. The thought crossed his mind that, horrible though it was, the brute was well-constructed. Almost alive. And painted a pinkish-yellow that, in the garish lights, looked like real flesh.

He nodded with satisfaction. He *had* hit something inside. The left leg was jammed rigid. Stuck. The other leg was pawing at the ground, but the automaton could only drag itself around in circles now.

Charles could escape.

John watched it bumping itself against the lamp-post. Then its foot caught in some heavy electric cables that snaked across the ground and — slowly, slowly, like a forest tree — it toppled over with a noise of crashing tearing, and crumpled up.

Barely ten seconds had passed.

Barely ten seconds.

He looked at it, pursing his lips, and thinking.

Tweedledum was no more than a pyramid of wreckage, but still stirring, still lifting its head, still looking this way and that under its wooden schoolboy's cap, the smiling lips on its wooden face still opening and shutting mechanically.

Who had made it? Who was controlling it? *Why?*

The scene he saw as he raised his eyes remained in his mind forever afterwards, as if it had been photographed onto his brain.

A second automaton, a second huge wooden schoolboy exactly like the first, was coming straight at him. Behind him was a fairground sign made of lights that blinked on and off. 'DUM AND 'DEE, it said. COMPUTER-PROGRAMMED BATTLES EVERY HALF HOUR ON THE HALF-HOUR AND HOUR. PLACE YOUR BETS HERE. An elderly lady was sitting at a small carved mahogany table underneath it, and she was pointing at him, her forefinger and little finger outstretched like

127

a pair of horns. The second and third fingers were folded in.

He did not need to be told who she was.

He raised the rifle, then thought better of it.

Luckily it had not been loaded.

There was a rattle as the old man's hand swept away the plastic ashtray with the two remaining bullets in it.

He was without ammunition.

A shrill blast screamed on a whistle, repeated three times. For an instant the shock made him freeze. He recovered, twice as alert.

"I have called the fairground police," said the old man's voice behind him. Cold.

Very determined.

"You will stay here until they come to get you. You have committed a serious crime, and you also owe me a great deal of money."

John swung the butt of the rifle backwards into where he judged the old man's stomach was, and felt a squelch.

He let it go and it dropped on its chain.

"Sorry," he said. *"And I mean that.* No alternative."

He ducked out the canvas flap at the back of the shooting-gallery as a giant wooden hand came across the counter. It missed him, just, and smashed the painted figures of the general and the shaven-headed boy onto their backs.

He was in the darkness, amid guy-ropes and machinery and parked trucks. Laughter, music and excited conversation came to his ears from the other side, from the world of lights. He had knocked against what seemed to be a mobile generator, and crouched behind it. It stank of diesel oil but was reassuringly heavy, like a kind of friendly animal. He had no idea which way to go.

They were being hunted.

Less than ten yards away a shadow moved across the yellow brilliance of that other world. The shape of Tweedledee. The monster boy was prowling about, looking for him, or perhaps for Charles.

Was that right? Did it have any senses of its own, any mind? Was it only a grotesque puppet, moved by someone else's will? Powerful but — on its own — as stupid as the wood, leather, metal, and paint it was made of?

John nodded to himself. Almost certainly the latter. In which case there was no reason to be frightened of it. It could chase, and grab, only if someone else was seeing for it, and thinking for it. The problem was, who was its master?

The answer was probably Megan. He thought of that withered figure, burning inside with a cold fire, that had raised two fingers and pointed at him.

Did she see with ordinary eyes? he wondered. Could she, perhaps, sense heat as pit-vipers do, and strike at the warm centre of life? Could she see by infra-red, like an army sniperscope, so that this darkness that seemed to hide him was no more than translucent grey to her? Did she have other senses entirely, senses that belong only to witches?

The giant shadow passed again, moving the opposite way. It was coming back, quartering the ground. It was going to be dangerous to stay put much longer.

Torches flashed twenty yards or so away, on the other side. Probing, stabbing. Torches that blinded you for a moment if they caught you in the eyes. He had forgotten. It was the police.

The police had answered the old man's whistle.

He was, he thought with disbelief, a criminal. He certainly didn't feel like one. But that was unlikely to make any difference if he was caught. He was old enough to know that the young are always guilty. In any case, the truth was unbelievable, a common fault with the truth. He wouldn't have believed his own story if he'd heard it from someone else.

One way of escaping from Megan might be to surrender to the police, and let them keep him in custody. No. Too risky. If something went wrong he would have lost all freedom of manœuvre. Most important, he couldn't leave Charles on his own.

Where was Charles anyway?

And Murgatroyd?

He glanced around, ears alert, the sharpness of all his senses whetted by danger. Then he slunk swiftly around the tailgates of the trucks, avoiding the alleyways of yellow-gold light that shone down between them. He found himself confronted by a board fence. Something on the other side was rattling and banging, coming close, then going away again.

He found a place for his foot in an empty knothole. Then he laid back sideways, flat against the fence, with his fingers hooked on a rib that ran down two inches proud of the planking. It was enough. He pushed off with his other foot, rose, then swung it so the heel caught the top. With a struggle he was up and over, and had dropped down into an alleyway.

The other side of the alley was a sheet of heavy canvas. He squatted on the tarmac and lifted it up to have a look.

What he saw made him smile.

Greenish skeletons were hanging from gantry-work inside. They were jerking about, and one, in particular, was taking its skull off its neck with one hand, making a sweeping bow with it — instead of a hat — then putting it back on its shoulders. The light was produced by shining ultra-violet on vaseline, or something like that. Under the gantry ran a narrow-gauge railway line. He had broken into the back stretch of the Ghost Train.

A recording of Paganini's 'Dance of the Witches' was scratching away in the distance: *meów-de-dee de-aów-oo, meów-de-dee de-aów-oo, meów-de-dee de-aów-oo, tshff deedee-de déedee-de eee....*

It was vulgar, and wonderful, and delightfully unlike the real thing.

He eased himself under the canvas, feeling safer than before.

A little way up the track he could see a graveyard, glowing in a purplish light. He padded towards it cautiously, keeping an ear open for a train coming from behind him, and sat down on a tombstone next to a large owl. The owl, so far as he could tell from flicking a fingernail against its feathers, was made of plaster of Paris. He patted it between the shoulders.

An unburied corpse was lying on top of the next grave, with a pile of earth at its head and a shovel stuck into the pile. The body was draped in a long white shroud, like a night-dress.

This gave John an idea. He bent down and tugged the shroud off the body over its head. It came off easily, because the 'corpse' hardly weighed anything. It was a shop dummy, with pink-brown plastic arms, legs, and torso. There was an unchanging smile on its face.

He lifted it up and rearranged the limbs so that it was sitting pick-a-back on the owl, unclothed and with its feet sticking out. Something for the people in the next Ghost Train to look at. It wasn't really very funny, but it relieved his nervousness.

Then he put on the shroud.

Disguise Number One, he thought. He shook his head wryly. Having just shot a wooden monster, I am now engaging in grave-robbing. Surprising how easily one gets into bad habits....

A wave of fear gripped him again, under the brave show of humour. Where was Charles? Where was the cat? It was a cruel situation because there was no one he could turn to for help. No one would believe him.

No one.

All right. *Alone, dammit, alone.*

He heard a rattling in the distance. Rattling, and gasps, and a scream or two. The next train was coming through.

He stepped clear of the track, pulled the shroud over most of his face, leaving a gap to see through, and stood still.

The train chuntered past, and there was some laughter at the dummy sitting on the owl. Then it faded away again. He was quite pleased that no one had paid any attention to him.

There was no sense in trying to go out the front and as likely as not being grabbed by the person on the gate, so he squirmed back under the canvas into the alleyway. When he had walked down to the end he climbed up to have another look around. Climbing on the inside was easy because of all the supporting timbers. As he surveyed the crowd milling along below — keeping his eyes open for Charles or Murgatroyd — he saw a small trestle stand. There was a sign propped up against it:

SPECTRE EXPRESS!
UNIQUE AND ORIGINAL
NOW IN ITS FIFTH SPECTACULAR YEAR
THE SUPER
SUPERNATURAL NON-STOP TOUR
OF
THE HIDDEN SECRETS OF THE OTHER WORLD!

A UNIQUE TEST OF CHARACTER
the only question is —
ARE YOU BRAVE ENOUGH TO FACE IT?
SEE : THE DANCE OF THE SKELETONS,
THE HAUNTED GRAVEYARD, THE SURGEON'S
CABINET,
THE DAUGHTERS OF THE DUNGEON,
&
MANY, MANY MORE GRISLY, SPINE-CHILLING, AND
BLOOD-CURDLING ATTRACTIONS!

Children under 14 must be accompanied
£1 the trip
Old age pensioners half-price on production of a currently
valid pensioner's card.

Precisely what he needed.

John tucked the shroud into his belt so he wouldn't trip on the hems. He slid down from the fence as inconspicuously as he could, lifted up the sign as smoothly as if it had always belonged to him, and walked — slowly — away from the Ghost Train. He looked like a billboard man, bored, and hired for next-to-nothing-an-hour to advertize it.

Now he had freedom of movement again, the next job was to find his brother.

He spotted Murgatroyd first. He was about to call out to him when some instinct made him stop.

The black cat was easy to identify because he was about twice the size of an ordinary cat, but the way he was acting did not seem to John quite like the Murgatroyd he knew, or thought he knew.

The cat was prowling around the metal stairs leading into The Hall of Impossible Mirrors, head down and sniffing, and peering at the tread of the steps. But it was not just that. Behind him was the thin figure of Megan in her black lambswool coat, a black silk scarf tucked in at her throat, and held with a serpent clasp of turquoise and silver. She was running the white-lacquered fingernails of one hand again and again over the back of the other. It was evident that she was in a state of barely controlled fury.

The two of them were working together. Occasionally the cat would stop sniffing, and look up and talk to her. She would spit a few syllables back at him, and he would cringe and return to work.

He hoped that Murgatroyd was just putting on an act to deceive her, but it did not look like that. He could not imagine — it made no sense — that Murgatroyd had betrayed them. Why should he? If he had wanted to stay on Megan's side, why had he helped Bear to become a Dreamguard? Why had he put spells around the house to protect them? Their friendship had been real, surely? Everything he had ever felt told him that. He could not believe he was simply wrong.

But. But. But.

Murgatroyd had been acting out of character this evening. Every trick he'd done in the fair had had a dark undercurrent of nastiness about it. That was not like him. And he'd been too anxious for them to come to the fair. Trust Charles to have sensed that something wasn't quite right. Something *was* wrong. But what?

A slight movement caught the corner of his eye. Something he'd seen before. Whose shape was imprinted, burned, in his mind. Tweedledee was standing half-hidden by a marquee not far away. That was the hand that had twitched.

The automaton fitted in perfectly with its surroundings. Being grotesque, funny, and improbable made it natural in a fairground. People glanced at it as they passed, and perhaps smiled or made a predictable sort of joke. But no one took it seriously, or was surprised by it.

John moved a little closer, keeping the billboard covering most of his face.

"My lady," he heard a familiar voice saying, "the sweetmeat is in there. I've found a part of a shoe-mark that's his, and I'm reasonably confident of olfactory identification."

'The sweetmeat', thought John. So Charles is a *sweetmeat*, and they're tracking him. I should have shot her when I had the chance.

Then he shook his head and rebuked himself: If I'd done that, I'd be even worse than she is. It's a no-win, either way.

And what are they up to now?

The witch had summoned Tweedledee to join her. The automaton shuffled up and stood outside The Hall of Impossible Mirrors, its reflections coming back from several directions, as if there were seven or eight of it.

Megan bought herself an entry ticket and walked briskly in, the cat sidling along at her heels.

Well, thought John, at least they've shown me where Charles is. The question now is, Do I leave him to look after himself — and he's adroit — or do I go in to try to help? If I do go in, what do I do? I can warn him, but he must already know they're after him.

He decided to wait. For the moment.

Time passed. Customers went in and out of The Hall of Impossible Mirrors. Not many, but a steady flow. Charles did not come out. Nor did Megan or Murgatroyd. Tweedledee stood motionless, waiting for its orders, a ludicrous but friendly figure to the passers-by, nightmarish to John. As always, he reflected, what you see depends on what you know.

John wondered if he'd lost the flow of the action. If they'd gone off somewhere else. Or if Charles had already been captured, helpless in the face of some quiet spell. If so, it was already all over.

He walked back and forth with the slow pace of the professional billboard man. Around him the fair continued. The Amazing Space Capsule whirled and rotated its counterbalanced bullet-shaped cabins at the end of rotor arms, rising and falling like a wave. Somendranath, the Bengali Strongman, thoughtfully flexed his abdominal recti muscles in front of a sign announcing that at 10 o'clock precisely he would allow an elephant to place its foot on his chest. The queues moved slowly into the fortune-tellers' tents. Madame

Ishtar, Babylonian Clairvoyante and Specialist in Star-Signs, seemed to be doing the best business. And perhaps also Mega-Druid — Your Future in Five Minutes. He watched the faces of the people coming out of the tents. They did seem a little happier, a little more excited. Maybe their money wasn't entirely wasted on such nonsense.

Tweedledee stirred. Its pink fists clenched. Its mouth opened an inch or two and it stuck its stomach out. Then it began to shuffle into the Hall of Impossible Mirrors.

The stout woman at the entrance desk bravely tried to stop it by pushing against its stomach and shouting for help. Tweedledee paused, gripped her in both wooden hands, lifted her level with its mouth, and smacked its wooden lips at her three or four times. Then it put her down and continued to walk forward. She seized her handbag, and a metal cashbox, and bolted.

John shook his head in sympathy. But for him there was no such choice. He did what had to be done, and followed the automaton into the world of mirrors, holding his billboard in front of him as both a disguise and a makeshift shield.

Everything inside was make-believe, and yet — it was also real. Dangerously real.

The Hall of Impossible Mirrors was a labyrinth of reflections, grotesque reflections with trick mirrors that turned your body into a stick or a pear, or made it ripple, or appear upside down. John could see himself, a white-shrouded figure, walking beside himself and towards himself, and away from himself, all at the same time, a ghost among ghosts.

The Hall was filled with statues, and the visitors wound among them as if they were all guests at the same party. There were statues of famous people, and statues of attendants, but the strangest were the imaginary animals, snouts twisting in the air like corkscrews, and the suits of fantastic armour with spikes on their kneecaps and talons on the fingers of their metal gloves. The empty eyes in their helmets looked both alive and dead.

Bluish-white strobe light flickered over everything, showing up the figures in flashes, on again, off again. It was hard to make out what anything was, thought John. No wonder Charles had taken refuge here. But it was also dangerous. Mischief could be done in a place like this and no one be any the wiser.

He could see Tweedledee at the end of a colonnade of reflecting pillars. The witch and the black cat were there, too, and talking. The witch seemed even angrier than before. He couldn't catch her words, but the tone was stingingly cold, like frozen fire. She was something out of Dante's Hell. Murgatroyd was cringing at her feet, his black fur rising like a spiny crest along his back. He seemed to be both terrified and wheedling her. It was not a pleasant sight.

John stood still, pretending to be one of the exhibits.

"Come nearer," said a whisper.

He looked about but could see no one.

"Left, and slightly back," said the whisper. "I'm in the black suit of armour."

John moved as indicated towards a two-headed man at arms carrying an iron conker with spikes protruding from it.

"It's not real, that conker," said the voice. "Tinfoil and paint. Put your finger under it and see how little it weighs."

"It looks real enough," said John.

"Of course," said the voice. "Good imitations often look more authentic than the real article."

"Only Charles could make a remark like that," said John.

"Thank you," said the whisper. "But I'd have thought you could have recognized my voice. Only place I could find to hide, this thing. I like your ghost-train get-up. Very crafty."

"What do we do?" said John. "We can't waste time in conversation."

"Get out," said Charles. "Once they're round the corner. They'll find us here in the end if we don't. By the way — very important — don't trust Murg. He's gone funny. I don't know how, or why. He's not his old self at all. It's heart-breaking."

"I'd guessed as much," said John. "After all we've been through together, too."

"After I got clear of Tweedledum...," said Charles. "Oh, I forgot. Thank you very much for that. If you hadn't had a rifle, and incredible presence of mind, I'd probably be inside her television set by now, giving her pretty vibes."

"Don't mention it," said John. "It's just useful, sometimes, that there are two of us. What happened next?"

"After I got clear of Tweedledum," said Charles, "and you'd vanished somewhere into the darkness, Tweedledee came after me instead. So I hid in the Lighthouse of Love."

"That's an awful place," said John. "Tacky."

"That's why I went there," said Charles. "I'd already seen Murgatroyd with Megan, and I figured that, with all the funny business earlier in the evening, something was wrong and he was mixed up in it. So I went to the kind of place I thought he'd think I wouldn't go. But he double-guessed me. Read my mind, or that's what it feels like. I was standing in line to kiss

135

Helen of Troy, or someone like that — she was probably an out-of-work waitress from the Godolphin Hotel — when there he was at my feet. And somehow or other he was able to let Megan know I was there, because that Tweedle-thing appeared a moment later, all smiling and smirking — it is absolutely horrible — and Murg actually said to me, 'Why don't you have a ride in it?' *Why don't you have a ride?* Can you imagine? Inside it? After being grabbed by it and as near as no matter digested? I said to him, 'Could you ask it if that would be all right?' and scarpered in the opposite direction. Caught him by surprise. I had about ten seconds start. It took every trick I could think of to keep ahead of them and get here. Double-backs. Disguises — I grabbed a girl's frock off a rack of them hanging up for sale. Using local knowledge — there's a cleaner's way out of the underground toilets on a spring lock that almost no one else knows about, but it was a gamble going down there, because, if the door hadn't been openable, I'd have been trapped. And all sorts of other tricks. John, it's been terrifying. I doubt if any fox has ever thought and fought as hard as I've had to over the last half-hour."

The brothers fell silent, thinking and waiting.

A number of customers wandered past. John wondered if they had paid. Probably not. Their reflections followed them around.

Then he heard Charles whispering again.

"I think, he said, "the best place to make for is about two shows down to the left when you go out. On this side. It's called Mackenzie's Time-Travel. Let's meet there if we get separated again."

"OK," said John, "but why there in particular?"

"Only place where there are disguises," Charles whispered back. "They fake time-travel with projected back-drops, but they've got three actors who put on costumes and pretend to be Elizabethan sea-dogs or whatever. You know, shouting "'Slids! 'Slids!"[3] and swishing their cutlasses about. There's a tent at the back where they keep the stuff. If we had enough time, we could make ourselves completely unrecognizable."

"What about our smell?"

"Good point," said Charles. "We'd better buy some perfume."

"And change our shoes," John continued. "Murg knows the patterns on our soles."

"Hmm!" said Charles. "I suppose cats live nearer the ground than we do. I'd not thought of that. OK. Shoes too."

---

[3] "God's eyelids."

136

In their excitement they'd been talking too loud.

John saw Murgatroyd's ears flick in their direction. He had forgotten the cat's powers of hearing. Then — worse — Megan's eyes.

The witch gave a gesture with her hands, and Tweedledee began to move.

"We've been spotted," he said to Charles. "The only thing is to run for it. Now. See you at Mackenzie's!"

Charles had to struggle to extricate himself from the armour fast enough. Luckily it was not real armour but a hollow cast, and quite a lot bigger than he was. But they lost time.

As they darted among the mirrors, the way out seemed to have disappeared. The flashing lights made everything confused. Time and again they found themselves facing their own reflections, hard up against a mirror, and had to choose a new route.

The cat's reflections appeared around them, hundreds of them, like a whole pack of black cats with green eyes. Sometimes the eyes seemed friendly, and a paw would be raised to show them the way to go. At other times the eyes were baleful and deadly, with fires burning within them, and they were glad they were only reflections.

Somewhere within all that illusion, Charles thought, is a real cat, but how does one know which one it is?

Tweedledee's reflections loomed above them. Its countless hands grabbed at the countless reflections of the boys. It lifted up suits of armour and shook them upside down. It overturned many of the statues and left them lying sideways on top of their reflections in the floor.

To John and Charles it was as if they were inside a huge kaleidoscope, mere bits and pieces tossed into different patterns from one second to the next.

Megan's eyes appeared, pursuing them through endless zigzagging ricochets of light-rays. It seemed there was nowhere to escape her. Mirrors mirrored mirrors till there was nothing but movement, and countermovement, and flickerings and weird distortions, but with *her* present in all of them. One moment she rose above them as gaunt as a withered tree. At the next she seemed like a doll darting about between their feet.

And then there were *two Murgatroyds*, one with them and one with the witch. And *two of themselves*. Two Johns. Two Charleses. And the reflections of all four. Running. Twisting and turning.

They stumbled round a corner and found they had reached the way out. The moving fairground that opened before them seemed, in comparison to what they had just left, solid and agreeably dull. It was an odd transformation.

They turned and raced for Mackenzie's Time-Travel. Close on their heels came Megan and Tweedledee. There was less than ten yards between them, and the distance was shortening,

The boys hit a flat-out sprint. John felt his muscles unable to do any more. He *made* them do more. Out of the corner of his eye he saw that he and Charles were drawing away from another John and Charles. And that one of the Murgatroyds was tearing along at their feet, the green light of battle in his eyes. A pure and extraordinary light.

The three of them swept into Time-Travel, breasting aside the small queue waiting for the next trip and the ticket-seller. Into the sudden darkness within.

A small tram with glass doors was standing at the platform. Its doors were closing. Just starting to close.

With a final surge of determination, John and Charles threw themselves through the narrowing gap, hit the other side with their shoulders, rolled, and turned back to see what was happening. Murgatroyd sprang with an arching leap through the last few inches after them.

The doors shut.

Some instinct hidden deep in Charles made him put his hand in his pocket and grasp his stegosaurus bone. What seemed like a ripple of light passed through the tram, and all the people sitting in it. There was a sudden silence, not an ordinary silence, but *complete* silence.

They looked back through the doors at what was happening on the platform. *John and Charles had been captured.*

The giant wooden boy had seized them, one in each hand, and a door in his stomach had opened. First one, then the other, was squeezed inside and held there. Then the stomach closed, and there was no more any sign of them, or that they had ever existed.

Megan flicked a peremptory finger, and the automaton turned round. Slowly it shuffled out of sight, followed by the witch and her black cat.

The platform was empty.

DARKNESS.

— Light again.

People walking backwards, through them, like ghosts.

"Yesterday," said Charles.

Night and day flickered outside. Faster and faster.

Strobe shadows, curving like scimitars, swept over the passengers' faces.

Then so fast, there was only a blur of grey.

But still luminous. Like the mother-of-pearl in a shell, held to the evening sky, late in the last dim light.

In the time-travelling carriage, the boys tried to believe that they *had* seen what they had seen.

Charles, in his pocket, rolled his stegosaurus bone over between his finger and thumb, secretly.

"The only way to make sense of it," he said softly, "is that we have split. Megan's captured half of John and half of me. We are our other halves who've escaped and are sitting here. One Murgatroyd is still her servant; the other is our friend."

He stroked a black cat, who was sitting on an empty seat.

"Can such things happen ?" he continued. "And, if they do happen, how?"

"People and cats are like diamonds," said the black cat. "When there is enough pressure they split down natural lines of cleavage. The Murgatroyd sitting here — me — is the one who was always faithful to you. And will now be always faithful to you. The pressure has lifted inside my heart. I feel as light as air. The black cat walking home with Megan, to lie sprawled out on the back of her armchair and who'll soon be watching her drinking in the beauties of you kids in her television set, growing young again on your smiles, is the one that betrayed you. And will be your enemy as long as he lives."

"Betrayed?"

"The other Murgatroyd, the other part of what was me, was under threat of a never-ending agony from the witch. So he betrayed you. It was that part of what was once me that planned Tweedledum and Tweedledee, that persuaded Megan to try it. That lured you to the Fair with his poisoned sweet-talk. It's the part who is sitting here who kept you safe from her spells when she was chasing you. You were incredibly resourceful — you have my full professional admiration — but even your wiliness and stamina would not have saved you from her if I hadn't jammed up most of her spells."

"Well, thank you," said Charles. "Both for the compliment and for the help."

His face was thoughtful, and more than a little grim.

"You have split, then, Murg, between your good and your evil inclination," said John, coming into the conversation. "But how have *we* split?"

Murgatroyd's eyes clouded over.

"For the moment, I have no answer," he said. "Time will probably tell us. But yes, I think we've all split."

139

"So we don't know who we are," said John. "What we have kept, and what we have lost."

"Find out by living on," said Murgatroyd. "I told you, I do not know."

"DO YOU REALIZE we're travelling through time?" said Charles. "That this is not a show any longer?"

"Witches can live backwards in time," said the cat. "Such journeys are not unfamiliar to me. You are right. But how do you know?"

"I know," said Charles, without explanation.

"The stars were rotating backwards," said John. "Before the speed got too fast for me to see the constellations. That's not at issue. The problem is, *why* is it happening?"

"The answer," said Murgaroyd, "is almost certainly in your brother's hands. That bone he is turning between his fingers in his pocket dates from the late Jurassic, more than a hundred and fifty million years ago."

"How do you know about my bone?" said Charles.

"I've known about it since I first came to live with you. It radiates time-waves: the time it lives by keeps rhythmically speeding up and slowing down compared to me. Yet it stays in one place. Weird, isn't it? I have always been sensitive to time-waves. The instant the carriage doors slammed shut, the frequency went towards infinity, then vanished. I've still got a headache from it."

"Meaning?" said John.

"Somehow Charles has tapped the gift of travelling through time. At the moment of utmost danger his mind unleashed a hidden power, a power he might never otherwise have known he had. This power has taken us — or part of us — to safety."

"It feels quite like that," said Charles. "But what about the split? I don't want to stay in two pieces forever."

He looked at the other passengers. Some were wide-eyed, some restless, some just talking to each other and paying no attention to anything around them.

"You can see we have a more immediate problem," he went on. "Or rather I have a problem. These people sitting here all think what they're seeing is special effects, courtesy of Mackenzies. What you are telling us, Murg, and I happen to know that you're right, is that this is *not* a special effect. It's *real*. What's going to happen when they find out? Panic? Fury with me? Despair?"

"What I do know," he added, "is that we got them into this mess, and that we are responsible for them. What do we do? There are more than twenty people in this carriage. I haven't any idea how to stop the process I seem to have started. Or reverse it"

"There will have to be an answer," said John. "We have to get back, too, to find our mother and set her free."

"Be patient," said the cat. "*Sbagliando s'impara.* One learns by making mistakes, as we used to say. Human history vanished behind us quite some time ago. We're back into rock-time."

"You seem very calm about it," said John.

"What else is there to be?"

"You know more than you're saying, Murg," said Charles

"No, I suspect more than I'm saying," said Murgtroyd. "Not know. For the moment just let me say that I have had a sort of waking dream: that even these extraordinary events were not entirely unforeseen. I think we have a chance of coming out the other end."

And the memory of a gold medallion twinkled for a moment in the depths of his mind.

steg

CHARLES WAS CLIMBING a mountain that no one had ever climbed before, or would ever climb again. It would be gone before there were human beings to set their feet on it.

Around him were trees that looked like gingkos, their many-fingered leaves hanging down like strips of green paper, but they were not gingkos. And there were trees that looked like pines, with heavy cones, but they were not pines. They had leaves, not needles.

A strange feeling took possession of him. A feeling of emptiness, a feeling of delight in this magnificence, but also a feeling of sadness and, at the same time, of exhilaration that he would be the only person — ever — who would see this.

He had no desire to give the mountain a name. Names were for telling other people. He was alone. The others had no courage to come to places like this. Not even his brother, John.

In fifty million years, or a hundred million years, it would have worn away. Its dark red-purple rocks would have been ground to dust, carried downstream by the rains, and settled on the floor of the coastal seas. And still there would be no people, none of his own kind. Not, maybe, for another fifty million years.

He felt at home here, drawn by a kinship he did not understand. That it was dangerous, recklessly dangerous, to wander off alone from the camp by the beach, he was perfectly aware. But calm filled him as he stood still, for a moment, in the sunshine among the ferns, and gazed at the view below him.

The Kauri pines stretched down the wrinkled slopes. Close to, their sleek paired leaves looked like millions of insects' wings, flying along the twigs. Their white cones glittered in the upper branches, as if they had been dusted with icing sugar. The wind, which had been blowing earlier in the morning, seemed to have stopped.

Beyond the pines lay the marshes, and their tree-tall ferns. Two hours earlier he had been down there, and slipped and struggled to find a footing. Small crocodiles, eyes in their bony orbits raised just above the water, had been lurking in the mud. He had walked by them carefully, watching them, keeping off the paths, paths made for other feet than his. Other purposes.

He remembered how, as he'd walked along, he'd run his fingers down the soft brown diamonding of the clubmoss stems. How he'd brushed their drooping twigs away from his face, almost in irritation. Their leaves, if they were leaves, were so fine they seemed no more than a green haze on the branches. He remembered, too, the squelch of his shoes in the mud.

He would have to go back that way. Better leave plenty of time for it, and plenty of energy.

In the distance the marshes ran out into the estuary. An estuary with long mudbanks that lay aligned with the flow of the water. The tides came in, bubbling and frothing over themselves, rising up with frightening suddenness. Then they ran out again, taking longer to do so, gathering themselves into the channels between the mudbanks, where they flowed faster. Some things had hardly changed.

In the hour before dawn, when he had been setting off, there had been flights of white pterosaurs, drifting like ghosts across the high tide, with one of them sometimes dipping down to catch a fish. He was too far away to see them now, even in the clear air. He could imagine the sunshine glinting on their wings. If they were still there. It looked as if the tide was out.

Somewhere below, on the granite shelf above the rise and fall of the sea, was Mackenzie's Time-Traveller, the beaten-up swindle-show from Saint Giles's Fair. He thought of it sitting there, like a Noah's Ark on another Ararat, and of the people who had come with him.

There were scenes from the English past painted on the Time-Traveller's sides. He remembered the apple-cheeked boys in smocks, and the apple-cheeked girls in embroidered skirts, dancing, motionlessly, around a Maypole. He called to his mind's eye the knights on their horses thundering across a drawbridge into a castle, watched by a startled ploughman. What message had they been carrying that could not wait? A last-minute rescue? Some matter of honour that would stain their lord's name through the ages afterwards if not, at once, avenged? Then there were the men in furs, their skins streaked blue, hurling down rocks from a cliff at panicking Roman legionaries.... They were easy to understand. So was the great king, Alfred, his head slumped in his hands before the flames of a cottage fire, thinking and thinking of a way to hold back the Danes, while, on the griddle the undersides of the goodwife's scones had charred to a black crust. Charles had often looked at him during the last four days, sitting there, unaware of the Mesozoic rocks, and smiled.

A stencilled sign was fixed above the glass doors:

MACKENZIE'S TIME-TOURS. SEE THE BRITISH PAST IN PERSON! — SEE NELSON AT TRAFALGAR, AND NEWTON HIT BY THE APPLE. SEE DRAKE DEFEAT THE

ARMADA, HENRY V RIDE FORTH IN SPLENDOUR AT AGINCOURT, KING ARTHUR'S LAST BATTLE AND THE TREACHERY OF MORDRED. SEE THE LANDING OF THE ROMAN EAGLES.... TWENTY CENTURIES IN TWENTY MINUTES, BROUGHT BEFORE YOUR EYES IN THE COMFORT OF YOUR OWN SEAT. GENUINE RELATIVISTIC EFFECTS. AUTHENTICITY GUARANTEED BY LEADING OXFORD SCIENTISTS. WE TAKE YOU THERE, AND WE BRING YOU BACK. FOR YOUR OWN SAFETY, PLEASE STAY INSIDE THE CARRIAGE WHILE IT IS MOVING THROUGH TIME. THE MANAGEMENT ACCEPTS NO RESPONSIBILITY FOR MISHAPS OCCASIONED BY THE BREACH OF THIS RULE.

W.R. & K.P. MACKENZIE (PROPRIETORS)

Good-natured nonsense. You could settle down in your seat, love it all, and expect to be entertained. He was sure they all had, Ken and Elsie, and the Yonders. And rest of them.

How the old fairground carriage had taken off into *real* time-travel that evening, he still had no idea. No idea, except that it had been his doing. Murgatroyd had said it was the stegosaurus tail-bone in his pocket, the one he'd stolen from the museum long ago. (It was a fossil, actually, not a real bone, but he thought of it as real.) Some sort of sympathetic attraction for which time had no meaning. The cat, of course, was right more often than not. He'd been a Prince over the Darkness in his life before, and knew a thing or two, including how to talk. So perhaps.... Perhaps....

But, really, that explained almost nothing, thought Charles. *How* had he been able to do it? *How* had he been able to lift the entire carriage, with his brother and Murgatroyd, and all the people in it, and hurl it across millions of years, entirely by the force of his mind?

All Charles knew was this. He had been fleeing from Megan through the lights and mirrors and shadows of Saint Giles's Fair that night, with John. He had been well aware, as she closed upon them, that the witch was hungering to suck on his soul. For her, a child's feelings were like a fresh stick of chewing-gum. She would have savoured them till the sweetness had vanished. Then thunked the dead, tasteless, wad — *him* — somewhere to be forgotten.

He had known very well the fate that awaited them if they were caught. Murgatroyd had shown them. A life, that was no life, as a pretty ghost playing bit-parts in that television set she had. Where she kept her childen. He would have been switched on and off, as it amused her to trifle with him.

Perhaps it had been the terror of that which had set loose a power inside him. A power he'd never dreamed he possessed. The power to fight back against *her*. And, when it came to the final encounter, the astonishing power to travel in time.

145

So, they'd escaped her. Or the older and harder parts of them had. The other halves of themselves, the gentler, dreamier halves, they had left behind in her power. The children halves, so Murgatroyd had suggested. Charles knew that, never in his life, whether it lasted long or left him in an hour's time, would he forget looking back through the glass doors of the Time-Traveller. Looking back and seeing two boys, *himself and John*, being crammed inside the stomach door of Tweedledee. The huge wooden doll, with its idiotic smile and clutching hands, alive with a kind of non-living life, as her magic had made it move. Tweedledee, lumbering after them through the fairground alleys, the painted boards and the shadows, dragging some of the booths down with its clumsy feet caught in the guy-ropes. It had cured him of childhood.

Nor would he forget Megan herself, black-coated, with her black silk neck-scarf, her turquoise-and-silver snake-brooch, and her white gloves, held loosely in one hand, so composed, so much the North Oxford lady, standing beside it, a smile of triumph on her respectable face.

He wondered what they had lost by this. — By losing the children within themselves. He felt himself almost the same as before. Delighting in this sunshine, in this other age of the world. But only almost. Maybe he was both more sober and more fearless. What lay about him was beautiful, but it was not his friend. Not his enemy either. Something other. To be treated with prudence. Hmm.

—Half of the cat had stayed behind with the witch. Rubbing up against her leg on the platform there, looking up at her with green eyes, eyes full of adoration. The evil half, doomed to be her familiar. The good Murgatroyd was with them, here. He only hoped that their half of the cat — so wry, so humorous, so happy — had some of his old black magic left. It was going to be needed.

Charles was proud of what he had done when the pressure was really on. If he had not won, he had still not lost. The trouble was, he had dragged all these others along with him, without meaning to. It would have been so marvellous if only the three of them had come, himself and Murgatroyd and John.

The others were just Oxford people, some decent, some remarkable. But they were not, as he was, enjoying themselves. Some were doing better than others, a lot better — some of them. But they thought of nothing but one thing. Of getting back home.

Charles didn't understand them. Wasn't it better to have seen this, this astonishing, beautiful world where everything was different — even if perhaps it did mean dying some time — than to plod on through everyday life with

146

millions of other ordinary people? What they mostly seemed to be scared of was missing the next morning at the office — the office! — or, in one case, the shop. The prison of tomorrow.

He watched the mayflies glittering above the cycads. Giant mayflies, with wings like rainbows. Maybe he was odd, but wasn't this worth any office, worth any shop?

Grandfather had told him that in a billion years the sun was going to blow up. The earth would be vapourized in a tide of fire exploding outwards. He'd been shocked at Charles's answer, but Charles couldn't see anything shocking in it. "Grandfather," he'd said, "I'd give almost anything to be around then, to see it happening." But wasn't that the obvious thing to say? Wouldn't anyone?

He thought of the people back in the camp. Of Ken Berrigan, all pipe and beard and bass voice. A history teacher, lost in a time outside of his history. And his sparrow-eyed wife, Elsie, with her mind like the patchwork quilts that she loved to make. And charming, polite Mr Shah, who ran the newsagent's near where they lived, and always ironed his papers before placing them, neatly, on the sales-rack. So concerned about the interruption of his deliveries. And Mrs Shah, who never said anything, but looked at you with enormous brown eyes.

And, of course, Harry Milman. Charles smiled to himself as he thought of Harry, the retired bartender, who sat with his back against a clubmoss tree reading and re-reading the same copy of *The Jewish Chronicle* — the one he'd had with him in his rain-coat pocket — and worrying about how to decide when it was the sabbath. Not easy in the Mesozoic.

Then there was Ellen, their Mackenzie Time-Tour Guide, in her blue and gold uniform. Her blouse was embroidered with golden stars, like the dawn in the sky. And a golden 'M' on the blouse pocket. She still thought she was responsible for them. As if they were childen at a party. Good on the journey, she'd been. The unwanted journey that had brought the old stories of their lives to an end. Always so calm, and so cheerful. Being in charge, thought Charles, can sometimes make people rise above themselves.

But what would happen when she realized that what was happening was — *really* — happening? A shadow of apprehension crossed his mind. That brightness was unreal. It could crack suddenly. He was worried for her, kind Ellen.

And what had all these people done — if anything — to be dragged along here with him? They had no stegosaurus bones in their pockets. Why these particular people? Why had they, and no one else, just happened to be sitting there when — whoosh! — he had rushed in, hot, and sweaty, and desperate, and their world had vanished? Was it just fate, playing its usual, whimsical, games? With all of them?

Charles looked at the different patterns in the veins of the leaves of the trees as he wandered by. Some veins were interwoven, like the cross-linked channels on a dried-out river-bed. Others were like straight lines combed in the sand, parallel and close to each other, but never touching. Amazing leaves. He wondered what the point was of such variety, and what difference it made. Why did evolution go to so much trouble?

Oh, well, the trip was a one-way ticket for all of them, so far as he could tell. He had no idea how he would set about travelling through time again, if he wanted to. And he didn't want to, particularly. Not just now, in any case. This world was too magical. This was *his* story.

He zigzagged between the V-shaped leaves of some cycads that rose above his shoulders, and looked, as he passed, at the orange-red seeds in their central cones. And the weevils crawling in them. Some cones were broken open, a few were rotting. Pity they couldn't be eaten. He wondered if there was any special way of cooking them that would make them safe.

After a time, he came out into the open again, and sat down on some rough volcanic rocks.

A butterfly was perching on a fern. Strange, he thought, — there are butterflies here before there are any flowers.

He was hungry. They'd been living on shellfish from the tidal zone of the estuary. Not just clams, but mussels growing in thick festoons in the cracks between the rocks, enormous compared to what you could buy in the Oxford shops. Billy and Ray had gone wading together one morning and caught some ammonites. Edible fossils. They'd been like plump shelly Catherine-wheels, and the biggest was almost a foot across. The taste was delicious when roasted, like escargots with a salty flavour. They'd have been better with garlic, though. Was garlic around yet? He thought of garlic. Must be some somewhere.

But he'd gone without breakfast to make an early start.

Not sensible.

He forced himself to stop dreaming about food. It was making his hunger worse.

So — where were they, on the map of the world? John had suggested it might be Antarctica. His brother had a memory for the maps of continental drift, that game of slow-motion dodgem-cars that the landmasses played across the oceans, and which took them millions of years. A couple of hundred million years ago — before Oxford time, that was — Antarctica had been quite warm, John said. Tucked in between Australia and South Africa.

Was this mid-morning world before him, with its hills and swamps and majestic trees and successful animals, going to be buried some day under thousands of feet of ice?

He shook his head. There was no point in jumping to conclusions. Nice to know, but it couldn't be said to matter that much. Not as much as finding something to eat.

He glanced at the watch on his wrist. The battery Seiko from Aunt Diana, with a local-time function, perpetual calendar, stop-watch, and alarm. It was a good watch, but the one thing the manufacturers had not included was a way of speeding it up. In the Mesozoic the days were shorter, and getting caught by the dark was something to be avoided.

The digital display said 0603, and it was easy to see from the sun that it was ten o'clock or later. In four days they'd already lost four hours.

So — the earth in these early times was turning faster. That meant, he reflected, that it must be smaller. When a skater spinning around on the ice pulls in her hands, she twiddles more quickly. When she stretches her hands out again, she slows down. The earth has to be the same.

But how did the earth get larger in our own time? he wondered. In Oxford time. By cooling down inside and crystallizing bigger, like ice? It seemed a little unlikely.

The problem was not what mattered. He stopped thinking about it. But it stuck, at the back of his mind, like a burr on a sweater.

He stood up again and began to walk along, in and out of the trees. It was a mixed forest, with peat-swamps here and there. He heard what seemed like bird-calls, and wondered if they were from archaeopteryxes, the earliest birds. Archies, he knew, were about the size of a pigeon, but with teeth and a bony tail. He searched among the branches for a tell-tale shape or two, catching the eye, perhaps, by flitting across the blue fingers of the sky. But he saw nothing. It was too soon for them, maybe, or the wrong place.

He was only a third of the way up the mountain, and he wondered if he would have the energy to get to the top before it was time to turn back. He stayed on a contour-level path, or what seemed like a path, to have a rest from the climbing.

The trees along it had been stripped of their leaves, to a height of at least fifteen feet. Tough, eating all that foliage, he thought, even if you do have stomach-stones to grind it for you.

Then he stopped in his tracks.

Motionless.

About thirty metres away a stegosaur was standing on his hind legs browsing on a small tree with leaves like long willow-leaves. His beak-like jaws were pecking at mulberry-shaped fruits that grew from what appeared to be ice-cream cones made of bark. Cones that sprouted straight from the trunk. The crunching sound was loud enough to be heard above the bubbling of a stream nearby.

The stegosaur's back was covered with pairs of what looked like greyish-pink dinner-plates, standing straight up. From the lower part of his back, all the way down to the end of his tail, sharp prongs curved backwards like rose-thorns made out of bone.[1]

When he saw Charles he dropped to all fours and began to amble over. For a moment Charles steadied himself to run. In less time than it takes to describe it, his mind had worked out a route over the boulders at the back, and up the cliff above them, ex-monkey that he was. His adrenalin went into overdrive.

Then he stopped, and laughed.

And began, himself, to walk towards the stegosaur, his hands raised in a gesture of welcome.

Without anything seeming to have happened, *everything* had changed. Without trying, *he knew*. This was *his* stegosaur. The one he had talked to in the University Museum, in the sunlit silence among the dusty cases. The stegosaur whose fossilized tail-bone he was carrying in his pocket.

Their world-lines, separated by more than a hundred million years, but linked by some mysterious affinity, had wound their way together. And joined.

Charles put his arms around the stegosaur's neck and gave him a gentle hug, as if they were the oldest of friends. As, perhaps, they had been for many years.

They talked together, then, but without a spoken word exchanged, in the criss-crossing shadows, under the long-fingered gingkos and the fruiting pentoxylon trees. The sun crossed the meridian and began its journey downwards, but they still, silently, interchanged their ideas.

Steg's mind was slow, like an old river half-asleep; but Charles found, if he was patient, that everything would become clear. He had to wait, first, until his own mind had emptied, and then sights and smells and sounds that he had never known before would begin to float through it. It seemed to be Steg's world, as he himself had experienced it.

From time to time immense muscles contracted in Charles's shoulders, muscles he knew he did not have. In his lower back he felt the twisting swing

---

[1] He was therefore, scientifically, a Kentrosaurus, a small southern member of the family Stegosauridae, and a close relative of the more familiar American Stegosaurus.

of a heavy tail. A tail that was not his. It almost seemed to him that he had two brains, one in his skull and one at the base of his spine, controlling different parts of him. At the next moment his heart throbbed with a flurry of fear, then his tail-spikes lashed. Then it steadied again as a shadow slid away. A shadow of flesh-tearing teeth and curved claws. So Steg had won a fight for survival, then. Good on him. He looked at the purplish-blue pentoxylon fruits and felt his beak watering.

It was harder the other way around, telling Steg about himself. The dinosaur only remembered the museum. The rest of the Oxford world was too far away. The world of roads and houses and tangled wires, and all the confusion of schools and railway tracks and television serials and wars. But Steg was fascinated by Charles's birds. The boy conjured up mind-pictures for his friend, pictures of splay-tailed hawks and sea-eagles, and of wide-soaring albatross. Sleek-necked cormorants, and multi-coloured parrots with nut-cracker beaks and a sense of humour, swinging themselves upside-down on the branches. Of modest brown thrushes and flitting wrens, and of ruby-crowned kinglets. Of the sudden flash of kingfishers. Perhaps he sensed his own kinship, as a dinosaur, with the birds, whose future was yet to come, as his own kind's was to end. And he met with Hippo and Tiger, too, and talked with them in his mind. He honoured them as Charles's friends. Like himself.

They came back at last to the present, having given each other their lives as best they could.

Charles then formed for Steg in his mind the image of the other humans near the beach. He tried to put over the idea that they were hungry. That they needed more to eat than shellfish. As he did himself. It was difficult to get this notion across. The world for Steg was full of food; and all one had to do, he thought, was eat it. In the end, though, after much explaining, he understood.

A smile appeared on the beaked face, and he indicated that Charles should climb onto his back, and make himself comfortable there, among the plates, where the warm blood cooled in the wind, so he'd have a good view as they travelled.

From a dinosaur's level the world was different. Like looking down from a truck-driver's cab, thought Charles, after having been in a car. It gave you a sense of control. Sometimes, though, he had to duck to avoid the branches.

The last ridge to the top of the mountain was treeless, just tumbled rocks and ferns. The sea beyond the estuary was in sight now, an explosion of gold standing straight up in the afternoon sun. He felt, uncomfortably, that something was missing, and wondered what it was. Something that should have been here, but wasn't.

Then he realized.

There was no grass.

It was too early in the world's life for grass, for the simple green blades underfoot, for the leaping straw-coloured tassels that waved in the wind, and the tangly roots that held the clodded earth together. And for all the things that went with grass, for deer and rabbits, and kangaroos that looked at you with wide black eyes, paws folded across their chests. And for raisin-bread, because wheat was a grass, and the whirr and roar of lawn-mowers on a Sunday afternoon.

No grass.

But a smell of honey was coming from somewhere. And a sense of pleasure was floating out of Steg's mind. Charles watched the heavy toenailed feet below him, edging across the tippy boulders. He sensed the tail behind him swinging, this way, then that way, for Steg to keep his balance. Conservation of angular momentum.

The honey smell grew stronger.

Steg had stopped and was munching gently on a thicket of dry-looking branches. Charles slid down his side to the ground, and broke off a twig. Sap oozed from the splintered end. 'Suck it,' said Steg's voice in his mind. 'Tastes good.'

A thickish liquid trickled down Charles's throat. His mind cleared, and he felt stronger. He snapped off another twig, and sat down with his back on a rock, looking out to sea. When he had sucked the stalk dry, and the fibres were rough and pithy, he threw it away and just sat there.

After a while he stopped thinking. He felt no need for it, just for the silences. For the wind, and the sound of Steg cropping the bushes behind him.

The sun set in front of him, moving to his left, and he knew, without working it out, that they had to be south of the equator. He was looking north. The light sank away along the horizon.

The river of stars was up again, as it had been the last three nights. But tonight there was the calm to look at it properly. None of the others knew the southern constellations well, not even John, who remembered the northern ones without missing one. John had seen no patterns of stars he recognized, from either north or south, and some of them, like Orion the hunter, can be seen at different times on either side of the line.

But no one had been looking, not really looking. Even Murgatroyd had been silent. Except for himself, Charles, they had been too shocked to do much. Just gather a few shellfish. To talk to each other as if nothing had happened. And — a few of them — to make a fire out of beach-wood and dead ferns, using Seb's cigarette-lighter.

They are here without being here, he thought. Only I am really here.

152

He searched the sky slowly until he had found what he was looking for. All the other stars had other, earlier, partners on the dance-floor of the skies. But not the two *nubeculae*, the Clouds of Magellan.

So now I am guessing no longer, he thought. I know where I am. A long way south. Surprisingly warm.

Charles's mind turned to Magellan then, the world-navigator, his pathway through the world-encircling seas still closed. You never made it home, Fernán, he thought, a great man cut down in a chancy squabble when landing for water. Can I do better? Shall I — shall we — return?

And after all is said and done, how much does it matter?

He leaned his head against Steg's shoulder, relishing the flow of warmth from the body, and slept. The dinosaur did not sleep, though, but watched the trees below. His hearing-holes trembled to the low-pitched notes that growled through them from time to time. Warning notes. He knew who was being hunted, who the hunters were.

Steg, too, was happy. His mind had no idea of time-travel, nor of a spherical earth, nor of Magellanic Clouds. It was enough, more than enough, that Charles was there, with him. At last.

WHEN CHARLES woke up, he was cold and stiff. His sweater was heavy with dew. Light was spreading around them, and across the moving pasture of mists that hid the forests below. Other mountain-tops appeared, and disappeared, among these fogs, some higher and some lower than the one they were on.

'Food,' he thought into Steg's mind.

The dinosaur barely stirred.

Charles ran his palm along the buff and brownish flank. It felt cold, like the skin of an old baked apple, left out overnight.

The picture of a sun came into Charles's mind, and a feeling of stretching and relaxing. 'Later,' said the message. 'Wait a while. There's no great hurry.'

Charles sighed. Then he eased himself to his feet and walked across to the bushes to break off a twig for breakfast.

When the sun had burned the mists away, they went down by the swamps. Bundles of honey-twigs shook on the spines that rose above Steg's rear legs. Charles smiled as he looked at them over his shoulder. He felt as if he were coming home from shopping. It had been quite a job, bundling those twigs up and impaling them so they didn't come off.

Tree-ferns grew by the edge of the blackish water. Their fronds arched up like umbrella-ribs from the crowns of their stubby trunks. Steg stopped, and sniffed and nuzzled at one. Then he pushed it over with his shoulder. There was a cracking sound, and Charles's mind-mouth filled with a taste like bitter artichoke. The picture in his mind came from Steg, pecking at the tree's heart, then looking up at him to see if he'd understood.

The splintered trunk was slimy with mud, prickly underneath. He lifted one end up, and levered and shoved it onto Steg's back so it rested between his plates. He was sweating when he'd finished, and filthy. On the palm of his left hand a moist trickle of blood was drying to reddish-brown.

'Looks like a battering-ram,' he thought as he looked at it, and his muddy face broke into a grin.

He didn't climb onto Steg's back again, but plodded along beside him, sometimes running to catch up, and watching the water-boatmen scuttering off on the surface of the ponds. The air was full of a rachet-like croaking, and Steg's mind told him what the creatures were that were making this noise. — Frogs. Olive-brown frogs with spotted backs and tails. Frogs *with tails*. But he couldn't see them with his own eyes. Just hear them chattering.

On the other side of a channel was a clump of bulrushes with swollen stalks. The taste that came into his mind's mouth this time was a mixture of fennel and celery.

He waded cautiously into the water. The wetness ran up his legs, and above his knees. He felt his denim trousers cling suddenly against his body. In the heat of the day it was pleasant to be damp.

With care, great care, he extracted his Swiss Army knife from his pocket. If it slipped in his fingers, that was probably goodbye to it forever. He levered the broad blade open with his thumbnail, and began to cut the plumpstalks — that seemed as good a name for them as any — one by one, and one after another.

When he'd crammed as many under his left arm as he could manage, he pressed the blade shut, one-handed, against his stomach. Then he slid the knife into his pocket again. He waded back to where Steg was standing, braided a few of the stalks around each other, and wrapped this rope around the bundle, tucking the end in under itself a few times. He wedged the plumpstalks between two plates, then clambered back on board himself. 'Beach, Steg,' he thought, filling his mind with a picture of the estuary. 'Beach, please. Others.'

Steg smiled, and picked his way through the horsetails, and across the swamps, until they came to the rocks, and the breeze from the sea was blowing in their faces. It felt warm and sweetish-salty.

Whenever it shifted direction a little, they could smell the pine-resin from the branches and needles in the camp fire. Steg put his nose in the air and stopped. Less than a hundred metres away the shape of the Time-Traveller rose against the sky, up there on its rocky shelf. Without asking, Charles knew that the dinosaur was unwilling to go any closer. He slipped to the ground, and, a little sadly, unloaded the food.

The image of a sun rising above the Kauri pines came into his mind. He nodded. 'Yes!' he thought back. 'Tomorrow morning. See you then. But not too early. When it's warm.'

Steg rubbed his beak against the boy's shoulder. Then he turned and ambled away, into the tall ferns.

"YOUR FRIEND from the University Museum?" said John.

Charles's brother was standing a few metres away, eyes twinkling.

"Of course."

"Thought so."

"How things here?" Charles asked. "Brought some vegetables."

"We could do with some of those," said John. "Look interesting. I've roasted all the fiddlehead ferns I can find for Harry."

"Still won't eat shellfish?"

"He'd rather die."

"Thought that was unrabbinical," said Charles. "Aren't you allowed to save your life by eating taboo foods?"

"Jonathan says you can. Anyhow, it's not necessary now. What are they?"

"Tree-fern heart. It's got to be cut out first. Plumpstalks. My name. Probably need to be opened up, pounded and done on hot stones, I'd guess. Honey-twigs for dessert."

"Can I try one?"

Charles bent down and snapped one off.

"You just suck the end," he said. "Then bite it off and suck some more."

"Mmm," said John. "Mmm. These are much better than they look. Very, very tasty. How'd you find them?"

"Steg showed me. They only grow near the top of the mountains."

John put the rest of his honey-twig in his shirt breast-pocket.

"Want a hand taking them up?"

"Uh. Let's do the plumpstalks first, and the twigs, if we can."

"Why?"

"Pterosaurs. They raid things."

"Right. If I cross my arms, can you load me up?"

"Manage that much?"

"No problem."

They walked up the granite boulders together.

"You never told me how things were," said Charles after a short while.

"No better," said John.

"They still don't think it's real?"

"No. They think we're in a safari park, or an experiment."

"Didn't they see me on Steg?"

"Seb and Musette did," said John. "That made it worse."

"Worse? How d'you mean?"

"We were sitting on the boulders when I saw you coming out of the ferns. Obviously, I told them to look. You know what Seb said?"

"What?"

"How unspeakably vulgar. That's what he said. *How unspeakably vulgar.* I asked him what he meant, and he said, 'If you ever needed any final proof that this is all a bad joke, that's it.' I still looked puzzled, and he said, 'If you still think it's real, John, you need your head examined. Suppose it were real, do you think your brother would be riding on a stegosaurus. Either the stegosaurus would be running away, or your brother would be dead, skewered by its tail-prongs. The only place kids ride stegosauruses is in theme-parks.' 'Seb,' I said to him, 'if you think it's a joke, why don't you come down and look? It can't hurt you.' When I said that, he looked at me with a very, very odd expression. Then he turned away and said, 'I have no intention of wasting my time on such stupidities. It's blatantly obvious it's a model. *It is a model.* That's all there is to it. There's nothing to be gained by confirming the obvious.'"

"Frightening," said Charles.

They had come to the door of the Time-Traveller. John dumped his armload of plumpstalks and honey-twigs just inside it. Then he leant back and stretched himself to unstiffen. Charles put his honeystalks in, at the side of the larger pile.

"Get the tree-fern?"

"OK."

They picked their way back down the rocks.

"Frightening," Charles repeated.

"Why?"

"They won't last long here if they don't realize that this is it. *This* is the world we're living in. Not something else in their minds."

"What about Ellen?" he added.

"Ellen's been great," said John. "Especially gathering wood off the beach for the fire. We've got a reserve now, in case we need it. Billy and Ray help, too, but just because they're friends. They treat it as a warm-up for training.

Katas[2] on the beach. Nobody else does a thing."

"Ellen happy?" said Charles.

John laughed.

"Nobody's happy here but you," he said. "I manage. I find everything interesting. You know me. But Ellen — no. Trouble with her is, I think, deep down she sort of knows it's real."

"That should help."

"It doesn't. Her boyfriend's a cripple, you know."

"I didn't, but what's that got to do with it."

"Apparently he's an amazing sort of person. Just sits there in his wheelchair and makes everyone around him feel happy. At least that's what she told me. We had a good talk. But he depends on Ellen. Totally. She's desperate inside, Charles, thinking about what may be happening to him. Outside she tries to smile. You know what a good sport she is. But inside.... I don't think anyone's fooled. No one who's got eyes at least."

"Well, fair enough," said Charles. "I mean, to be upset over something like that. My friends are here, like Steg, or live outside of time, like Tiger and Hippo. Be careful with that tree-fern trunk. It's got sharp bits on it under the mud."

"Thanks."

They carried it up the rocks, panting too hard to continue talking.

Below them, the tide was turning. The long mudflats seemed to be rising up from the departing water, cut through by hundreds of short-lived streams pouring off them, and joining together into momentary rivers as if they were part of a real landscape.

The day's meal was served late in the afternoon. Succulent warm tree-fern heart, cooked by Charles and Ellen on hot stones. Each piece was wrapped in a clean leaf. With sea-salt. And individual helpings of roasted plumpstalk in clamshells, one each, garnished with mussels. There were twenty-one people there, sitting round on the rocks and on the doorstep of the Time-Traveller, twenty-two if the black cat was included. He had his own meal, though, a small mammalian shrew he'd caught somewhere.

The water was passed from hand to hand whenever someone asked for it. Tim had found a yellow plastic bucket under a seat in the Time-Traveller. Probably left by a cleaning-woman. John had spent hours one morning scouring it with sand and sea-water to get the detergent out of the scratches, then

---

[2] Set-pattern exercises for karate.

rinsed it in the stream to remove the taste of the salt. It was the only large container they had.

They munched in silence for a time. The food was tasty but tough, and the sunshine pleasant. When Ann Fellows had finished, she began to talk to them, just as she would have addressed the City Council, of which she had been a member for half of her fifty years.

"As I said last night," she began, "there is going to be need for a law to ensure that crimes like this are not committed again. When I get back I intend to raise the matter with Sir Matthew Klompen — who is an old friend of mine — with a view to having a bill laid before the House."

"Isn't it against the law already?" said a small white-faced woman with untidy black hair. Charles seemed to remember that she'd said she was a viola-player. Her name was? — Oh, yes — Louella Swarf.

"Of course it is," said Ann. "What I have in mind is a compulsory register for the operators of time-travel shows, and the deposit of a sum of money before they are permitted to operate."

"How would that help?" said a solid-looking man in a roll-necked pullover. His name was Gus Ladd. He ran a rock-shop called Minerva Minerals. John had often enjoyed looking in his display-window.

"The fund would be invested," said Ann, "and the proceeds would provide compensation for those who suffered from temporary disappearance, and their families."

"It's not going to be so easy as that," said a man who appeared to be about seventy. "This is big-time we're in. Government level. Someone has kidnapped us, and has put us in here to test us. Maybe to see how we react under stress. Mental stress as much as physical stress. That's the kind of thing intelligence services like doing. I used to work in security, before I retired. I know something about these things. We are probably being watched through one-way glass as we sit here, talking. I wouldn't be surprised if the rocks we're sitting on were bugged."

"If it's the government," said a thirty-year-old man with a pipe in his hand, "it's not going to be so easy stopping it. Didn't the CIA drop the germs for a mild 'flu over San Francisco in the 1950s to see how easily a disease could be spread?"

"Oh, please," said Ellen, "it's not that simple. Bob Mackenzie's drunk half the time these days, since his wife died, and Ken spends his time at the races or the dogs. I practically run the show myself, with Lucy at the gate. There's no way something like this could be set up by someone without my noticing. The Time-Traveller is crammed in among other shows, including the Wall Of Death pantechnicon. You couldn't pull it out without causing complete confusion, and tangling up all the power lines. Something really odd has happened. Something really odd. If you ask me, I think we've really travelled in time."

"It's very loyal of you to defend your employers, Miss Roy," said Ann, "and I don't blame you for it. But we have to opt for the least unlikely solution. I do not like to have to agree with Mr Yonder that it could be the work of the intelligence people. I have a high regard — a high regard — for our security professionals. I much prefer Mr Amplemain's theory that we have been transferred to a safari park, perhaps for the amusement of high-paying Japanese businessmen. You must be aware of Japanese television shows where audiences have fun watching pain being inflicted on volunteer victims. It would be entirely in their character if they were to enjoy seeing us tormented. But Mr Yonder's theory is within the bounds of what is possible. He may be right. Your theory cannot be correct. Time-travel is not a possibility."

"I see it differently," said another middle-aged woman with a disdainful face and a voice like wet sandpaper. She was wearing a broad-brimmed hat, and sitting up with such a straight back it was uncomfortable to look at her.

"Mr Yonder may be correct about the electronics," this woman went on. "I cannot speak to that. I am, as you know, a painter. A fairly well-known one, if I may say so. Visual illusion is one of my professional skills. This is not an illusion. It is considerably more horrible."

She looked around her to see if she was holding them.

"In my view we are in Africa," she continued. "Note the absence of grass and the humid climate. This place is, in all likelihood a reserve set aside for genetic experiments. Some multinational company has done a deal with one of those governments that have followed the downfall of our Empire. Their scientists can come here, out of sight of the animal rights' movement, or the press, and pursue their experiments without interference. The monsters that some of us have seen are, in my view, quite real. They have been bred. Quite deliberately. Like the Minotaur in the Greek legend, but this time in reality, by genetic manipulation. We have ourselves become the victims of those whom we have foolishly allowed to torture animals, and whose morals have been destroyed in the process."

"But my dear Elaine," said Seb, "who benefits from this? What use are we — here — to scientists like those you describe?"

"There are many possibilities, Mr Amplemain," said Elaine Quainton, fixing him with a stare. "They might want us to breed with them. They might want to feed us to them. You cannot tell with scientists."

She turned her eyes on Ellen.

"And there is something else that I have noticed," she added. "Only the

159

employee of Mackenzie's maintains that no crime has been committed. Only the employee of Mackenzie's has remained cheerful throughout this entire harrowing experience. Why? I do not wish to make unfounded accusations, but I would be less than honest not to confess that the thought has crossed my mind, *How much is she being paid for this?* Is she here to keep a watch on us, perhaps? Would you care to explain, Miss Roy?"

There was a silence.

Ellen's face showed a mixture of horror and disbelief.

"Excuse me, Miss Fellows," said Charles's voice in the silence. "May I have your permission to serve the dessert, please? We have honey-twigs tonight. They are delicious, and John and I have cut them up specially."

Ann Fellows looked surprised. Then she recovered herself and smiled.

"That would be most appropriate, Charles," she said. "May I say how much we really do appreciate your hard work, and your brother's. Yes. Please do serve the dessert. Honey-twigs sound delicious. I do not think we have had them before. We can resume our discussion in due course."

Sometimes, thought John to himself, even politicians earn their keep. He moved swiftly to help his brother.

"FIVE WATERFALLS," said John, half-dreaming. "Five."

Murgatroyd's eyes glowed beside him in the dark. The light from the fire danced in his green lenses.

The driftwood had been weathered into ungainly shapes. Sometimes it seemed as if crouching monsters were burning there, the flames flickering along their backs.

John tossed on handfuls of pine-needles, and some cones and dead ferns. The fire leapt suddenly, sending monster-shaped shadows running across the monsters' shoulders. Then it died down again, and the half-burned logs lay there, smoking on the embers. The embers squirmed slowly with their own heat.

"Five waterfalls," he repeated. "We had a croft on the edge of the beach in those days. When you went outside the front door you could see five waterfalls. They came off the cliffs, almost into the sea. I sat on my father's shoulders, and he would walk along to where one of the streams ran out across the shingle. Then he'd turn, and climb up the boulders, very carefully because I was still on his back, until we got to where the waterfall came down. We'd stand there, looking up at it, enjoying the spray on our faces."

"Where was it?" said the cat.

"Sound of Mull," said John. "The north shore. At the end of a seven-mile dirt road that ran among huge trees. There was a storm the next year that blew most of them down. Some of them across the road."

The memories came back to him then, of summer evenings that never seemed to end, and the brown-purple hills asleep above the empty sea. A time when his father and mother got on with each other. When their half-sister still lived with them.

"My father says my first proper word was 'waterfall'," he added. "We used to say it so often."

The cat made no reply. The tide was at the ebb. He was listening to the waves on the mudflats, and thinking of the four-armed starfish — not starfish really — with the whiplashes at the end of each arm, and the thumb-sized prawns, lying there or emerging from the ooze.

The twenty others were asleep. Only the two of them were keeping watch, as they had done, every night, since the Time-Traveller had arrived.

"Cetiosaurs still over there?" said John after some minutes had passed.

"Moved off some time ago," said the cat. "When they were near us I could feel the rock trembling as they walked. Can't you tell how still it is now?"

"Not really. I don't have your paws. Anything else?"

"Some small dinosaurs in the swamp," said Murgatroyd. "They seem to be resting up. It's easy to smell them now the wind's coming off the land."

"Know what sort they are?"

"No," said the cat. "But something like *coeluri*. Three-fingered hands probably. Catch lizards, or small mammals like me. I think I can hear land-crocodiles, too."

"Land-crocodiles?" said John.

"Yes. Run faster than you do. If you get chased, your only hope's to get up a tree."

John laughed.

"Lucky the firewood ring's in place now," he said.

"No luck about it," said Murgatroyd. "You built it."

"With Ellen," said John. "And help from Billy and Ray."

"You persuaded them," said the cat.

"And you persuaded me," said John.

He paused, and sighed.

"It's odd," he went on, "being the only ones working. The others just sit there and talk, as if they're on a cruise-ship. Actually, that's not quite fair. Harry's apologized for not helping. He's got a bad back. Something to do with the war."

"Harry escaped from a death-camp," said Murgatoyd. "He can be excused, at his age."

"Oh," said John softly. "Oh."

He leant back, resting his head on his cupped hands, and gazing at the sky above them. Somewhere up there, he thought, are the great southern stars — Canopus, Antares, Fomalhaut. Which ones are they?

"It's an odd situation," said the cat. "A thirteen-year-old boy and his twelve-year-old brother looking after a group of grown-ups. In many ways more grown-up than they are."

"What's happened to them?" said John. "I mean the grown-ups. Ellen, I guess, excepted."

"They don't believe what's happening to them," said Murgatroyd. "That's what. So their eyes turn off, and their minds turn off. They don't see what's in front of them. If they do see it, they misunderstand it on purpose. When Charles told them there was no way the sun could be faked, nor the fact that everyone's watch was losing an hour a day, remember what Mr Yonder said?"

"That it could be magnetism," said John. "A mountain full of iron nearby, or something like that. Is that possible?"

"It wouldn't affect all the watches the same," said the cat. "The more expensive ones are anti-magnetic. Like Mrs Dalrymple's, or Gus Ladd's."

"Why are Charles and me all right, then?"

"One reason," said Murgatroyd, "is that you minds aren't set yet. Grown-ups inside, maybe, but you still don't really know who you are. So, when the story changes, you just go along with it. Like pine-cones floating in a stream."

"Musette's younger than Charles," said John, "but she thinks we're in a theme-park, or somebody's experiment."

"She's still a child and believes her mother, and her brother," said the cat. "But if she stays here long enough, she'll wake up."

"Beautiful hazel-brown eyes she has," said John."What's the other reason?"

"The other reason?" said Murgatroyd. "Oh," — and he chuckled — "simply that you and Charles are you and Charles."

John looked landwards into the darkness of the forest and the swamp, and thought of the *coeluri* and the land-crocodiles.

"Are we going to be attacked?" he said.

"It's bound to happen in the end," said the cat, "but there's no telling when. That's why it's important to keep watch."

"But if Charles brought us to the Mesozoic," said John, "why can't he get us back to Oxford?"

"Lots of times you can do things once," said Murgatroyd, "but you can't do them a second time. Factorial *n*."

"Well," said John, "I know, but.... "

He stopped, then resumed.

"I was chased by a bull two years ago. I didn't know he was in the field until I heard him coming for me. Had to jump a five-foot hedge to escape. Or, rather, I sort of rolled through the top of it in my windbreaker. When I came back next day with my mother, to show her, from the outside, and when I looked at that hedge — it was over my head — I didn't believe what I was telling her. She didn't either. But I know it happened. I wouldn't be here otherwise. But I couldn't have done it again, on purpose. Unless, maybe, I was being chased again."

"Adrenalin," said the cat. "When you're scared for your life, you can do these things."

"I don't think Charles wants to go back," said John. "I think he likes being here. Does that mean we're stuck here forever?"

"My magic doesn't extend to time-travel," said Murgatroyd. "So we either get on with it, or we give up."

John clicked his tongue.

"In that case," he said, "what about building a fish-trap?"

"Fish-trap?"

"Remember the croft?" said John. "On the beach below there was a rough half-circle of rocks. Between the high tide and the low tide, running out and making an enclosure, about as high as I am. My father told us what it was. The ruins of a fish-trap built by the people who used to live there. The fish came in with the tide, over the top of the wall. Then, when the tide ebbed out, the water ran back through the gaps between the rocks, but the fish were caught, unless they were very small, I suppose. At low tide, all the people had to do was to walk down and pick them up as they flapped about on the mud. Of course, by our time, a hole had been broken in it."

"So your idea's to build a fish-trap on the beach here, is it?" said Murgatroyd. "Won't it be difficult, moving rocks that are heavy enough?"

"Yes — on my own," said John. "But Billy and Ray will help, I'm sure. Think what a fish-trap would mean. Fresh food forever, with no need to hunt for it."

The black cat gave a chuckling purr.

"I've got enough magic left to help you, I think," he said.

"Could you make us a fish-trap?" said John.

"Yes, but I won't," said Murgatroyd. "If it just appears one morning, like a Sultan's palace conjured into existence by a genie, they'll never believe this place is real. What I will do is make the rocks lighter — while you're moving them. How about that?"

"Useful," said John. "But, but — oh, I don't know — there's something in me that makes me want to do it myself. The hard way."

"I don't have to help you," said the cat.

"No, Murg, please do," said John. "We haven't got too much time and it's important."

He thought for a while.

"Best place for it would be under the cliff," he said. "The shingle's pretty solid there. If we put the rocks on sand, the base'll get sucked away and they'll sink."

"Correct," said Murgatroyd.

"All right, then," said John, "let's go and have look at it before we make our minds up. I wonder what we'll catch. Ostracoderms?"

"They're meant to be extinct by now, the armoured fishes," said Murgatroyd, "but some of the ones with the squarish scales of thick enamel, like bathroom tiles — they might be around still."

"What about those beasts who haul out on the rocks at the end of our estuary?" said John. "The ones that look like reptile seals, though my seal wouldn't thank me for saying so."

"What about them?" said the cat.

"I was wondering," said John, "if we mightn't find our fish-trap being raided."

"It's bound to be," said Murgatroyd. "By the pterosaurs, too. We just have to be there first. Hey. What's that?"

The two of them came wide awake, cat-senses and boy-senses trying to pierce the darkness of the vegetation less than two hundred metres away.

"It's a pack of something," said the cat.

"I can hear running," said John. "Shall I light the fires?"

"Yes," said Murgatroyd. "Quick. Get three or four more going."

John rocked to his feet, picked up the bundle of dried ferns and twigs lashed to a pine-branch that lay beside him, and thrust it into the main fire. In an instant a torch was blazing in his hand. He moved around the perimeter, pushing it into the kindling laid ready in four of the fires in the defensive line.

The flames leapt up around them, reflected in the glass doors and the windows of the Time-Traveller. He could see Murgatroyd now, clearly, sitting on his folded sweater, green eyes intent on the blackness beyond the flickering blaze.

Seven or eight shapes passed by, moving swiftly in the moonlight.

"What are they?" said John. "Any idea?"

"Something more like *deinonychus*," said the cat. "Pehaps an early form. They've got lethal teeth and claws, and hunt in packs. Worse, they can think."

"More fires?" said John. "Shall we close the line?"

"No need," said Murgatroyd. "They're after something else at the moment. "Just stay ready, in case they change their minds."

The bigger logs in the fires were catching now, and the glare and the crackling intensifying.

One of the doors of the Time-Traveller slid back, and Gus Ladd put his head out.

"John," he said, "what are you playing at? It's dangerous to have fires burning like this. The Traveller's made of wood. Think what would happen if it caught alight, with people sleeping inside it."

"There are animals out there, Mr Ladd," said John. "We need the fires to scare them off."

Gus's face thickened up, like a sauce. He was still half asleep, and struggling with his annoyance. But he was also trying to be fair.

"Look," he said after a while, "it's not really on the cards that whoever is behind this damn-fool joke is going to let us get hurt. You should come inside and take some sleep. Huh? One fire's enough. Pull those others apart, and then turn in. You'll be a wreck in the morning if you don't."

"Mr Ladd," said John, "they're *deinonychus*, or something like them. They're dangerous. We need the fires."

"John," said Gus Ladd, "you're a wonderful fellow. You know all the names and everything, but that doesn't mean that you know what the world is like. Also, you mean very well. Otherwise I'd be angry, which I'm not. But believe me, we are *not* in the Mesozoic. *Not, not, not.* I work with rocks and fossils. I sell ammonites, and iron pyrites, and garnets to tourists every day of the week. I know about these things. There is no way we could have travelled in time. It *has* to be something else. You've heard us talking about it. We don't know exactly what — there are several possibilities. But the one thing it isn't is the real thing. OK.?"

"What about the ammonite Billy and Ray got hold of?" said John. "Wasn't it alive?"

"People used to think the coelocanth was extinct," said Gus, "until one day some fishermen dredged one up off the coast of Madagascar. And there it was, plump-bodied, fleshy-finned, with a three-lobed tail, and a mere three hundred million years out of date. These things happen from time to time. You can't prove time-travel from one living ammonite."

"What about my brother's point?" said John. "That the days here are shorter, by at least an hour."

"If a battery runs low in a watch, the watch runs slow," said Gus. "We can't be sure the days are really shorter."

"And the night sky?" said John. "There's not one constellation we know.

Only the Clouds of Magellan. And how did we get to the southern hemisphere? There's no land like this so far south in our own time."

Gus Ladd drew in a breath. Then he looked up at the stars above them, crystal bright, as if they had been needle-pierced in a metallic blackness.

"We have been confined in some kind of gigantic planetarium," he said. "We are being played with, very very skilfully."

"Mr Ladd," said John, "you may be right. You certainly know lots more about the world than I do. But don't you think that, if they've spent so much money on this experiment, they may not be prepared to kill us? Like lab animals?"

"Or like gladiators in a Roman circus," said a woman's voice behind Gus. "Maybe we're being made into a video. Live."

It was Ellen. There was a dead look in her eyes, and her voice had lost its music. It had an edge to it.

Oh, no, thought John. Oh, *no*. Outwardly he nodded.

"Something like that," he said. "Don't we have to look after ourselves, whatever the truth of it is?"

"What's a *deinonychus*?" she said.

"Two metres tall," said John. "Three metres long. Runs on two legs, with a heavy tail. Has a special long claw on its feet, for slashing...."

"And exists," interrupted Gus, "exclusively in museums, television shows, and John's imagination."

"John," he added, "would you please stop upsetting people and do as I ask. Pull the fires you've started apart. We need to be able to sleep."

John glanced at Murgatroyd.

The cat looked back at him, unblinking, and — just perceptibly — nodded.

"OK, then, Mr Ladd," John agreed. "I'll bed them down. May take a few minutes."

He began to look around for a long hooked stick.

"Thanks, John," said Gus. "We'll see you in the morning."

The glass doors closed with a click, and John, with deliberate slowness, started to pull the burning branches out of one fire and then another.

"They've gone in any case," said Murgatroyd when the boy sat down beside him again, panting, and smudged with soot. "So it saves firewood for next time."

John rubbed his forehead with his forearms to stop the sweat running into his eyes. Even at night the weather was warm.

"Suppose they had attacked us," he said. "What would Gus have thought?" Murgatroyd grunted.

"That it was a blunder by the management, I suppose," he said. "Or a deliberate part of the experiment. There's always some sort of answer if you're determined not to understand. There's no way we're going to change his mind."

"I know," said John wearily. "I know. Are you sure we're right, Murg? I mean, in believing this is real?"

"Can you fake an ocean?" said the cat. "Can you fake the sun? Can you imitate the tides? Even if you might bring a few dinosaurs back to life from the gene-code preserved in fragments of their eggs — and no one's done it yet — you can't manufacture a whole world. Not with rains and winds, and real-sized mountain-ranges. Not unless you are God."

John gave the cat a wry smile in return, and settled back drowsily against the rock. The tide was rising, and he was already dreaming of his fish-trap, and ostracoderms.

The moon was beginning to set. The light shone slanting across his forehead, the tumble of uncombed hair, the smudges of soot, and the closed eyes. Murgatroyd glanced at him with fond admiration, and resumed his vigil through the last hours of the darkness, alone.

THE SUN WAS UP when Charles came by, sucking on a honey-twig.

"Morning, Murg," he whispered, so as not to wake John. "What happened last night?"

"Pack of *deinonychus*, or something like them," said the cat. "John lit some extra fires, but they went off."

"Interesting," said Charles. "I'll ask Steg to show me the footprints."

"What are you two up to today?" said Murgatroyd.

"Panning for gold," said Charles, with a twinkle in his eye. "Steg says there's a river with sands that glitter from the gold in them. About a day's walk from here. His walk, not mine."

"So you'll be gone some days?"

"Oh, probably," said Charles. "Don't worry about me."

He stroked the cat.

"Isn't it beautiful here!" he said. "Beautiful and exciting!"

"What are you going to do with the gold when you've got it?" asked Murgatroyd.

"Nothing," said Charles. "Just have it."

He gave the cat a smile and disappeared down the rocks.

Murgatroyd looked at the pterosaurs gliding above the estuary waters. Then he stretched himself, digging his claws deeply and luxuriously into John's sweater as he did so.

167

John, beside him, opened an eye.

"Hey, Murg!" he said. "That's mine! Treat it nicely."

The cat stopped in mid-stretch.

"I didn't know you were awake." he said.

"That's not an excuse," said John.

"Oh, come on," said the cat, "I've been keeping watch all the time you've been asleep, and I'm stiff. There's nothing like chunky knitwear for giving one's claws a good work-out."

"As a punishment," said John, "you can come with me to look at the place for our fish-trap."

He stood up and flexed himself. Wrists bent back, fingers pushed slowly against each other, toes curled up, then down....

"On your shoulder?" said Murgatroyd. "I can see better from there."

"Oh, all right," said John. "It's easier to talk that way."

The cat landed with a thud, and John swayed in the other direction to balance himself.

"You win every time," he added. "Mr Murgatroyd."

Then he picked his way down the rocks till they reached the line of loose sand, and seaweed-entangled driftwood, that marked the highest reach of the sea. The wind was tossing the sand into his face, but in his present mood he paid no attention to it. Up above he could hear the others' voices as they came out of the Time-Traveller — Tim, Mrs Dalrymple, Louella, Ann, Seb, Elsie and Ken, and old Caleb. They seemed to be complaining about the wind. Oh, well, he thought, let them. They have nothing else to think about.

As the cliff turned west it rose higher. John and Murgatroyd were soon standing under a hundred feet of overhanging rock. Trickles of water clung down it, leaving dark stains, and feeding the patches of orange and grey-purple lichen.

"We're not going to be trapped by the tide here ourselves, are we Murg?" said John. "The beach is getting narrow."

The cat surveyed the shoreline from John's shoulder.

"No," he said after a while. "We're in no trouble."

"Oh, dear," he added, "look at that. Is it what I think it is?"

John hooded his eyes to a sharp focus.

"A body," he said bluntly.

"I feared so," said the cat. "We had better examine it."

John walked uneasily towards the awkward tangle of limbs. Then he stopped again. The blue clothing was only too easy to recognize.

"It's Ellen," he said.

"Get closer," said the cat.

Reluctantly, John closed the gap until he was standing above her, looking down. The head was bent back at an impossible angle. One of the legs was broken and buckled.

He squatted to let Murgatroyd off, then lifted one of her wrists to feel for the pulse.

"Not a tremor," he muttered. "Murg, can you do any magic?"

"Not on people," said the cat. "I wish I could."

He licked Ellen's forehead a few times to remove some sandy grit.

"She's getting cold," he added. "Must have been here at least an hour."

John stood up again and shook his head.

"Poor Ellen," he said. "She really tried to help us. What happened to her, do you think? Happened to her inside, I mean."

"She knew the truth," said the cat, "and it was more than she could bear. Charles told me he was worried about her. He sees these things from a long way off — as you know — but I can't imagine he thought it would happen so fast. He wouldn't have left on Steg this morning if he had. He had a great regard for her, Charles had."

John knelt and eased the strap of Ellen's handbag from her fingers. It was black plastic leatherette, with gold-coloured plastic edging, and a metal twist-snap fastener.

"Do you think we should open it?" he said.

"Why not?" said the cat. "She won't mind."

"I know she *won't*," said John, "that's obvious, but *would* she have?"

"I don't think so," said Murgatroyd. "She was an understanding person. We may learn something; and, if we ever do get back, we'll have to tell her family. And we don't even know who they are."

John unsnapped the bag. Inside, a double-folded scrap of paper was wedged between a powder-compact with orange-yellow glass marigolds on its lid and a purse. A name was written on the outside.

"'Mr Nicholas Delsey'," John read. "'50 Sommelier Court, Oxford. Please Forward If Possible'."

"I think that's the name of her boy-friend," he said. "He was certainly called Nicholas. I remember her saying so. Do we look at it?"

"We look at it," said the cat, "and we forward it, if we get the chance. What does it say?"

"I'm not sure I like doing this," John muttered, but he unfolded the note.

The writing was uneven, and the ink was stained in a couple of places, probably with tears:

Dearest Nick [John read]

I don't know if you'll ever get this. I don't think you will. But I'm writing it in case you do. So you can know what has happened and, I hope, still remember me. If you are reading this, I shall have been dead two hundred million years. Don't bother putting up a memorial to me. I had never realized how futile these things are till now.

I mean two hundred million years, which sounds strange, I know, but if you do get this — and just the thought of you reading it almost makes me happy again — though I'm nearly certain you never will, I suppose — someone will probably have explained what has happened.

Our Time-Traveller took off into real time-travel. I don't know how, but it did. Everyone else keeps pretending that it hasn't, that it is just a trick by scientists, that we are just being experimented on. How I wish I could believe them! You have only to look around here, Nick, to realize that this has to be real.

So, in a way I am dead already. I am cut off from everyone who matters to me, from everyone that makes my life make any sense at all. The people here accuse me of being paid by the Mackenzies to be a sort of secret agent in charge of the experiment from the inside. It's so stupid it really shouldn't matter to me. But it does. I don't care anything for any of them any more, and I've tried so hard to help them ever since it happened, whatever 'it' is, I don't know. And without them to care for, or you, or Mother, what's the point of my going on? There isn't one.

I suppose the two boys are all right really, but they live so much in their own world, I don't seem to have anything I can do for them either.

So — I am saying goodbye to everything, Nick. Don't be angry with me, and don't be sorry for me, because it won't help. I hope the rest of your life goes well, and you are able to make someone else happy. I love you, and I wish that someone could be me — but it will never be.

Being in this place gives me an understanding of these things, too terrible for me even to want to try to tell you.

With all my love, my darling,
            forever,   Ellen.

"They killed her," said the cat. "Adults are like that. You're hitting the grown-up world head on. Welcome. I just hope you can handle it."

"What do we do?" said John after a long silence. "Bury her?"

"It makes no odds," said Murgatroyd. "One way or another, slow or fast, she will pass back into the earth, be reabsorbed into it, be recycled, be forgotten. All that will remain of her is her spirit in that letter."

"Don't we want to keep the pterosaurs from her?" said John.

"I know how you feel when you say that," said the cat, "but if it really matters to you — really — then you still lack understanding of what it's all about."

"Maybe I do care," said John. "Maybe I do."

He kicked a mass of small stones and shingles together, then scooped them up with his hands and covered the body. The cat watched him motionlessly, saying nothing. When John had finished, he wiped his hands on the sides of his trousers, and picked up the handbag.

"That's it," he said. "Perhaps we can do better later. Let's go back and tell the others."

As he trudged along on the return journey, the cat swaying on his shoulder, the wind blew from behind them. It lifted up sandy swirls of dust that danced away down the beach.

THE SUN was shining far away in the mountain valley. A river meandered along between expanses of grey-white sand on alternate banks, and overhanging branches. Steg was cropping the red pear-shaped fruits hanging from a tufted cyclomeia tree. Charles was working on the riverbank.

Strips of bark cut from clubmoss trees lay beside him in a pile. They looked like huge brown carpenter's files, with their surfaces scarred by the broken bases of old stems. Charles had spent the morning in the swamps below, slicing and levering them off, and loading them onto Steg.

Now he was busy with his knife again, smoothing the inside of a hollow half-trunk. It lay, at a gentle angle, on a ramp of piled-up stones. Beside it a pipe made of horsetail stems gushed water into the sand. Charles had cut the stems from one of the clumps at the edge of the river, rammed the soft membranes out of the septs inside with a thin branch, and wedged the ends into each other. They were rather like bamboos, Mesozoic bamboos. The upper end of this sectioned pipe was fed from a side-stream only a few strides away. All he had to do, when he wanted to send water down the trough was to lift the last section up and rest it on the lip at the top.

He wasn't quite ready yet. The trough needed more smoothing, and grooves had to be cut so the strips of bark didn't slide out once they'd been placed inside.

At the bottom end of the trough was a massive, odd-shaped, limestone rock with a shallow basin in it. Steg had had to work hard to roll it all the way to where it rested now. Charles's idea was that the basin might help to catch some of the last grains of gold that had failed to stick in the bark, before the downrush of water poured itself back into the river.

When he'd finished making his gold-trap, he sat on a sandbank, chewed on a honey-twig and looked at it, wondering if it could be improved. Steg wandered over, and he tried to explain it to the dinosaur by letting pictures of it working float through his mind. Steg was fascinated but puzzled, so Charles gave up and patted him on the beak instead.

'You'll see in a minute,' he thought. 'It's your placer as much as mine.'

Sand-coloured hoppers were jumping around his legs as he sat. Funny creatures, he thought. You can't see them till they move, and when they land you think you know where they are, but — you can't see them again. He amused himself by flicking his foot in the sand and making showers of sand, so the hoppers leapt up. After a while he grew bored with this and stopped.

"OK, OK," he said out aloud to himself. "Let's get it going and see if it works."

He picked up a piece of curved bark. Then he waded into the river. The water curled and broke around his ankles, running away in two long shaking Vs downstream until it merged with the flow again. Out of the side of his eye he saw an animal cross over the sandbanks and vanish into the undergrowth. But, by the time he had looked up and focussed, there were only the branches shaking.

He scooped up a dollop of sand. It glittered in the sunshine. In two ways. The light catching on the wetness, already drying out fast. And on the gold. Countless minute particles of gold, whose glitter held steady.

He smiled, waded back to the bank, and flopped the sand down on the top end of his trough, like a bricklayer splatting a trowelful of mortar onto a course of bricks. The sand bulged a little under its own weight, and a trickle of water began to ooze down from under it over the strips of bark. Not only the gold was sparkling, but little black-blue specks of mica and tiny whitish crystals.

He waded back in for a second scoopful. Then a third and a fourth.

Panting slightly, he put the bark trowel on the dry sand at his feet and wiped his gritty fingers clean, back and forth against his calves. Then he lifted the end of the stem pipe with the water gurgling out of it. The pipe twitched a little in his hands as he wedged it under a stone at the top of the

172

trough, adjusting its angle so the water ran over the sand, washing it away, and carrying it down the hollow half-log as a thin buff-yellow slurry. He watched it build up in the basin-sized hollow in the rock at the bottom, then brim over, spilling down onto the bank and back into the river.

It was an old idea. He'd seen it in one of his father's books, full of woodcuts about German mining long ago. Diagrams with letters and keyed-in explanations. Drawings of ladles and basins and waterwheels. And men in hooded jackets doing things among the rocks and streams, turning windlasses and pushing carts along wooden rails. Read one sleepy summer afternoon in Oxford, with Hippo — as always — on the sofa-arm, reading it over his shoulder.

Gold is heavy. Sand, and almost everything else, is light in comparison. So, as the water runs down, it entrains the sand-grains effortlessly. But the gold is dragged along grudgingly, sluggishly. It barely leaves the bottom, and — sooner or later — it sticks in the ridges of the bark.

Charles watched the mound of sand wash away.

When the water was running down clear again, or almost clear, with only faint streaks of sand along its lines of flow, he freed the pipe and let it gush out to one side. A criss-cross pattern of gold-laden crevices shone up at him from the bark strips in the trough. He felt the pleasure of a dinosaur mind flowing through him as Steg gazed down at it beside him.

'Beautiful, isn't it?' he thought back in return.

He prised out the trough-bark strips with his army knife. Then, using the water-pipe as a hose, he washed the gold off them, section by section, into the rock basin. Once the particles of gold had had time to settle there, he sloshed out the remaining water with a fresh piece of bark. When he'd finished, there was a pile of wet gold dust at the bottom of the basin, enough perhaps to fill a teaspoon.

After a moment's thought, he gave a slight smile, and fished a polythene sandwich bag out of one of his windbreaker pockets. With very deliberate patience, he nudged the gold into it with a dry leaf, using his forefinger nail to scrape the last flecks off the limestone. Then he twist-tied a knot in the top, shoved it into a zipper pocket, and flopped out onto the sand, exhausted.

The dinosaur listened to the river, and to the water still trickling from the pipe. Cicadas were chirring from the groundpines, non-stop, as they had been doing all day. Once in a while there was a splash. Probably a crocodile catching something. Evening was coming on. Long shadows stretched across the sandbanks. But Steg's mind was full of gold. He had loved this river since the years when he was young, its fast-flowing riffles and its barely moving pools, always sparkling, like nowhere else in his world. That's why he'd told Charles about it, and shown him the way here. But he'd never dreamed that his friend would know a way to coax its gold from the river's sands. His astonishing friend from another time.

Charles spent the next three days placer-mining. He filled his wind-breaker pockets with gold-dust until the jacket was too heavy to be wearable. But the morning of the fourth day he felt ill.

There was nothing wrong with the day. It was still sunny. Mayflies were dancing above the water like clouds of transparent rainbow commas. There were dark grey lizards warming themselves on the rocks, delicately curved, like the *f*-shaped slits in the sound-box of a violin, elbow-legs out sideways and ready to vanish at the slightest rough noise. But he felt cold inside. There were hammers beating in his head.

'Steg,' he thought to the dinosaur, 'we've done enough. Can we get back now? I've got to see the others.'

Steg lifted his beak, a little surprised.

The image of tree-ferns came into Charles's mind, and the warm delicious taste of tree-fern heart.

'No,' he thought back. 'Not this time, Steg. No time to spare.'

He lifted the heavy wind-breaker onto the dinosaur's back.

'Why so fast?' Steg seemed to be thinking. A scene of sunbeams through the trunks of Kauri pines, moving past them gently, and the smells of wood rotting in swamps, and pentoxylon fruits, drifted through Charles's thoughts. He gave a look at his trough, aslant on its pile of stones, and the horsetail pipe, still spurting onto the sands. A thought came into his mind that the river had no name. That it would never have one.

'Why so fast?' came Steg's questioning again.

Charles began to wonder himself. Then — abruptly — his inner vision filled with fires, and confusion, and black shapes rearing and tearing, and last of all his brother John, standing alone with a huge flaming branch in his hands, his mouth set grimly shut, but the look of death in his eyes.

'That's why,' his thoughts shot back, as he swung himself up between Steg's plates. '*John is why.*'

But there had been no need to answer. The message of the mind was home already. The earth had begun to shudder under the dinosaur's footbeats. The trees seemed to rush at Charles both ways back and forth. As the heavy tail lashed for counter-balance, he gripped to hold on, using all his strength, and only just managed. Bush-growth and swamp-waters plunged, splintered, and splashed beneath them. Steg was running now, up on two legs only, his huge strides thundering on the ground, and he was going at a tremendous speed.

174

"NEVER PLAY CARDS, me little 'uns, with someone you don't know," said the warm, North Irish voice.

Billy Rush's face had broken into a smile.

He put out a huge but sensitive hand, and cupped it around the two shells that lay on the flat-topped rock. Two white ammonite shells. He pulled them to the edge of a large pile of other shells already stashed up in front of him. Black mussel-shells, pink-and-white sea urchin's casings, long razorblade shells gleaming with mother-of-pearl inside, brown cowries with openings like toothless smiles, more ammonites....

Tim, facing him from the other side, shook his head and combed his hair back with his fingers. His blue-grey eyes looked puzzled.

"Nineteen to your twenty," he said. "I thought the odds were pretty good for me, but you always seem to go one better. Well, that's all my shells gone — till I gather some more."

"How do you always know what's in our hands?" said Musette.

"A misspent youth, me little 'uns," said Billy. "You need to concentrate more."

"Concentrate?" said Musette.

"Keep your mind on one thing," said Billy, smiling again. "Like our Mr and Mrs Shah up there. They haven't been out of the Time-Traveller except to eat and you-know-what for the last two days. Talking about which young man to marry their daughter to — when they get back to Oxford of course. I don't think they've ever left Oxford — in their minds, that is."

"It sounded more like quarrelling to me," said Tim.

"They're scared," said Ray Honeykick. He was lying on his back next to Billy, with his head on a pile of ferns and his knees swinging idly back and forth. "They like to pretend they're back home. In that newsagent's shop of theirs. Selling chocolates to schoolboys whose parents have too much money."

"What's this Queen of Spades doing in front of me?" said Musette suddenly. "How did it get here?"

The card was lying on the rock-table where no card had been before. It was smiling up at her.

"You took your eyes off me fingers, me dear," said Billy, his Belfast accent half mocking, half-friendly. "So she'd thought she'd pay you a call, you see. While I'd made you think about Mr and Mrs Shah."

He flicked the Queen back into his palm. Then he picked up the deck, tapped the edges on the rock to make them square, and slipped it back into its case. The blue Irish mountains and golden wheatfields on the back disappeared.

The case he dropped into his shirt breast-pocket.

"Aren't you going to show us how you do it?" said Tim.

"Me? Show you how to cheat other people?" said Billy, putting on a serious look. "That wouldn't be moral of me, would it now?"

But his eyes were twinkling.

"Did you see the Queen get there?" John whispered to Murgatroyd.

The two of them were sitting on an outcrop just above the rock that served as a card-table, and looking down.

"Of course," the cat murmured back. "But it's a terrible temptation."

"What's a temptation?"

"To turn it into the Queen of Plesiosaurs," Murgatroyd whispered back. "I'd love to see how he reacted."

John smiled, then his face went sad.

"Did you see what happened this morning?" he said. "Out in the bay. The fish-lizard?"

"I did when I saw you looking at it," said the black cat. "But it's just life, John. They live on the plesiosaurs."

"I'm not sure I always approve of life," said John.

He put his hand on the cat's shoulder, and they looked in silence across the mudflats.

"Like being in prison, isn't it?" said a deep voice beside them.

Ken Berrigan was standing there with Elsie, looking at them.

Murgatroyd began to wash his whiskers by wetting his paw with his tongue, as if he'd heard nothing.

"Why prison?" said John. "You can go where you want to here, can't you? If you've got the courage — like my brother."

"This whole place is a prison," said Ken. "I thought we'd agreed on that. A singularly nasty experiment, with us as the laboratory rats. Or a peepshow for sadistic Japs. Isn't that right?"

"The whole thing about prisons," said Billy, glancing up at him, "is to try to forget you're there. Just let it be, till something happens. Just let it be. Why don't you tell us some more of your stories? You've got a mind full of stories, like a shop full of TV sets, all playing different programs. Keep us thinking about something else. Come on now. You're the professional."

Ken smiled with his lips, not his eyes, and leaned against the card-table rock. Elsie sat cross-legged at his feet and leaned her head against his leg, smiling. Murgatroyd went on pretending to wash.

The history teacher took a pipe from his pocket and held it in the palm of one hand. Then he put it away again.

"I guess I had better just imagine the smell of tobacco," he said with a regretful smile. "Imagine the sweet-smelling tar, and the mind growing clearer and clearer. But my pouch is almost empty. Best saved for later. When I really need it."

He closed his eyes, and opened them again.

"Suppose it's not an experiment," he said. "Suppose it's real. Suppose this *is* the Mesozoic. What's the point of history? What's the point of my life? Does it matter here — or not — if Columbus joined Europe and America?"

"Doesn't slavery matter, Ken?" said Elsie softly.

"Sure, it matters, love. But what I like doing — really like doing — isn't anything that matters. I just like telling stories to kids. Being an actor. Making the past come alive. Making them see how complicated everything really is."

"Like slavery?" said Ray.

"Good example," said Ken, not noticing the edge in the karate expert's voice. "I make some of them play the parts of the West African chiefs who captured other Africans, and sold them to the whites. And I say to them, imagine you've just been captured. What's it feel like, being captured by one of your own people and sold? Or doing the capturing? Maybe they enjoyed it? Maybe. Imagine it. Or whipping someone? Is it exciting? Or disgusting? Or both? And then I have a rebellion on shipboard. The blacks break out of their irons and take control. So I say to the kids, OK!, you can kill the captain if you want. He's evil. But what are you going to do with the sailors?"

"Kill them too," said Ray.

"In that case, you've got problems," said Ken. "Without officers, you can't navigate the ship. You're lost in mid-Atlantic. You can't even sail it, without sailors. That's one set of problems. The other is, most of the sailors have been press-ganged. Seized when drunk and forced to work on the slaver. Or been so poor they've had no choice. Should you really kill them? Really?"

"What's the answer, then?" said Ray.

"There is no answer," said Ken. "All I try to do is to show them how complicated life is."

"What would you have done?" said Ray.

Ken looked disconcerted. He pulled his pipe out, and sucked on it, cold.

"I don't really know," he said after a while.

"Aren't you paid to tell them?" said Ray.

"No. No," said Ken. "No. My job as a teacher is to make sure they know what the arguments are. Not to tell them the truth."

Ray raised his eyebrows, and a strange sort of smile flickered across his black face. But he said nothing more.

John's eyes, with what was now habit, quartered the hills in the distance and then the nearer forests, searching them systematically. He was only half-listening.

"I liked that other story you told last night," said Billy. "About the wily Chinese general and the empty city. And his enemy who was so intelligent it was possible to fool him. Remember?"

"Oh, Zhuge Liang," said Ken. "Yes."

"I didn't understand it," said Musette. "How is it possible to be so smart you can be fooled?"

"Yes," said Tim. "Why didn't that other general — you know, the swaggering one with the metal eyes on his kneecaps and belt-buckle — why didn't he just march in when Zhuge opened the gates to him?"

"While Zhuge sat on the city wall above the gate," added Musette, "smiling down at him, with a slave-boy at his back, and playing the zither. Ghostly harmonic notes, just letting his fingertips rest on the strings."

"Because," said Ken, "General Zhuge was famous for his trickery. So, when his enemy, General Sima, rode up and stopped the length of a bowshot off — that was old Chinese army safety regulations — and he saw the gates open, and the old rogue twanging away, what do you think he thought? Hmm? *Hmm?* — Obviously, that it was a trap. He didn't know that Zhuge only had about thirty soldiers with him, and that this was a trick, born of desperation. So Sima told his army to retreat. At which point, Zhuge's men, hidden in the thickets by the roadside, banged on their gongs and thumped on their drums. Sima's men fled in panic until they realized no one was chasing them, and by then old Zhuge had escaped in the other direction."

"So, if Sima had done what his stupid son had told him to do," said Billy, "and just charged in and grabbed Zhuge, he'd have won. Right?"

"Of course," said Ken. "But Sima was too clever to do that. That was why Zhuge was able to trick him."

"That story could still come in useful, even here," said Billy. "I don't think you should worry about being a historian."

"I wish I thought I was still some use," said Ken. "But it's we who've been tricked. We're caught here like the fish in your tidal trap at Point Ellen. We *are* in a kind of prison. Whatever it may look like. Real world or not."

Billy shook his head, and gave another smile.

"Ken," he said. "You've never been in a real prison, or you wouldn't say a thing like that."

"Sounds as if you have been in prison, Billy?" said Tim, "the way you said that...."

"Three years in Reading, little 'un," said Billy. "How right you are. With time off, of course, for good behaviour."

"What on earth did they put you in for?" said Ken. "You don't seem like a criminal to me."

"You're not a police officer," said Billy. "You are not at war with the human race. They put me inside for two offences, two very serious offences as they see them — me Irish temper and me sense of justice."

From habit John was still watching the Kauri pines, even while he half-listened to the others talking. His eye caught something stirring there, about where the trees ended, and the ferns began. Something hard to see, but which worried him.

He looked sideways at Murgatroyd.

"What are they, Murg?" he murmured under his breath.

"Six ceratosaurs," the cat murmured back. "Your eyes are improving."

"Are they dangerous?"

"Extremely."

"What do we do?"

"For the moment, nothing. If they come within about two hundred metres, the perimeter fires will need lighting."

"Gus Ladd says I'm not to light them."

"If they attack," said the cat, and his eyes glowed suddenly with a ferocious green light, "*you* will be in charge, as the only person here who understands what's happening. Forget what he says. I will back you up, if need be."

John nodded but said nothing. His face was growing grim, not so much at the thought of the ceratosaurs, but of having to give grown-ups orders. He began to ponder on the few resources they had for defence.

It seemed almost unthinkable in the midday sunshine, with the breeze blowing gently, and the white-furred pterosaurs rising and falling above the estuary waters. It really was like a theme park.

Or Calypso's island. But no Zeus to order their escape.

He began to think harder: there was only limited firewood. If they lit the fires to keep the ceratosaurs off, they might burn for a day or so. Then the fuel would be gone, and there would be no more defences. What was needed was something more active.

He slipped away from the card-table rock and paced to the top of the rise above where the Time-Traveller was lodged and looked down at the beach below. Forty to fifty feet. It was probably enough of a drop. A hundred would have been better.

He turned to look down the slope, beginning with the mosses and gravels under his feet, and the finger-sized ferns curling beneath the boulders. He was rearranging the lines of fire in his mind until the pattern looked right. A deliberate weak point just seaward of card-table rock. A wide curve around the Time-Traveller. A separate fire-block on the outer edge to force them higher up. *And over.* That would do it.

He nodded. They would also need burning branches as prods. Better get them piled ready.

He hoped there was time. Just possible if Murg helped him.

He glanced across at the fern-covered slopes. The ceratosaurs had not moved. — Not yet.

He walked down the slope again to discuss the details with the cat. To make sure they would work. To make absolutely sure.

In his own mind he knew he had already taken over.

"Be serious," he heard Ken saying. "A sense of justice is hardly a crime, is it?"

"You've a point, maybe," said Billy. "It was more a mistake on my part. I mean, going to a football match by myself, that is. I'd no friends in Cambridge, none to speak of anyhow. I'd just quarrelled with the girl-friend — that's why I was there in the first place. Waste of a train-fare. She lived in Bateman Street. I just thought I'd take my mind off things by going to a game that afternoon."

He fell silent and looked at the sky.

"Are you making this up, Billy?" said Elsie.

He hooded his eyes and pretended to be considering the question.

"All of life's a story, isn't it, me dear?" he said. "Of course I'm making it up. Crims always talk themselves up, don't they? Romanticize the crime. Innocent and hard done by. Never to blame. You can believe it or not, just as you choose, me dear. How's that for generosity? I don't even know, meself, if I believe me own memories any more. But one thing's on public record. It cost me two and a half years of me life."

"Leave out the worst bits, Billy," said Ray.

"Have you heard it before, then, Ray?" said Elsie.

"Course I've heard it before," said Ray. "And more than you'll hear."

"Is it true?"

Ray shrugged.

"Billy don't ever tell a lie," he said. "Not while I've known him. I wouldn't be his friend if he did. But that doesn't mean that what he says is what you call true. Things can look more different than you can believe, seen from different points of view."

"Well," said Ken, "what's a real prison like then?"

"First of all," said Billy, "there's the little matter of how I got there. Me a loyal Protestant, with a picture of Her Majesty in me bedroom, and paying her me respects every night before I say me prayers. Think of it."

"Not that it's much of a room," he added. "Lowest rent in Mrs Pratley's boarding-house."

He rested his chin on his hand and seemed to be lost in memories of some sort.

"As I said," he went on, "I was watching this football match, and a fight breaks out in the stands. Two gangs. Nothing very special. Bit of razorwork on the face, broken-off ends of bottles — you know, jab, twist, that sort of thing. Nothing to do with me. I was just watching, 'cause fights sort of interest me professionally. Standing well back. Behaving meself.

"Then the police came in, with orders to break it up. Problem was, they didn't have the guts to do it. There are some good coppers, but most of them aren't trained. So they pick on easy targets. And that was me.

"Tried to arrest me. And that made me really angry. 'You just leave me alone,' I said. 'I'm nothing to do with this fight.' Answer was an amateur half-nelson on me arm. 'Let me go,' I says. 'I'm doing nothing.' Then he puts a burn on me wrist, twisting his fingers round in opposite directions.

"This is kid stuff, and it's enough for me. I spin, break his arm off me wrist with me forearm, stamp on his instep, elbow-smash his chin, and that's it. He's on his back and takes no further interest in anything."

"Did you kill him?" said Musette.

"'Course I didn't kill him," said Billy. "I'm a professional. I don't believe in doing more than's necessary."

He looked genuinely shocked.

"All right, then," he went on. "Here I am, walking away, minding me business, and thinking I'd better get out, when six of them come for me. With their night-sticks. Well, that is a challenge. I move away, S-bending so they stumble in each others' path. I spin outside the outer one and side-kick his knee in. That crumples him up. Catch the ear of the next chap coming for me. Pull him towards me. Turn and kick his jaw in as he goes past. And then — one motion — a spin and a back-kick with the same foot into the groin of the one coming after him. Block a night-stick coming for me head with a wrist-block, then coil me arm round his so I swing him in front of the last one. Bend his wrist, dislocate the arm and grab the stick as it drops. Use it to smash in the head of number six as he stumbles in front of me. Nice taste of his own medicine. Three needs another kick or two to keep him down, and that's it. About thirty seconds. A perfect demonstration. I can remember every move like a film in a film-editing machine. Frame by frame."

Billy was smiling to himself now, reliving it.

"Why didn't you get away?" asked Tim.

"Because, Tim me lad, you can't argue with three guns," said Billy. "I'll take on two, if I have to. Use the karate shout to nerve-freeze 'em, win a split second, and kick the weapons out of their hands. It's very risky, but it's possible. But not three. And they had three on me."

"You were lucky not to be shot," said Ray. "Give the Cambridge cops some credit."

"At the time," said Billy, "there was me thinking I might have done better to be shot, and get it over with. What they did to me in that wagon, once the doors was shut, doesn't bear telling about. It was a month before I walked again. Only thing that kept me going was contempt. Their techniques are so crude you'd think you were in a playground. But contempt, that's a powerful thing. Gives you strength to go on."

The veins were swelling in his neck, and his face had flushed red.

"But Billy," said Tim, "didn't you explain to the judge what had happened?"

The karate expert broke into laughter, his face relaxing, and he patted Tim on the back with great affection.

"Little 'un, little 'un," he said. "You're a treat. A treat. Do you really think that any English court would believe a word I said, and me with me Belfast accent, even if I do live in Oxford? And no friends to back me up? And the police all lying through their teeth and covering for each other, as they're trained to do? I'll say this for the smarter judges, though — they know the police are liars in court. But what can they do? If they don't accept what the police say, the whole system collapses, doesn't it?"

He was still laughing.

"It makes me angry," said John.

"It made me more than angry," said Billy. "But when it was over and the judge had sentenced me, I felt crushed. Like someone had taken a pen and drawn a line through my life. Like someone had said to me, that's three years you're dead. Three years you don't exist."

"Is that what prison's really like?" said Musette. "I can't bear to think of it."

"Not in the least," said Billy, laughing again. "Prison's great fun. Just so long as you're on the right side. There was me, on me first day in, shuffling along by the counter hatch to get me meal, face like a ghost I'm told, and a voice says to me, cheery-like, 'Oxford, aren't you, mate?' 'Yes,' I says, 'and so what?' 'Oxford rules here,' he says, giving me a wink, 'and to begin with, that's double helpings for you. That's what.'

"Gangs, me little 'uns, that's who rule the insides of prisons, whoever may rule the outsides. And the Oxford gang ruled Reading. So I'd landed on me feet. I was on top, from day one on. Got what I wanted, did what I wanted — everything except get out."

"I thought the warders were in charge," said Tim.

"If the screws want a quiet life," said Billy, "and some nice pickings — and have you ever met a screw as didn't want pickings? — we give 'em both. They leave the gang alone. We run the prison for them. Everyone is happy. Only dangerous time is when the gang leaders have done their time. Then there's a war, with the other gangs trying for the top spot. That's when people get killed — sometimes. Towards the end of my time, Oxford was running down, losing its hard men, see. It didn't take too much to see the Jamaicans getting ready for the big push. They're a fierce mob — like old Ray here — but they didn't move till Billy — that's me — was out and away. Then — biff! — it was over in a day and done with."

"Did anyone get killed?" said Tim.

"Not that time," said Billy. "But that was more luck than good judgement."

He leant back and munched on a half-chewed honey-twig.

"Stay out of those places, me little 'uns," he added. "Only fools get caught. Or people like me, people with a sense of justice and no control of their tempers."

SOME HOURS LATER the sun was sinking.

The smell of fish, cooking, spread from the two cooking-fires as Billy and Ray turned them slowly on their sticks.

The others were sitting and, with one exception, doing what they had been doing all day, and the day before, and the day before that. Pretending they weren't there.

The fire-trails, however, had been re-laid.

John was also sitting now, with Murgatroyd beside him, and licking the salt taste from the sweat around his lips. His shirt still clung to him, wet. He flexed his back muscles and shoulders from time to time to stop getting cold. It had been hard work.

Long clouds hung above the hills inland. The indigo-blue hills. There were clouds of many shapes and textures. Clouds like moving grained wood and like moving cross-bedded sandstone. Like turtles and soft ungainly animals. Like fish-lizards and poodles. Clouds like castles rising above other clouds, some deep-shadowed and some shining. Clouds pointed upwards like white stalagmites, and clouds like dark jellyfish trailing tentacles of rain.

The weather was changing.

After a time John gently pulled his sweater from under the cat, and tugged it on over his head. The cat stretched stiffly as if he had intending to get up. Then he sat down on his haunches once more.

"They are coming closer," he said after some minutes. "I can see the crests on their heads."

"Time for stage one yet?" said John. "We don't want a false alarm."

Murgatroyd focussed his eyes on the distance.

"Can't be sure," he said. "But my best guess is that they are making for us."

"Right, then," said John.

He stood up, clenched his fists slowly, then let them relax.

"Let's get the others inside."

He took the hardest first. Ann Fellows was talking with Caleb Yonder and his wife, sitting on a palm-fern trunk not far away. Something about the policy of the Conservative Party towards small businesses. When John came up, they paid no attention to him. He waited a moment or two, then interrupted them.

"Miss Fellows," he said, "and Mr and Mrs Yonder, we are being approached by six ceratosaurs, extremely dangerous animals. I have to trouble you to make your way inside the Time-Traveller, please, at once."

Caleb Yonder bristled.

"I don't see anything," he said. "I am not in the mood for...."

"At once, if you don't mind," said John. "I have to move on now to tell the others."

There was a flat authority in his voice. After a moment, Caleb found, for reasons that he could never explain to himself afterwards, doing what he had been told. All he could remember was that stray cat looking at him with an odd expression in its eyes. The others followed after him.

Harry Milman was next. John was gentler with him.

"Harry," he said, "do us a favour, old friend. There is danger approaching, and you'll be better off inside. Could you make your way to the Time-Traveller, please."

The old bartender folded up his newpaper nervously.

"What is it, John?" he said. "I was just in the middle of this article."

"I've no time to explain, Harry," said John. "Behemoth, perhaps."

Harry smiled.

"I have sat here," he said, "and seen Leviathan. Seen him with my own eyes, sporting in the waters, as it says in the writings. You understand these things, so it is always a delight to talk with you. Now you say Behemoth...."

"Harry, please."

The old man sighed, and rose to his feet.

"We can talk about it later," said John. "But I have to move on quickly."

"Is it really safer in that wooden box?" said Harry.

"A little," said John. "But the other reason is that you have to give us room to manœuvre. It is going to be very dangerous outside."

Harry nodded.

"I understand," he said.

John smiled as he watched him walking, a little awkwardly, up the slope. The others laughed at Harry, but John did not. It was not for nothing that the old hero could draw on three thousand years, or more, of experience of survival.

He found Seb Amplemain writing a poem, sitting on a stone overlooking the estuary, and determined not to be interrupted. John looked over his shoulder and read from the flowery scrawl

What is
is not
what is.
Rich turbulence of other suns forfends
the god-like artifice
— displays
peacock laboratories, heart-cold experiment
till we, mere mice, yield up
our lives — statistic blood
a dud run set aside
— skilled scalpel-fingers fumbling, selves mis-cut
a millimetre wide
whatever truth was sought
mislaid
forgot

"Seb," he said, "you can write that stuff just as well indoors."

The poet gave an arrogant toss of his yellow hair and stared at John. He had a swollen, unpleasant face.

"You know nothing about it," he said. "Move off."

"If you ever want to write any more poetry," said John, "get into the Time-Traveller at a brisk walking pace. Now. There is danger approaching. Lethal danger. Ceratosaurs, if you want to know. They're not electric toys from Hong Kong either. There's no second warning. Make your own mind up."

He walked away, with Murgatroyd at his heels.

Seb looked at John's back with pride-wounded rage. The jumped-up little skunk.... His mouth opened and shut without his saying anything. Then his cowardice got the better of him, as John had known it would, and he began to walk up the hill, rather too hastily, stubbing his pointed Italian shoes on the rocks and ashamed of himself for being so nervous.

John glanced towards the Kauri pines, and began to move slightly faster.

Elaine Quainton was scratching a portrait of Louella Swarf on a slab of thin slate using a piece of flint. It was rather beautiful, catching something in Louella that was there but difficult to see.

"Ladies, excuse me," said John, "but would you be so kind as to join Miss Fellows and the others in the Time-Traveller to wait out the period of approaching danger. We have a ceratosaur problem."

"Is this a request from Miss Fellows?" said Louella.

"In effect, it is," said John. "And I am sure she would wish me to convey to you something of the sense of urgency that she feels about the matter. Once the danger is past, everyone will be free to resume their work."

"Since it seems to be Ann's wish, I am sure we should go at once," said Elaine. "Thank you, John, for coming to tell us."

"A pleasure," said John. "If you will excuse me, I have to move on quickly."

"We quite understand," said Elaine.

She wrapped her silk neck-scarf around the slate.

"It's a beautiful portrait," said John.

"An interesting new medium," said Elaine. "One has to salvage something from the wreckage, or they get too arrogant."

She looked at John and began to draw him in her mind, her right hand moving in slight sketching strokes as she did so. The line would bend this way to catch the bend in the collar. It would come out like that for the sag caused by the two open buttons at the top. His weight was on his left foot as he stood, looking back at her. So the fabric pressing a little tighter on that side. The light curving along the forearm and up the cheek. It was unusual to draw with light, not shading.

Then she saw he was anxious.

"Don't worry," she said. "We'll be coming shortly."

John nodded.

"Thank you, Miss Quainton," he answered, and glanced round for the cat, who was sitting on a rock ahead, a little impatiently.

"Excuse me," he said again.

"You're getting to be quite a diplomat," muttered Murgatroyd to John, once they were out of earshot. "Misleading people without quite telling lies."

"Sorry," said John. "I didn't know what else to do."

"Don't apologize," said the cat sharply. "I'm full of grown-up admiration."

John pursed his lips and looked around, up and down the small hill.

"So far as I can see," he said, "Gus is already in the Time-Traveller, with Mrs Dalrymple. Same for the Shahs, I think. Apart from Billy and Ray, and us of course, no one's been going very far from base. That just leaves the Berrigans, then, and Tim and Musette. Billy and Ray are cooking. We'd better get the three reserve fires going now, Murg, please, so we have some of the big branches burning."

The cat nodded. There was a hiss and a spluttering, and then in three different places flames leapt into the air from three piles of branches stuffed with dried ferns.

"What's up, John?" Ken asked as John approached. "Seems like everyone's getting into the Time-Traveller. We going home or something? And why the extra fires?"

"Not home yet, I'm afraid," said John. "We've got six ceratosaurs moving in on us, and the only safe place for you and Elsie, and Tim and Musette, is inside. Could I trouble you to get in please."

The history teacher looked down at the thirteen-year-old.

"Are you trying to give me orders, lad?" he said.

"It looks as if we are going to be attacked," said John, "by half-a-dozen ceratosaurs, each weighing about half a ton. A plan of defence has been made, and fire-trails have been laid. The idea is to deflect them over the cliff. It may not work, but that's our only chance. This plan requires that you, and Mrs Berrigan, and Tim and Musette, too, are inside and, as far as possible, out of the way. So, no, I'm not giving you orders. I'm telling you what has to be done, and asking you to do it, please. We don't have much time."

Ken swallowed and said nothing. Murgatroyd fixed his green eyes on the man's face. Then Elsie took him by the arm.

"Come along, Ken," she said, "don't let's make trouble."

"Amusement arcade stuff," said her husband irritably. "I don't know why we have to put up with it."

But he went with her, climbing slowly up the shrug-shouldered slabs of granite.

"What about us?" said Musette. "Do we really have to go? It's horrible inside the Time-Traveller. It stinks of fish and sweat and unhappy people."

"Musette," said John, "listen, please. It's like not having non-players on the football field. We have to avoid confusion. Just try to help me. It won't last long."

"But it's not real," said Tim. "You don't think they'd actually let us get hurt, do you? John, you're on a trip. All this rushing around and being practical and playing at being in charge. It's make-believe, and it's getting irritating. I am quite a lot older than you, you know."

"Look down *there*," said John. His voice was like a spade digging hard into gravel.

The small pack of ceratosaurs were less than four hundred metres off. They were crossing the broken ground where the last big ferns ended. Their pace was slow, but they were coming straight for the rise on which the Time-Traveller stood.

"People are going to need to eat," said John, "whether that lot are real or cuddly rubber look-alikes. Please, if you would, get the fish off Billy and Ray and take them into the Time-Traveller where everyone else is. Wrap them in glossopteris leaves, if there are any left up there. Musette, could you give him a hand?"

"At least that's being useful," said Musette, her hazel-green eyes flashing. "Come on, Tim."

Murgatroyd rubbed himself against Tim's leg, and the boy gave a sudden shudder.

"OK," he said. "I'll do what I can."

Left alone with the cat, John studied the scene below. His eyes narrowed to lines.

"Except for us," he said, "everyone's inside the inner ring. So — let's have the inner fires on, please, but low — so as to save fuel. And leave a small gap for us to get in and out of."

The cat nodded, and yet more smoke began to encircle the Traveller. A dark haze from the leaves, as they spurted and flared, swirled up in the off-sea wind and blew across its windows and over the curved carriage roof.

"Last step before it starts," said John. "Let's talk to Billy and Ray."

The karate experts watched him and Murgatroyd climbing up to the small plateau where the cooking fires were burning.

"I don't make out that cat," said Billy. "I never have. It seems to have a mind of its own."

"John says it lives with him and his brother," said Ray. "He never calls it 'his' cat. Never. It lives *with* them. That's all. Seems its name's Murgatroyd."

"It sits on his shoulders when he walks on the beach most days," said Billy. 'And remember, it sat watching us all the time we were building the fish-trap."

Ray nodded.

"I think there's something special 'bout that cat," he agreed. " And look how powerful he's built. But what's special — I can't tell you. It's just a feeling. Just a feeling."

"Well, John," said Billy. "You're panting. What's it all about? You going to ask us to go inside?"

John shook his head, and waited till he had his breath back. Then he looked at them, hard and steadily.

"You and I, gentlemen," he said, "are the ones who stay outside. The ones who make it happen. Unless you disagree. — I find it hard to imagine that you do."

He pointed down the slope.

The six ceratosaurs were clearly visible now, not much more than two hundred metres away.

Ray nodded.

"That's not a fight we can run away from," he said in a cold voice. "Even if it doesn't look too much like one we can win."

He drew a deep breath.

"So it's real, John, isn't it?," he added. "After all. And you were right. All along. Who'd have thought so? Who?"

"Gojuryu takes on the dinosaurs," said Billy, softly, a light shining in his pale Irish eyes. "And me life has a meaning at last. I wonder if any of them old Okinawa masters who fashioned our Hard-Soft School, learning to use their hands to smash through the armour of the knights of Satsuma, could ever have imagined the final end their mastery'd be put to. We shall do them honour, Ray, even if no one lives to remember us."

"Karate is the last resort," said John. "Please. Not the first. The basic plan is to use fire to stampede them over the cliff-top. They come in through the planned point. The gap down there. See? That's my job. And then we drive them with burning branches up that line to the right there. See, between the mounds of branches? They'll be burning soon. Then we swing them back, round the seaward side of the old Traveller, and, with any luck, over the cliff at the top. That's your job. Clear?"

"Clear enough," said Billy. "But the fires round the outer edges aren't burning yet. Shouldn't we be lighting them up, too?"

"Fuel is scarce," said John. "We shall wait till the ceratosaurs are at a hundred metres. Arrangements have been made. Let's hope they work."

He crossed his arms and leant on a boulder, watching. Thank heavens for the real professionals, he thought. Nerveless and practical. We might just win this one. Might. Just.

"Murg," he said softly. "The best place for you would be near the top, so you can see what's going on, and shift the fire around. There's a rock near the Traveller with an overhang not much higher than you are. Would that give you cover?"

"It should keep them from trampling on me," said the cat.

"Right," John went on, "that's your command post, then. We'll have the outer fires on when the first 'saur passes that flat white stone down there. That make sense to you?"

"You're cutting it fine," said the cat. "But — yes — I think that's acceptable."

John watched him lollop up the last short stretch of hill. Like a shadow cut loose from its object, he thought. — So, we're ready. There's nothing more to do now but wait. Of course, they might always get bored and go away.

The six carnivores were already close enough to look terrifying. He guessed two metres at least to the mouth. Two-legged. Forelegs armed with three tearing claws. Heads that were almost all jaws. Multiple rows of what looked like curved-back teeth. Like the crusher at the rear of a garbage-truck, only not rotating. He could see their eyes clearly, now, and the gold-brown double crests above them.

He watched the flat white stone down below. As the first ceratosaur passed, there was a splintering sound. Blue and yellow flames encircled the perimeter. Tearing and roaring and crackling flames. The ceratosaurs were already trapped between two lines of fire. Billy and Ray glanced at each other.

"Impressive," muttered Billy under his breath.

"Yeah, impressive," said Ray. "This guy *thinks*."

In the Time-Traveller high above, Musette pressed her face against a window. It was like watching a fireworks display. Only it was real war, not an imitation.

She watched the ceratosaurs milling about below, huge shadows against a backdrop of flames.

A hand gripped her shoulder. She knew, without looking, that it was Gus Ladd. She wasn't angry but just wished he'd keep his hands to himself.

"Don't be too impressed by it all, Musette," she heard him saying. "It's just a show. Have you ever seen a natural fire switched on like that? Of course not. They must have gas-burners under them to make them flare so evenly, and all at one and the same time."

"I'm worried about my seeds, Gus," said Musette, without moving or even looking at him. "You know, my night-flowering stock? The packet I had with me?"

"What's the worry?" said Gus. "You planted them correctly. They'll come up."

"That's what I'm worried about," said Musette. "That they will come up. Maybe there's a chance that the ceratosaurs will trample on them. I do hope so."

"Musette, what are you talking about?"

"I don't want to muck evolution up," said Musette. "As you once told me, there are no flowers in the Middle Mesozoic. So, if I've gone and started some off, it may throw evolution off course. That's what worries me. Look! Something's beginning to happen down there!"

"My dear, sweet girl," said Gus, "this is not the Mesozoic. I thought I'd explained that. It can't be. Can't. Can't. Can't. You are looking at some sort of simulation."

"It's just as real as all the funny fish the boys catch in the fish-trap," said Musette. "How many extinct species do you have to see before you believe your own eyes? What's the problem?"

"Logic," said Gus. "Just logic. This doesn't exist."

Billy and Ray and John had armed themselves with heavy branches spewing flames and smokes from their leafy ends. They waited some way back . The ceratosaurs were hesitating, uncertain which way to go.

If they don't get moving soon, thought John, our fuel will run out, and if they attack again, then we're done for.

"Wait here," he said to Billy and Ray. "I'm going to give them some encouragement."

The two karate experts watched in disbelief as John edged out and round to the back of the second largest ceratosaur. This was cold courage at the limits of the possible. They saw him drive the burning branch at a low angle upwards, in behind its tail. The beast towered over him, almost half again his height. Then it gave a low gurgling roar, like the bass-pipes of a church organ filled with blood, and rushed into the rear of the ceratosaur ahead.

The group began to move up the trail. All but one, the largest, which stayed put.

Billy and Ray fended off the group from one side, guiding them up. John edged back to keep control of the last ceratosaur. So far his master-plan was working, but this one was a problem.

He watched with quick glances from the corner of his eye as his friends worked the herd up past the Time-Traveller. He knew they must be within a metre or two of Murgatroyd, secure — he hoped — in his granite bunker. Whirling light danced from the burning branches like the twisting streamers from a many-armed Indian goddess, dancing a dance of magical destruction. Another Murg touch.

The last ceratosaur, however, the one now facing him, seemed to be watching too, waiting to see what happened. Neither retreating or advancing. He had the uncomfortable impression of intelligence. Of thought behind those eyes. How much experience, he wondered, did such a dinosaur have of fire? Maybe it was not as frightened of it as he had reckoned it would be? Or, could it learn?

The night was beginning to fall. The circles of fire seemed brighter by the minute, and the dark shape stranger and more menacing. He kept his burning branch levelled in front of him. So far it seemed to be effective. After ten or fifteen minutes, though, he knew he would have to retreat to pick up a replacement.

A cry like the tearing apart of the world came from the beach at his back. It was a cry so hideous, so pitiful, and so unrestrained that nothing he had ever heard resembled or approached it. He did not need to be told what it was. It was the death-cry of the first ceratosaur driven over the top of the cliff, mortally wounded but not yet dead. Death would come soon.

Another cry cut through the night. Agonized bellowing echoed and re-echoed from the cliffs, drowning the roaring of the sea. Then another cry, and another and another.

Billy and Ray had done their job. Five were over. A repulsive, necessary job.

Then a thin and hysterical human screaming came from the Time-Traveller. He checked, with flickering sideways glances, that nothing was wrong. Indeed, the fires were dying down to red embers. The carriage looked untouched. Ugh, he thought contemptuously, trust them to start screaming when the danger's already gone.

Or almost.

It was at that moment that the last ceratosaur gave an answering roar and charged at him.

John wheeled, gripping his flaming branch, and turned it as it passed. But it spun, and came back from a new angle much faster than he had expected. Again he turned it, this time the other way. But his arms were hurting already. Its power was such that even a glancing blow was the limit of what he could take.

A third time it charged, but two other blazing branches, driven in hard, deflected it this time. Billy and Ray were down to help. They must have run hard to make it, he thought. The battle was turning their way.

But the last ceratosaur would not be driven uphill. Instead, it made straight for Billy, and ripped his branch away in his jaws. Billy leapt aside to avoid the danger.

As he leapt, another cry arose, a sound so chilling and so cruel that for a second John felt himself freeze. It was the *kiai*, the shout with which, so it was said, the Japanese warriors knocked birds out of the sky. John saw Ray rise into the air, and rise, as if lifted by magic. He saw the sword-hand drive into the dinosaur's eye and blind it, even as Billy stumbled, a gash along his side.

John moved to cover Billy.

"Get a new branch, if you can," he said. "We're covering you."

Billy rolled to his feet, his hands in guard.

"Keep the brute there," he gasped.

The dinosaur lunged again. John blocked it, but as the jaws came down, and the teeth tore through flaming foliage, Ray rose in the air once more. As he rose he smashed out a flying kick. It broke the ceratosaur's jawbone, and sent the bite skewing sideways.

With one eye gone, and in pain from its twisted mouth, the beast was even more dangerous than before.

Two of their three fire-branches were out, or almost, no more than smouldering twigs on an unburnt trunk. Only John's still flared with a usable flame. He positioned himself between the ceratosaur and his friends, who were stumbling back to the fires where the replacement branches were. He would need to hold for a couple or minutes, he reckoned. He wondered if he had the strength left. He steadied his elbows on his stomach, and watched for the next charge.

He was, for the moment, on his own.

The ceratosaur snapped and bit at his branch. John danced backwards, weaving and jabbing. It snapped again. No doubt about it, the brute could think. He could manage a minute more. A minute and a half perhaps. The pain in his arms was almost too much to endure. And the flames were low. Without fuel to work with even the cat could do little. And where was the cat? Did he realize he was needed?

The ceratosaur came in for the kill. Straight in, and ignoring the flames. Then, as it charged, he heard the thunder of footbeats, and glimpsed the whirl of a four-pronged flame above the ceratosaur's head. For a moment he saw, or he dreamed that he saw, an incredible sight. Charles riding his stegosaur, high on its neck, and the stegosaur twirling and swinging its four-pronged tail like a ballet dancer that slashed, then skewered, the ceratosaur's throat.

After which everything vanished.

He was there, wide awake and in pain, but his will unbroken, still gripping a smouldering branch. He could hear the tide lapping, out there in the dark on the mudflats. He could feel a cool breeze running over his face. He had neither won nor lost, merely suddenly been forgotten.

The ground in front of him was churned to a muddy filth. The circles of periphery fires were still burning around the Time-Traveller, the inner one just a dark red halo of embers. But the ceratosaur had vanished. And of Charles, and of Steg, there was no sign.

Three flaming branches, a forest on fire, were coming down the hill. Reinforcements, but now no longer needed.

"Where's he gone?" said Billy, panting. "Look, we brought you a fresh branch, too, but it doesn't look you'll need it. Did he run? Where's he gone?"

John put down his branch, to give his arms a rest.

"You won't believe what happened," he said. "I don't believe it either. All I can say is that what seemed to happen was this. He came in for the last charge, for the kill, unafraid of the flames — the ceratosaurus, that is. And then — then ... Charles came. *From nowhere.* Riding high on that steg of his. Steg struck through the brute's throat with its spiked tail. Then all three of them vanished. It took hardly five seconds. Less."

Ray said nothing. He stalked up and down the muddy ground, with his branch held over his head to give a light.

"I don't know what a stegosaur's hooves look like," he said, "but there are two sets of different prints here. The long, almost bird-like ones, are ceratosaur marks, that's for sure. So it could be that what you saw happen, did happen. I don't know 'bout the disappearance, though."

Billy propped his fire-branch, still blazing, against a rock. Then he sat down wearily on the ground, and pulled off his shirt over his head by gripping the collar with his right hand. He wrapped the shirt round his left upper arm to stop the blood spurting out.

"Gojuryu boys won," he said. "That's all that matters. It was Ray, of course, not me. But we won. We didn't let our masters down."

"Even so," said John, "you're going to need penicillin to stop that wound turning poisonous. I wonder if there's any way of finding some."

IT WAS MORE than a day later.

The Time-Traveller was moving through time again, driven by the power of Charles's mind. A soft blue light flowed out of everything in the carriage, and the carriage itself, a light not from the outside but from the inside. The denser the material, the brighter it was. The heads of the iron nails shone like jewels in the wood of the seats. In the windows and doors the glass was dark, but the metal frames and steel handles gleamed. So did the floor underfoot. And the bones in people's skulls, and in their fingers, gave a blurred glow through the dimmer flesh around them, like X-ray photographs reversed.

Gold rings were most brilliant of all. When Mrs Dalrymple moved her hands, several blue diamonds flashed. And Charles's windbreaker, crumpled up on the seat beside him, was a swirling wave of blue foam.

They'd seen nothing like this on the journey out, and John guessed it was a bow-wave, the effect of speeding fast-forward through time. It made people's faces seem weird, like expressions floating on bowls of illuminated water.

He stood with his back to the control panel, where Ellen — alas! — had stood on the way out. This was real life, with no happy endings. He surveyed the other passengers. Ordinary people — not in the least ordinary. Caleb Yonder's mouth was set in grim determination. He was clearly intent on vengeance — just as soon as he got back. But Helen, his wife, was asleep, her head on his shoulder, the look on her face like that of a forgotten rag-doll.

Ann Fellows was talking to Elaine. Her lips seemed to twist like water-snakes, with a life of their own. And Elaine kept nodding in reply, but without saying anything. More vengeance, he thought.

Ken's face was sunk in his hands. He no longer believes in his history, John mused. He knows, now, it's no more than a ripple lost in the ocean of time. Elsie, beside him, was stitching intently in something tiny. Her face showed no feeling. She, too, he thought, is finding a way to keep the world out.

No one seemed happy. And no one, he reflected, had thanked him for what he had done. Or even mentioned it.

He shrugged. If that was the way it was, then that was the way it was.

He no longer had to be told that he was only an adult now. A once-whole person whose child-half had vanished from him. No matter how young he looked. No matter how instantly he could charm Elaine with his dimples and long lashes, and a toss of his hair. He was a grown-up.

He was not enjoying the experience. The sooner he could become at least partly a child again, the sooner he could dream again, the sooner he could talk to Bear again, the better. He wondered how his other half was living, his child-half, entangled in the emprisoning sweetness of the television world. Somewhere in Oxford — he didn't even know where. A self with everything provided for, nothing to worry about. Without this thankless responsibility for other people....

He found it hard to imagine that his two split selves had anything in common with each other any longer.

Only Musette had a smile on her face, he thought. She looked like an angel lying there asleep, on the seat in the next row, her hands closed round her ceratosaur crest.

Ray's flying kick had knocked it loose, and John, fossicking about in the mud after footprints, had found it later. The two of them had agreed at once to give it to Musette. In case, Ray had said, with one of his rare grins, "anyone dare make fun of her and say she's crazy 'cause she tells them she's been on a time-journey. Then they gotta explain *that*." And he'd jabbed his finger down.

Only Musette, so far as John knew, had even watched everything that had happened.

The crest was a weird thing, of hollow, bird-like, bone. In daylight it was brown and gold, but now only a dim blue, lying there like a shadow between her brighter fingers.

Billy had a fever. The sweat-drops moved down his face like dark spots. He shook from time to time. Ray had his arm round his shoulder, to steady the shaking, and kept saying things to make him laugh. And Billy kept trying to laugh. But John knew, and he knew Billy knew, it was going to be a race to get him to a hospital before the infection from the wound killed him.

Gus's face was wry and puzzled. The curving wrinkles on his forehead rose and fell in exasperation. John knew he was trying to make sense of things, and for a moment he wanted to sit down beside him and just tell him the truth. Gus was an honest man, an everyday sort of scientist. But it would have been too dangerous. If Gus had learned what Charles was doing, his mind might have broken.

Best let him go on thinking the whole adventure was mischief on the part of the Mackenzie brothers, or the government, or a Japanese television company.

Silence was the price of everyone's survival. More unwanted adult wisdom.

He remembered what his brother had said to him:

"I never meant to disappear. I didn't even know I knew how to, when we left the gold-panning creek to come to help. But when that ceratosaur turned back to attack Steg, my heroic Steg, who was struggling to drag his prongs out of the brute's neck, and I saw those jaws, and that one terrifying eye — my God, Ray must be a hero to have taken that thing on with his bare hands — I was filled with such a desire for us to be somewhen else that — *we found we were*, with the monster still attached to us. I've no idea when it was. A few years earlier, I think. So I mind-flashed a message to Steg: *Get clear for half a second, that's enough, and I can wrench us free.* So he twisted round like a top, flinging the brute to one side, and the prongs came out, and I had my half-second. Enough! Enough to skip to somewhen else again. To leave the ceratosaur behind, marooned, and, I hope, to die. But it was also a moment of fantastic elation, because I knew then that we could do it whenever we wanted to."

"'We'?" John had said.

He remembered the strange look in Charles's eyes just then, and what he had said next:

"John, I think I have had my life already. To you it seemed less than an hour, I'd guess, before I came back, and I came back alone. But where and when do you think I had been in that hour? Time-travelling with Steg, and by my reckoning for about a year. We went through the Mesozoic everywhen, and then a long way earlier. There are no sign-posts up telling you when you are. We have seen everything — the slow amphibians with sails on their backs like Chinese junks, whole herds of Triceratops thundering over the prairies, the earliest birds and sweet-smelling flowers, and the first leaves that fall in the autumn. There is only one rule. You can never be a second time when and where you were before, or even too close to that point. We tried, and you can't.

"We became unafraid. As long as we kept our wits sharp, and acted fast, there was always time to escape into. We were not, like everything else, imprisoned like insects in the glass wall of the present. You people seem to us now like pressed flowers, flat between pages of newsprint, yesterday's edition and tomorrow's, or like Chinese paper cuts, sculptured from nothing. Without any substance, thin almost to the point where you don't exist. I'm sorry, but that's how it is."

"How did you say goodbye to Steg?" John had asked. "I'm happy for us you came back, but it must have been an unbearable parting."

"There was no goodbye," Charles had said. "No goodbye as you usually understand it.

"Steg and I lived in each other's mind for a year. Don't be surprised if I tell you he learned the art of moving through time from me. He can do it now for himself. He only likes to use it gently, for a few years, or a century here and there. He is not consumed, as I am, with the desire for endless horizons and for what is, forever, futher on. Or further back. What he knows how to do is how to look at things, to see all the details that I miss. A few metres along a forest path can keep him happy for an afternoon.

"So it was not goodbye. When two minds can both travel in time, then, John, they can both be with each other all the time. I don't know how to ex - plain it, but we have never had to say goodbye. And even when we have both passed away, we never will. Sounds unbelievable, I know, but there it is."

John continued to look down the carriage, lit with its strange blue light, and these words still in his memory.

He saw Harry studying his watch. Then he saw him nod, and heard him begin to hum. In the silence the words were easy enough to hear:

Shema' 'Isra'el, 'Adonai 'Eloheinu....

So was a new day beginning, or something, in Harry's calculations? It was a weird world, and the people in it even weirder. He hummed the end of the phrase with Harry, to keep him company:

... *'Adonai 'ekadh.*[3]

Then he looked across at Charles, whose eyes were half-closed in concentration. He certainly seemed a year older, almost John's own age in fact.

"What's happened to your windbreaker?" he said. "It weighs a ton. And it shines."

Charles opened his eyes and smiled.

"Packed with gold-dust," he answered. "Mesozoic gold. Unique in the universe."

---

[3] "Hear, O Isra'el ! The Lord our God is the one God."

• label land

"TRANS-TIME VELOCITY approaching the standard rate of happening," said Charles. "*S* plus five, *S* plus four, *S* plus three...."

Sunlight and shadow began to flicker. Dazzle and shadow stabbed at their eyes.

John, at the back of the carriage, braced himself for that moment, already so familiar, when the flickering would stop, the blue light vanish, and the heartbeat of day and night take up its rhythm again. His mind went back to their flight from Oxford. A few seconds after Ann Fellows had left, stepping out angrily onto the platform, Murgatroyd had whispered: "The only safety is in the future. *They* are still there. Quick!"

Charles had jerked the three of them away. Even before the glass doors had shut. Yes — it had been Megan and the other Murgatroyd, glancing back at them. And the lurching wooden puppet, its hand on its stomach. Jerked them away —

— into a time when, from the Oxford point of view, nothing had happened yet.

The world they'd lived in disappeared in that moment's thought. Harry, Musette and Tim, Billy and Ray, Gus, Ken and Elsie, the Yonders, Elaine and Louella, the Shahs, Seb, Ann, Mrs Dalrymple — and Ellen, of course. They'd gone as if they had never existed. A sense of loneliness had come over Charles from that time on, a loneliness without an end, or any meaning. He realized that he had been indescribably fond of them. Perhaps because he had fought so hard for them.

Gone. Like melted snow. Like dead blossoms. Yesterday's wind.

And now the three of them had spent what seemed like another life-time among the broken islands of time-space — all that seemed to be left of the future, why they had no idea — wondering where to stop. Changing their minds. Going on. Going on again. Leaving behind them oceans shrunken to muddy runnels at the bottom of dried-out shadow-filled canyons. Dead cities encrusted like collars miles high up along the ancient coastlines. Metal bubbles the size of small moons, with millions of windows glowing light, trapped like fish in floating wire-mesh nets far above the Earth's surface, feeding them with power from the Sun, detecting the signals from the universe around them. Fragmented, unsustainable, meaningless.

So why here? What had persuaded Charles to stop here?

As always, it happened before he was ready for it.

THE CARRIAGE lay at rest. Above them an unmoving sun shone down. No trace of their journey remained. It was as if they had always been where they were, drifting down the current of the present moment, trapped in the same unchanging spider-web coordinates of space and time.

A dusty-green field of unripe wheat could be seen through the windows. Its stalks were swaying in the wind. The bristly ears were brushing against the glass. Their sound, the first outside sound from this new time-world, was a faint and squeaky whispering. Then the heat of a summer day began to filter through the walls, stirring the wood-molecules in the wooden panels, and warming them with a new energy of internal vibration.

Charles had slumped across a bench at the front. He needed to recover. The outpouring of mind-power needed to travel across so much time had exhausted him. John glanced around impatiently. How soon would his brother be strong enough for them to venture out together?

He noticed something.

A shadow had fallen across the polished brass runner that gleamed on the back of a bench. He tensed. Was there someone else in the carriage besides the three of them? Someone who had not got off at Oxford? Or someone who, a moment ago, had not been there?

Behind the shadow something stirred and turned. A pair of eyes appeared. John gazed into them and found it was the face — of all people — the face of Bear! The dreamguard looked rumpled and sleepy, as well as surprised. But that slow, gentle smile could only be his. Ripples of sunlight, reflected from the wheat, ran over his brown fur, but the medal that gleamed from his chest had a steady light, deeper than the sun's. He was who he seemed to be. But how had he entered real life?

"Bear," said John, putting his hands round one of Bear's paws, "this isn't a dream. How have you managed to get here?"

"This is one of the handful of futures in which I am real," said Bear. "The probability of it happening is lost to sight at the end of a string of countless zeros behind the decimal point. Yet — here I am. So much for probability."

John was still looking at him in happy disbelief.

"Your magic powers? Do you still have them?"

Bear scratched his head with the other paw.

"Some of them," he said. "Not all. Don't count on anything. But who knows what I could do if I were really up against it! Even in this place-time, where I feel I'm a stranger to myself. I'm still an Official Dreamguard, once and forever, remember. We have our standards."

He peered through the window.

"Seems a tame enough countryside," he observed. "Why don't we take a stroll? Even make a friend or two?"

"Charles," said John, "are you coming?"

His brother shook his head.

"Need to recover some more," he muttered. "See you both later. I seem to be still dreaming."

Bear slid back the carriage door and stepped with a crunch into the wheat. John jumped down beside him and filled his lungs with the air.

"Good to be free again," he said. "Time is a prison, however fast you move through it."

Bear nodded and looked thoughtfully about him.

"It's incredible," said John, "having you with me like this."

"Yes," said the dreamguard, "but I like it this way too. Odd place."

He continued to look about him. Then he said:

"*Very* odd."

"What's odd?"

John could see nothing unusual. The sky was an almost painted blue. Neat white clouds were drifting over the hills. What seemed to be a road wound away in the distance towards a grove of poplars.

"Look at a stalk of this wheat," said Bear. "Any stalk."

He broke one off and handed it to John.

John stared at it and turned it over.

Seems like plain wheat to me," he said.

"Look at it more closely. At the stem just below the ear."

The boy held the tubular stalk to his eye and squinted along it. He saw why Bear had been surprised.

A tiny transparent label had been stuck there. It was printed in microscopic type, and said: '*Semi-ripe wheat*'.

"*Semi*-ripe?!"

"Semi-ripe," said Bear. "Do you see what that means?"

John raised his eyebrows.

"Re-labelling each stalk when it ripens?"

"Not only that. It means first labelling each seed. Then each sprout. And picking off the old label each time. It's quite, quite crazy."

"Your eyes are sharp," said John. "I would never have spotted it."

"There's a label on every stalk of wheat I've looked at," said Bear. "It's neither an accident, nor a joke."

He dropped onto all fours and nosed about among the roots, then scooped up something delicately on a claw.

"I thought as much," he observed, standing upright again.

John examined the upturned cup of Bear's paw. Between two of the pads was nestled a minute clod of soil, with fragments of hairy roots. Stuck into the clod on a pin was a tiny flag. It said: *'Light arable loam. Low acidity. Grade C2'*.

Bear tossed it aside and it caught on the awn of a wheat-ear, glinting like an insect. He groped under his zippered armpit. Out came a steamer rug checkered in red and green and brown and white, which he spread on a patch of crushed wheat. Then he produced a white cardboard flag the size of a postcard and mounted on a long steel needle. He thrust this through a corner of the rug. The lettering was sharply engraved — black copperplate — and said:

'COMFORTABLE STEAMER RUG FOR HUMANS AND
BEARS. GRADE A'.

Hanging from this card on two strands of thread was a smaller card that read:

'LABEL FOR A COMFORTABLE STEAMER RUG FOR HUMANS
AND BEARS. GRADE A'.

Dangling from this second card on a single thread was a scrap of triangular paper which said, in letters almost unreadably small:

'LABEL FOR A LABEL FOR A COMFORTABLE STEAMER RUG FOR HUMANS
AND BEARS. GRADE A'.

John broke into laughter and Bear chuckled too.

"When in Rome," said Bear, "do one better than the Romans do. Sit down. Let us have a swig of some hot unlabelled coffee. This needs thinking over before we stir any further."

He produced an orange plastic thermos and two grey stoneware mugs. The coffee aroma was reassuring to sniff, so they sipped slowly and watched the steam drift off over the wheat and lose itself in the warm air of the late morning.

"Steam," mused John. "There's no way of labelling steam. So what do they do about the clouds? Or the wind for that matter?"

"We can soon find out," said Bear. He took out some American Army Surplus binoculars from his zip and peered at the four little clouds that hung over the hills, twiddling the focussing wheel until the image was exact. Then, without saying a word, he handed them to John, who looked in his turn.

"'CUMULUS'," he muttered. "One on each one. How in the name of real life do they manage that?"

"Projectors," said Bear. "Very powerful projectors indeed. Probably each labelled 'VERY POWERFUL PROJECTOR INDEED'. If you look really hard you'll see some transparent balloons catching the sun as they float across the fields. One of them at least has the label 'GENTLE WIND'. Your questions are answered."

He dematerialized the thermos, the mugs, and the binoculars.

"To fix all those labels," he commented, "and to keep them all up-to-date, must take every hour of working life these people have."

"*It has to,*" said a man's hard voice. "*With subversives like you around.* Get up! Both of you! Place your hands on your heads. You are under arrest."

Four more-or-less human faces were looking down at them. Four faces behind the barrels of what looked like laser-guns. The guns were pointing at their hearts.

Taken by surprise, John and Bear stood up stiffly and put their hands (or, in Bear's case, his paws) on their heads. They could see their captors properly now. They were short, stocky men (if men they were) in black uniforms. They had white plastic badges on their chests, with red letters: 'LABEL POLICE'. The one who had spoken wore an arm-flash saying 'SERGEANT'.

"This is not a very friendly way to greet visitors," said Bear.

"You are not labelled as 'VISITORS'," said the sergeant. "Therefore you are nothing of the sort. We have been observing your activities since you appeared here a few minutes ago. In that time you have committed ten major offenses against Etiquette."

"Etiquette is good manners," said John. "We've not even spoken to anyone. How can we have shown bad manners?"

"Etiquette," said the sergeant, as if he were reciting something, "is wearing the correct approved labels, acting in exact accordance with the correct approved labels, and respecting the correct approved labels of others in behaviour, speech, and thought. I will now charge you with your crimes."

He flipped back the cover of his notebook sharply to express his relish at what he was doing.

"One. — You are not wearing labels."

"Excuse me," said Bear. "I *am* wearing a label. This gold medallion on my chest describes me as an 'OFFICIAL DREAMGUARD BEAR'."

"By 'label'," the sergeant snapped, "I mean — of course — a correct approved label. We can't have everybody putting on any label that happens to catch their fancy. The label 'OFFICIAL DREAMGUARD BEAR' does not appear in the *Official List of Correct Approved Labels*, current edition as issued — under Authority — to serving members of the Label Police. Therefore— it does not exist. Neither has it been affixed by an entitled etiquette officer. Therefore — you are guilty, by your own admission, of wearing an incorrect unapproved label illegally affixed. Your friend is label-less."

"My friend," said Bear mildly, "is not label-less. He is merely modest. He wears his labels inside. Show them the name-tape on your shirt, John."

"It's inside my collar," said John, careful not to take his hands from his head.

The sergeant strutted over and turned the collar back more roughly than was necessary.

"'JOHN'," he read. "What kind of a category is that? What is a 'John'?"

"It's my personal name," said John. "There's only one of me."

"Individual names are forbidden," rasped the sergeant, and began to recite again. It was obviously something he had learned by heart.

"Only categories are permitted," he droned, "because only categories can have prescribed qualities. Without prescribed qualities, correct behaviour is impossible to define."

"No wonder you were hiding your label," he added. "Individualist labelling and failure to display are more serious offences than being label-less. I will alter the charge-sheet. Accordingly."

He scribbled self-importantly.

"Crimes two, three, and four," he continued, "relate to the mode of conveyance in which you have arrived. This object carries the label 'MACKENZIE'S TIME-TRAVELLER. 3d PER CENTURY'. This is not a correct approved label. The style of lettering is also ornate, flowery, unclear and so liable to corrupt and confuse. Finally, it is situated in a location designated 'WHEATFIELD' and not 'LANDING-STRIP'. This has caused the unauthorized destruction of several thousand stalks of wheat — the precise number to be determined at a later date — which are now incorrectly labelled, and will have to be relabelled 'CRUSHED WHEAT'. In other words, you are culpable of the creation of confusion."

"It had that name when we took it over," said John. "But what else would you call the old thing? It comes from a fairground, it belonged to two drunks called Mackenzie, and we use it to travel through time."

"Fairs are forbidden," said the sergeant. "Names there do not correspond to reality. They are breeding-grounds of illusion. But time-travel — you confirm that you said 'time-travel'?"

"Yes."

"Time-travel confuses the proper sequence of past, present, and future. It makes a nonsense of progress. It is a crime so revolting that the right to a label is withdrawn, the right to any label. Extinction is mandatory once the offence is confirmed. So! You will have to be taken to a Capital for examination by a Label-Lord."

While the sergeant had been speaking one of his officers had been looking closely at the three-part label on the steamer rug.

"I've found something even worse, Sergeant," he said. "I have the duty to report detection of subversion of Etiquette. This here is a label of a label, and the little one underneath it is a label of a label of a label."

The sergeant looked at the card with a smaller card hanging from it, and the triangular tag dangling in its turn from the smaller card. His face went mud-coloured with anger.

"Let me see!" he grunted.

He held the three labels by their rims, one after the other, as if anxious not to be contaminated. Then he turned them over.

"'BACK OF A LABEL...'," he began to read. His voice suddenly rose to a scream.

"Impound them!" he barked. "Under a 'HIGH SECURITY' label. Evidence of unutterable filth and depravity. This is not just crime. It is heresy. To be precise, it is Referentialist Regressionism. The price of progress is unceasing vigilance. As the *Handbook of Etiquette*, current approved edition, correctly informs us, the most dangerous of all forms of Anti-Labellism is Ultra-Labellism. And why, men, why? Because to side-track the heroic efforts of label-loving people into the meaningless labelling of labels is counter-labelutionary sabotage! It undermines our historic task, which is nothing less than the labelling of the entire world. It is a crime against the Glorious Future."

"It was meant to be a joke," said Bear.

"A joke? A joke! *A joke!!*" shouted the sergeant, unable to control himself. "You unnatural, anomalous, improperly labelled object, you will soon see what happens to people who make jokes. If anything is worse even than heresy, it is humour."

He spat and glowered at Bear. Then his voice became slower again, and ugly.

"I shall behold your decategorization with pleasure," he said. "Do you understand, with real pleasure? My only regret is that it will be metaphysically impossible for you to be decategorized more than once."

He consulted his noteook again.

"Further felonies of a serious nature," he went on, biting off each syllable as he said it. "Five: breaking a stalk of correctly labelled wheat without having the authorization to do so. Six: failing to report this event to the nearest Label Emergency Office. Seven: neglecting to affix a temporary label indicating 'Current Label Status Inapplicable' to both crushed and broken stalks of wheat."

"We don't have such labels to hand," said John. "We only arrived here a few minutes ago."

"You should have thought of that before you came," said the sergeant. "It is a punishable offence not to carry a reasonable supply of CLSI labels at all times. Everyone has the labelutionary duty to patch and report anomalies when and as they occur. Igorance of the correct procedures is no excuse. It is an offence. Do you confirm your confessions?"

"It can't make much difference after all the other so-called crimes we are said to have committed."

"Not *said*," snapped the sergent. "Not said. *Observed* to have committed. Do you confess to failing to carry a reasonable supply of correct and approved CLSI labels as required by the *Handbook of Etiquette*?"

"Of course," said John, shrugging.

"Good!" said the sergeant. "Cooperation will be noted as a point in your favour. The first one so far. We will now proceed with the charges. Eight: removing a correct and approved soil label without the authorization to do so. Nine: throwing away the said soil label in an unauthorized direction, thus wilfully risking labelling some other object in incorrect and unapproved fashion. Ten: having charge of, or in some respect being responsible for, an object labelled, as stated under the second head of indictment, a 'Mackenzies' Time-Traveller', this being an incorrect and unapproved designation. This item is to be given a temporary cover label and taken into custody as evidence."

Two of the Label Policemen pulled out wads of sticky labels saying in black letters on a Dayglo-orange ground 'RECLASSIFICATION PENDING'. They moved towards the carriage. Charles was, however, watching them through the window. Just above his shoulder was a second pair of eyes, green and unwinking, and set in a black whiskered face. As the officers approached, Charles smiled at them and vanished — *pouf!* — together with the carriage and Murgatroyd.

A bronze-gold globe the size of a football glinted above the wheat where they had been, and then slowly went out.

The silence of the four policemen was painful. The two officers stood there with the sticky labels flapping in their hands. Their mouths hung open. But John relaxed. He could smell again. A hot indefinable odour of moisture and sunshine was coming out of the ground. He felt reassured. The world of his senses had come back to him, like remembering a life he had almost forgotten in the mind-prison of label-talk.

"What was that?" said the sergeant, pointing to where the globe had been.

"A time-buoy," said Bear. "They left it there, so they'll be able to find us again."

"They?" said the sergeant. "They? Where did *they* go, your accomplices?"

"Into the future," said Bear, "or perhaps the past. The carriage is correctly labelled. It travels across time."

"When it appears again," said the sergeant, "we shall annihilate it. Deliberate avoidance of labelling is the only crime for which no further permission is required to disintegrate the offender."

"All world-lines end somewhen," said Bear, "and so must ours and so must yours. But, somehow, I doubt if they have travelled the oceans of night, and seen the stars be born and die, learning the minds of many peoples, simply to be snuffed out in your backyard."

"We could snuff the pair of you out right now," said the sergeant, patting his laser-gun.

"Not so," said Bear. "We are important criminals. We have to be reclassified by a Label-Lord."

The sergeant looked at him sourly. If this, he thought, was an 'ANIMAL', and that of course remained to be determined by the labelling authorities, then it had no business being able to talk, let alone to argue with him.

"My arms are hurting," said John. "May I put them down, please?"

"Pain is a privilege," said the sergeant. "The beginning of re-education, and beautiful to see. Keep them up! It will do you good."

"Officers!" he continued. "Affix 'OBJECT IN TRANSIT' labels to these unidentified entities, and escort them to the Reclassification Centre."

"I am a human being," John protested. "Not an object."

"*You*," said the sergeant, "will be whatever *we* define *you* to be. You aren't even alive, unless we say you are. Keep your feet off the wheat! Do as you're told! Quee-*eeck* march!"

Unwillingly, John and Bear did as he ordered.

Not far away was an asphalt road, marked at intervals with white signs on wooden posts bearing the words 'ASPHALT ROAD' in black lettering, neatly painted.

"It's like a child's colouring book," said John. "Everything has to be enclosed in an outline. Neat and complete. No gaps allowed. What do they do about shadows?"

The sergeant simply scowled at this. His men's faces remained impassive. They trudged along.

"Feeling emotion seems to be a privilege of the bosses," muttered John to Bear, he hoped inaudibly. But the sergeant heard him.

"Emotion," he snapped, "is nobody's *privilege*. A member of a category feels the emotions proper to him or her, under the circumstances. Love, rage, sorrow, and joy are to be experienced on the occasions proper to them, and not at other times. To be without emotion when emotion is correct is evidence of possible decategorization. I am enraged with you, you filthy mob, because it is appropriate that I be enraged with you. The Label Officers are sternly dutiful because that is the part they have to play. You two should be hanging your heads in shame, not making smart-aleck remarks about the labelling of shadows, something beyond your walnut-brains to understand. Keep your hands on your heads there!"

They marched on in silence. The road was clean and bare. The few lizard-like cracks were all labelled. The occasional clumps of dandelions along the verges wore label-collars, each of their puffballs enclosed in a small polythene bag. They were overtaken once by a truck with a badly adjusted engine smelling heavily of oil. Otherwise there was no traffic.

"You are also wrong about bosses," the sergeant resumed. "There are no bosses in our society. It is totally classless."

"Classless!" said Bear. "What about all those labels on people?"

"Categories are not classes," replied the sergeant. "Any child knows that. With categories there is no exploitation, no superiority, and no inferiority. Think of it like a machine. A smoothly-running machine. We are different parts, different categories whose only difference is that we have different jobs to do. How can one say that a fan-belt is superior to a fly-wheel, or a nut to a bolt? Ours is the most beautiful, the most equal, and most perfect society that has ever existed. And not for the likes of you. You contaminants!"

He stamped his metal-rimmed boots down on the tarmac to emphasize his ideologically correct feeling of detestation.

They left the wheatfields behind, and passed through some woods until they reached a chalk-quarry. The air was smoky with white dust that had settled on the leaves of the trees. These all had brass labels screwed onto their trunks saying 'CHALK MAPLE', 'LONDON PLANE', 'BLACK LOCUST', and so on.

"Handy for nature-walks," murmured John. "No need to wonder any more what a tree or flower is. No need to have to look it up in a book when you get home."

"Where's the fun, then," Bear disagreed, "if you can't scratch your head sometimes, and try to make up your own mind if a spike of yellow florets is melilot or agrimony?"

"Why bother with flowers at all if you don't want to know their names?" said the sergeant without turning his head.

John and Bear looked down into the quarry as they went by. The workmen were all in pairs. One man in each pair was labelled 'QUARRYMAN' and the other 'LABELLER'. As fast as the first cut out a lump of creamy-coloured chalk with his chisel and hammer, the second banged a label onto it with his staple-gun.

"Does everyone work in pairs like that?" John asked.

"Not always," said the sergeant. "A faster worker may have two labellers assigned to him, or even three."

"So you use less than half your workers actually to do anything," said Bear. "Doesn't that reduce output?"

"Economics is an abstract science not related to the real world," said the sergeant. "I belong to the Label Police and it is not within my categorized duties. According to experts, however, output does not exist as output until it is so labelled. Therefore, the more labels, the more output. Simple enough logic, I would have thought, even for you."

John smiled when he heard this. He lifted his hands of his head and let them drop to his sides.

"Put your hands up again," said the officer behind him.

"What hands?" said John.

"Them repulsive pink dibblers dangling by your buttocks," said the officer. "Onto your bleedin' head, and be quick about it."

"I am simply an 'OBJECT IN TRANSIT'," said John. "Objects in transit don't have hands, or heads, or anything else, until given a new, correct, and approved label."

"Sergeant," said the officer, "permission requested to inflict pain."

John darted a glance at Bear. Did he have enough of his Dreamland powers to help? Bear shook his head slowly. 'Not for the moment' seemed to be the unspoken massage. John swallowed. He realized he was probably going to be hurt.

The sergeant brought them all to a stop, then turned.

"Not just yet," he said. "The stages of persuasion have to be properly observed."

He strutted up to John.

"You there," he growled, "Hands on your head at once."

"I don't have any hands," said John. "I don't have a head, either. I am classed as an object."

"You are wasting Label Police time. Put them up."

John looked the sergeant in the eye.

"Can you label pain?" he asked.

"No," said the sergeant. "We cannot label your pain. It is therefore not real. We *can* label your shrieks, and your screaming and squirming around, all of which will be highly enjoyable and make up for long hours and low pay. How else can I relieve the tension in my men? I advise you to put your hands on your head."

John's answer was to sit down with his back against a paper-bark maple. Bear removed his paws from his head, too, and sat down beside his master. The sergeant gave them a glance, then said something to one of his officers, who set off at once down a path into the quarry below.

"Can you deflect their laser-guns?" John whispered.

"So long as they don't catch me by surprise," Bear whispered back. "They may have other weapons. Play it cool, very cool. We'll just have to see what happens."

A siren went off in the quarry. Its wailing seesawed up and down through the sunlit dusty air and through the green gloom of the trees.

"What's that for?" John asked.

"Your meeting," answered the sergeant. "The people are going to tell you what they think of you, and why. Come with me down to the quarry."

John slipped a questioning look at Bear, who nodded, unperturbed. They clambered to their feet again.

They could see as they came down, feeling for footholds, that work had stopped. The quarrymen and the labellers were standing in two separate groups, facing them. Two standard-bearers in each group were holding up a banner sagging between two poles, one saying 'QUARRYMEN' and the other 'LABELLERS'. Others had placards with slogans like 'Victory is certain!' on them. It looked like a trade-union demonstration. — Without the good humour. The workers' faces were streaked with dust, here and there washed clear by a runnel of sweat.

"The sweat isn't labelled," said John.

"Not necessary," said the sergeant. "The labelled whole includes the part in cases specified in the *Official List*. It is in the nature of quarrymen and labellers, as defined, to be sweaty when they work. A clean face would be inappropriate, and require a special label. You are still talking as if you think that these matters had not all been carefully examined by those wiser than you will ever be, long ago."

"Now then!" he barked. "Objects in transit! Objects in transit will stand to attention, with hands on their heads!"

John and Bear continued to let their hands swing by their sides. When the quarry-workers saw this they began to murmur angrily.

"The people do not like what they see," said the sergeant. "They say that you are defying the Label Police, which is ungrateful and wicked. They are also saying that they want to go back to work, and that you are preventing them. Do you want them to lose their wages and have nothing to eat tonight?"

"I am not preventing them from working," said John. "So far as I am concerned they are welcome to continue."

The sergeant snapped a riffle of thick fingers on his left hand. He pointed to one of the quarrymen.

"Come here!" he shouted.

A quarryman moved forward, his eyes shining.

"Tell these objects here," said the sergeant, "how you feel about their disobedience in not putting their hands on their heads."

The quarryman, in his chalk-dusted overalls and white-besplattered boots, came closer. He suddenly laid a hand on John's shoulder. It felt grimy and friendly.

"Without labels," he said earnestly, "we wouldn't know what we are, nor what we have to do. If you defy the Label Police, it's like trying to bring the world to a stop. The whole world. Do what they ask. Do it!"

"What's your name?" said John.

"I am a quarryman," said the quarryman, pointing to his own label.

"I don't mean your label," said John. "Don't you have something you call yourself, you and you alone? A name that makes you different from everyone else in the world?"

"But I'm not different from other quarrymen," said the quaryman. "If I was, it would be terrible."

"After work," said Bear, "don't you go home to your own home, to your own wife, and your own children, who have eyes only for you? Don't you have some favourite dish that you particularly like to eat?"

"Of course I go to a home," said the quarryman. "I check at the door, as the rules say, to make sure it's the right category, and that somebody else isn't there first. If there is, I go next door till I find one with a place for me. Wives and kids do the same."

"You mean you go home to a different wife every night?" said John, somewhat shaken.

"They're not different," said the quarryman. "A wife's a wife, isn't she?

So long as she's in the right category. Same as a quarryman's a quarryman. One member's got to be as good as any other member. Has to be. That's what belonging to a category means, don't it?"

"But," said John, baffled, "don't you have a feeling inside you that there's something there that exists nowhere else? Something that will go out of existence when you die?"

"Nothing goes out of existence," said the quarryman. "How can it? Matter's indestructible, isn't it? Just gets rearranged different from time to time."

"I suppose so," said John, "but you can't remain a quarryman for all eternity. Don't you have accidents, or get old, or die?"

The quarryman pointed at his own chest.

"If you mean that some time or another this body has to change category, of course it does. It might become a 'PENSIONER' or a 'CORPSE'. But the categories don't change. If this body has to be reclassified, there'll be a vacancy and some 'APPRENTICE' will be transferred to 'QUARRYMAN'."

"Surely you feel some sort of 'me' inside you," John persisted.

"That's a daft sort of idea," said the quarryman. "The words 'you' and 'me' are just for the convenience of pointing at people. They aren't labels. You can't label a 'me'. So how do you know it exists?"

"I'm bewildered," said John. "But tell me something else. Why does it matter so much to you whether Bear and I put our hands on our heads, or not?"

"Because you've been told to by the Label Police. It's their job to see labels are correct, and to dispose of unlabelled objects. That's what you are. If you don't let them do their job, that stops them being what they are, if you see what I mean. You're messing up a category and creating confusion."

"Has it occurred to you," said Bear, "that if everybody acted like that, then a category could die? That even a category like 'LABEL POLICE' could vanish?"

"To think thoughts like that," said the quarryman, "is to look into a black hole. If they went, nothing else could exist. Nothing. People wouldn't know what things were."

"You see why he's angry," said the sergeant. "He is entitled to be angry. Indeed, it is correct for him to feel angry."

"More than just plain angry," said the quarryman, "like what you feel when you step on a rusty nail and it goes through the sole of your boot, or you hit your thumb with a masonry hammer. We can't go back to work while you continue to disobey. What that means is we shall get no wages this evening, have no food, and the wives and the kids go hungry. Is that what you want?"

"It's blackmail," said John. "I have no intention whatever of giving in to it. If the sergeant wants you to eat, all he has to do is to take back his order. He is responsible, not us."

"Your human feelings are dead," said the quarryman. "Small wonder they need to relabel you. But it's our duty to try to persuade you first. Maybe there's still a spark or two of fellow-feeling to be fanned alight. Look at what's going to happen to you, over and over again, if you don't stop refusing."

The quarryman tugged out his broad-bladed chisel from his belt-strap, unbuttoned the top lefthand strap of his overall, pulled back the unwashed shirt underneath, and, before Bear or John had realized what he was going to do, or could check him, plunged it in six or seven inches between two of his own ribs, grunting and twisting and struggling to push it in further. He crumpled onto the ground, his blood spurting out onto the white chalk, then rolled over on his back, still gritting his teeth. Bear tried to grab him, but two officers gripped his paws to stop him moving. In any case, the man was clearly going to be dead in a minute or two.

The sergeant snapped his thick fingers again, and pointed to another quarryman, who stepped forward at once, his eyes shining.

"No. No," said Bear, aghast. "Some things are too much. — John! We will put our hands on our heads and do as they say."

"I am glad that the moral power of appropriate action was able to touch you," said the sergeant. "I had thought you both completely inhuman."

"You seem to have us where you want us," observed John. "I couldn't face any more of that."

"Our spirit is superior to yours," said the sergeant. "We believe our arguments."

"Will no one mourn for our quarryman?" said Bear. "Will no eyes fill with tears to think that he will never again step across the threshold of his home, to make the room warmer with his smile?"

"Of course no such thing will happen," said the sergeant. "All that has occurred is that there is a vacancy in his category. We shall probably have it filled by this evening. The footsteps and the smile will be assured. As to the corpse, it is a routine relabelling job. Any one of them would have done the same."

As they walked, the afternoon grew warmer, then gradually cooler again. They trudged through hamlets of small identical houses, and once they paused to watch the evening milking of some cows in a barn. Up in the half-darkness of the rafters, two boys in T-shirts were climbing, looking for new spiders' webs to label, and the occasional unspotted bird's nest. The milkmaids sat with their labellers beside the cows, swiftly pulling out the white fluid, *ping-*

slurp-slurp!, into the galvanized pails. 'EMPTY PAIL', 'PART-FULL PAIL', 'FULL PAIL' .... There was no rest for any of them for an instant.

A mixture of dung and straw covered the floor, strewn with labels saying 'MIXED LITTER', and smudged with bootmarks where the workers had carelessly tramped across them. Flies were buzzing drowsily around the cows' flanks, bestirring themselves from time to time, jsut enough to avoid, mostly, the efforts of four determined little girls to capture them with jam-jars. When they did get hold of a fly, they took it to a battered old table where one girl held it down with a pair of tweezers while another pulled a loop of thread with a label on it, 'FLY', tight between its abdomen and thorax. Then they proudly let it go and watched it buzz away.

The sergeant shook his head with disapproval.

Messy business, farming," he observed. "Barely under control. I much prefer factories. Machines do what they're supposed to do, and stay where they're put."

Later still there was a sunset over a lake dotted with floating buoys saying 'LAKE'. Then the stars came out. John looked at the constellations, but not one of them could he recognize. They had travelled so far into the future that the positions of the stars had changed relative to one another. There was no Orion the Hunter, no Archer, no Great Bear.

Oh, well, thought John to himself, I suppose they were only ever chance assemblages of stars. Stars that never really had anything to do with each other. But they seemed so fixed, so dependable. Ah, well.... He sighed and noted that the River of Stars, the Milky Way, was still up there. The rim-edge view of their local galaxy.

"Why aren't the constellations labelled?" said Bear mischievously.

"Because you are still in the country," said the sergeant. "In another half-an-hour we shall reach the city. You will see that everything is as it should be, there at least."

The city was a dull, almost unlit, conurbation. It seemed to have been put together out of grey Lego-bricks by some unimaginative child. Everything was rectangular and repetitive. Along its wide avenues flowed crowds like some sort of sticky fluid, catching on the edges of buildings, breaking free again, twisting in little knots against the main current, backing up alleyways or spilling out of them, but always moving along, moving along, an intermingling of thousands of identical journeys, by categories, not people. Above the highest buildings hung a gigantic transparent dome. Here and there along its curves it shone with light reflected from the city below. To

Bear's sharp eyes it was apparent that this dome was turning to match the slow rotation of the stars above it.

Every single visible star had a label engraved on this dome.

"'RG'," read Bear. "That must stand for 'Red Giant'. And 'WD' for 'White Dwarf', I suppose. What's 'SG'? 'Sub-Giant'?"

"Correct," said the sergeant.

"Don't you have any constellation names?" said John.

"You are forgetting," said Bear. "Individual names are forbidden. The stars here, too, are only labelled by type."

"What's the Milky Way, then?" said John, pointing. *"That."*

"A multi-stellar conglomeration," replied the sergeant. "It is labelled — 'MSC' — as you can see if you look closely. There are many of them. It is simply the nearest."

"You can't catch them out so easily," Bear murmured to John. "They've been playing this game for a long, long time."

They strolled in silence, washed over by a sea of labels. 'AVENUE', 'LANE', 'DEAD-END', 'ALLEYWAY', 'HOUSE', 'APARTMENT BLOCK', 'DORMITORY', 'PENSIONERS' RESIDENCE', 'HOSTEL' .... over and over again.

"No addresses," said John. "Eerie."

"See that theatre?" said Bear. "All the poster says is

'TONIGHT! ROMANTIC LABELUTIONARY TRAGEDY. TWO GRADE-A STARS, GRADE-B CHARACTER ACTOR, PLUS C-GRADE SUPPORTING CAST!'

Not much of an attraction, is it? Suppose, once you've gone in, it turns out you've seen the play before. Do you get your money back?"

"Why should you?" said the sergeant. "Each particular type of play produces the same correct and appropriate emotions. You don't object to eating your favourite food twice."

"What about the element of surprise, then?" John put in.

"The desire for surprise is a disease of the mind," said the sergeant. "We find our pleasure in predictability. That is what people need, and therefore what they are obliged to want. If labelling is correct, surprise is impossible."

"Because surprise means a loss of control?" said Bear.

"By definition," agreed the sergeant. "If a romantic labelutionary tragedy had anything surprising about it, it could only mean that it was not romantic, or not labelutionary, or else not tragic. In such a case it would be mislabelled, and the audience would be right to ask for their money back. One of our jobs is to see that this does not happen."

The signs went by, repeating themselves: 'HUNGER RECTIFICATION CENTRE', 'CORRECT ENJOYABLE BEVERAGES OUTLET', 'PREDICTABLE PINBALL PARLOUR', 'APPROPRIATE ARTIFICIAL INTEGUMENTS — CATEGORIES 17 TO 54' (a clothing shop, by the looks of it).... Many were closed, as it was already late in the evening.

The group turned a corner and came face with a well-lit window. A red neon sign flashed on and off above it: 'LUCKY'S LABELS' it said in slinky letters that looked like handwriting. 'THE ONLY PLACE IN TOWN'.

"The *only* place?" said John in surprise. "How can that be?"

The sergeant was scowling.

Everyone pressed against the plate-glass to look inside. The display was elegantly laid out on glass and platinum trays, in contrast to the perfunctory arrangements in the other shops. The goods on offer consisted entirely of labels, but what labels they were! The materials of which they were made were some of them luxurious, like ebony, mother-of-pearl, gold, and liquid crystal, but most of them were downright weird: engraved potatoes, winking Christmas-tree bulbs, and polished teeth set in red plastic mouths.... The lettering was equally queer: the svelte swirling loops of fashion script, the billboard style where every capital letter swaggered about on Mickey Mouse boots, the pure mathematical sanserif with no little twiddles at the end of each little line, the pompous bloat of Circus Style, with cute weeny stars in the middle of the thicker lines....

At the centre of it all was a sign on Z-flexed steel struts:

'TIRED OF YOUR OLD LABEL? THEN CHANGE IT TODAY AT LUCKY'S! ANY NEW ONE ABSOLUTELY FREE! THE ONLY QUESTION IS — WOULD YOU DARE TO GET AWAY WITH IT!?'

"I have not seen this place before," said the sergeant. "It is counter-labelutionary on at least four counts. It is stylistically corrupt. It violates the principle that members of each category should be indistiguishable. It incites to discontent. And there is no indication of approval by Authority, displaying which is mandatory."

He tried the door-handle. It was shut.

He yanked out a whistle on a lanyard and blew a fierce high-frequency note. In less than a minute some seven or eight Label Police officers appeared. They stood to attention in front of him. The sergeant jerked a thumb in the direction of 'LUCKY'S LABELS'.

"How long has this been here?" he said.

The officers who had come at the call of the whistle stared at the red neon sign, and the window of tempting labels, and the little sign. The lights above the window went on winking on and off, almost insolently.

They broke ranks to confer with each other.

"Sergeant," said one of them who was acting as spokesman, "we have not seen this shop before. We are certain it was not here an hour ago. There is some reason to believe that it is unlikely to exist."

"As I thought," said the sergeant. He pointed to two of his own men. "You! Report this anomaly to a Label Lord at once, then come back here. You others! We shall effect entry in an orderly fashion."

He kicked at the glass door with his boot, and to his surprise it immediately swung open. He led his posse in, with John and Bear, forgotten about, bringing up the rear.

Cases and shelves inside the shop glittered with more alluring labels. All of them were temptingly open. One of the officers fingered an ivory and jet badge saying 'SERGEANT OF LABEL POLICE', and offered it to the sergeant.

"It'd look really handsome on you, sergeant," he said.

The sergeant gave him a savage look.

"That there bauble," he snapped, "is not a correct and approved design. It is filth. Trash. Give it to me. I shall impound it as evidence."

He stuffed it into his pocket.

"Don't ever make such a suggestion to me again," he added.

"Yes, sergeant," said the officer. "Sorry, sergeant."

Bear glanced at John. His eyes were twinkling.

"You can put your hands down, now," he whispered. "No one is going to notice us for a while."

The policemen were rummaging through the labels, pretending to note what was there. They were horrified, fascinated, and one after the other succumbing to the urge to pocket the best ones for themselves. Badges, and stickers, and brooches, and pins lay higgledy-piggledy all over the floor.

"You old rogue!" whispered John back to Bear. "You really have sown the seeds of merry chaos."

He patted his burly shoulder.

Bear smiled a smile of seraphic beatitude, and tried to stop his eyes from twinkling quite so much.

"There are shops like this all over the city already," he said. "And every single one of them is being looted."

The arrival of the Label Superintendent caught them unawares. All of a sudden, there he was on the doorstep of Lucky's, backed by a dozen or so scary-looking officers whose labels proclaimed them to be 'LABEL EMERGENCY SPECIAL FORCES. GRADE ULTRA.' The superintendent was calm, grey-eyed, and polite. His men's eyes looked like they would waste anyone he told them to, with the coldest of cold pleasure.

"Good evening, Official Dreamguard Bear and John," he said, with the slightest nod of his head.

"Good evening, superintendent," said Bear, bowing. "And thank you for using our approved and correct designations."

"The pleasure is mine," returned the superintendent. "If you would be good enough to come with me, we can assure you of agreeable quarters and a dignified welcome, appropriate to your category."

Bear hesitated.

"Official Dreamguard," continued the superintendent, "please be reassured. We are not attempting to take you into custody. The Special Forces are, if I may so put it, a guard of honour. Let me assure you that we intend to treat with the greatest of respect any entity possessing powers like yours capable of causing so much confusion in so brief a space of time."

"Words with two meanings, superintendent," said Bear. "One may treat an enemy with respect, even while seeking to destroy him. Before we go with you, let me remind you of two things. First, we are not your enemies, unless you choose to make us such. Second, you would be wise to treat us with a certain caution. We are not alone. Were we to be hurt, vengeance would strike you from a quarter that you cannot parry: from the time that lies just about you, almost infinitesimally near, yet completely beyond your reach."

The superintendent smiled.

"You are bluffing a little, Dreamguard," he said. "You would speak less grandly were you entirely confident. But be at your ease for the moment. You shall discuss such matters more fully with a Label Lord."

Slightly warily, Bear and John went with him down the ill-lit streets. As they walked, John had a vague sense that the night-air was full of moths. From time to time he would glimpse a flurry of wings against the globe of a street-lamp. Once at least he was sure he saw the flash of black letters on a moth's wings. The Special Forces seemed uneasy, too, glancing this way and that as if they were half-aware that something uncanny was developing. Only Bear was serene, his gold medallion now glowing at full power, like the beam of a lighthouse above the dark sea.

GREY MARBLE covered both the floor and the walls of the corridor that led to the apartments of the Label Lord. Oil paintings in golden frames were hung at intervals, each one simply labelled 'MASTERPIECE'. One showed the delicate tracery of electric pylons crosssing the meadows beside beds of peony flowers. Another showed blue-overalled girls in yellow helmets struggling ecstatically to turn huge handles and stop-cocks controlling the pipes of an oil-refinery. John noticed that in none of these paintings did any person or object cast a shadow across any other person or object.

"Don't you ever put the names of the artists under the pictures?" he asked.

"I think you know us well enough now," said the superintendent, " to realize that each painter of a given category paints pictures appropriate to his grade, no better and no worse. A painter who paints too well may at times have to be punished."

"When that happens," said John, "are the labelling authorities not to blame? Like guidebooks to museums that only give a two-star rating to a three-star picture."

"A labelling authority can never be wrong. That follows by definition, as your friend the sergeant would say, but it has a deeper meaning. We make up right and wrong, of course. In a sense they are arbitrary. What we decide is less important than our making the decision. The agreement that we create is the glue of stability in our society. Any disagreement, any crack in unanimity, is like a crack in a dam. What begins as a miserable trickle of water hardly moistening its face may widen and swell until suddenly it brings the whole structure down. Now — when someone performs worse than he is meant to perform, that means he is incompetent, or lazy, or at worst obstinate. Punishment is necessary, but does not have to be severe. But to do better implies arrogance, impudence, even rebellion. It never happens without the person doing it knowing what he is doing. It is making a crack in the dam wall. There is no excuse for it, and punishment has to be exemplary."

John was slightly dizzy with the lines of pictures passing by him. He was therefore not certain that he had seen what he thought he had seen: a creamy-white moth with rectangular wings, settling on top of a picture label. He was even less certain about what the letters on its wings said, but he could have sworn they read 'CHOCOLATE-BOX RUBBISH'.

They climbed some dully gleaming steps and passed through several doors that opened by themselves, and then closed again in the same way. In the end they found themselves in a circular room with glass walls through which they looked down at the night-time city. A Label Lord was seated in a high-backed black chair. He did not rise, but gestured in the direction of a low black sofa.

"Travellers from Time," he said. "Won't you make yourselves comfortable? Thank you most kindly, superintendent."

The superintendent bowed, and withdrew with his men.

The Label Lord looked at John and Bear for a long time without speaking. He had a face of kindly cruelty, like a judge's, with high cheekbones and piercing eyes. His mouth was like a thin wire, continually changing its expression, sometimes thoughtful, sometimes mocking, concerned, wry, doubtful, and sardonic by turns.

"I have studied your dossiers," he remarked at last, "with — shall I say — a certain historical nostalgia. Your actions and your way of speaking bring back the flavour of a world that has now disappeared for many thousands of years. Your pre-labelutionary taste for confusion, and for individual names, reminds me of how much the human race has accomplished since those times."

"What do you think has been accomplished?" said Bear. "To us it seems that the richness has departed from your lives. The unnamable splendour of the world surrounds you, but you can no longer see it, or enjoy it."

The Label Lord regarded him with a quizzical expression.

"In your time," he said, "men and intelligent animals feared death. They lived in terror of the extinction of something-or-other unique and individual that they called 'the self' or 'the soul'. Or the 'personality'. They were so much in dread of its disappearance that many of them even talked themselves into believing that this imagined something-or-other was immortal. Was this not so?"

"Very approximately," said John.

"We have abolished this age-old fear," the Label Lord continued. "We have annihilated the individual. Thus there is nothing — or, if you prefer, no one — to die. In our world, only categories are imperishable. That they are outside time is self-evident, since they are abstract and symbolic, untouched by the rust or rot of decay. When a member of a category ceases in some way or other to be a member, he — or she — is simply replaced. Even a category that is for the time being empty, remains as a potentiality, ready at any time to be filled. A category cannot die."

"Unless perhaps it is forgotten," murmured Bear, but the Label Lord either did not hear him or chose to appear not to have done so.

"There is another problem that we solved long ago," he resumed. "In your day there was a philosopher who had — if you will excuse me — the individual name of 'David Hume'. He argued that no argument could derive what one *should* do from what were merely *facts*. Or, as he put it, one could not get an 'ought' from an 'is'. This argument was like an acid of the mind, dissolving old certainties both in religion and philosophy. It made both 'good' and 'bad', and 'ought to' and 'ought not to' seem no more than matters of

220

custom, or individual taste."

"And your solution?" said Bear.

"To make certain that all names correspond exactly to reality. If, at all times, everything is correctly labelled, then it cannot, in fact, be what it ought not to be. Let me give you a simple example. A 'MOTHER' is a female who is kind and loving, in a principled way, towards her children. You have a mother. Would you agree?"

John smiled and sighed.

"Yes," he said.

"That is how we define a 'MOTHER' label," said the Label Lord. "Now you, with your out-of-date views, might argue that there could be such a thing as an unkind and unloving mother, in other words, a 'bad' mother. To us, this is nonsense. A female who behaves in this way towards her offspring is no longer labelled a 'MOTHER'. She is something else. As we put it, recategorized. No true 'MOTHER' *can* be unkind or unloving. By definition, because 'mothers' aren't. Just as no 'CORPSE' can be alive. Again, by definition. Thus nothing can be what it should not be. No person can be what she should not be. The label has changed, provided society is vigilant. If someone is not what she *should be*, then, as it were, she *is not* that someone. Put this way, our achievement sounds very dry, very philosophical, very far removed from life, but this is not the case. It has, for example, enabled us to abolish crime."

"If that is so," said John, "why do you still need Label Police?"

"To ensure that the labelling is exact," replied the Label Lord sharply. "This requires a constant dedicated effort, even when the system is not being messed about with by intruders like yourselves."

"I think your system is repulsive," said John. "I shall never forget the quarryman who killed himself this afternoon just to make us put our hands on our heads."

"Please do not forget him," said the Label Lord. "The memory will help you appreciate both the beauty and the power of our system. Let me show you a little more. Here is what we call a 'Deeposcope' of a recategorization as we like to do them."

He leant down and pushed a switch set into a small table at his side. Then he punched a number on a panel of digit keys. One of the huge curved panes of glass that surrounded the room went cloudy, and was transformed into a three-dimensional video screen.

A vast arena spread before them. It was like a sports stadium, with television cameras, flags flying, and a crowd of sections of identically labelled people. The bent figure of a man stood, stooping, in front of three others, who had braced themselves self-importantly. The Label Lord turned up the sound. They could hear a voice, flat yet biting, coming over the public-address system:

"... this entity, heretofore wearer of the correct and approved label for the category 'SOCIAL WORKER', which category is a subset of the categories 'HOMINID' and 'LIVING BEING', among others, is to be removed from these three categories afore-mentioned, and all wholly subsumed subcategories of the same, to be totally de-labelled, and thereby forfeit all entitlement and obligation to display any correct and approved label now, or in time to come, other than 'NULL', the grounds being behaviour inappropriate to the categories afore-mentioned."

One of the three erect figures stepped forward. He tore a label from the chest of the stooping figure, who collapsed at his feet. The crowd, like a beast with a hundred thousand separate throats but a single soul, let out a sigh of satisfied hatred. The man's body quivered a little, then lay motionless.

An officer of the Label Police swiftly affixed a new label to the cadaver, and two uniformed figures removed it.

"He's dead?" said John huskily.

"In your old-fashioned language, that could be said to be so," said the Label Lord. "For us, there never was anything called 'he'; so nothing of this sort has disappeared. When the world changes, labels must change with it. Conversely, when the labels change, the world changes with them. You will have noted that nobody laid a physical hand on that entity in its previous form."

He switched off the Deeposcope, and the window cleared again.

"Was he given a 'CORPSE' label?" said Bear.

"That would have been for the death penalty," said the Label Lord. "This was an annihilation. For an annihilation we affix a 'NULL' label. It makes a deeper impression on the crowd."

"I thought you said you had abolished crime," said John. "Didn't the social worker commit a crime?"

"The moment a certain embodiment of the category 'SOCIAL WORKER' acted inappropriately, he ceased to be a 'SOCIAL WORKER'. He became a 'NULL' — the action, by the way, was shockingly incorrect. What you saw was not an execution, but a public and formal rectification of a label. The implied rectification took place at the moment of the incorrect act. Thus there was no crime. A 'NULL' cannot, by definition, commit anything."

"Your system makes government easier," observed Bear grimly. "If that is all that matters."

"What else can matter for a government?" said the Label Lord. "Political problems have vanished. So have conflicts of interest, and competition, and ideological discontent. None of them can exist."

"What about numbers?" said Bear, sucking on one of his paws. "I noticed you punching some numbered buttons just now. Isn't each number unique?"

"That is not something with which we have any difficulty," replied the Label Lord. "You can have as many two's or three's as you want. Unlike individuals, who are once-off."

Bear went on sucking his paw.

"Mathematicians in our time," he went on, "talked about things called 'real' numbers. Actually they were almost as unreal as you could imagine. They were infinitely long strings of digits after the decimal point. My point is, though, how could you label one of those? You can't have a label that is infinitely long."

"You can label any number that you actually use," said the Label Lord. "You can either write out as many of the digits as you want to be bothered with, or you can use a formula, like one of those for π — the ratio of the rim of a circle to its diameter. And a formula only has a limited number of letters and figures and signs in it, which are its label. In this case the label *is* the entity itself. The power of labelutionary theory is remarkable. It not only solves all the problems of society, it can also solve mathematical problems as well."

"An example?" said Bear.

"In your dark times," said the Label Lord, "mathematicians went mad. They argued that there were an endless number of infinities, each one infinitely bigger than its predecessors. Thus the first infinity just meant counting forever, like a girl skipping on a rope: 'one, two, three, four...', and so on. The second was all the points in a length of straight line, which was said to be infinitely bigger than the first one, and impossible to put into a single countable sequence, because for any countable list of these numbers you could always find another number not in it, and so on. Can you think of anything more crazy?"

"Easily enough," said Bear, "but why do you think it's wrong?"

"There is only one infinity," said the Label Lord, "that of the numbers that can be labelled. Labels can be put into a single order, first by the number of letters and numerals in each one. Then, within each set of a given length, by alphabetical ordering like that in a dictionary, 'a' first, 'b' second, and so on. There are countless labels for each number, but if you can't find a label for a number, you can't use it. Certainly not in a computer. You can't really even talk about it. *If it doesn't have a label it doesn't exist.*"

"If you have two formulas, like two of the many formulas for π, that give the same result," said Bear, "they'll be of different length, or at least have different places when you order them by the dictionary system. You've got to know which formulas give the same result when you work them out, so you can knock out of the list all the ones longer than the shortest. How do you decide which formulas give the same results? It might take forever on a computer to find out even about one."

"A very good reason for not trying anything so half-witted," said the Label Lord. "The basic axiom of modern mathematics is: 'Labels first, numbers second'. Labels are primary, numbers mere by-products. In the single countable infinity of all possible labels, there will be an infinite number of formulas that will produce every single so-called distinct number. '2 + 2' or '3 + 1' or '-8 + 12' all give 4, for example. You see how much more powerful labels are than numbers! If you *begin* with the labels, why worry about the fact you can get any number an infinite number of ways?"

Bear had no answer, but thought to himself that not all labels gave you a number. What about '? + *'? or '$ - ‡'? or 'aaaa", for example?

"Labelutionary theory has not only abolished the individual and death," said the Label Lord. "It has not only secured social stability, and put an end to crime. It has cleaned up the follies of the philosophy and mathematics of your time. Do you understand, now, my dear travellers from Time, why we cannot permit you to disturb it?"

As John looked once more into the Label Lord's face, he was filled with a cold terror. It was not just the face of a hanging judge, who relished the wrenched neck dangling from the gibbet. It was the face of a madman, closed off in a self-contained world, free of any doubts, moving in the circles of a self-justifying system of ideas. Nothing could, or ever would, trouble its certainties.

But Bear, the Dreamguard, pointed to the city that lay, almost all asleep, outside the circular windows and below them.

"Underneath all that order," he said, "underneath all those labels, lies chaos. Not just the ordinary uncertainties of tiny differences in where you start leading to immensely differing journeys. Two railway lines that point in only the most slightly different directions will end up, after enough miles, as far apart as you want them to. No, the chaos of clouds of interacting waves of probabilities that guide the paths of microscopic particles. You can't even label the same particle twice with certainty. Let alone hang a label on a wave that carries nothing but a sort of information."

"Again, you have misunderstood," smiled the Label Lord. "Waves of probabilities are only a way of thinking about the readings of pointers on the dials in scientists' laboratories. All of these can easily enough be given their correct and approved labels. Only the stupidest of Ultra-Labellists would be demented enough to wish to try to hang labels round the necks of individual electrons."

224

Bear shook his head, and smiled, thinking of the litttle girls in the barn chasing flies.

"We have learned much from you and your subordinates, Label Lord," he said, "but it is time for us to be going. We shall not trouble you again."

The Label Lord shook his head in return.

"You have caused too much chaos for us simply to let you go. You offer us a chance of a kind that comes too rarely in our well-ordered society, the chance of a show-trial to satisfy that monster we call 'the public'. It is good for them to relieve their tensions and heighten their vigilance against false labelling. It also reminds them of how much they owe to us who are in control. We really cannot afford not to make some use of you."

"So what do you propose to do?" said Bear.

"The details will take time to prepare," said the Label Lord. "Maybe as much as a year or two. In the meantime we shall see to it that you live comfortably, though it will have to be in seclusion, I fear."

"And the show-trial," said John, "will that mean a change of category for us?"

"How could a show-trial have any other purpose?" said the Label Lord. "But there's no need for it to be particularly painful. Our purpose is to help ourselves, not to torture you. Any pain will be incidental."

Bear looked at their adversary through narrowing eyes.

"My Lord," he said, "why have you become a 'SLAVE'?"

The eyes of the Label Lord turned down sharply toward his chest. His 'LABEL LORD' label, black letters on shimmering marble grey, had gone. In its place was a grubby cardboard stencilled badge saying 'SLAVE'.

"Change it back," he said curtly. "I do not care for vulgar conjuring. There are five laser-guns pointed at you from hidden holes in the wall."

"Before you fire them," said Bear, "let us look one last time at your Deeposcope screen, and see what will happen."

No switch was turned, no digital buttons punched. The huge screen lit up of its own accord. They could see below, from about the height of a first floor, the streets of the city moving swifltly by beneath their feet. Around them flew millions of white label-moths. Millions more were breaking the silk of white cocoons spun under cornices and in the ironwork of the street-lamps. All of the moths had black lettering on their wings spelling out labels: 'EMPEROR', 'MADMAN', 'MAGICIAN', 'SAINT', 'SOOTHSAYER', 'CLOWN', 'TROUBADOUR', 'PROFESSOR', 'WITCH', 'POET', 'LOVER', 'GAMBLER', 'PROPHET', and countless others. As they watched, the moths alit on the labels of the people in the streets, folded their wings, and merged into the old labels, changing their messages.

225

Surprise spread in waves through the crowds, then embarassment, then confusion. Last of all, fits of wild laughter. They tore at their ugly clothes; they exulted, hugged each other, and began to sing. Some of them tried to act the new parts assigned to them. Some of them fought, and then collapsed into laughter again. Wider and wider still spread the white moths, carrying chaos like a plague. John doubled up with laughter at the sight of a Label Policeman turning into a 'SIDESHOW FREAK', squatting, pulling gruesome funny faces, and scratching for imaginary fleas under his armpit like a baboon. An 'ARSONIST' lit bonfires at the street-corners, and orange sparks flew into the sky among the moths....

"Seen enough" said Bear.

"A repulsive saturnalia," said the Lable Lord. "Turn it off. And give me back my label."

The screen went blank, then transparent. The night-time city reappeared.

"As you realized, it was an illusion," said Bear. "Yet it could be real. The moths are already there, waiting."

He opened his paws, and a moth fluttered out from between them. Its wings were cream-coloured, spotted with blobs of gold. It flew to the window, perched and folded itself into a rectangle. The black letters on its quivering wings read 'ILLUSION'.

"If it is really there," said Bear, "then it is not an illusion, and its label is a lie. If it is not really there, then its label is correct and appropriate, and it is an illusion. But, if it is an illusion, then there is no such label, and there is nothing to be either correct or appropriate."

He stood up.

"Harm me," he said, "and they will no longer be under my control. All that you have seen will come to pass. And worse. For your own sake, you must let us go."

The Label Lord's face knotted itself like a twisted cloth into a spasm of rage. He jerked. Five hidden laser-guns loosed their beams at Bear and John. But Bear had been ready long ago. The photon-streams curved around them, held in two time-fields of negative space. To the eyes of the terrified Label Lord, they seemed like twin spheres of incandescent black light.

He groped for the switch, and with a shaking hand turned it off again.

As he did so, the time-travelling carriage materialized into the circular room. The doors slid back and Charles popped his head out.

"Get in! Quick!" he said. "I've never seem a time-buoy blaze through space-time like that before!"

"John and Bear were aboard in less than an instant. Charles's mind flicked them into the safety of the future. Murgatroyd looked up sleepily from one of the benches. He had been having a siesta.

"Mad place you chose to visit," he commented. "We chased you as best we could, lost the trail in the city, and ended up by mistake at a football match. You'll never guess what was going on."

John grinned.

"One team was labelled 'WINNERS' and the other 'LOSERS'," he said.

"How the HSM did you know that?" said Murgatroyd, swishing his tail with annoyance.

"After a day in Label Land, you learn a thing or two," said John. "Bear! How about some jasmine tea for a change?"

But Bear had gone. His improbable world-line had twisted away once more from the real to the imaginary, and he was back among his dreams, caring, with his all-but-infinite care, for everyone in trouble.

The two boys and the black cat were on their own again.

Searching for the way home through the broken time-space islands of the universe to come.

• funworld

"HOW DO YOU DO IT, Charles?" asked John.

"Do what?"

Charles lifted his head from the control panel. Dark rings showed under his eyes.

"Travel through time."

Charles gave a faint smile.

"We are always travelling through time," he said. "We are alive. Things are happening. Clocks ticking. Outside us, inside us, the twinkling of cause and effect never stops. That *is* time, passing."

"But you can make *our* time shift compared with others' times," said John. "This gaudily painted caravan of ours, covered with scenes from English history flaking away on its panels, this ramshackle time-traveller, W.R. & K.P. Mackenzie, proprietors, from a fairground in a place called Oxford, dust long ago, has been back in the Jurassic. And now it's somewhen in the future. Somewhen when our grown-up lives are already behind us, empty nothings forgotten by whatever history there still may be. I often wonder what sort of lives we had. How is it done?"

"Ordinary timeshift happens by itself in the world of speeds close to light," said Charles. "Anyone interested in these things knows that. Seen from the outside, the faster something like a clock goes through space — from here to there — the slower it *seems* to us to go through time — from one tick of its own clock to the next. So long as you're outside, watching it. At the fastest speed of all, the speed of light itself through empty space, its time seems just to stand still — for us, outside, watching it. Its clock doesn't seem to move, *ever*, from the beginning of the universe till now."

"And our clock seen from its time?" said John. "The same?"

"Of course. And other people's time runs slower and slower still the nearer they are to huge stars, but space grows wider there."

"That's not what you're doing to us, though," John insisted. "You're doing something else."

"I am," said Charles. "I don't know what I'm doing. I just found that when I had to, I could do it. Birds fly. They don't study aerodynamics. Fish swim. They don't take classes at school in the physics of fluids. The same with me. To go into the future, I slow down my own rate of happening, my clock inside me if you like, and the rest of the universe rushes by."

"And to go back?" John wanted to know,

"Need to flip in my mind into a mirror of myself first. That's why it's so much harder. I'd never have known what to do if I hadn't split in two when we were being chased by Megan."

"Mirroring's dangerous," said the cat. "You can burn up meeting events coming at you the other way through time."

"That's why you need to take some of your world with you," said Charles. "Like this Time-traveller. Bits do get burned off the edges when you stop or start."

"Doesn't it worry you," said Murgatroyd, "that you might, all of a sudden, forget how to do it? That you might leave us stranded in the middle of nowhen, millions of years from the last Mozart symphony, and the last human smile, — not to mention the last other cat?"

Charles shook his head, and smiled again.

"No," he said. "Not that. The travelling's easy now. The problem's finding my way around. Everything is moving relative to everything else. The earth spins. And it circles the sun. The sun drifts through the footloose stars. The galaxies alter among their ever-changing selves. Clusters of galaxies form like foam, or spiders' webs, then dissolve again. What tracks can I follow in this wilderness of time? Each signpost is here, then gone, from one instant to the next."

"You've done all right, so far," said the black cat. "You've stayed with our earth."

"So far," said Charles. "So far. But every second our earth is less and less its old self. Mountains melt away like waves. Oceans and orange-red deserts swirl across its surface like scum. In the end, when we see it again, how shall we recognize it? How shall we say, *This was ours, once?*"

"No way," said Murgatroyd, his green eyes burning with a strange intensity. "No way. It isn't."

THEY TRAVELLED ON silently, and without apparent movement. Only Charles's eyes, hooded with concentration, and his tightened lips, showed how fiercely he struggled within himself, to hold his course on the twisting paths of time. One dim light burned at the end of the bulkhead, powered by a car battery. Everything else was a ghostly blue again, even their equipment piled against the seats, its hundreds of shadows criss-crossing on the painted panels above it. Sir Francis Drake, still at bowls on the Hoe, high above Plymouth bay. The young knights still smiling at the maidens before they put their helmets on to joust. The weary legionaries peering through the mist and sungleams north of the Emperor Hadrian's wall. On the watch for the dangerous Scots. Dreaming of Roman sunshine and olive-groves, and Roman girls. How soon would it be before they, too, turned and began the run home?

And then, to what end? Was there any real hope of doing what they had set out to do when they had left Oxford again, vanishing the moment Ann Fellows, the last of the others to make her way out, had stepped down onto the platform of the time-travelling show, and looked out, with a City Councillor's anger and disbelief, at the unchanged world, barely half a minute on the clock after they had left it? — To come back to their own world *from the future*? To find their other half-selves, their children selves, whererever they were, drugged, overmastered, sweet powerless playthings for Megan, in her prison-box of delights and torments? To set free those beings who were both themselves, and no longer themselves, from the respectable North Oxford lady, to whom the policemen spoke so politely, and who was in her black, rotted, heart the witch-empress of illusion? To become again whole and complete?

It seemed a hopeless dream. Those other selves, perhaps, no longer even existed.

The black cat surveyed the two boys and thought to himself. *They are no longer just boys. Except, of course for their looks. They are hardened now, harder than many grown men. Already they have a little of that power, the power of otherness, the lonely power that comes from understanding what others do not, will not ever, understand. But, when it comes to the moment of decision, to meeting head-on with that hideous mind of infinite self-delighting evil, the mind of Megan, are they hard enough? Can they take the strain, and the strain again, and still not seek the relief of submission?*

And John, eyeing Murgatroyd, so casually relaxed on his folded sweater, for his part also wondered, *Could he be leading us astray? Perhaps without knowing it himself? What does his heart really follow after under his many truths, his many lives, his many selves? Maybe it follows nothing at all? Would we be wise to forget our other half-selves? What use are they to us anyway now? Do they, and we, share anything in common any longer? Two names? Two faces? A handful of memories? A mother?*

"I'm tired again," said Charles. "Tired of tracking this elusive planet that's meant to be our home. We're going to have a short rest, friends. Let's just hope it's safe. One Label-Land was more than enough."

He relaxed, and leant back in his chair. As he did so, the blue light darkened, and the flickering began. The time-traveller was returning, returning to bright day and starlit night, which alternated — even now — only a little slower than the age-old rhythm into which they and their ancestors had been born. It grew slower, and slower still. Charles gave a grin.

"Another paradox," he said. "We're both slowing down and speeding up. Our speed across others' time is almost zero now, but our own internal time is quickening. A few minutes back each second that ticked on our clock meant the passing of a billion of theirs. We must have seemed as slow and forgetful as the granite rocks to them. Now we're living so fast we're almost in phase with them. *There.* We *are* in phase."

The time-traveller juddered. Its dusty windows had filled with a brilliant light.

"Gentlemen," said Charles, standing up and stretching himself, "let me hand you back to real life. So-called real life"

THEY HAD COME to rest in a palace of glass and girders. A tracery of steel soared upwards and outwards in uncountable transparent repetitions. Up and down the walls ran straight pipes, millions of spiderfine lines coloured white, or orange, or deep blue. Plates of bright bronze hung on long steel wires, trembling. From time to time, as they moved, one or another would angle back a sudden reflection of light. Multiple streams of water slid down a black rock, pushing each other, then joining and sliding and breaking apart as they dribbled into a pool.

People were everywhere, but seemed tiny in this immensity. Neat dog-toothed lines of visitors rose past them on moving staircases, or descended. On the levels below, loose groups were milling about, bumping off each other like the molecules in a gas. The Traveller seemed to be on a small green hill, and surrounded by a circular walkway.

"I have," said Murgatroyd, " a curious and uncomfortable feeling."

"Of what?" said John.

"Of being an exhibit in a very large exhibition hall."

Charles gave an amused smile.

"Convenient," he said. "If you're right, we won't have to explain who we are. That gave us a lot of trouble last time."

"Let's see, then," said John. "Are we correctly labelled?"

The cat coughed.

"Not so fast," he said. "We must move cautiously."

He had spoken too late. John was already out and walking down some dark green plastic steps.

The old Mackenzie's Time-traveller, he discovered, was indeed on a

232

stand and separated from the public by plaited ropes of white and scarlet thread, rising and falling between small knee-high posts. There was a sign on one of these posts, but with its back to him. He stepped over a rope to read it. Charles, with Murgatroyd perched on his shoulder, watched through the open door from above.

The two brass posts between which John had passed began to pulse with a violet light. Murgatroyd frowned, held up a paw, and muttered something that sounded like 'Oki-yameh'. The pulsing faded away.

"Why'd you do that?" Charles asked.

"Security device," said the cat. "John triggered it when he stepped across the rope. We don't want to start our visit here by having him arrested."

"Call him back?" asked Charles.

"Not yet," said Murgatroyd. "I want to know what our label says. In the meantime, look at some of these people, if *people* is what they are. We seem to have come to a very peculiar place indeed."

Charles, being Charles, stayed outwardly composed. Inside — once he'd seen what Murgatroyd had noticed — he felt his tummy sucked empty by a vacuum cleaner. *Oompf!* — Not a single one of the people in all the crowds that filled the concourse had, so far as he could see, a normal body. They all had extra limbs.

Extra arms, third and fourth legs, doubled heads, multiple bodies even — as if they were sprouting vegetables.

But every one of them was elegantly dressed, mostly in sharply creased slacks and block-printed shirts, or even tailored suits neatly cut to accommodate the extra limbs. And they moved with such well-fed ease that one scarcely noticed — until one did notice.

"Weird, weird, weird," mumured Charles. "Do they grow them, do you think, or graft them on?"

"My guess," said the cat, "would be grafting."

"Why?"

"If you look closely," said Murgatroyd, "you'll see the bits don't match. If I grew a second head, or some more front paws, they'd look like my present head or paws. Or at least I hope they would. See that fat woman over there?"

"The one eating strawberry ice-cream with one mouth," said Charles, "and cramming in black-currant water-ice through the other?"

"Yes. That one. Look at her two faces. The left one's got high cheekbones and alert grey eyes. The eyes in the other face are piggy. They're sunk in the flabby cheeks. And the jawbone's slacker. Ugh."

"It would be funny if it wasn't so disgusting," said Charles. "There's one over there with a male and a female head, kissing itself."

John had finished reading their sign and came back up to join them. The alarm did not pulse again. Probably Murgatroyd's magic had disabled it.

"What's our sign say?" said Charles.

> " TIME-TRAVELLING CAPSULE
>
> EARLY SCIENTIFIC ERA [*CIRCA* +21ST CENTURY]
>
> MODE OF PROPULSION UNKNOWN. THREE CREW-MEMBERS (TWO BIPEDAL,
>
> ONE QUADRUPEDAL) SURVIVING FROM A PROBABLE TOTAL OF TWENTY-ONE.
>
> THIS IS
>
> THE ONLY CAPSULE OF ITS KIND PRESENTLY KNOWN.
>
> GIFT OF THE LADIES THESBAIN NISBET BARTON MÜLLER ACKROYD
>
> CHATTERJI.
>
> PLEASE DO NOT TOUCH,"

said John. "That's us. You're right, Murg. We're an exhibit."

"How long do you think we've been on show here?," said the cat. "In their time, that is."

"A century or two," said Charles. "Just while we were slowing down a few minutes ago. Remember?"

"Unnerving," said John.

"Talking of that," said Charles, "have you looked at the people?"

"Not yet. What's the matter with them?"

"You'd better take a look," said Murgatroyd. "They are — shall we say — interesting."

John began to survey the multi-level concourse. He gave a start, and then controlled himself.

"Intriguing," he murmured after a while. "Makes you think of all sorts of possibilities."

"It's unpleasant," said Charles. "Like some forced evolution. And where do you think all the bits and pieces came from?"

"As a musician," said John, "I can see some use for it. If I had two heads, I could sing duets with myself. One tenor and one baritone. See all that white wrought-iron furniture down there? And that sort of person-thing next to it? It's a one-person string quartet. Two male heads, one bearded, chins on their violins. A long-haired female head on a body linked at the midriff, drawing a viola-bow back and forth. And a large extra pair of hands and arms, without

234

any head, for the 'cello. It's ingenious. You can hear them, too, or it, above the hubbub. *Blah-tah-de-ráh-do-teee, Roh-tee-dee-diddle-rummm, Dee-dee-dée-di-rohhh, Tee-deedle....*"

"Shut up," said Charles. "It's monstrous. It would even look ugly in an Indian temple. How do you think it lies down at night? Or goes to the bathroom?"

"I am glad to see that they do not use animals for their experiments," said the cat.

"That well-proportioned gentleman over there," said Charles. "Yes, that one with two pairs of legs, one just behind the other, with neatly tailored trousers in mid-gray with maroon-and-white pinstripes, and the crisp creamy shirt with a floppy knotted purple bowtie, that one — looks not unlike a horse with four shiny leather shoes."

"I suppose he does," said the Murgatroyd. "But not a real horse. Oh, my God, I believe she is coming for us."

A woman was smiling up at them. She had two heads, each flowing with golden hair. Her four white arms were bare, and perfectly matched. Her two necks joined together like the arms of a candlabra and plunged into a bodice of beige crêpe that rippled down over dozens of breasts. It seemed as if a massive bunch of pinkish-creamy grapes was breathing and swelling under the soft fabric.

"Which face does one look at to be polite?" muttered Murgatroyd. "Tell me that."

The lady lifted one of the braided ropes with one of her many fingers and thumbs, and neatly hooked it back on itself. She climbed halfway up the green plastic steps, and then stopped, still smiling.

"Seventy-two teeth!" said Murgatroyd under his breath.

"Hi!" said the heads in unison. "Hi there! I'm Glorma. Welcome to Funworld! We just love time-travellers."

"How do you know we're time-travellers?" said the cat. He was still perched on Charles's left shoulder.

All four of Glorma's blue eyes blinked.

"Say!" she said. "Delicious! Did you folks body-blend animals' heads in your time? Does it feel good?"

"I couldn't tell you," said Murgatroyd. "Being still detachable."

He leapt down onto the dark green plastic plinth, stretched — a little rudely — then sat upright, flicking his tail round his front paws.

"How did you know we were time-travellers?" said Charles, repeating the cat's question.

"That's a real shame," said one of Glorma's heads, looking down at Murgatroyd. "You looked so cute together."

The other head answered Charles:

"The boss told us he saw you coming out of the time-capsule," it said. "Do you breathe oxygen? Are you in credit?"

"We breathe oxygen, mixed with nitrogen," said John to Glorma II. "Do your visitors sometimes breathe something else?"

"It's a question of whether you can afford it or not," said Glorma II, while Glorma I observed in conterpoint:

"Sometimes it's culture-shock. We've been sent to make sure you boys have a real nice time here, and don't misunderstand us. You enjoying yourselves?"

"We've not really had the time to yet," said Charles, "but thank you all the same."

"I hope cats are included in the treat," said Murgatroyd, while John added: "Perhaps you could show us around, if you're not too busy?"

"My! Oh, my!" said both of Glorma's heads. "You can all speak together, just like a real person. Yes, of course. This *is* going to be fun!"

"Of course cats are included," added Glorma II. "I haven't seen a cat for centuries. It's darlin' to have a cat along again."

"I hope your time with us will be a pleasant one," said Glorma I. "We get very attached to visitors."

She held out two of her hands to John and Charles. Murgatroyd sprang back onto Charles's shoulder. He made quite a zip and a thud. Smiling with one head each at each of the boys, Glorma led them down the steps and into the crowd, who looked at them with fascination.

"Why did there *used to be* cats," hissed Murgatroyd into the ear of Glorma I, "and there aren't any now?"

Glorma I allowed her baby-blue eyes to gaze for an instant into his dark green ones.

"We just had to concentrate on human beings," she said. "That's our thing."

"I don't think I quite understand you," said the cat. "Can you explain?"

"We love to feel good," said Glorma I. "Feeling good is bein' a human bein', all through and all over. We hadn't got the resources for dogs and cats and birds and all that. It wasn't that some of us didn't like them, but it cost money, and bein' us was — well — just so sweet a sensation, I guess, we just had to do without them. So we did. Same with trees and flowers. They're so different from us. In the end — we didn't see the point of them. So we let them go. Just kept food animals."

"Don't you get lonely without animals?" said Charles. "I can't imagine how I'd feel without animals to talk to."

Glorma ignored him. Or maybe she didn't understand what he meant.

"Let's go get a meal," said Glorma II. "A delicious meal fit for several stomachs. Home-toasted apple-flaked Mount McKinley Baked Alaska with Boysenberry topping and coffee-chocolate twiglets. That's what I love about this time of day, most days. Other days I have Macadamia-nut Mauna Loa banana sundae with pawpaw and passion-fruit, and an eruption of hot-cherry lava sauce splashed all over the top. And we'll meet some friends, and explain everything you folks might want to know."

Bubbling with what seemed like enthusiasm and sincerity, Glorma steered them round group after group of human composites, who stared back at them at them with a curious hungry interest, as if wondering what they would be like dismembered, especially the black cat. They watched two four-handed people playing ping-pong with two balls at the same time. They lingered, unable to stop looking, beside a roped-off ring where two three-torsoed bodies, linked at their bellies but with only a single head each, grappled and grunted in a wrestling match. The limbs dripped oil and sweat under the low-hung hooded lights, each arm and leg seeming to lead its own life as it coiled and twisted against the others. When they tore themselves away they found themselves among tables of chess players, each of whom had seven or eight heads. Some of the heads nestled on their owners' shoulders, deep in thought, while others scanned the board restlessly or looked across, bored, at neighbouring games.

Not all the additions were so obvious. Often they had to look embarrassingly closely at some suave gentleman or some serenely superior lady before they noticed — this one had a doubled pair of ears set neatly in parallel, that one had twin noses canted at a discreet angle to each other, and that other one again had two pairs of hands, all four hanging from clean white cuffs, palm facing palm, like fleshy tongs.

The restaurant was a glass-floored boat, hung from golden hawsers, and festooned with dark green plastic foliage and pink plastic hyacinths. The curved glass seats were filled with the bodies of gourmets. These were double-stomached men — and a few women — most of them with a pair of heads, one for the wine and the other for the solid food. They sat by themselves, their pairs of gobbling faces half-hidden behind heaped platters of shellfish and crushed ice, or copper pots, wreathed in steam, full of Mongol-style mutton, beancurd, capsicums, and herbs.

Glorma found them an empty table where they eased themselves in.

237

"Isn't it just luscious?" she said. "Isn't it just fun?"

To Charles's surprise their waiter had a normal body. He had expected him to have at least a dozen arms, each carrying a tray. He glanced down at the boys, and the cat, but spoke only to Glorma, who ordered for them. Charles felt uncomfortable at this, and muttered to himself: "He can't think we amount to much — only two arms, two legs, and a head each."

"Nor are we," Murgatroyd whispered. "Not compared to Glorma. She's got thirty-eight breasts. I've counted."

"Nothing indeed," smiled Charles. "Not compared to such magnificence."

"What was that you were saying?" asked Glorma I.

"I was observing," said Charles, "that we feel inadequate compared to most of the people here."

"Well, so you are," said Glorma, "but you've only just arrived in Funworld. The great thing about it here is that there's hope for everyone. If things go well for you, soon you can be doing some body-building, too. Here's to your success!"

Glorma raised two glasses, one of raspberry fizz and the other a hot mint soda, to both of her mouths and drank both of them at the same time.

Charles shook his head.

"I think I'd prefer to stay me," he said.

"But you will stay you, only better," insisted Glorma II. "You can get into anything you like. Into hands, or bodies, or legs, or other things. Whatever you like. Of course you stay you."

Murgatroyd had been lapping at a saucer of what the menu called Goldenherd Meadowsweet Nutrient-Free Blended Milk Delight. It was not particularly tasty, certainly not as good as its name suggested. Now he raised his head.

"Look here," he remarked, "a certain amount of clarification is needed. To begin with, how did you people first get into this business of extra hands and heads, and what-have-yous?"

The Glormas looked at the cat, then at each other. It was Glorma I who answered, while II listened:

"Some centuries back," she said, "we had a pleasure crisis. Those days, there were lots of resources, least for developed peoples like us. Everybody had everything. Two motorboats, hands-on feely videos, everything. But we didn't *enjoy* life any more. So somebody said — and the talkshows'll tell you it was Jo Trud but I think it was just in the air — mind you, I wasn't all there yet — so somebody at last asked the basic question. *What is pleasure?* Once you ask it, the answer's obvious. Pleasure isn't in *things*. It's in *bodies*. If you wanna enjoy food twice as much, it's no use eating twice as much. Like as not that'll just make you sick. What you gotta have's a second mouth and a second stomach so you can get it all down. Then thirds, if you wanna real symphony. Can you imagine it? Sweet and sour and salt all trickle-tickling down three different gullets all the same time? And *all you*? It's stupendous. I'm going to go triple soon as I can get the kreds. Anyway, that's how body-building started — with the gourmets. Like the people here."

"Once it had started," she went on, "people soon saw the possibilities. Athletes got in real deep real fast. Till you've seen a twelve-armed boxing match, you've seen nothing."

"They must look like sea-anemones," said Murgatroyd, with a dead-pan look on his face, "waving all those arms about."

"It's so fast, and so exciting," said Glorma II, "it just makes your adrenalin spit. Fights always end in knockouts. Guy gets hit on the head with three or four fists at the same time, no way is he going to survive. He gets crunched, and good. Them old-time slugfests, they were real dull. Fifteen rounds — can you imagine? And decisions on points? Yuck."

Both Glormas laughed.

"You talk as if you'd been around a long time," said John, "but you look so young and beautiful. Have you solved the problem of living for ever as well?"

"Not quite," said Glorma I. "After the pleasure-crisis we had the eco-crisis. Resources ran out, and most of the planet was unlivable in. So we stopped having children and began to recycle bodies. It was cheaper than growing a lotta new ones and having to educate them and all that."

"What exactly do you mean by 'recycle'?" asked Murgatroyd.

"Well, suppose someone has an accident, or gets real sick," said Glorma I, "we salvage the good bits of her body, and divvy them up round her friends. It's less wasteful than burying people or burning them. Canya imagine burning a perfectly good hand? That's what they used to do. Cremate people. Amazing. Say I go mad in my head. OK, my head's no good to anybody. It's gotta be scrapped. But why waste a good body as well? My friends, they can have bits of me. I can live on — with them, as part of them. Everybody benefits. Right?"

"I can see that," said John. "Once you get used to the idea."

"Do you have to wait for a friend to die to get your hands on a new ... er ... bit?" said Murgatroyd. "Seems slow and accidental, doesn't it?"

"People sometimes get to swap," said Glorma I.

"Or sell?" inquired Charles softly.

"It's a free country," said Glorma II, putting her hot mint soda on the marble-topped table. "If you wanta sell, there's nothing stopping you."

Charles shot a glance at the cat, who nodded slowly back.

"Doesn't it cause a crisis of identity to have a second head?" said John. "Who's the boss? Or do you make decisions equally?"

"The surgeon in the body-shop will arrange for one of us to dominate," said Glorma I.

"Which one?" John continued.

"The one that pays for the operation, of course," said Glorma I. "But there'd be no point in having a second head, if you didn't give it a chance to do its own thing sometimes."

"After all," added Glorma II, with a radiant smile, "our interests are identical now."

"From what you are saying," said Murgatroyd, "the population must be getting smaller. Doesn't anyone have children?"

"Ugh, children," said Glorma II, "they're illegal. We do have some specialists, you know — ladies that like that sort of thing — who give birth to babies for tissue-replacements. Up to eight or ten kids at a time. They really charge for their services, too."

"We don't let them appear in public," added Glorma I. "We don't like to be reminded of that kinda thing."

A feeling of digust welled up in Charles. He pushed his Cream-Foam Banana-Gondola Mint-Leaf Delight with Angelica Straws to one side, unable to think of finishing it.

Glorma II draped a cool white arm round John's shoulder.

"Whaddya really like doing, huh?" she whispered.

"He's a musician," said Charles, to show he'd overheard.

"A mews-ician," murmured Glorma in a honey-trickling voice. "That's real cool that is. We can do a lot for mews-icians, John. Whadd'you play?"

"Drums," said John. "Piano, synth. Guitar, and others."

"Hand instruments," said Glorma II. "That's nice. Easier than winds.It's messy getting extra lungs and lips. But hands.... Think what you could do with a third hand, John. A skilled musician's hand. Imagine all the extra harmonies, the trills, the little extra comments at the top of the keyboard. Mm?"

"The thought had occurred to me already," said John. "when I saw that quartet."

"John!" said Charles sharply. "You can't possibly be thinking of such a thing!"

"Why not, younger brother?" said John. "It's not a chance I'll get again."

"You might pick up blood poisoning from the other person's arm," said Murgatroyd. "Or cancer. If someone has to sell himself, he's not going to be too healthy. The risk's not worth it."

Glorma II shook her head, and her golden hair danced and swayed in the light.

"They're just wonderful, our surgeons are," she said. "They can build a body better than nature ever could. You're not going to have any of those problems."

"If there just happened to be a good hand going," said John, "I really wouldn't mind having it."

"No girl would look at you," said Charles. "With three arms?"

"Arms are in this year," said Glorma II. "He'd look real cool with three arms. Perhaps a black one. And he'd hug good, too."

"If she liked my music, she'd understand," said John. "If one's to be a professional, one has to make sacrifices."

Glorma II let her fingers caress John's neck.

"I know of a *very* good musician's hand that's coming on the market soon," she said. "It's not for sale yet, and I might get it for you cheap."

"You mean -," said John, "I have to pay?"

Glorma II smiled at him, while Glorma I sucked at her raspberry fizz through a golden glass straw.

"You don't expect a guy to give up his arm for nothing," she said. "Not an arm like that, do you? Then there's the surgeon's fee. And transfer tax. And insurance. But it's still cheap. For you, seein' what you're getting."

"What will he do without his arm?" said John. "The donor, I mean. Won't it be difficult for him?"

"That's his business," said Glorma II. "I expect he'll buy another arm. One that's more useful to him, maybe."

"Or go without, and starve," said Murgatroyd.

John reached inside his jacket and pulled out a small bag, made of washed leather. He let it drop on the glass tabletop in front of him with a thud.

"You can't use that," said Murgatroyd. "That's your share of our reserve."

"What is it?" said Glorma I, pulling her mouth away from her straw.

"Gold dust," said John. "The best trans-time currency ever invented."

The eyes of both Glormas grew larger, and the pupils swelled within them. John loosened the drawstrings and folded back the crumpled leather.

"Look!" he said. "Gold from the Mesozoic. The only such in all of space-time."

He watched, with a faint smile, while the Glormas stirred the heavy yellow dust with their finger-nails. Then he said:

"How much?"

"Half the bag," said Glorma I. "For everything."

"It's Steg's gold," said Charles. "You can't use it, John, even if it is your share. Not for this. It's not fair to him. Or me. We spent days in the mountains panning that stuff."

John seemed not to hear him.

Slowly, Glorma I's eyes shrank again. They were now icy-cold.

"We are unique in time ourselves," she said. "There ain't nowhen else you can pick up a good musician's arm. The price is one half-bag."

"There's enough sticking to your fingers alone," said Murgatroyd to the Glormas, "to meet any reasonable price."

A look of unhappiness crossed John's face. He sighed and looked away, and then seemed to be preparing himself to say something.

"One-eighth," said Glorma I quickly. "Don't miss your chance. You can have it for an eighth."

John brightened.

"That could be a deal," he said. "But on one condition. If I don't like the hand, the price covers the surgeon's fee to take it off again."

"You're on!" said Glorma I.

"Give us the gold!" said Glorma II.

"Not so fast, ladies. Not so fast," said Murgatroyd. "Cash on delivery. We hang onto the dust till the operation starts."

Charles was about to explode, but the cat quelled him with a sudden flash from his eyes. The younger boy clenched his fists, but kept his silence.

Glorma I shook her head.

"We gotta have the dust in advance," she said. "We have to pay the surgeon to take it off. We have to pay the guy to let his arm go. He's gotta be sure we're playing fair. Dust's up front, pussycat."

"Fair enough, in principle," said Murgatroyd. "But not in practice. We have no idea what we're buying. We want to see this arm. We want to hear it playing. On its present owner. If we're satisified that it's what you say it is, the deal's on. If not, then nothing's lost except a little time."

"Rules don't allow donors and grafters to meet," said Glorma I. "We gotta have the money in advance, or it's no deal."

"I don't believe it is against the rules," said Murgatroyd. "I wouldn't buy a head I'd never met. Would you? — *Did you?* And even if it is against the rules, you can bend the rules for an eighth of a bag of Mesozoic gold. It is still a stunning bargain."

Glorma II looked deep into John's uneasy eyes.

"The gold," she murmured. "OK if I take it now?"

John smiled back at her but put his hand firmly on top of the bag. He shook his head.

"Murg's right," he said. "I've got to see what I'm buying."

Glorma pursed her lips.

"Since you folks are visitors from the out-time," she said, "I will see what I can do for you. As a special favour. But don't expect too much. It's gonna take time."

"How long, then?" asked John.

The Glormas thought.

"Six hours," said Glorma I. "Seven maybe. You can wait that long?"

"Easily," said Murgatroyd before John could answer. "We're tourists here. Six hours would give us time to see something of this place. This concourse, marvellous though it is, can only be part of the picture. Can you fix us up a tour outside? Then we can come back to have John's arm done."

"It's much more fun in here," said Glorma I.

"We're not interested in fun," said Murgatroyd. "Can we go outside, please. Or shall we just go by ourselves?"

"You can't," said Glorma II.

"Why not?"

"Because you'd choke," she said. "There ain't enough oxygen no more. You can breathe outside for, maybe, ten minutes. Then you choke."

"What do people do when they leave the hall?" said Charles.

"We put on oxy-packs with mouth-tubes," said Glorma I. "It's real expensive. And it's dangerous. There's lots of unimproved folks out there, and they don't treat us gentle."

"Fit us up with packs, please," said Murgatroyd. "We'll pay for them."

Glorma II shook her head.

"Couldn't guarantee your safety," she said.

"Well, what do *you* do when *you* go out?" said Charles.

"Hire some cops," said Glorma II. "And that's real expensive, I'm telling you."

"We'll hire an escort in the same way," said Murgatroyd. "Would you be kind enough to put us in touch with someone reliable."

Glorma's two heads looked at each other. After a while they smiled.

"Sure," said the first. "We'll fix you up. Everything you need. Three oxy-masks, and our favorite cop. It'll cost you one-sixteenth of that bag of gold-dust."

"We can't afford that," said Charles.

"Yes we can," said Murgatroyd. "This is an unrepeatable opportunity. Give me a plastic sachet."

Charles pulled a small transparent envelope from his pocket. It was one of the ones he used to keep his stamps in. Reluctantly he pushed it across the table. The cat shook out a sixteenth of the bag into it, tapping it delicately with a half-extended claw. Then he licked the flap with a sweep of his pink tongue, pressed it down with a paw, and nudged it over to Glorma I.

"Cash in advance this time," he said. "No problem."

Glorma dropped the sachet into a pocket hidden by the folds of her skirt. Then she clapped both her pairs of hands to summon a waiter.

"Get Luigi," she told him. "And three snifferators for my friends. They're going to out."

The waiter bowed.

"My pleasure, Madam Glorma," he murmured. "I shall see to your needs at once."

He was back a few minutes later, followed by a man with four heavily muscled arms, all of them with rolled-up sleeves. The man's face — just a single face — was weary but tough, with a small downturned mouth. Four holsters bumped against his stomach with odd-looking guns in them. Probably stun-guns, thought John. People here are too valuable to be killed.

"Luigi," said Glorma I, "wantya to meet my friends from Science-time. This is John. John, Luigi. Luigi Motorola. My personal cop. Charles, Luigi. And this is Murgatroyd, Luigi. Yeah, he speaks, too. Big vocab."

"Ah. Timeys. I see," said Luigi.

He shook the boys' hands and stroked the back of Murgatroyd's neck.

"Pleased to meet y'all," he added.

He remained standing.

"Luigi," said Glorma I, "they want to out."

"I figured that," said the cop. "You told 'em what it's like, yet?"

"Yeah. General idea," said Glorma I.

"Listen, timeys," said Luigi, "Out is not the kinda place you folks should be wasting your time on. Why'nt you stay in here? It's beautiful. Clean. Safe. Fun. You got business or something in Out?"

"We thought we'd like to see something else," said Murgatroyd.

"Some things," said Luigi, "ain't fit for decent people to see."

"What's so bad about it?" said Charles.

"Out there there's so much filth you can't even breathe the air," said

Luigi. "You've gotta have an oxy-pack. Glorma, you order snifferators for the timeys?"

"Coming," said Glorma I. "And, uh — forgotta tell you. These folks are offering you twenty kreds for six hours."

Luigi looked startled.

"That's paying good, timeys," he said. "And I hope you can afford it. For your sakes. It's not good for the health, being shorta cash here. But money ain't everything. For twenty kreds, I don't wantya to be disappointed. Don't wantya going back whenever it is you're from and telling your folks you had a bad time here. I sure know what I'd do with twenty kreds to spare. Spend 'em here, right on the inside."

As Luigi finished speaking, the waiter reappeared. He had two large back-packs with brass cylinders on them for the boys, and a small one for the cat.

"Right or wrong, Luigi," said Murgatroyd, "we want to understand this place."

Luigi shrugged, and raised all four of his hands slightly up and outwards as if to say 'what-can-you-do-about-it?'.

"I tried, Miz Glorma, I tried," he said. "It's goddam crazy, wasting twenty kreds just to see a lot of no-hopers. I mean, you could get a real good ear for less."

He said nothing more, but led them to the down-escalator. Its gold and glass steps hung in a curve like a rope, moving endlessly towards the concourse a hundred and fifty feet below. It dropped so fast at first it took their breaths away, but then levelled off to deliver them at a walking pace at the bottom.

OUT REALLY WAS unpleasant. Water ran across the streets, smelling of acid. Sickly rainbows gleamed from puddles of oil. Mounds of detergent froth choked the sink-holes of the gutters. Above this foot-level mess rose buildings. Some were eyeless cylinders of smoked glass, others corroded spines of metal armour and grilles. To John they seemed like the insides of an old-style wireless set, its thermionic valves and condensers swollen to a gigantic size. Or like overgrown metal vegetables.

Khaki-green fog gusted past their faces, smelling of burning rubber. The tops of the buildings were half-hidden in its haze. They sucked on their oxy-tubes, relieved at the relief.

People limped past them, trying to go faster than their bodies would let them. Only the four of them were looking around — tourists, taking their time.

These men and women, grim and hurrying, were like a different species from the good-timers in Funworld. Many had only one arm, or bumped along on a crutch and a single leg. Others had an ear or a hand missing. Charles watched a legless man sitting on a skateboard, and leaning down and pulling himself along the street with mudstained hands. Another legless person looked out from a pram, as a friend with one eye wheeled her along. Now and then a policeman could be seen walking by, like a zoo-keeper, with four arms and two heads, one facing in either direction. Once in a while they passed a normal person, who gave them a frightened glance. Everyone else was missing something.

"So this is where the extra limbs come from," said Charles. "From the poorer people."

"They should have such luck," said Luigi, tugging out his oxy-tube and spitting on the sidewalk. "Think it through from their point of view. A guy runs outa money. OK.? He can't afforda to breathe no more. He can't afforda to drink. He can't afforda to eat. So how can he go on living?"

"He doesn't," said Charles. "Not unless someone helps him."

"Right," said the cop. "You got it. He dies. But if he can sell an arm or a leg to someone with money, he lives. Right? And the other guy gets to develop himself."

"If you're short of a hand or a leg," said Charles, "it's harder to make a living, wouldn't you agree?"

"Sure is," Luigi agreed, pushing his oxy-tube back into the corner of his mouth. "When you're doing good, smart thing is to build up a reserve. Like I don't really need four arms, though they come in handy at times. Take too much extra feeding. But suppose I need cash quick, I can always sell one. Better than money in a bank, ain't it?"

"Do people without hands ever make it up the ladder again?" Charles went on.

"Oh, sure do," said Luigi. "Sometimes. But they gotta have character. Lotta character. See that movie-house over there?"

He pointed.

Charles gave a nod.

"That title in lights out the front," said Luigi. "You read it?"

"THE MAKING OF A MAN?" said Charles.

"That's it," said Luigi. "It's a true story. Very, very moving. Or that's how it got me. 'Bout a guy who loses both arms, both legs, his unmentionables, and an ear. But, you know what, he makes it back. Today he's got the greatest body in Funworld. You should see it. Three torsos. Beautiful muscles, real sleek. Shine widda oil. Twenty-eight arms, matched in pairs. Other things, too. Can you imagine just the feeling of bein' him? I know some friends of mine wept when they saw that film. It's emotional. You wanna see it?"

"No thanks," said Murgatroyd. "There's not time."

"How did he do it?" said Charles. "With next to nothing left?"

"Sang," said Luigi. "He sang his way back."

"What would have happened," said Murgatroyd, "if he hadn't had a good voice? Like mine, for instance. What if nobody had liked his singing?"

"No one ever dies round here," said Luigi, "if that's what you're thinking. People who don't make it good, they just get redistributed. So they live on, but as parts of other people. Wouldn't you prefer that, if you were going to die?"

"I think I might find it difficult to know who I was," said Charles.

"Charlie, dontcha think dying might remove that altogether?" said Luigi. "Think of the economics. You throw away a body, it's just a waste. All that feeding, all that training, all that work you put into makin' it, and you wanna throw it away? Not me. I'd rather become part of some guy who's a success, and feed nice and be dressed good. Wouldn't you?"

"In other words," said Charles drily, "if you can't beat 'em, join 'em."

"That's it," said Luigi, not realizing Charles had made a joke.

Murgatroyd coughed furiously into his snifferator, trying to hide his laughter.

John did not react. He had said nothing all this time. He walked along, with his eyes screwed up, drawing deep breaths on his tube, and looking more and more unhappy.

"Is there anything else going on," he said, "beside the movies? Somewhere we could drop in and see a bit of life?"

"Life?!" said Luigi in disgust. "No. Not really. People only come out here when they got business. Or when they got no place else to go."

"Hey, you!" he growled as a one-legged passer-by lurched into him. "Where d'ya think you're going?"

The one-legged man took two more hops. His stick buckled under him, and he collapsed on the sidewalk. He lay face downwards, and the blood trickled slowly out from under his forehead. Luigi knelt down and examined his back-pack.

"Same old story," he said. "Run out of oxygen. Good-for-nothing, that's all."

He riffled through the man's pockets, using two fingers like a pickpocket to fork up an old plastic billfold. He flipped it open.

"See," he said. "No money. No oxygen. An' too damn proud to go to a body-shop while there was time. We'll just have to do what we can."

"Going to help him?" asked Charles.

"Nope," said Luigi. "I ain't. You help people, they stop trying. Or they depend on you. No oxy, he's a goner anyway. Guys like this make me puke, wasting their bodies. Their beautiful, valuable bodies."

He pulled out a flat black case and snapped back the lid. Inside there were surgical instruments. Silver-steel scalpels nestling in black velvet depressions, clips, curved needles, and a couple of blood-stained rags. He fished two long plastic socks from an outside pocket, and Charles realized what Luigi was going to do.

"You can't dissect him, " he said. "He's not even dead."

"Look, timey," said Luigi, "I don't get his arms off while he's still fresh, then he goes to waste. One hundred per cent waste. Wise up."

He worked fast. First he slit the clothing below the neck, then he cut and pinned back the skin, and disentangled the nerves and muscles. A small crowd gathered around, but not to watch.

"Jackals," said Murgatroyd. "Human jackals. Waiting for their turn."

John and Charles turned away, unable to look at what was going on.

It didn't seem long before Luigi clapped them both on their shoulders.

"All done," he said cheerfully. "Let's go. I gotta find a body-shop. Get these beauties dumped inna the freezer."

Two arms, pinkish-grey in their transparent plastic bags, swung on cords from his shoulder like salmon. The boys had no choice but to follow him, this way, then that way, round several corners. There was one freshly painted store- front in a long row of grimy buildings. Only one. It was here that he headed. The window outside, brightly lit, was like a real-estate agent's. Glossy colour snaps were pinned to boards, and the prices were neatly printed underneath, giving the price in kreds and the history of the donor.

Once glance was enough. The boys and Murgatroyd refused to go in. They waited, their backs to the window, till Luigi reappeared with a smile of satisfaction on his face.

"John," he said, "you wanted to see a bit of life. My friend in there just reminded me — there's a dive near here. *The Laughing Cripple*. Wanna give it a try?"

"What is it?" said John.

"Sorta night-club. Good music, lousy drink, other things if you can pay for 'em. Talk if you can't," said Luigi. "Fulla failures. Helpin' each other to hide it from themselves. Makes me feel sick justa see 'em. But you said you wanted to see everything? Right? I guess this is part of everything."

"Let's give it a go, then," said John.

The Laughing Cripple was in a basement at the bottom of winding stone steps with black slime on them. It would have been easy to half-slip and turn an ankle. Just inside the door they were stopped by a burly one-armed man. His face looked crumpled, like a pushed-in paper bag.

"Hiya, Jampole," said Luigi. "How's business?"

"Dyin', Mr Motorola," said the one-armed man. "Dyin'. Pianist's quittin'."

"Crabfingers quittin'?" said Luigi. "He can't afforda retire. None of us can. Where's he off to?"

"Better ask him yourselves," said Jampole. "He ain't told the rest of us nothin'. Quarter kred for four airs."

He held out his single hand.

"For air?" said John, surprised.

"Yuh. Don't need your oxy-pack inside," said Luigi, "so they gotta charge us for the air. Be my guest. I made a nice profit already this trip."

He slipped the doorman a hologrammed token, and Jampole waved them in.

"Have good time, folks," he said. "While you can. We ain't none of us in one piece for ever."

It was darker inside, and more than half empty. Scarred wooden table were scattered about, and a few cane chairs. The guests were sitting in separate groups, taking no notice of each other. Up on the stage a black man with iron grey frizzy hair was drawing a tune — slowly, ever so slowly — out of an upright piano. A saxophone lay on a chair nearby, but no one was playing it. In the corner stood an unattended bass drum, a snare-drum, and a pair of high-hat cymbals. The atmosphere was weird. Life seemed to be moving at half its normal pace.

"That's old Crabfingers," whispered Luigi. "Crabfingers Odum. Kinda cool, dontcha think?"

John did not answer.

He was listening.

The old man wasn't just good. He was *incredible.* He was leaning back on that rhythm so it pulled and pulled on your heart, without ever letting the inner beat weaken. And the tune was sad. Sad beyond anything he had ever imagined. The high notes floated out, over the bass, as if they had a life of their own. Every now and then one of the people at the other tables would shout, "Hear ya, Crab! Hear ya!," and the old pianist would lift a hand in acknowledgement.

A waitress appeared and served them four glasses of lemonade and a plate of biscuits. Her face was sweet but weary. Her brown hair came down loose to her shoulders, but didn't quite hide that her ears had gone.

"Gloomy hole, ain't it?" said Luigi. "I think folks should enjoy themselves more. Don't know what's wrong with 'em. Had enough now? Wanna be moving?"

"*No*," said John. "I want to get to the bottom of this."

He stalked up onto the stage, crossed it, and sat down behind the drums. He remained motionless there, gathering his thoughts and waiting. Crabfingers seemed not to have noticed him, but he had. Unobtrusively, he shifted into a complicated double rhythm, two speeds running against each other. It was an unspoken challenge. Read that, man, if you can. Read that.

But John had his measure. Softly, effortlessly, the way a wind first starts to blow, he let the wire brushes echo a background, sometimes across the drums, sometimes on the cymbals. The bleak and difficult piano tune became a duet, as if two people were walking along together where only one had been walking before.

Little by little, John let fiercer sparks of sound break in. Crabfingers responded. Thick jagged chords, like handfuls of rock-crystal. Melancholy was becoming defiance. And then *boum*! The foot-pedal beat on the drum for the first time. Like a tremor from the depths of the earth. Like an earthquake awakening. *Boum*! Crabfingers poured back a cloudburst of runs. Spattering, shattering, up and down the keyboard. Up and down, up and down. *Boum*! *Boum*! *Boum*!

And suddenly stopped.

The same instant, exactly, the drums were silent. By some sixth sense, John had known it was coming. All had been said.

No clapping came out of the darkness below. Only a hush. Crabfingers stared at the keys. He shook his head. John got up and walked over, putting his hand around the old man's shoulder.

"Maestro," he said, "come and have a drink with us."

Crabfingers looked up.

"Who are you?" he said.

"John."

"Where you from?"

"Not where," said John, "but when. We are travellers in time — myself, my brother Charles, and our cat, Murgatroyd. We are from what you call the Early Scientific Age."

Crabfingers smiled. His brooding, frozen face broke into a wide smile of some secret inner triumph.

"It is explained," he said. "Explained. No one, no one livin' in this age could play along with me like that. And no one, no one ever before, has known exactly when I going to stop. So, yes, John, I will have that drink with you. With you, it will be an honour."

It was clear, as he sat down, he didn't care to have a cop at the table with him, but he treated Luigi with a dignified, distant courtesy.

"Talkin' cats common in your time?" he asked Murgatroyd.

"No," said the black cat. "There was only me."

"How could that be?"

"Once," said the cat, "I was a Prince over the Darkness. And I committed the Great Disobedience. *I foreswore all evil.* It was not my part to do so. Not my destiny. When I did, I angered the Master of Darkness, and worse, the greater power that set him there and gave him his task. For evil has its part to play, and if its servants renounce it, as I did, they have nowhere to go. I am the last shadow of myself, nothing compared to what I used to be. Surviving only because of my insignificance."

"You serious?" said Luigi. "you never told me anything like that."

"He is entirely serious, cop," said the old pianist. "I can tell you that. I have heard the voice, the voice outa the whirlwind, tellin' me my pain is nothing to the pain that could be, and yet be survived. Soon, I going to be next to nothing, too, but thinkin' on the glory of all that is, I shall survive. Survive somehow."

The policeman raised his eyebrows, then shook his head.

Crabfingers smiled again.

"Don' worry," he said. "I don't expect you to understand a word I say."

A long silence followed before John resumed the conversation.

"They've told us you're leaving tomorrow, Mr Odum," he said. "That true?"

Crabfingers nodded.

"I been made an offer I cannot refuse," he said. "Five thousand kreds. On money like that my family and myself, we can live for many years, if we're careful. I'm in debt just now, as it happens. I going to have to sell myself, sooner or later."

"A family?" said Luigi in disbelief. "You people out here still have *families?*"

"We have families. 'Course we have families," said Crabfingers. "You live entirely for yourself, life becomes meaningless."

He stretched out his right arm and right hand, and let them rest on the table.

"See that," he said. "I been offered five thousand kreds for this hand and forearm. By the agent of someone who wants a musical hand. Buyer's going to inspect it a coupla hours from now. Y'all just heard my last piece. And, John, thank you. I'd never have believed it, you walkin' in just that moment. From somewhen outa another time. You made it one of the greatest — no, the greatest ever."

Sickness welled up in John's heart. Rage at himself. He mastered his feelings with the utmost difficulty. Then he pulled out his wash-leather bag, with the Jurassic gold-dust in it. He gripped the old man's enormous fingers, and stuffed the bag between them.

"This is gold," he said. "Gold from the Mesozoic. It is unique in all of space-time, except for the few other bags we have. It is worth at least half a million kreds, from what I have seen of prices here, and probably far more, if you know how to drive a bargain. For a certainty, no less. Take it. Use it as necessary. Look after your family. And play, as long as life lasts, with both your hands. *Your own.*"

He got up from the table and began to walk unsteadily towards the door, picking up his oxy-pack as he left. He just remembered in time to turn it on as he began to climb the slimy steps, in a daze, back up into the street.

Tears, which he wanted no one to see, were running down his face.

In the basement he left behind him, sitting at a scarred old table, in front of a half-drunk lemonade, Crabfingers Odum staring at the gift that had just changed his future.

"You tell me what this means, please," he said to Murgatroyd.

"That you have been saved," said the cat, "and that John has been saved, from something unspeakable. Don't try to understand it further."

"Oh, no," said Crabfingers, "I understood it already. Glory be to all that is. An' believe you me, I already forgiven him a thousand times. Once he had understood, fully understood, there was no trace of evil in him. Only generosity, unbounded generosity. In music, there's a great friendship, and a great healing. I never going to forget I played with him once, and I believe he never going to forget that he, too, played along with me. And gratitude is equal, both ways, for, to tell the truth, I, too, done him a service."

He stood up, shook hands with Charles briefly, bowed to the cat and Luigi, then shuffled off into the darkness. He seemed strangely smaller than he had been before, as if all the energy had drained out of him.

"Your brother," said Luigi to Charles, "is the most stupid, goddammed idiot I have ever seen, if you'll pardon me saying so. If he stays round here much longer, he'll end up as scraps."

"We can talk about John later," said Charles. "I'm just glad he's still my brother. Now we'd better get back, please, to the glass palace and cancel

252

Glorma's contract."

Jampole gave them a big smile as they said goodbye to him.

"Pianist's stayin'," he said. "Don' know how ya did it, but thanks a million."

"Nobody knows how or why we came here, and nowhere else," said Charles softly. "All I can say is, I suppose that's why we came. Or, maybe, were meant to come."

They made their way up the steps to the outside again, Murgatroyd sitting on Charles's shoulder, and Luigi following along behind.

They began to suck on their oxy-pipes, and settle into their stride for the long walk back to Funworld through the unbreathable air.

———————

• home time

IT WAS LATE in the afternoon in Oxford. The sun shone aslant the witch's garden. Bent-over roses projected their crooked shadows across the uncut grass. New fleshy branches pushed out of the stump of an elder-tree. Clusters of runner-beans hung down unpicked, too old and rough for eating. Their tendrils writhed around the bamboo poles, strangling each other with affection.

Megan closed her curtains, and the autumn day vanished behind the velvet darkness. She turned on her television, watching the flickerings in the abyss. Then she tiptoed to her chair, a thin smile running to the corners of her mouth. Her black cat stretched his way over the carpet, and rubbed against her legs. After which he, too, sat still and watched.

A glade had opened in front of them. Charles was fencing a boy with red-auburn curls. Their crossing swords flashed like water in a mountain torrent. Tree-branches heavy with buds hung low over the grass. Between the roots grew fragile yellow flowers. A herd of deer browsed in the distance, unconcerned.

The duel was fast. Feints, parries, lunges, ripostes, and deflections followed without a moment for thought or inner doubt.

"Beautiful, those cruel swords," murmured Megan to herself.

Her breathing came faster. Two hot spots darkened along her cheeks. She felt a fizz, like warm electricity, run through her body.

She had the delicious illusion that she was alive again.

"What a pity it would have been to have let him escape," she whispered. "One of them is going to be killed soon."

"The chase was more thrilling than an easy capture," said the cat. "The darkness made darker by those feeble fairground lights. The growing terror of our victims until, when the end came, they almost welcomed it. And the Ferris wheel turning above us all the time like an eternal torture."

"Ixion's wheel in Hell," said the witch. "What a mess the fairground people leave at the back of their tents. Piles of boards, electric generators resting from their labours, guy-ropes.... It wasn't so easy for Tweedledee to follow you through all that. He's inclined to be clumsy. I thought we were going to lose them among those lemming-like adults and mindless music."

"But the capture," said the cat. "The capture. Wasn't *that* satisfying? The click of the latch closing on the wooden stomach, when you knew you'd got them? I loved it when you gave them a dab on the back of the neck and they went limp. The way a spider does it."

"There was no other means of — forgive the term — squashing them in. A design-fault in your monster, my obsequious cat, as you will be obliged to concede. Spider-poison liquefies its victims. It would be — shall we say — unfortunate if it appears to have impaired the quality."

"To me, Madam, they seem the sweetest of electronic delicacies. I trust I am not mistaken."

"Adorably destroyable, yes. Yes. But there is still something missing. Some I-know-not-what in the after-taste. *Too* sweet, perhaps."

She turned her attention back to the television set; and the cat, wisely, kept his mouth shut.

"TIME," said the other Murgatroyd, far away in the future. "Time we returned. Your other selves are still caught in Megan's television set, becoming less like you every day. You need to rescue them."

Funworld had vanished, like Label-Land before it. The world flowing past outside the Time-traveller was four-dimensional. They could *see* time. Like shining twisted lengthwise-corrugated streamers the lives of mountain ranges spread out in their minds as *single things* all the way from their moment of birth to their last dissolving shreds of existence. The same for whole planets. And even for burning clusters of stars, forming from dark swirls of dust, then bursting into flame, exploding in far-flung helical tentacles, growing dark again. Complicated single things in the four dimensions of space and time. Change seemed an illusion.

"What if we don't?" said John.

"We become ghosts," answered the cat. "Like the Flying Dutchman, we wander through space-time forever. We belong nowhen."

"Couldn't we just go back to Oxford the way we are now?" said Charles. "And forget about the John and Charles captured by Megan?"

"If your friends had been caught by a witch, would you let them down? — No? So, are you going to let yourselves down?"

"For your friends you have no choice," said Charles. "For ourselves, we do."

"What would happen to them and us," said John, "if each of us went our own way?"

"I'm not certain," Murgatroyd replied. "Something is missing in both of you now. I used to be able to feel that something. It's gone. A kind of warmth, a kind of spontaneity. Everything you do now is determined, thought-out. Impressive, too. But I miss the boys I used to know."

"Do we get it back if we rescue our other selves," said Charles. "Or is it something that gets lost when you grow up anyway?"

"It's that warmth that Megan absorbs out of her children. She needs it, the way a sick person needs a pain-killer. You will never be completely yourselves again unless you recover it. With luck it will only be hidden as you grow older, not dissolve."

John looked at Charles. They understood each others' thoughts.

"Right, then," said John. "We're going back."

"Oxford," muttered Charles. "How do I find it? What will it seem like after we've been away so long?"

"No one understands his home but the traveller," said Murgatroyd. "The citizens of Uruk of the baked-brick walls — who knew what they really were but Gilgamesh their king, returning from his journey? Who but the home-coming travel-stained Odysseus, familiar with the minds of all peoples, could discern the true nature of his own Ithacans?"

"Oxford will have changed," said John.

"Less than you will have."

"I'm not just searching for Oxford," said Charles. "I'm looking for a house I've never seen before. And for one room in it, with a television set. How do I pinpoint it, with what seems like all eternity around us here?"

"Affinity," answered the cat. "Response across time and space. Think of your other self. Of that frightened face on the other side of a closing glass door. The first law of magic is that 'Essences that are similar will seek each other out'. You can be drawn back to yourself, even across the abyss."

Charles nodded, and closed his eyes in concentration.

"What will our other selves have become?" said John softly to Murgatroyd. "Is it possible to join with them again. Could we take over each others' memories? Remember things that never happened to one of us? Will we have to live like twins, the same but not quite?"

The black cat shook his head.

"There *are* new things under the sun," he replied. "This is something I've never seen before. Never even heard of."

"Suppose our other halves don't want to be rescued. Suppose they are happy where they are?"

"That might be a problem. Most of her children love being in her garden, until near the end of their internment."

"If so, what do we do?"

"Don't make plans. React. In Megan's world, what it is depends on the state of your mind."

John pursed his lips. Success, for him, had to be built on planning. How else could he have laid the lines of fires that had saved the time-travellers from the ceratosaurs? But he said nothing more.

THE WITCH, whatever she had pretended to her cat, had relished the hunt. Water hitting a throat parched desert-dry was nothing compared to the inner ecstasy she had felt at that double capture. Now she was enjoying them in a gentler way.

So full of life! Such handsome sweating faces! Such exuberance in just being themselves! That inner springtime that the young have, but are unaware of. Which the old can only hunger after.

She pressed her fingertips against each other, and watched Charles fighting Berklak.

Megan had not guessed that the boys and the black cat had split. It did not occur to her that the boys might have adult halves, still free. Such things had almost never happened. The thought that they might be planning to rescue their child selves from her power was not even the possibility of a possibility. Her mind was relaxed and unwary in its enjoyment.

Surprise was complete.

The duel disappeared from the screen. Three youngsters appeared in its place, sprawling on a Persian carpet. It was a magnificent carpet, she noted, full of dark blues and rusty reds, decorated with dull orange-coloured lozenges, and diamond-shapes of a glittering black. Above it, round fruits and dark green leaves sparkled fiercely in the sun. Like a tapestry.

The girl was black, with mischievous eyes. She was sitting cross-legged, wearing dirty white shorts and a crumpled, once-white, sweat-shirt. A silvery-white kitten dangled from her hand by the scruff of its neck. She kept laughing. The witch knew well enough who she was.

The other two looked like John and Charles. And also not like John and Charles. Their faces were edgy and uncertain.

"*What's this?!*" said Megan sharply.

The cat simply looked at her.

Puzzled.

"I did not change channels," she added.

"Then what's happened to the duel?"

"That is not apparent. It was a fencing-match with a nice taste of reality. Both swords were sharpened this morning. They helped each other do it. And — there is a death coming. I like deaths. So — *final*. I hope I haven't missed it."

258

She turned off the power. The huge screen melted to a mid-grey blur.

"I'll try it again in a moment," she explained.

Before she could lift her hand, *the screen lit up again.* First the other Charles, then the other John, the black girl, and the silver-coloured kitten reappeared. The humans were arguing about something.

She could hear them, but had no intention of listening to what they were saying. Her eyes were hard. She kept running a white-lacquered fingernail along the milled edges of the knobs, making her cat wince at the sound.

"The power is off," she said. "How can the picture be there still?"

She twist-clicked three other knobs. Back and forth. Nothing happened.

"There's no voltage coming through, either," she rasped. "I can't get any feelings."

"Turn the set back on," said the cat.

She looked at him sourly, and did so. When she next spoke, her voice was harsh and shaking, like clinker being raked out of a grate.

"It makes no difference. Feeling's dead. Something has got into the set. Invaded it. Some force is keeping it from my will."

"Impossible, Madam."

"Stop soothing me," the witch snapped. "It is evident enough what has happened. An alien will is after my children. I shall have to enter the set myself, and destroy it."

The black cat's jaw dropped open.

"But what if you were turned off from outside," he said. "It's too dangerous."

"You will remain outside," said Megan, "to ensure that that doesn't happen."

"As you command, my lady," he murmured.

Then his voice began to quaver-miaow.

"Look.... Look at the set again."

"What is it, you querulous creature?"

"Madam, if you meet with a black cat inside, I would beg you please to remember that that cat is not me. I have never disobeyed you. I am devoted to your interests."

The witch peered again at the screen. Hmm! She hadn't seen what her familiar had seen. Sitting quite still in the shadows was a majestic black cat. He looked like her own Murgatroyd, but he was heavy, not scrawny. His eyes were almost the same, too. Their green was not cloudy, however, but clear and unfathomable.

"*Two of you!*" she said. "Two of you. I never put a cat in there. How did he get in?"

She reflected, pursed her lips, and frowned.

"Two of you. So, I wonder if perhaps there are two of them? Tell me, do you see anything different about these two boys? — The ones that are giving me no heart-thrill."

The cat looked them over professionally.

"As you are aware, Madam, I do not feel thrill. So I can only say that they look older to me. Grimmer, and with a certain melancholy."

The witch interrupted him.

"Do you recall that time-travelling carriage? The one at Saint Giles's Fair?"

"Indeed, Madam, I do. A vulgar piece of painted-up nonsense, and close to falling to bits."

"Do you further recall that it vanished, just as we were compressing the two victims' little bodies into the wooden stomach?"

"It came back. Almost at once. Away for half a minute, at most."

"In half a minute," said the witch, "a million years can pass. If they really travelled in time."

"My lady," said the black cat, "with the greatest of respect, that is the kind of delusion that normally afflicts human beings, rather than an enlightened entity like yourself. Surely it was the fraud that it appeared to be? Fairground humans make their living using contraptions like that to fool standard-issue members of the human public."

"A transparent deception may at times be the subtlest disguise," said the witch tartly. "Hide real magic in a conjuring show, and who will believe that the magic is real? You have overlooked a critical consideration."

"Please remember," said the cat, "that whatever I may have been in my previous lives, I am now only your humble inferior. What have I overlooked?"

"When that little group of humans came back, just as we were guiding Dee off the platform, they were unkempt and dirty. They smelled as if they had not washed for weeks. Their clothes were grimy. The men had scruffy beards. The eyes of the women were open too wide. They had looked at death, their own death, face on, and had not yet recovered from surviving it. All that in an ordinary half-minute?"

"There was rather a charming little girl," said the cat. "I remember wondering if you'd enjoy her. She was not wide-eyed with fear, but delightedly happy."

"I did indeed enjoy her," said the witch. "Just looking at her. But do you recall what she said, and what happened? — 'Mummy, when can we see the dinosaurs again?' A harmless, if silly, request, if all they had seen were some projected pictures. But her mother began to slap her, and shout. Even for a human mother, that surprised me. They had seen something, that lot, and been scared witless."

"The projections are good," objected the cat. "They do Hannibal crossing the Alps with his elephants. They do slaves strung up on crosses all down the Appian Way after the crushing of Spartacus' rebellion. There's even a charming tableau of Adam and Eve cuddling under an apple-tree in the Garden of Eden. Brings back the past remarkably, even if some of the details are absurdly wrong. Why shouldn't the dinosaurs have made an effect on them?"

"Men don't grow beards watching films. But forget that. Do you remember what happened next?"

'Not too well. There was a City Councillor woman making a fuss about something. Wanted a new bye-law against dinosaurs, or licence fees for Time-travellers, or something. Why?"

"Not that, my muddle-brained familiar. After the doors on the carriage had shut again, what happened?"

"Rolled off down a siding, I think."

"No. It did not," said the witch. "It vanished again. There were still two boys inside it, and a cat."

"What do you mean. The boys were in the monster, and I was on the platform with you."

"What I mean," said Megan, "is that what appears to have occurred is that you all split."

Moonlight falling on drifting pack-ice was warmer than her smile. Two little television screens danced reflected in her eyes.

"For the last four days," she said, "you have been the perfect servant, something you have never been before. The new mixture of servility and insolence has been a constant delight to me. You have even taken pleasure in your work. Extraordinary. Even as late as last week I was beginning to suspect you of insubordination."

The cat sat very erect, looking up at her.

"I am devoted to you, my lady," he said. "Devoted, believe me, heart and soul."

"It is just as well for you that you have neither," said Megan. "As I was saying, I was wondering last week — needless to say, only as a hypothesis — if the best place for you wouldn't be a closed time-loop, a little half-hour that went round forever and ever, like a loop on a faultily programmed computer."

"HSM," sad the cat plaintively, "who trapped the pretty morsels for you? Who dreamt up for you Tweedledum and Tweedledee? Who sweet-talked the reluctant youngsters into coming out at night?"

"Bad Murgatroyd," said the witch. "Just as it was Good Murgatroyd who devised all the difficulties, without which such a complicated plan would never have been necessary. Who betrayed my secrets? Who put protection spells around the house? Who tricked my wind-hands? And who, my dear familiar — now grovelling so ingratiatingly — invented that gruesome Stuffed Sleeping-Bag Bear?"

The venom in her voice made her seem like a coiled rattlesnake lusting for a bite.

"Nothing is wrong with me now," said the cat, miaowing and cringing. "I was just trying to win their confidence."

"You will have to lie better than that to persuade me," said the witch. "It's lucky there's nothing right with you now. That is how I like it. You have split between good and evil, haven't you?"

Her hand ran lovingly down his back. He arched in response and blue sparks of static electricity crackled in his fur.

"Do you think John and Charles have split the same way?"

"Unlikely. They've not had enough time for evil to mature in them. Each being is like a raw diamond. If it splits, it splits along its lines of weakness. Good/Bad splitting I've seen, but this is something different."

"How have they split, then?"

"I'm not sure. That is another reason why I must go into the set and see for myself."

She opened a drawer in the low table at her side, and picked out some white silk gloves. She pulled them on, tugging each one tight, like a surgeon preparing for an operation. Ripples began to flow inwards on the picture, which was still moving on the television screen. They were like water gathering and vanishing at a central point. Faster and faster they converged and disappeared. The witch rose from her chair, stood suddenly straight, then arced like a diver into the heart of the scene in front of her. As she entered it, she became invisible. The ripples closed behind her feet. The picture continued calmly, the two boys arguing with the black girl under the tree laden with fruit in the sunshine. The cat sitting in the shadows.

But Bad Murgatroyd stared after her. He glanced nervously over his shoulder. Then, as if pouncing on a snake, he leapt on the wire leading to the power-socket. His paw raked across it, and tore it free from the set.

Nothing happened to the picture.

He pushed the power-switch off and on, and off again.

Still nothing happened.

He fled in panic.

NO WARNING TOLD the time-travellers they were entering Megan's set. No black-and-white wheel of nights and days flickering to a stop. No jolt and shudder that signalled the end of the journey. They found themselves there suddenly, in a landscape as bright as a painting. Charles's mind had taken them home directly.

They swung the doors open, and paused at the doorway to breathe. The air that filled their lungs was sweet, heavy, and alive. Bracken beneath them sparkled with dew. They stepped down onto it, feeling only the lightest pressure under their feet.

This world was more subtle and beautiful than any they had been in before. Everything here could be seen to be made of tiny spinning globes, if you kept your eyes on it intently enough. Some of the globes were bright, some dark; and their colours kept changing. Nothing had clear edges. Each thing merged into the other things around it. A single flow of light and shadow ran through the gently stretching trees and through the secretly purposeful streams. The trembling ferns and the self-admiring flowers were made from the same fabric as the birds who perched and darted and perched again, as if they were tearing free from and then rejoining the pattern. Heavy bees voyaged down invisible corridors of air, corridors only created by their voyaging. The wary deer were a part of the meadows where they nibbled at their leisure and from time to time looked up The sharp-eyed pine-martens were indistinguishable from the shadows in which they hid.

Compared to this rich polyphony of colours, thought John, what had Label Land been but a child's painting-book with the outlines to be filled in by the numbers? What had Funworld been but a travel-poster come to life — plus some of the sights that travel-posters don't usually show you, but are usually there.

Nothing stayed still. Even time itself was irregular. They watched some lilies. Maybe they watched an hour. Maybe ten minutes. The buds undid themselves. The petals folded back, each honey-coloured layer disclosing another layer beneath. Stamens thust forth. Heavy, orange-golden, tipped with pollen. Then the flowers hung limp, the honey hues staining with brown, like tassels on an old cushion. The stalks grew dry, then crumpled.

From the distance it looked like time-lapse photography. Close to, it was a dance. A dance of millions and millions of spinning globes, minute, but possible to see. They swirled in patterns along hidden lines of force; and these patterns rearranged themselves from time to time in little jerky shifts, or else suddenly disintegrated.

Sometimes the skyline seemed to move. Observed directly, it stayed still, like the hour-hand of a watch. When you glanced away, and then glanced back later, it had shifted. The rock-strata crept upwards like frozen sheared-off breakers, and the screes beneath the cliffs sneaked themselves slowly downwards like a milling scrum of motionless stones.

"In Megan's Garden of Delights," said John, "there are no separate things. Only spinning globes and happenings."

He pointed at a blackish shape.

"That was a tree-stump not so long ago. While we've been talking, it's been dissolving. You can see bits of it, or what used to be bits of it, flowing into those fat amber mushroom and those sponges of hungry red mould. Look at the ferns behind it. They're not ferns. They're millions of tiny particles conspiring to look like ferns. They sprout their heads, curled tight like the scrolls of little fiddles. They unroll themselves like fragile lace. They dry out, cast their spores, and crumble to brown-red dust. Are we changing like that ourselves, do you think?"

"Who knows?" said Murgatroyd. "Where do we find something changeless with which to measure change?"

"Is science impossible here, then?" returned John. "Would our wooden rulers sprout leaves, or sing like flutes? Would our weights grow cloudy and evaporate off the scales? Would our clocks have fits of hiccups, or spin their hands like propellers and lift themselves whirring into the sky?"

The cat laughed.

"You've caught the spirit of the place," he said. "This is a world of the mind. Remember the painter Seurat, who painted in nothing but dots? Thousands upon thousands of dots of the purest primary colours: red, yellow, and blue? His canvases swim with light. Somehow in your mind the dots turn into luminous, misty, presences that you see as the bodies of bathers, or trees. We're in a picture like that now. One that the witch is dreaming. Things float through us as we float through them."

"Could she switch us off?" asked Charles.

"She could, but don't let it worry you."

"Why not?"

"Because she'd have to switch us on again before long. She needs her fix. Her fix of kids' feelings. If the set's off for long she gets irritable. Hunger gnaws at her inside. Her fingers find their own way back to the knobs before she even knows what they're doing."

"Doesn't she sometimes hurt her children?"

"When they're old and coarse, and not cooperative. A dose of pain can jolt them into giving her some emotions."

"Could she come in here and confront us directly?"

"Yes."

264

"What would happen?"

"I don't know," replied the cat. "What would happen to a painter who became a figure in one of his own paintings? Or an author a character in one of his own stories? Would the other characters be able to take their revenge, if they felt hard done by? What would Tess say to Hardy if she had him at her mercy?"

"We had better get moving," interrupted John. "The sooner we do so, the better the chances that she won't notice us."

Charles felt a moment of panic in his stomach as the Time-traveller disappeared.

'If we can't find the old thing again,' he thought to himself, 'how are we going to get out? Me, maybe. But how do I take the others?'

He looked back and tried to fix the shape of the path in his memory. But there was nothing distinctive about the place. It was just a path, winding in and out of ash-trees, and elms with their serrated leaves, and a few old apple-trees. A red-berried snow-plant grew at his feet. Someone had ringed it with rocks. He knew it would be gone by the time they came back. Probably the rocks, too.

Murgatroyd sat on John's shoulders as they walked under immense pine-trees. The trunks rose above them, branchless for fifty feet, then spread into fan-vault tracery. Here and there the blue sky sparkled through the dark green.

The path ran out eventually into a moorland valley, where it vanished. Gorse bushes grew around them, bright with yellow flowers. On the other side of the valley, dim white mists drifted about on the hillsides. Dark-white wild horses wandered in and out of them, silently.

Then the valley deepened into a gorge. They found themselves strolling beside a river whose shallows were full of chattering pebbles. You could cross on accidental — or were they accidental? — stepping-stones. Further on came plunging rapids, followed by deep, clear pools where the water almost came to a standstill until the current had gathered its strength again to pour through the way out.

A wildcat with sulphur-yellow eyes watched them from a tree-branch, but only Murgatroyd noticed him there.

Along the bank, the path reappeared. They saw a boy and a girl looking at the river. As they came up to them, they could see the boy's face was pale, and his eyes dark and restless. Curls broke along his forehead in little waves. The girl was black; her skin shone the colour of coffee-beans. Muscles rippled lazily in her long arms, and she looked like an athlete. Her eyes were sometimes thoughtful, sometimes mischievous. When she flashed her white teeth, they seemed mocking. Her stained sweatshirt was half-tucked into a pair of crumpled shorts. The boy was bare to his waist, with his shirt rolled up and knotted around like a belt. Both of them were barefoot; their feet dirty with dust.

Some yards apart, all four stopped and looked at each other.

The girl raised her eyebrows.

"What *you* doin' here, Charlie?" she said.

Charles started at the mention of his name.

"Gone zombie," said the boy. "Berklak must have killed him."

"I'm alive," said Charles. "Touch me if you want."

He held out his hand, but the girl shrank back, looking at him.

"You was fightin' with Berklak when we left," she said. "You couldn'ta gotten here faster than us. Unless you's a ghost."

The boy walked slowly around Charles, very close. Charles could feel the heat coming off his body. The air between them began to dance like the air above a hot road on a summer's day. Then the boy moved away, and Charles felt cool again.

"He's older than Charles," he said, and the voice sounded musical and soft. "He's seen more. He wouldn't risk his life, or anyone else's, just for the fun of it."

"What's your name, then?" he added.

"The one you just gave me, and then took away. Charles. What's yours."

"Chardon. A worthless plant that grows in waste places. She's Daphne."

"Don't you recognize me?" said John. "There are two of me, too."

Chardon opened his dark eyes and looked at John. Then he half-closed them and seemed to sink into a trance.

"Are you someone we know?" he asked. "I can tell you've been wounded. A wound that will never quite heal. You know something of the sadness of the world. And its beauty. Beautiful because you know you are going to lose it."

"All musicians know that," John broke in. "Before music can become what it is, it has to vanish. You can't tell what a note is meant to say, how short it is, or how long, or how high or how strong, until it has already disappeared."

"We've no musicians like that around here," said Chardon. "I don't think we know you."

"My name is John. Is there no other me here?"

His face fell.

"We do have a John," said Daphne. "And his face does look a bit like yours. But he's a wild guy, with a real beautiful smile. Dimples, too. He climbs trees, an' rocks, an' scrambles up waterfalls. Water come streamin' down over his body, but he don't mind gettin' wet. Just laughs. He can do all kindsa strange things. He can take a snap of someone you know, lay it on a table, an' hang a nail on a thread above it — holdin' it 'tween his finger and thumb — an' then tell you by the way it swings roun' whether that person alive or dead. You do that?"

"I used to," said John. "I'm not sure it always works."

"What our John says," said Daphne, "is that if a person don't believe it, then it don't work. No better than chance. Perhaps you both right."

"Perhaps we are both right," said John with a sigh. "I used to climb trees. Even waterfalls. He's me all right, even if I no longer smile the-way he does."

There was a silence. The river resounded below them. A smell of wet mud and old leaves rose from the path, merging with the scent of birch-bark and sun-warmed rocks. A blue-jay rattled above their heads. Murgatroyd had been following some way behind. Now he gathered himself and sprang onto Charles's shoulder.

"Don't move!" said Chardon. "Don't frighten him and he won't hurt you."

Charles gave a slightly twisted smile.

"I'm sorry," he said. "I forgot to introduce you. There are three of us, Chardon, not two. This is Murgatroyd, our cat."

"I like cats," said Chardon. "They're beautiful, like me, and they do what they like."

He rubbed Murgatroyd under one of his cheeks.

"Hello," he said.

"I've seen him before," said Daphne. "Don't know where, though. Makes me uncomfortable to look at him. Maybe somethin' I don't like to remember."

She shivered.

"*I* remember *you*," said the black cat. "You used to wear a cotton frock with an apple-blossom pattern, and roll up the sleeves of your woolly jumper. It turned her on when you got angry, or cried."

Daphne looked at Murgatroyd coolly.

"So you's a talkin' cat. What d'you mean, 'It turned her on'? Who's she?"

John was impressed. She didn't shock easily.

"We're in a television set here," said Murgatroyd. "At that time, I was outside it, with my mistress, a witch called Megan, looking in. How else do you think I knew what you used to wear. She keeps you and Chardon, and the other John and Charles, in here for her amusement. Don't you know that?"

"You is outa your mind, pussy-cat," said Daphne. "This is the real world here, the real beautiful world. Not a television set."

"Look at those dark red paint-brush flowers," said John. "You can see they're made of little particles, like dots. Doesn't that tell you it's a television set?"

"The world's like that," said Chardon. "Everything's part of everything else. Like whirlpools spinning in a stream, coming together, breaking up. That doesn't tell you it's a TV."

"Come and sit down with us a moment," said John. "We'll give you our story, and maybe you'll believe us then. Even if you don't believe us — and why should you? — it's a good story."

He led them away from the river, following his feeling for the lines of force hidden in the ground, till he came to some granite boulders. They sat down there, with their backs to the rocks, letting the warmth flow into them. Chardon undid his rolled-up shirt and wedged it behind his head as a pillow. He flexed his toes into a fist-foot once or twice, then closed his eyes.

The rock-surfaces glistened with black and white specks, and a few green flecks of glinting mica. From time to time or or two of them would disappear. Otherwise, nothing seemed to be happening.

Time stops and repeats itself when a story is being told.

JOHN BEGAN with the bearded Dr Homely-Sage, who had come to dinner, hypnotized their mother, stuck a deadly needle into Tiger's heart, and then taken their mother away in his car, tied up in shimmering webs of words. He explained how he and Charles had answered an ad in the local newspaper, and how Murgatroyd had appeared, a well-spoken cat, looking for a friendly family, and with a number of magical tricks.

"He was of course Megan's cat," he added, "collecting children for her television. When children have just lost their mother, their soul-force is weak, and they are easier to capture. She feeds on imprisoned children's feelings."

"I think that Murgatroyd said Megan is a witch," said Chardon. "That right?"

"Correct," said the cat. "And also the witch who put you in here."

"I came of my own will," said Chardon. "No witch put me here."

"Let me finish our story first," said John. "For some reason, Murgatroyd betrayed her, and decided to help us instead."

"I admired you," said the cat. "The horror of what had happened would have broken most kids. You just fought back; and you really tried to take good care of me. You even refused to buy yourselves anything with my beautiful fake money. The deepest reason was that I still wanted, or part of me wanted, to be good, if I could."

"Sounds like me tryin' out what it feels like to be bad," said Daphne.

"I have always known what *that* feels like," said Chardon softly. "The best and the worst in me cannot be separated."

John took a breath and went on. He told them how Megan had devised one plan after another to seize them, even giving him orders in his dreams. His voice deepened as he recounted her defeats at the paws of Bear, Official Dreamguard. (And he thought to himself, how strange it is that even mentioning Bear's name makes me feel stronger.) As tactfully as he could, he explained why Murgatroyd had then betrayed them: the witch suspected him, and he feared he would be imprisoned by her to the end of time in a never-ending living death.

"How come you've forgiven him," said Daphne. "I wouldn't have."

"Murgatroyd is no longer what he was then," said John, "a mixture of evil and good. I was about to tell you how this happened."

He described the horrors of the night-time fair, and how he had used a rifle from a shooting-gallery to disable the huge wooden puppet, Tweedledum, when it had seized his brother. He spoke of the chase in the halls of mirrors, and how it had ended at Mackenzie's Time-traveller, where they were cornered by the witch and Tweedledee. He concluded with the splitting of their world-lines, when their adult selves had escaped into time, leaving their child selves prisoners, and how Murgatoyd had divided into his Good and Evil Inclinations.

Daphne was fascinated.

"Do you think I could travel through time, too?" she asked.

It was Charles who answered, taking up his part of the story:

"Long ago I stole a stegosaurus bone from the University Museum. Evil, too, you see, has always its part to play in the world. I had a feeling for that bone, as if we'd been old friends, maybe in a previous existence. I couldn't leave it there in its case."

"A feeling I know only too well," smiled Chardon. "Things do speak to one sometimes, and persuade one to liberate them."

"I always keep that bone in my pocket," Charles went on. "As Megan and Tweedledee closed behind us, I touched it by accident. We began to travel through time as I did so, together with all the other people sitting in the time-travelling carriage. They had a rough time, poor people, while we had a wonderful one. There are few experiences so upsetting as knowing you're buying a fake and then finding it's real. To the end, most of them didn't really believe what they saw; and I doubt if they ever will."

He then described his meeting with Steg, a friendship that made a hundred million years seem nothing, the forests and swamps of the Mesozoic, the giant dragonflies, and the mountains he had climbed once but which had now vanished forever. He spoke of how he had panned for gold; returned with Steg in the final desperate moment to help John and Billy and Ray defeat the last of the ceratosaurs; then brought the bewildered and unwilling time-travellers back home. He finished with their long loop through the future, undertaken partly to escape from Megan, and partly to attack her the only way a witch could be attacked — by coming at her backwards through time. In passing he said a few words about Label Land and Funworld, adrift in their closed-off islands of space-time and in their own unanswerable closed-off madnesses.

"I begin to see you more clearly," said Chardon. "You are prisoners of the past. You want to become what you once were. Why don't you just live on, like me?"

"Success in setting ourselves free is only the beginning," said John. "Beyond Megan lies the real goal — Grayach. That is Dr Homely-Sage's true name. We have, somehow, to find him and set our mother free as well."

"What happened to your mother after she was wrapped in those spider-webs?" said Daphne.

"We're not sure. She's probably in a soul-cage."

"Makes her sound like a song-bird," said Chardon.

"She sings for his pleasure," said Murgatroyd. "It is by no means a bad comparison."

Chardon shuddered.

"I couldn't bear to lead your lives. All this is so long ago, and everything will have changed. Suppose you do manage to set your mother free, do you know that she'll thank you? Maybe she's happier where she is."

"She's still part of us," said John. "It's like rescuing our other selves."

"Which you won't succeed in doing," said Chardon. "They won't want to come with you. They're like me. They live in the present, for the present. Call it what you like: illusion, enlightenment, imprisonment in a witch's electronic playpen. It's all the same to me, so long as I can really *live* it."

"You both have histories, too," said Murgatroyd sombrely. "Histories that you have forgotten. Until you remember them you will remain their prisoners."

He turned his full gaze on Daphne, and something exploded in her brain.

"Why, yeah. Yeah," she muttered. "I do remember now."

THE BLACK GIRL was smiling like a nun dreaming of God. Her voice became younger, her Caribbean accent stronger. She was being possessed by a spirit, her own younger self, who began to speak through her:

270

That day, yeah. We was roun' back of the verandah. We was puttin' weedkiller dust in the eyes of this white kid when his ol' man turns up, and we has to run for it. There's a crab-apple tree growin' by the wall. So I climb up in the branches. That big man's fingers, they grab at mah skirt an' tear it. 'Cos I jerk away, hard. I'm not lettin' him hold onto me. But he grab at me some more, so I has to scramble higher. Don't let go the branches. Not for anything. My knee's scraped an' bleedin' like someone been planin' the skin with a cheese-grater up an' down along it.

He starts to climb, so I gets real scared. I crawls out on this big branch, like a cat. Goes over the other side of that wall. Crack! an' all of a sudden I's crashin' to the ground, with a torn-off branch tuggin' about in my hands. So I lets go quick, an' all the crab-apples they come bouncin' down all over me.

That ol' woman, I think maybe she was out workin' on the beans. Dressed like she been in the Oxfam shop, but her eyes, was they fierce! Fierce like you feel she can see under your clothes. An' that's where I seen you before, cat. You was the big black cat sittin' on an upturned wheelbarrow. Lookin' at me, and' sayin' nothin'.

But that voice. So bossy an' so sweet, all at the same time.

"You go into the house, my dear," she says, "and I will deal with the gentleman."

Those her words. An'

"Wash your hands in the bathroom downstairs, and then you may help yourself to a boiled sweet. The glass jar is on the shelf. Only one, remember."

I wonder what she ever do to that man. Put him in prison? Maybe he was too scared to come on into her garden. There's a terrace there, real elegant, with purple irises growin' out of bulbs like a white boy's toes half stuck in the ground. An' real French doors. Carpets inside. Carpets.

Later on she comes in, puts me in a bath, and wraps me up afterwards in a fluffy towel. Makes a long speech in an accent makes you think she must be part of the govm'nt. Like this:

"I have yet to meet a mother who looks after her own children, let alone looks after them properly. What can be expected when parents are not professionals, and have other things on their minds? No doubt, when you're sixteen and can earn her some money, she'll turn up and pretend an interest in you. I've seen it more often than I care to remember. Some of them even bring birthday cards. 'Don't forget your own mother, who's never forgotten you,' and all that sort of pretence after years of neglect. There is nothing that one can do to stop it, of course. It would be improper to undermine a child's

271

faith in her mother, however misplaced. Meanwhile, my dear, you'll be staying here with me. As long as you give satisfaction, you will find it agreeable."

She really did talk like that, so I knew I got to do what she say. But I never see her again afterwards.

"WHY WERE YOU putting weedkiller dust in that boy's eyes?" said John.

Daphne came out her trance.

"Felt good," she said. "Revenge. Hurt someone else. He screamed real nice."

"Aren't you sorry?" asked Murgatroyd.

"Wouldn't make sense to be sorry. I'm not the same person as the girl that did it. I doubt if there's even one bit of me that's the same. Even my teeth all changed."

She lifted her hands against the sun. They were the colour of dark warm chocolate. Along the edges of her fingers they could see her atoms whirling and leaping like the corona around an eclipsed sun.

"I changed," she said, "See, I'm still changing."

"You have memories," said Murgatroyd. "Isn't that continuity?"

"You made me bring them back," she answered. "You made me go visit the graveyard. You got me talkin' like a zombie-girl. But it wasn't me. *I* wasn't talkin'."

"Who was, then?" asked John.

"One of my dead me's."

"When you talk like that," said Charles, "you make justice impossible. You have taken away any responsibility for anything. If we followed your way of thinking, people could do anything they want. It makes punishment meaningless."

"It is meaningless. You can't punish a woman who's done a murder. I mean that. Listen. Suppose you catch her — except it's no longer her. Suppose you try her — except it's no longer her. Suppose you hang her by the neck till she's dead. Except it wasn't her you hanged. What you done? What's the 'her' you dealing with? It's someone different each time. The woman that did the killing, she's slipped through your fingers. She don't exist no more when you catch the woman you catch. And the woman you try, and the woman you hang, they're different again. It's the same with the little black girl who helped her friends have fun putting weedkiller dust in the eyes of a little white boy. She's gone. So's he. There's no way you can get her back to punish her. She's just not available."

272

"Punishments often don't work," said Chardon. "I was sent to a school where they beat you. The boys who were beaten became heroes, so long as they could swank and swagger, and pretend it hadn't hurt. If they made fun of the masters, and dared them to beat them again, they became super-heroes. To the other boys, of course. In the changing-room, we all wanted to see the marks on their legs. The more horrible the better."

"Is that what happened to you?" said John.

Chardon laughed.

"Not me. I was different. Didn't ever intend to get caught or punished. I stole things for kicks. Not because I wanted them. Oh, sometimes I did, of course. In special cases. But I loved to be being looked for. I was only happy when I felt like a hunted animal. My senses came alive. I could think faster. To be being pursued, and not being found, that was the most exciting thing in my life."

"So that's how she got you," said Murgatroyd, turning the full depth of his eyes into Chardon's.

SHE DIDN'T get me [replied Chardon]. I got myself. For once there was something I really wanted. Wanting clouds one's mind. One shouldn't — ever — *want* anything.

It was a tapestry. A tapestry of a girl. Her eyes were wide and sweet. She was sitting in a field of lilies talking to a unicorn. Her little dog lay at her feet, with his head up, listening. I'd wandered into this church, and spotted it hanging in a corner. All dark where nobody could see it properly. The little girl told me it was all right by her if I took it away.

So I lifted it off its hooks, rolled it up, and put it on my shoulder. Then I walked out of the church, casual-like, pretending to be workman. The graveyard outside was peaceful and sunny, with a smell of new-mown grass. Several fields away a tractor was chugging, just loud enough to hear.

I was excited by my new prize, but calm at the same time. Fond of everyone in the world. Then I heard this grunting.

Grunt. Grunt. Grunt.

Someone was grunting behind me, so I swung round to look. It was the vicar. He was trying to run. He was a fat, unfit, sweaty man in a shirt that had stains under the armpits, and his flannel trousers were held up by a tie instead of a belt. What a way to spoil a tie.

And he was spoiling my morning by grunting.

I realized I ought to drop the tapestry and run. It would have been easy. But I couldn't believe anyone would care so much about such a thing, except maybe me. It was just a bit of old carpet, really. I was still thinking these thoughts when he came a bit quicker and grabbed me.

CHARDON SMILED ruefully and shook his curls.

He began to slap me. He couldn't slap for toffee of course, and I told him to try harder, so he'd lose control and I could wriggle myself free. He went a revolting beetroot colour, and slapped me even more wildly. It wasn't really very nice. His hands were so sweaty. I thought, why couldn't he wash them first?

I baited him some more, telling him it still didn't hurt. But he kept his grip, so I dropped the tapestry, hoping he'd let me go so he could pick it up, but he held onto me.

Well, all this was going on, and we were getting nowhere, when an old lady turns up. She's wearing a snobby hat of dark blue straw, with a bouquet of silk flowers and cherries round the rim on one side of it. Her eyes were horrible eyes, very upper-class.

At least that's what I thought at first. Later they seemed to change and go all spaniel-like when they looked at me.

'What has the child done?' she asks in a voice like squeaky sand-paper.

The vicar stops pummelling me and tries to get his breath back.

Poof! Pof! Poof! Pof!

He starts to tell her about the tapestry, but she cuts him short.

'This wretched boy is a runaway,' she says. 'He has escaped from the Heritage Orphanage, an institution to which I devote some of my time as a governor. I shall take him back with me. Be assured, dear vicar, that we shall inflict condign punishment on him for the damage he has done to the treasures of your beautiful church.'

So the vicar lets me go, and makes off with my tapestry. Yes, mine. The little girl, the unicorn, and the dog were my friends, not his.

The old lady then gives me a nice shock. She strokes the top of my head and says in a quite different voice:

'Come along now! We have to get you washed and some nice new clothes on.'

She takes a barley-sugar out of her bag, uncrinkles the wrapping for me, and pushes it slowly into my mouth for me to suck. I remember thinking, That's nice! She's sweet on me, so I can con her real good.

I give her one of my winning smiles, and I think she likes that.

CHARDON paused, then continued:

She had a nice house, too. Full of things to steal. I saw a silver tray with two snakes wriggling round the edge. The handles were their open mouths, fangs showing, reared up one at each end. To pick it up you'd have had to put your fingers inside.

"AND NEVER got them free afterwards," said Murgatoyd.

I SORT OF GUESSED as much. There was also a small gold clock whose dial went anti-clockwise. The minute-hand was a sword. The hours were marked by little heads, with numbers engraved on their eyes. As the minute-hand passed them, they rolled back and forth, as if it had cut them off.

I also noticed a porcelain bowl. It was full of little balls made of ivory and ebony, each showing a different phase of the moon. I was wondering whether or not to pop a few in my pocket when she made me go upstairs for a bath.

"NEW ARRIVALS always have to have a bath," explained Murgatoyd. "Once a boy or girl has taken off their clothes, and put their heads back under the water, they lose their wills, and do what she wants them to do."

I ENJOYED my bath. Lots of suds were floating on the surface, and she gave me a magic duck to play with. It dipped its head and drank the bath-water. After ten dips it filled up, turned its tail to the ceiling, and plunged to the bottom. After that you could empty it out and start again.

After a while she came over and looked down at me, sitting there all grimy, even in the foam, since I never fussed with washing myself, and messing about.

'Your hair needs a wash,' she said. 'Lie back, and I will do it for you. That's right. Knees up and head under.'

I did it without thinking. But the moment my head was under the water, the wetness vanished. I was here in this world where we are now.

"NOW YOU KNOW you are in prison," said Murgatroyd, "do you want to get out?"

"No. I like being here. I just wonder why she never comes to see me. I thought she liked me."

"She relishes you," said the black cat, "and admires you all the time. It's just that you don't see her."

Chardon looked disconcerted, and a long silence followed.

275

"WELL," said John, "we have to get on. Can you tell us which way we should go to find our other selves?"

Daphne stood up and stretched.

"We'll take you there, if you like," she said. "I've never seen anyone meet themselves before. Could be kinda interesting."

THEY LEFT the circle of rocks, and time speeded up again. It was early in the winter. A side-path took them up into some squat hills. From the summits they could see the cold earth-browns and deep indigo-blues stretching away to the horizon. The season was the time in the year when everything waits in silence for the snow, but day after day goes by, and the snow doesn't come.

They went past lakes shining like anvil-metal, hard but full of light. The path beneath their feet changed back and forth from slabs of rock to leaf-mould, purple-black, wet, and sludgy.

Walking through a forest once again they came to a pasture, cleared long ago, where the bramble-bushes were growing back, the height of a man. Two grey wolves, one slightly larger than the other, trotted out of the woods towards them. When Chardon stood still, they came up and sniffed at the back of his outstretched hand.

John sensed rather than saw the eyes of other wolves in the trees behind them. His hand strayed to the handle of his sheath knife; it was all he had to defend himself with. He noticed that Murgatroyd's tail was flicking, this way that way, this way that way.

Chardon didn't seem to feel the cold or have any sense of fear. He stood there, bare-footed, the arms of his knotted shirt swinging from his waist, talking eagerly with the two animals.

"Ten days. That's a long time to go without food."

The wolves were looking him in the eye, and he nodded.

"Yes. Quite near here," he added.

Their heads cocked, questioningly.

"Up the gully. Where the white-barked birches grow. Go down-wind first, or he'll catch your scent. Turn back up the slope, through the sugar-maples. Come out onto the open land at the top, where the standing stones are. He's in a depression in the ground near there."

One of the wolves gave a growl, and John's hair rose on the back of his neck. But Chardon was smiling.

"Fully grown. Enough for all of you."

The larger wolf half-opened his mouth and steam drifted out into the cold air. Abruptly he turned, and loped away. His companion followed. Then the whole pack moved after them through the woods. As he watched them, John thought of the shadows of railway carriages that ripple along the ground beside them, flowing over bridges and over streams, along embankments rich with ragwort and fireweed, over furrowed fields, over blackberry bushes, leaving them all the same as they were before, once the train has gone by.

"What were you talking about?" he asked.

Chardon grinned excitedly.

"*This*," he said.

He dropped onto his hands. His shoulders grew thick with muscles. His forearms lengthened out, and his fingertips hardened into neat black hooves. His thighs swelled into haunches, so his trousers burst and their shreds dangled off his back, showing an elegant pair of hind legs. Fur sprouted, grey with flecks of white, and spread downwards onto his chest. His throat became a deep curved neck. Last of all, his face bulged into a muzzle whose nose twitched, sensing the wind. He was no longer Chardon, but a buck whose dark eyes seemed both frightened and excited.

The buck bounded up the hill into the undergrowth. There was a sound of crashing and breaking branches; and they saw the tops of the bushes shaking. Howling arose in the distance. Then yelping. A stag's voice, belling, could be heard for a moment. Then there was silence.

In John, something snapped. He raced up the pasture, into the woods, his will dragging the others after him. But the path was already hard to follow. The broken-off branches were healing. Dried sap was closing up the wounds; new bark thickening around the scars. Bent blades of grass were restraightening themselves; new tendrils feeling their way outwards in open space and sunlight. Signs that anything had passed that way were vanishing.

John read the last few clues — fresh soil under a dislodged stone, a dead branch kicked sideways, a hoofmark in the clay edge of a puddle — and led them out onto the moor.

The wolves were trotting off, bellies sagging. The rocks nearby were splashed with dried blood that made shapes like cave-paintings. Scraps of carcase lay about among the tussocks, with scrums of maggots writhing over them. Horn-armed beetles were burying the smaller bits of bone. A few minutes later the first curled leaves of flowers were poking up here and there, lush with the nourishment.

"Why?" panted John. "Why did he do it?"

"Wolves hadn't eaten for ten days," said Daphne.

"He fed them on himself."

"Chardon gave as easily as he took — that's one way of looking at it. He didn't feel he was separate from the wolves — that's another. It gave him a kick to do something extraordinary — that's a third. He had no sense of time, of a past or of a future, of memory or planning, of looking back or looking ahead — any moment was the same as any other — that's still another way of seeing it. He was all of those, none of those, and maybe something else as well."

"Won't you miss him? He was your friend wasn't he?"

"There are no friends in this world," said Daphne. "We don't even exist ourselves."

"I think I exist," said John.

Daphne shook her head, and ran her hands over herself as if she was smoothing the wrinkles out of a length of fabric.

"Here's a pretty brown body. Me. But what is it really? Atoms bouncing off each other. Changing at each instant. It's only you looking at it, and thinking about it, that makes it exist."

"Hard to believe Megan would let him go so easily," Charles broke in. "It costs her a lot of trouble to catch her children. Right, Murgatroyd?"

"If he was a real boy, yes," agreed the cat. "But she fills this set with simulacra for the real kids to play with. Imaginary beings, dream-children. They can be tossed away, and made again."

"I don't think Megan would have known how to invent Chardon."

"I'm inclined to agree," said the cat. "I think he was real."

THEY TRUDGED on, subdued except for Daphne. She seemed exhilarated by what had happened.

The summer appeared, and the landscape changed again. They were in a valley planted with groves of orange trees. A Persian carpet was spread out beneath one on the grass not far away.

"That looks nice, don't it?" said Daphne. "Let's have a rest there. I wanna laze awhiles, an' feel good, just like an animal."

She squatted down on the carpet, rolled over, and lay looking up at the sky twinkling through the leaves. Since they depended on her to lead them, they had no choice but to sit down, too. Murgatroyd sat upright at the edge of the carpet, and swished his tail impatiently.

"I like it here," said Daphne, stretching herself to get comfortable.

Murgatroyd sniffed at the air. Tiny spheres were drifting off the fruit in clouds, floating away, vibrating and glowing orange. Some of these streamers were carried upwards by the air currents, some dissolved, some sank into the ground. He sniffed again — and caught a familiar hot-and-sour odour. Another cat! He glanced around and found her, a silky-haired kitten with sad little blue eyes. Looking across at him from the other side of the carpet.

Who you? he thought in wordless cat language.

Don't know.

Course you do.

No. Really. I think I've only existed a few minutes. She made me up. I'm wanted for something.

The kitten directed a glance at Daphne.

Dpahne was having an argument with John.

"Still upset about Chardon being eaten, aren't you?"

John nodded, lips tight together.

"Your thinkin' needs straightenin' out. We've both changed since we met. You agree?"

"I feel much the same," objected John.

"Don't figure. You've had new experiences, met me, so you got new patterns in your atoms. 'Nough to make a difference."

"If a camera takes new pictures, it's still the same old camera."

"But the film changes, don't it? Take my hand."

John held her hand, a little unwillingly at first.

"Feel anythin'?"

"Warm cream pouring up my arm and into my body."

"Beautiful feelin'. For me, too," said Daphne. "Now look at our two hands and see what's happenin'."

John observed his pinko-white fingers lying in her coffee-coloured palm. Where they were in contact he could see particles mixing and whirling about.

"See? We's becomin' each other. Slowly. Little by little. Wait long enough and we'd be mixed, you bein' as much me as me you. Even since we started talkin' we's changed."

"I've got to find my other half-self before I become anyone else," he explained with a smile.

"*Your?*" said Daphne. "You've not been listenin' to me. Haven' I jus' been showin' you there's no such thing as *you?* Listen to a story then. Perhaps that make it plainer."

WHEN I WAS jus' a stupid little girl, my auntie use to make us all go to church. That church! Roof was corrugated iron. My goodness did it get hot inside in summer! When I think of it now, whaddo I remember? — The smell of the dust. Yesterday's cookin' comin' from the house next door. An' how dim it was.

There was a few rays of real sunshine fallin' from a window. Way 'bove my head. Everyone sittin' still, except me.

There was trains, too. Used to go by, time to time. So noisy you couldn't hear what the preacher was tellin' you. He used to shout, an' his voice got all cracked from tryin' to make himself heard.

Long as you all good, he said, you goes to Heaven. I used to look round at the folks there, an' I'd ask myself, What age are you when you's in Heaven? See that baby, little face all crumpled up, sleepin' in his mammy's arms. He's too young for somethin' difficult like Heaven. What 'bout that schoolgirl with her back goin' straight up an' down, and still *tryin'* — unlike me? Maybe she's the age you best go to Heaven. Too young for things to go wrong. Time she gets be Tanya's age — Tanya, she's my big sister — she'll be smoking pot an' foolin' with the young men.

Gets worse later. I'd feel sorry for those big, sad mammies tryin' to drag their men to church. Who'd wanta be them for ever? Let alone be like one of them old women, too old to get any fun from the place when they get there. Just complain, complain, complain. Kids throw things at the old women in the streets down here, and they might be spared that in Heaven, I suppose. Best kill yourself when you're about eleven, I used to think. Otherwise it's too late.

"ISN'T HEAVEN outside time," put in Murgatroyd. "Why should your age matter there?"

THE YOU THAT GOES there's goin' be different dependin' on how old you are. Cats change, too, don't they? Human life's a mess. Goes up a little bit, then goes down the rest of the way. One day you find you must be grown-up because all you want to think about is men. You want them to stay round, but they never do. You bring up the children, maybe find another man. They go off, maybe he goes off. In the end you forgotten. Body goes; mind goes. The world float round like you is sick all the time, you know what I mean? You start to do silly things. First of all people is kind to you. Then they get impatient, and start to wish you wasn't here.

Like you go to the shop, put things in the wire basket, and come to the counter, and open your purse. Oh, dear! There's no money in it. Maybe you left it at home, on the dresser. Maybe you got no money any more. They don't know, you don't know, and others is waiting in the queue behind you, dear. Could be the shop-girl's nice and lets you have the things anyway. But when you gone out the door, she gives a smirk like she was saying 'Dotty old thing!' She apologizes to the other customers for the trouble you been causin' them. They say it doesn't matter, and put on soppy smiles 'cause they wanta show how understanding they are. Maybe also 'cause they frightened one day they'll be like that and want people to treat *them* good. Underneath, they don't like old folks. Makes them remember they goin' to die one day, too.

"PERHAPS YOU'RE the right age for Heaven right now," murmured John, not really thinking what he was saying.

Daphne tightened her tummy muscles and sat up with a jerk. Light was jumping out of her eyes like sizzling fat bouncing off a hotplate on a stove.

"You telling me I should die, little whitey?" she snapped. "Little patronizing whitey. What do you know about life?"

She grabbed the white kitten by the scruff of its neck and held it out in front of her. It dangled there, miaowing, like an ornament on a Christmas tree.

"See this kitten, whitey? Perhaps I'm going to kill her. Wring her scrawny little neck till it snicks. Unless, little whitey, you gives me one reason, jus' one good reason, why I shouldn't."

"She's got as good a right to live as you," said Charles. "Why shouldn't someone wring *your* neck."

What right?" said Daphne. "I see you's wearing cow-leather shoes, so you ain't a vegetarian."

She tightened her grip, smiling venemously. The kitten miaowed again.

John was deep in puzzled thought.

"Well," he said at at last, "Give me a good reason why you *should* kill her. I'm sorry you don't like my sense of humour."

He turned his eyes full on her, and his voice hardened a little.

"One good reason."

"I gotta reason," said Daphne. "I wanna teach you the way things is. I wanna make you *see* the world, not jus' think about it."

"There is no argument that works," said Murgatroyd to John. "Suppose you say, all right, now you see things her way. She'll still say she'll have to kill it so you can *feel* the truth. To shock you into a real understanding."

The tip of his tail began to flick.

A will-o'-the-wisp of mischief was dancing in the black girl's eyes.

"I's waitin'," she said. "I's waitin', but I can't wait forever. Can't control myself forever."

"*Nor I*," said John from behind her.

He'd moved so fast she hadn't seen him coming. His foot was in the small of her back, his fingers locked round her neck, one thumb-knuckle pressing against the artery taking blood to her brain.

"Give me a reason," he said in a voice thick with anger, "why I shouldn't choke *you* instead. One *good* reason."

But Daphne began to laugh. She dropped the kitten, which wobbled towards Murgatroyd as fast as it could.

"Hey, hey," she said. "I made you come alive, didn't I. I like you a lot better now you no longer patronizing me. An' I taught you somethin': jus' talkin's not worth much, is it? Doin' is different."

But John strengthened his hold on her.

"The reason?" he said. "I'm still waitin' for the reason."

Daphne laughed some more.

"There's no reason good enough." she said. "You feel like sending me to Heaven, I don't mind. You jus' told me I's the right age. You wanna be my friend, that's great, too. I got nothing against you. I like you now."

"Of course I don't want to strangle you," said John, letting go, and pushing her away gently.

Daphne gave a spit-snort of disgust.

"You's soft after all. Thought you might amount to something, but you gives up half-way. Next you'll be telling me you're sorry."

THE WORLD BLANKED OUT.

THE ORANGE-TREES, that had been as bright as the illuminations on an ancient manuscript, vanished. The colours in the carpet, multitudinous as the hues in a Moroccan bazaar, vanished. The fruit-smells, grass-smells, people-smells, cat-smells — vanished.

There was an absence of everything. They seemed to be floating in a grey glycerine mixture that was neither warm nor cold, and to be neither awake nor asleep. Their minds became mirrors reflecting emptiness. Outside and inside became indistinguishable. Memory was only a memory of memory, without movement.

Only Charles fought back. He had no intention of accepting the soothing nothingness.

He concentrated. Patiently, detail by detail, he remade the world. First dark green leaves. Then the oranges. He put in the jigsaw of shadows. Next, the children. Daphne, with her mind like that of a wood-nymph being chased by a god, both in love with reason and running from it in terror. John, with the music in his mind like waves beating along an invisible shore-line. Murgatroyd, soft and ponderous, with his hidden goodness and his dark past. The scared white kitten. He made her larger than she had been before; and the kitten knew it and gave him a grateful look. He brushed in the forests and the hills that rose and fell on the horizon, and above them the sky blazing in cloudless splendour.

THE WORLD CAME BACK.

"She turned us off," said Murgatroyd.

"And I brought us back."

"Come off it," said the cat. "She turned the switch on again."

"Look at Selina, if you don't believe me," said Charles.

Murgatroyd looked at the kitten, magnificent in her new fur and gazing at him with admiration, but also a confidence that had not been there before. He nodded.

"You gave her a name, she says. That's wonderful. And more than interesting. It means we have a weapon to fight back with. But also, it means danger. Now Megan must know we are here. No mere child, and almost no adult, has the mind to do what you've just done. She will attack us. Sooner rather than later."

"Which way do we go, Daphne?" asked John.

"Any way you like," said the black girl. "I'm bored with the whole business."

She picked up a fallen orange, then lay on her back, cutting the outer skin into segments with one of her sharp fingernails. That done, she pulled the flesh apart. When the fruit spurted into her face, she just rubbed the juice off with the back of one of her hands.

"Which way do we go?" John repeated.

Daphne shrugged.

"We'll have to look after ourselves," said Murgatroyd. "Come on. Time's running out."

As they moved off, she glanced up from the half-eaten fruit and spoke:

"You don't belong here. I hope the witch gets rid of you."

SOME MILES later on, they found themselves in a rain-forest. Everything was happening fast. Flowers swelled up and fell to pieces before their eyes. Caterpillars lengthened on the leaves, nibbling and gorging until they were fat, poisonous, and as bristly as spiny hairbrushes. Later they bundled themselves up into chrysalises, and hung like cloudy glass bowls by sticky threads from the branches. If you peered closely you could see their separated parts swilling around in a milky soup, being reassembled. Soon they were butterflies, biting free from their cocoons, resting trembling on twigs until their wings dried and they could fly off. Airborne, they flashed and fell like confetti at a wedding that never stopped.

A leopard leapt out on a fawn and bit its neck. The energy from the hot, dead, body flowed out of it like heat flowing out of a fire. The leopard's coat began to shine more brightly as he ate. Nothing stayed still for more than a moment or two.

They almost missed the other John. He was hanging by a bent arm from a rope of creepers twenty feet above their heads.

"John!" hissed Murgatroyd, surprised.

"That's me!" the climber sang out cheerfully.

"We've come to rescue you," said the first John, looking up at him from the ground.

"Rescue me? What from?" said the climber. He flicked his bare foot expertly round the rope to make a temporary stirrup, and eased the weight on his arm.

"I know it doesn't seem like it," said the first John, "but this place is a prison. Do you remember being caught?"

"Perhaps," said the climber. "I think it was a dream, really. I was with my brother at a fairground, at night. A long time ago it seems now. We were chased by a witch, put put us in a huge doll. Into its stomach. It was lightless and horrible inside. I used to have other dreams about being chased. By oily dark bronze statues, and other things. They would come alive on their pedestals, leap down, and run after me, getting closer and closer. I think it was like that."

"It wasn't a dream," said the first John. "It was real. You were trying to get into a Time-traveller when you split. Half became you. The other half is me."

"I don't remember splitting," said the climber. "I feel like all of me, not a half."

He kicked his foot free, and pulled himself, on the other arm, a little further up the creeper.

"Come down," said the first John. "I can explain it later. We're in a hurry. The witch knows we're in here."

"The witch vanished long ago," said the climbing John. "I've never seen her since."

He flexed himself up-and-over like a pole-vaulter, and landed on a broad branch festooned with hanging moss. He squatted there, looking down at them.

"Why don't you join me up here?" he said. "It's beautiful. Higher up, it's more beautiful still. Orchids grow on the branches, and tree-frogs live in pools of water in the branches' armpits next to the main trunk. Right at the top you can see for miles over the treetops. Swarms of insects shine in the sun like glass beads."

"You've not been listening," said the first John. "You and I are the same person."

"I don't think so," said the other John. "If you are, climb up."

He gave a grin. Then, with a wriggle, he disappeared into the green canopy above their heads.

"What can I do now?" said John to Murgatroyd. His face looked haunted, and his breath was choked.

"Are you sure he's really you?" asked Charles.

John nodded.

"Absolutely. I recognised him at once. He's everything I've lost. The smiles. The climbing. The living for the moment. I don't know why he didn't recognize me."

"Leave him for now," said Murgatroyd. "We know where he is. Let's find the other Charles, and see if we do any better with him."

THE TREES opened out, and they found themselves in the northern woodlands, wandering through the springtime. Short-cropped turf sparkled in a glade among oaks, poplars, and sycamores. Flowers were opening here and there, orange crocuses and white star-anemones. Deer grazed in the distance, but a snowbank, still frozen, lay under the overhanging branches. From somewhere beneath it came the trickling melody of the snow-melt. Two youngsters were fighting on the slippery grass. They had real swords, and were trying to kill each other.

"That's me," said Charles grimly. He pointed to the one with light brown hair.

The duel was fast and skilful. Thrusts were met with parries. Lunges were turned by blocks, ripostes guided away by deflections that became new feints. Each move happened without a moment's thought. Then the auburn-haired boy hesitated, a passing instant of blank mind. It was all Charles needed. He skewered the other's neck, tippled him over onto his back, and skipped out of the way of the last downward slash. He pressed his foot against the other's chin, and took out his blade with a firm twist of the wrist. Then he plunged it in again, between the other's ribs. He pushed it in deeper and deeper, and held it there, breathing hard. The body beneath him thrashed like a fish. Then it lay still. The face, with its open eyes, seemed calm and thoughtful. They wondered why it didn't say something. The auburn curls lifted and stirred in the wind.

The younger Charles tugged his sword out. He wiped it a couple of times on the grass, then dried the blade carefully on his handkerchief. He threw his head back and walked over to his other self.

"Fun," he said with a grin. "And really close."

"Fun?" said his tight-lipped other self. "Killing a friend — is that fun?"

"More than fun," said the younger Charles. "It's magic. Magic to be alive afterwards. Look at this sunshine! This turf! All these trees! I can feel them without even touching them."

"You've killed him," said the time-traveller. "Brought his world-line to its end."

"That's the whole point. He'd have killed me if he'd been able to. That's why it's so amazing to be alive. Kiddy stuff's no good. Blunt blades, buttons, padded suits, having another chance when you've made a mess of it — it isn't real. No kick in it."

He threw his arm around the other's shoulder.

"I thought you'd understand," he said. "But you're timid. Domesticated."

"Megan certainly gets her money's-worth," muttered Murgatroyd to John.

"I do understand," said the time-travelling Charles."Don't you ever think that, some time, you might get the worst of it?"

The other nodded.

"Of course. That's why it's exciting."

He pointed.

"See that butterfly? Look how he wavers, this way and that, stitching a crazy hem between the rows of grasses."

It seemed to have become summer. They were standing in a meadow among thick-stalked hay-grass, heavy with seed, and ragged blue corn-flowers.

"What about him?" said the older Charles.

"He's motionless. It's us that are tilting back and forth. We're veering left and right. So are the trees, the ground, and the sky. Can't you feel it?"

"I'm not a butterfly. Are you?"

"If you can't be a butterfly," said the fencer, "you're almost dead. If you've just survived a fight, the simplest things are miracles. To you that dried-up dock-plant's probably ugly, useful at best: somewhat dark green leaves and thick, red-veined stems whose juice stops nettle-stings itching. And the sorrel down the path is commonplace enough. But they're all I need to be happy at a moment like this. A half-withered dock-plant and an old rusty sorrel."

"Listen," said the time-travelling Charles, "don't you know who I am?"

The fencer stepped back and regarded him.

"I thought I knew you at first. I'm not so sure now. What's your name?"

"*Your* name. Charles. We have *that* in common."

The time-traveller pulled a small piece of tail-bone out of his trouser pocket. It was a stegosaurus vertebra. He let it sit on his palm.

"Well?"

"That's *my* bone," said the younger Charles. "My lost bone. Where did you find it? It's been missing ever since I came here."

"I didn't find it. I've always had it. At least since it left the Musuem. Remember the glass case in the Museum?"

Like a snake's tongue flicking at a mouse, the younger boy's fingers picked the bone off the older boy's hand.

"*Mine*," he said. His eyes glinted. "Want to challenge me?"

"It's ours," said the time-travelling Charles. "*Ours.* We are the same person."

"You aren't like me at all. To begin with, you're scared."

"Of many things," said the older boy. "You would be, too, if you knew what I knew. Let us go back to the Museum again. Doesn't it come back to you? The hot glass cases. The silence. The guilt. The excitement. Was there anybody else there when we took it?"

"You're reading my mind." said the fencer. "Keep out."

"If we're not the same person, how do I know about the Museum? We never told anybody, did we?"

"What are you playing at?" said the younger Charles. "I'm not going to get mixed up with you. Nor with anyone else for that matter. People don't split in two and live. It's impossible."

"I'm not sure I want to get mixed up with you, either," said the time-traveller, "if I may return the compliment. But that's the way it is. Let me explain some more."

He never had time to do so.

A golden light flashed. Grey-bright steel lifted to meet it. The scream of metal rose like a rotary saw. There was a crack, then a hail of splinters.

The older Charles leapt back. A razor-sharp golden discus, more than twice the width of a dustbin lid, was spinning away from his head. It carved through the branches of the trees with a crisp whirring, as if they were made of paper. The boughs and foliage came crashing and thudding down into the grass. The discus banked in a circle and swung towards him again.

His younger self stood braced to meet it. A shattered half-blade stuck out from his hand, and the older boy realized he owed his life to that incredible speed of reaction.

"Unthink it," said Murgatroyd's voice, harsh and urgent. "There's no other way to stop it."

Time-travelling Charles bent his mind on the golden disc. It shimmered like a heat-mirage. Then, as when a splash breaks a reflected sun into fragments, it shattered and vanished.

The swordsman glanced at his older self with a sudden, awed, respect.

287

"Stay ready, both of you," said the cat. "We are under attack. She has come."

As he spoke, the greyness struck.

The others dissolved. They dissolved into the shadows of what was possible, not what was real. Only the older Charles remained.

Mind-hardened as ever, he took stock of what was happening. Oaks, poplars, sycamores, and meadow-grasses were fading to grey and white. They were flickering like an old movie seen through a snowstorm. Hard edges softened as blankets of shadow were laid over them. Smooth movements broke apart, their little eddies shuddering off in no particular direction. Clear sounds sank away into dry whispers.

He looked left and right. It was the same everywhere. The trunks of the trees were shadows laid on shadows, like those of the banisters on the staircase long ago. The forms of John and Murgatroyd, and his younger self, and the dead Berklak, wavered like statues in an underwater museum.

It was a world without solid things. Without people. Without minds. Without events, except the random flickering of light and dark. A world without differences, empty of usable energy.

And unacceptable.

Around his feet he willed a patch of lawn, green, pleasant, and alive. At the edges he added ferns, uncurling themselves. Then hundreds of bluebells. Behind he placed boulders of gneiss — grey-black, unyielding, metamorphic rock. And towering above the boulders a grove of sugar-pines, whose giant branches sagged with two-pound cones.

The mists did not vanish, but just fell back a little. He wondered if he dared imagine the others back into existence again. But the witch's voice spoke to him before he could reach a decision. It was cold, and it came from no one single place. With a shudder, he knew at once — it spoke for the power behind the void.

"You alone," it said. "You resist. You must tell me how you do it."

A voice that expected to be obeyed. It took all the will he had just to think in his own way.

"We are not resisting you," he said. "We just want our own lives back."

"What makes you think you have any right to your own lives?" said the voice. "I have authority over you. Answer the question."

Charles of course did not answer. He enlarged his domain with two sequoias. They were huge and sleepy trees, with many-fingered fronds that trembled even when there was no wind. He made them as he remembered them from Mesozoic times, a species no longer on the earth today. He wondered if Megan would be sharp-eyed enough to notice.

"Since you are disobedient," said the voice, "you will be punished."

In his thoughts Charles shaped a white pterodactyl. He made him perch on a low branch, his eyes darting to one side then another.

"And doubly punished for showing off," the voice went on. "I have been to museums, too, to listen to the voices of the dead. I am not impressed."

So, thought Charles, she can't time-travel. That's worth knowing. What else can we find out?"

He began a series of feints.

"I am sorry for you," he said. "We all are."

"It is not your place to have such sentiments," said the witch's voice sharply, but he could tell he had surprised her.

"Won't you die, or wither, with no more children's feelings to feed on?"

"I get all the children I want."

"In this grey waste-land?" said Charles. "Where are the kicks for you here? Your sweet kicks, that keep you alive?"

"They are memories just now," said the voice. "I will call them back when I feel the need for them."

"Let the two of us go free, with our cat and our other selves, whom you have been holding prisoners, and you can have the rest of your childen to yourself again."

"You little huckster," said the voice, "what makes you think you can bargain with me? I like your arrogance, but making you suffer for it is something I shall enjoy even more."

"While I remain here," said Charles, "you cannot even budge those sequoias."

IT WAS AS WELL that he was ready for her attack. His mind hit something like a wall. He hardened his concentration to a point. He drew on the strength of all his voyagings, on the millions of years across past and future time. The wall collapsed. The green fingers of the trees shivered, but the giant trunks stood firm. It had been a wise decision to challenge her over something from the distant past of which she had no experience.

"Hold us," he said, "and as the days pass you will shrivel. Let us go, and your world is yours again."

Sweat ran in a sudden cold trickle under his arm. He was pretending to a confidence he did not feel.

"You know too much," said the witch's voice. "I shall punish you first. Then I shall smash your mind. Like the cobweb of wires inside a light-bulb when the current burns too hot, I shall overload your brain, and then I shall blow it out."

A huge black window opened slowly in the greyness.

"Look!" commanded the voice. "Look! And a fire shall start to burn in your heart, a pain that nothing can put out. Look, understand, and be destroyed!"

Two figures appeared in the blackness, brightly lit. They were naked and flawless. One was a young man, beautifully muscled. The other was a girl, eager and delicate in her movements as a deer.

They gazed into each others' eyes, drinking and devouring the other's soul. Their lips were trembling, fierce and red. Suddenly they kissed each others' shoulders. The two passionate mouths closed on the flesh with a hiss of steam. The bodies shuddered. Both skins were stained with a rust-red burn.

They drew back, gasping with pain and a still unsatisfied delight. But only for an instant. They closed again, sinking their teeth, greedy with longing, in the backs of each others' necks. Steam hissed again, and hung in thickening clouds. Blood was dribbling down their shoulderblades. They jerked apart, quivering with the torment.

Passion drove them back. Merciless passion. Again and again. They stabbed each other with burning kisses on every part of their bodies until only two bloodied hulks remained, groping slowly and helplessly for the touch of each others' arms. The compost-heap of flesh smouldered, dissolved by an inner heat. After a time, the heap sank down. A twisted mess of ash, like an old barbecue pit, was all that was left.

"Enjoy it?" said the witch's voice.

Charles said nothing. His mouth was dry, but he forced himself to swallow.

"It's for our amusement, of course, not yours," the voice went on. "That's what human life is for — to keep us entertained. You will make your contribution, I'm sure."

"Illusion," said Charles. "Like everything here. Like a television set. Patterns of dots that your mind gives meaning to."

She laughed. It sounded like a viper slithering through dry leaves.

"There is nothing more delicious to us," hissed the voice, "than destroying hope. Imagine the feelings of a saint, just escaped from his corpse on a cross, when he comes to us and finds.... What? — That his feelings were just to give us a good laugh. Or Jews from the Shoah, what a merry pantomime! And teenage martyrs in the Holy Wars of Islam — best of all, Holy Wars against each other — manipulated like marionettes by crazed old men — delicacies for the connoisseur! They die in agony and ecstasy, for what? To find that they were just stage extras in one of our little plays."

290

There was another spasm of dry laughter.

"The dead get so insulted, it's quite comical. Best of all are people like you, people who think they're enlightened. We enlighten them a little further. Look again!"

THE BLACK WINDOW opened on another scene. A mother sat on a block of marble. She was naked and beautiful, her breasts full, and a baby on her knee. He laughed up at her, and she smiled down at him with all the sweetness of a face in a holy picture. She lifted him to her breast, and he began to suck. Or, rather, he began to lick her. Under his eager little tongue her body melted away like a statue of yellow-white candy. Her fingers flowed into each other. Her plump legs merged. She shrank and shrank as the baby grew bigger, lapping and snuffling at her like a fat-cheeked puppy. Now her face smiled up at his, with gentle affection.

His teeth crunched into her knees. Her expression changed. At last she had realized what he was doing. But it was too late. He sucked in the rest of her body, and munched contentedly on the fragments.

The baby finished, and licked his lips. He looked about him, and an anxious expression appeard in his eyes. "Mummy!" he called. "Mummy!" No answer came. He started to whimper. Still no one appeared. He screamed. He lay on his back, kicking his legs angrily. It had no effect. Little by little his well-nourished body shrank. He looked like an old plucked chicken left too long on the slab in a poulterer's shop. He was dead. Of starvation.

Charles kept his face impassive. Like the granite features of a carved Pharoah from ancient Egypt who presides at the high end of a museum gallery, indifferent to lesser exhibits, he gave away no hint of his thoughts. And the witch wondered who this boy might be, so untouched by her horrible illusions. She had thought that some rival evil had invaded her set, something of her own hungering kind. But he seemed ordinary, and yet — unlike any other child she'd known. In some way, he was not a child at all.

"Callous little beast, aren't you?" she remarked. "Suffering seems to mean nothing to you. I wonder how you'll feel about your own father. Have a look and see how he keeps us entertained."

THE BLACK SPACE scrolled past. Then it re-filled. An aged body hung there, unclothed and twitching about like a leaf used as a hide by a spider in her web. The eyes glared. The hair on the beard and chest stuck out in tufts. It was, as she had said, Charles's father. He was impaled on steel rods that came up out of the darkness below, and were moved by invisible hands. One rod went through each knee, and one through each elbow. They ended in

291

small L-bends to stop the body sliding off. The fifth rod protruded from his breast, while the sixth went into his head and stuck out from his forehead like a unicorn's horn.

The head was being waggled back and forth. His arms and legs tugged at the rods in a useless effort to break free. Pulsing waves of blue-white heat flowed down the metal to inflict spasms of pain in a musical rhythm.

"Isn't he dancing a pretty caper!" said the voice. "Like a Javanese rod-puppet. He is giving us such pleasure, but not enjoying it at all."

Charles gritted his teeth; controlled himself. He was not going to be be goaded into striking back. She had to be shown her conjurations were powerless.

"Don't feel a thing for your father," said the voice. "Perhaps he isn't your father? Who knows? But have a glance at your mother. What's happening to her is a delightfully appropriate fate for an artist. She's dead now, too, you know. There's no point in going looking for her anywhere else."

THE WINDOW went black again. The voice continued, with its hissed consonants and its contemptuous upper-class rise and fall:

"She was under the care of Dr Sage before she passed away. Dr Sage calls himself a word-therapist, and changes into a spider at night. He has an Institute on the top of a building in the City of Fogs and Machinery. Its concrete walls are cracked, because the old mine-workings underneath it sometimes suddenly slump. There is no lift and no staircase. Patients, that is to say, his victims, are carried up and down by another means.

"Her ambition was to write. So he filled her soul with poisonous, glittering words, a whole dragon's hoard of them. Soon she could see nothing, hear nothing, taste nothing, feel nothing but these wonderful words. She would shake the kaleidoscope of her mind, and think it was creation. The world had become invisible.

"He gloated over her ruin. He was jealous. Her talent would have been so much greater than his. When she died of disillusion, she came to us, as they all do. Have a look."

The window contained a new image. Charles saw a frail woman with mouse-coloured hair. A person who was in his heart. He shivered, but just controlled himself.

She was seated, with the body of a 'cello gripped between her knees. But only the body of the instrument. Instead of the box that holds the four tuning-pegs, she used her head, bent back from her neck. The ebony finger-board ran up and merged with her chin, like a narrow beard. Her chin served as the fret. Over it ran four shuddering, heavy strings. Then they splayed out.

The two central ones plunged into the sockets where her eyes had been, pressing furrows into the flesh of her cheeks. The two outer strings lay across her jaws, and from there were anchored inside her ears. To keep them all taut she had to keep her head thrown back, and clench her teeth with the endless effort.

The spike of the 'cello went through her left foot. The bow was impaled on her right hand, and she guided it with a forefinger and a thumb. At each legato outward sweep a flurry of drops of blood was flung off into the shadows. The tone was heart-breakingly sweet, but the notes were out of tune, uncouth and flat. Her neck-muscles were not strong enough to keep the strings at the right pitch, except for a moment or two.

"She is blind and deaf to the world outside," laughed the witch's voice. "She only hears the tune that she plays on herself. Each note carries its quantum of pain, but she cannot stop playing, or death would become meaningless. So she plays, and becomes her own torturer. Tastefully contrived, is it not?"

Charles's stomach rose. It was both his mother and not his mother. Nor did he believe she was dead. With cold fury he wiped the image away, checking himself from saying "Sorry!". It was only an image. He removed the black window, and steadied himself for war.

FIRST, HE WILLED the witch to appear. She materialized as a moving X-ray photograph, white lines of bone twisting in a grey-black cloud. Her shoulder-blades seemed to lie across her chest, which meant that her head had been turned back-to-front.

On a sudden she became an Oxford lady. The cloud was covered by a black jacket and skirt. A flounce of lace spilled out where the throat was. Wrinkled skin crawled across her flat shining skull. Two eyes transfixed him with hatred. A diamond brooch, stabbed into the depths of the lace, glowered like a third eye, as loathsome as the others. Her shadowy hands were covered in long white gloves.

"Megan," said Charles, "your attempts at terror are futile. I have been deep into the past. I have been far into the future. I have seen too many dreams of life, too many of the stories in which people live and mistake for reality, to believe in any of them.

"For every faith, and for every science, certainty is different. When one comes from the outwhen, as I do at all times now, all places, belief is only the local madness, persuasive because agreed upon and doubters murdered.

"Being mad does not mean they are wholly wrong. Mad people often see a few things more clearly than we do. But never more than a few. No one who merely lives through time can imagine how many perspectives there are on life. Life is like waves. You can take a wave apart into other waves in as many ways as you like. There's no limit. And added all together once more, they make something not unlike the truth."

"So we're showing off again, are we?" said the witch in a nanny's voice. "Been reading our parents' books on popular science, have we? How do you ever think you can measure yourself against me, child?"

"I have seen the science, not read it," said Charles. "I am younger than you, *but also older.* I have been when you will never be, and when you have never gone. For all of what you think of as your 'experience', your cruel little tricks, your magic that weakens each time it is performed, your life flashes by me like the glint off a turning mayfly's wings. After a day-long dalliance in the air it falls in the water and is snapped up by a trout. Behold!"

He opened his hands, and the Mesozoic appeared around him. A thousand panoramas passed before their eyes. Continents and islands merged and broke apart, rising from the waters and being sucked under again. He summoned up vast prairies of ferns, and warm inland seas. Stampeding herds of stegosaurs filled the air with dust. He called on groves of redwood trees to show themselves, and canyons layered with rocks from the time when the only life was so small it was invisible. Amphibians barked from the swamps, the earliest crude voices. Dragonflies the size of schoolboys teetered in currents of air above foaming rivers. Through the branches the first birds flapped clumsily, shaking loose scented odours as they brushed against the green fingers.

Megan contracted with terror. Her eyes flicked from side to side as she watched for an attack. When nothing more happened, she recovered herself and drew out a small stained knife. She took a quick step forward. Charles blocked her with his mind.

The witch smiled.

"I always leave the blood on it from last time," she said. "It's a handy little knife, and has done some mischief in its time. And will again."

She tried to move forward again. It took him an effort to hold her. He withdrew his energy from the world he had made around them, and it blurred like scenery seen by a short-sighted person who has taken her glasses off.

They mind-wrestled. Megan tried to advance. Charles tried to throw her back. Arm-wrestlers sitting at a bar-room table, with the veins bursting from their forearms, and their fingers white with pressure, never fought with such remorseless concentration. Neither gained the advantage.

Then Megan advanced another foot.

Charles shook his head. He struggled to drive her back. She wouldn't budge.

He sneaked a hand into his pocket and felt for the stegosaurus bone. It wasn't there. He remembered — the younger Charles had taken it. No escape through time was possible. His mind flickered with the first alarm.

Megan used this moment of weakness to come two steps closer. Charles blocked her again. He summoned up a surge of panicky energy and tried everything he knew to drive her back. Her body shivered, but did not shift. He was fighting against a ratchet.

He kept his concentration unwavering, and simply held her. Time passed, and his strength began to go. He could feel it draining like the fine downward fall of sand through the funnel of an hour-glass. He knew, with an unselfpitying clarity, that in due course it would have vanished.

Megan stepped forward once more, smiling tightly. Her white gloved hands stroked the blade softly, She thought she was winning. And there was little doubt that at this point she was.

Where were the others? Was there anything else he could do? His mind raced. No. There seemed nothing else for it. He gathered the inner power, the *ch'i* he had learned for karate. Its full use would destroy her — but also him.

The fern-prairies and the seas blanked out. The sequoias returned to the shadows. The green grass shrank to a patch around his shoes. But now he had the *ch'i.* It began to burn in his fingertips, deadlier than any knife. It was his last weapon, and he had no choice but to use it.

"Not yet, Master, not yet!" said a powerful voice at his feet.

A warm, friendly presence was pressing against his knee. A surge of happy ferocity ran through his entire body. He chucked Megan back with contemptuous ease, sending her tottering. Then he looked down, and his breath stopped.

Broad-shouldered, indomitable, green-furred, level with his knee, stood Hippo. *His* Hippo. Not stuffed, not silent in the company of grown-ups and other children, but alive, amazingly alive, the glint of battle in his eyes.

"You!" he said. "How did you get here?"

"Don't let her go," said Hippo. "She'll try to escape now. We've got her."

"If she goes, so much the better," said Charles.

"She'll come back. Hold her! Good! That's it! She's pinned. You can finish her later."

He paused and looked up at Charles.

"You wanted to know how I got here," he said. "I'll tell you, but it has to be brief."

"When I was made," he went on, "cut and stitched in the factory, I was given my destiny, like all my brothers and sisters. My share of fate. I got almost everything. Exceptional strength and intelligence, a crazy sense of humour. I was given a well of invention that never runs dry, and a will that cannot be broken. Only one thing was lacking. One only. That was reality. I was left a creature of dreams. Of your dreams and mine. A mere stuffed nothing."

Charles shook his head.

"That was the hand I was dealt," said Hippo. "My hand of cards to play. But there was a Joker in it. Ten minutes of real life, ten minutes to be taken at the time of my choosing. Ten minutes only. There was a riddle, my Master, for me, the master of riddles. When should I take them. Can you think of a harder choice? But the riddle is broken now. All else is a might-have-been. There! Hippo has played his card. *Moriturus*, my Master, *te saluto*.[1] Listen to me, before my moment ends."

"I can easily hold her now," said Charles. "But how do I finish her off."

"Time," said Hippo. "Time is your weapon. Take her back in thought to the Beginning. Give her the whirlwind of the stars."

He was silent a moment. The he added:

"Never give in. She will struggle of course. Witches are hard to kill. You must always have something more. Something more to be done or dreamed of. You will defeat her now. For the honour of the Night-Club, you must. It shall not be said — No! it cannot be said — that Hippo once played his highest card in vain."

His body slumped. The fur went chill. As he passed back into the world of dreams a shock-wave from his dying field of force induced in Charles a new field as it vanished, a field of fury that fed on itself till it exploded.

He forgot where he was. He forgot Megan. His mind became all that was, and is, and will be. It bubbled with galaxies and super-galaxies, numberless as the possible patterns among his trillion nerve-cells. Each galaxy was fleeing from the others. The farther away, the faster they moved. At the limit they were going at the speed of light. So they still appeared as they had done at the Beginning, untouched by any happening.

His mind went beyond any one place or moment. He saw each point of time and space as it seemed from every other point, influencing every other point, dreaming a manifold of mind-destroying complexity.

-----

[1] "I, who am about to die, salute you!" Said by Roman gladiators to the Emperor as they stepped into the arena.

The witch's brain froze. Like a schoolgirl faced with some impossible problem, she felt it lock and refuse to move. She tossed like a withered leaf in the mind-storm raging around her.

Charles mirrored himself and reversed the direction of time.

At first nothing seemed to happen, except for the subtle shifting of colours. Then light imploded on them. An infinite density of stars. Charles's body vanished. Only his mind remained, like a ghost that is less than something, but more than nothing, at a point that was both the beginning and end of all things.

Yet Megan was laughing, a dry, ironic laughter. He couldn't tell where it came from, nor how he could hear it.

"Didn't you know," it was saying, "that a witch can never be destroyed? Banished, confined, perhaps, but never extinguished entirely? You can't go on doing this forever. Sometime you must weaken. Then, like the spore of an old illness hidden in the lungs, I shall grow strong again, and consume you."

He heard the laughter again.

What were Hippo's words? There is always something more. How could there be more than this?

Then it came to him.

When he had first travelled with Steg some way towards the Beginning, first seen the whirlwind of the stars begin to close in on him, he had had a glimpse of something else. Something he had never dared to speak about to the others. Not even to Steg. Something he knew well but could never describe, and that both frightened him and drew him on. Reluctant and fearful, he had no choice.

He dreamed this last, unnameable vision.

"Behold," he said, *"what lies beyond both Beginning and End."*

SHE DISSOLVED. He felt her go. The last tatters of evil will unravelled, blowing away like lambswool across a moor on a windy, sunlit day.

His own mind emptied. The vision had passed, and the total silence. Blackness had returned. Then thundering and crashing. Light flooded in, the everyday light of the autumn sky. Familiar surroundings reappeared around him. Dust-smells, and the buzz of a lazy fly.

The appalling journey was over.

HE WAS SITTING on a carpet among heaps of electronic wreckage. Smashed cathode-ray tubes, cracked circuit cards, loud-speakers, and tangles of colour-coded wires bristling with capacitators and transistors, and other units he couldn't recognize, lay scattered about the room. All that was left of the television set.

Not far away, John was sitting up and rubbing his head. Near John was Murgatroyd, looking through his fur for splinters of glass.

He knew where they were. He'd been here before. It was Megan's sitting-room. The French doors had been blown open, dragging the curtains out with them, and letting in shafts of sun. The sounds of traffic rose and fell in the distance. He smiled with relief at how ordinary it was.

"Look at all the things to steal," said the voice of another boy.

Chardon's eyes were alight with excitement. He was moving stealthily from one shelf or table to the next, putting objects he fancied into his pockets or inside his shirt. His shorts stuck out at bulgy angles.

He held up a gold-and-enamel egg with a shepherdess and a shepherd-boy painted on it.

"Mm. Nice," he said, pushing it into a back pocket.

"This, too," he added, picking an ivory case off a Russian wooden cabinet. The case was Chinese, deep-carved with tiny pagodas and verandah walkways. Mandarin ladies chatted under parasols, or leant langorously on the balustrades to admire the goldfish ponds. Each minute fingernail and parasol strut was cut with fascinating precision.

Murgatroyd chuckled. A purry cat-chuckle.

"My dear Chardon," he said, "you don't know much about witch's houses, that's plain."

Chardon put his hands on his hips and tossed his curls.

"What don't I know?" he challenged.

"When you walk outside," said the cat, "that pretty egg will look like a stone with slime on it; that delicate ivory case will turn out to be no more that a piece of pitted driftwood."

"Rubbish," said Chardon, and went on collecting.

Daphne was sitting in an arm-chair, one of her legs drawn up underneath her. She was shivering slightly. Leaning on the back of the chair just behind her was the auburn-haired Berklak. He looked pale and subdued. There was a scar on his throat.

"Bastards," said the black girl. "You interfering bastards. You've mucked it up, the most beautiful world that ever was. That's all it is now, a heap of junk."

"That's all it ever was," said Murgatroyd.

"Yeah, but what am I going to do now?"

"It's better than being dead," said Berklak.

"You can go home," said Daphne. "I don't even know if I've a home to go to. And, if I do, I don't know if I want to go there."

She looked at John.

"Pity, when we rubbed that weed-killer dust in your eyes, we didn't make a better job of it."

John stood up slowly, and brushed some bits of glass off his shirt and trousers.

"Let's get outside," he said. "The atmosphere in here's still poisoned."

He helped an exhausted Charles to his feet.

"Come on."

"Just a moment," said his brother.

He bent down again and picked up Hippo off the rubble.

"Mustn't forget him," he said, rubbing Hippo affectionately on the nose.

"You soppy kid," said Daphne. "You couldn't even shit for yourself, without a stuffed animal to help you."

"You and I," said Charles, "owe our lives to Hippo, as does everyone else here. He gave us his own brief time in reality to save us. A gift there will never be any way of repaying. Just don't forget it, that's all."

"Outside," said Murgatroyd, a little sharply. "John's right. We'll start quarrelling if we stay here. Keep going to the gate, and don't look back till we get there."

He sauntered through the open doorway, and the children followed him. As they went down the flagstoned path towards the road, they smelt the wooden fencing at the edge of the property giving off a warm smell. For no reason they could think of, it was comforting. A small car rushed by on the road. Spiky green casings of horse-chestnuts lay tumbled about at their feet. Some had split open to reveal the shiny brown conkers inside.

Last through the gate came John. He pulled the lift-and-drop latch shut with a click.

"Okay," said Murgatroyd. "Take a deep breath. Then look back and see where you've been."

Hesitantly, they turned. There was no sign of the house out of which they had just come, nor of the garden through which they had hurried. What they saw was an allotment. A badly tended allotment, full of old stalks of Brussels sprouts and couch-grass. Tags of silver-foil tied to strings crinkled and jingled in the wind to keep the birds away from vegetables that were no longer there. Some cloches with broken glass stood in a line above what might have been supports for tomato-plants. The walls of a battered toolshed, leaning aslant, were patched with pieces of tarred roofing-felt. A muddy path ran from this shed to the gate where they stood.

"So she *was* a witch," said Daphne slowly. "My mum, who comes from

Jamaica, used to tell me stories about things like this. I never believed her. Didn't believe you before."

She put out her hand to John.

"Sorry," she said. "'Bout everything."

John shook her hand and smiled.

"I know," he said. "Thanks for telling me. Past history."

Chardon reached into his pockets. They were crammed with slimy stones. He tossed them back, one by one, into the allotment. The last one clanged on a piece of corrugated iron leaning against the shed.

He reached inside his shirt, and pulled out a piece of pitted driftwood. He flipped it, spinning, through the air, and it landed on a clump of chives, where it shattered a couple of the purple flowers and stuck, at an angle.

"It was a beautiful case," he said. "I'd like to be able to make things like that one day. Even if it is only a thing."

John and Charles looked at each other quizzically. After a while, John said:

"How much do you remember?"

"Everything. Label Land. Killing Berklak. Everything."

"So do I," said John. "Drumming with Crabfingers. Swinging through the jungle canopy. All that."

"Then we've done it. You and I are together again."

He felt himself: chest, arms, legs.

"Seems like an anti-climax, doesn't it?"

John nodded.

"All that trouble, just to be oneself."

"Of course!" exclaimed Chardon. "I knew there was something wrong. There ought to have been four of you."

"No longer," said Charles. "See this?"

He took a small bone from his trouser pocket.

"*Ours*," he said.

THE CHILDREN AND THE CAT walked along the street in silence. Cars passed by more frequently. They could hear the sound of the morning rush-hour building up on the main road.

"What happened to us, Murg?" asked John.

"Only *you* can tell *us* that," replied the cat. "What does it feel like?"

"Hard to say. I feel young and old at the same time. Something hard and bitter has melted inside me. I've come alive again. But I'm wiser. I can see under the surface of things in a way I never did before."

"Same with me," said Charles. "Everything is the same as it used to be, but different, if you can understand that. This ordinary world, this street lined with trees, these houses with lovingly tended front gardens full of too-bright flowers, families out walking, kids on bicycles, is also quite extraordinary. That's something I never saw before."

"We can put the puzzle together now," said the black cat. "The halves that escaped from Megan became, as we suspected, grown-ups. You may not have noticed what was happening. I did. You reasoned. You thought ahead. Your warm affections, little by little, turned into cold ambitions. The here-and-now began to lose its savour.

"This hardening had its uses. Megan tormented Charles with visions of Hell. He withstood it. A child who was only a child would have gone mad in a few moments. Few adults could have endured it for long either, unless hardened by deep meditation. The halves that were captured were eternal children, incapable of growing up, but spontaneous, lovable, and immediate. Without this half, the heart dies. You saved yourselves when you rescued yourselves."

"Mightn't we have been better able to face Grayach," said Charles, "if we'd stayed adults?"

"Maybe. Maybe not. You might no longer have cared to make the effort. You have not lost your experiences. Nor the knowledge about Grayach that you surprised out of Megan. Crucial information."

They had come to the main road. Daphne stopped.

"I gotta go the other way from you," she said. "I wonder if they still remember me?"

"They will," said Murgatroyd. "Witch's time runs differently from human time: sometimes faster, sometimes slower. In your case, you've not been away for long."

Daphne still hesitated.

"Come and see us soon" said John. "I told you where we live. There are one or two points of philosophy we still have to settle."

The black girl's face opened into a grin.

"That's for sure," she said. "Be seeing you."

She began to walk away, but Murgatroyd called after her:

"You'll find Selina waiting for you. That is, if you're interested."

Daphne nodded hard, smiled a wonderful smile, and broke into a loping run.

Chardon left them a few minutes later.

"I think I'll stay with someone I know," he said. "I don't fancy going home at present."

He waved, smiled dreamily, and disappeared round a corner.

"Bit of an alley-cat," murmured Murgatroyd, once Chardon was out of earshot.

"He's strange, but I rather like him," said John. "He makes everything certain seem open to question."

Last of all, Berklak said goodbye. He had hardly spoken to anyone all this time, but now he smiled and shook their hands.

"I think," said Murgatroyd, after he'd gone, "that being killed by Charles was a shock to him. Like having a dream in which you're guillotined, and your head drops into a basket in front of your nose, or in which you're shot by a firing squad and look into the eyes of the people shooting you. You feel frightened when you wake up, as if you are not really there, and don't have any right to be alive."

"We were mad," said Charles. "He was unlucky to lose."

They walked past the playing-fields of a snobby school where a schoolmaster's wife was out excercising two badly behaved cream-coloured retrievers. Then they turned onto the towing-path beside the slowly-flowing Thames.

"What's happened to the other childen in the set?" asked John.

"Gone home to where their hearts were," said Murgatroyd. "Like the white kitten. We stayed together, because our strongest feelings were with each other."

"And the Time-traveller?" asked Charles.

"A casualty."

"I only need Steg's bone to travel through time," said Charles, "and some sort of protection. But I shall miss the old thing with its odd paintings. Oh, well, may what's left of it rest in peace."

When they came to their own house, he noticed weeds in the gravel drive and frowned.

"Not like George to overlook weeds," he observed.

A curious feeling had come over them, a feeling that they were ghosts. It seemed to them that they were coming back to haunt the house where they had once lived. They felt uneasy as well as happy. Would something have changed?

"Here we are," said John, as they came down the drive. "Back to square one."

Murgatroyd raced across the grass and clawed his way twenty feet up a tree, then slithered and jumped down the other side.

"I remember," he said, "when Gilgamesh came back to Uruk, grim-faced because he had lost the plant of immortality that was to be his gift to his subjects. I remember when Odysseus had to slip back into Ithaca

302

disguised from his own countrymen."

"You remember?" said Charles.

"You forget," said the cat. "I was there."

"Let's hope we get a better reception than Odysseus," said John with a laugh. "That man of wiles who learned the minds of many peoples."

"We will," said Charles.

He ran up the steps and gave a long, long, ring on the bell.

———————

DREAMGUARD
the trilogy

continues...

...in VOLUME 2

¡Tiger's Island

- Egger
- the sunken galleon
- Hereza
- the night club
- the sea of bones
- Sacramento

available now

...and in VOLUME 3

The Word Spider

- the city of fogs and machinery
- the gift of the Itilgi
- the hungry images
- Keml, Ngraa, and Paari
- Emer

available mid 2000

TO ORDER: *make cheques payable to Samara Press*

AUSTRALIA: post-free from Samara Press,
Mayfield Road, Tarago, NSW 2580
A$ 19.99, set of two A$ 34.99; add 10%
GST after July 1 2000.

UK: from Cathie Brooks-Burridge,
22 Wilverley Crescent, New Malden,
Surrey KT3 5LN   £ 7.99, set of two £ 12.99

USA: from Autumn Stanley, Trillium House
241 Bonita, Los Trancos Woods,
Portola Valley, CA 94028
US $12.99, set of two US $21.99.

VISIT: dreamguard at www.dreamguard.org for
summaries, extracts, current prices and credit card
sales or email <John.Dutton@bigpond.com>